Ghost Writing in Contemporary American Fiction

David Coughlan

Ghost Writing in Contemporary American Fiction

palgrave
macmillan

David Coughlan
School of Culture and Communication
University of Limerick
Limerick, Ireland

ISBN 978-1-137-41023-8   ISBN 978-1-137-41024-5   (eBook)
DOI 10.1057/978-1-137-41024-5

Library of Congress Control Number: 2016956886

Cover illustration: © Trigger Image / Alamy Stock Photo

Printed on acid-free paper

This Palgrave Macmillan imprint is published by Springer Nature
The registered company is Macmillan Publishers Ltd. London

To my grandmother,
Mary Coughlan

ACKNOWLEDGMENTS

This book began life as a research project, "Ghosts of American Writing," supported by a Government of Ireland postdoctoral fellowship awarded by the Irish Research Council (then the Irish Research Council for the Humanities and Social Sciences) and undertaken at the School of English, University College Cork. I gratefully acknowledge this support, as well as that of the Arts, Humanities and Social Sciences Faculty Research Committee and the School of Culture and Communication (previously, the School of Languages, Literature, Culture and Communication) at the University of Limerick which, in addition to making available conference and research funding, granted me a book completion award and sabbatical leave. Without these, I would not have been able to finish.

While writing this book, I spent a memorable month at the Department of English, University of Stockholm. My thanks to Claudia Egerer, Paul Schreiber, and Francesco-Alessio Ursini for being wonderful hosts and especially to Adnan Mahmutović for sharing his desk and his home with me. I spent some time also in the Humanities Reading Rooms at the British Library and in the New York Public Library, and I am grateful to librarians in both institutions for their assistance.

Many people have helped to shape this project, but I am most indebted to my friend and mentor Graham Allen (another who was kind enough to share his office with me). It was with Graham that I organized a conference on *where ghosts live*, and it was Graham who introduced me to the tremendous group of people who taught me what it means to read Jacques Derrida: Chiara Alfano, Clare Connors, Thomas Dutoit, Mika Elo, Jacqueline Hamrit, Sorelle Ann Henricus, Margit Hesselager, Maebh

Long, Martin McQuillan, Jp McMahon, Forbes Morlock, Dag Petersson, John Phillips, Nicholas Royle, Roy Sellars, Mauro Senatore, and Sarah Wood. This book would not be this book without them.

I would like to thank all my colleagues and friends, past and present, at the University of Limerick, but especially those in English, including Michael Griffin, Yianna Liatsos, Sinead McDermott, Tom Moylan, Tina O'Toole, Emma Bidwell and James Carney, Louise Sheridan and Niamh Hehir, Jack Fennell and Jason King, Cathy McGlynn and Maggie O'Neill, Carrie Griffin and Graham Price, Meg Harper and Tina Morin (fellow followers of ghosts), Caroline Magennis and Stanley van der Ziel (for coffee and more), and Kim Arnold and Clair Sheehan. Special thanks go to Patricia Moran, for her valued friendship and support always.

I would also like to thank everyone I know in the Irish Association for American Studies and the American and International Comparative Literature Associations, my much-appreciated academic communities. And life, whether academic or otherwise, would be very different and much the worse without the friendship, energy, and ideas of Erica Bartlett, Derval and Sam Cromie, David Huddart, John and Joan McSweeney, Belinda and Leo O'Donovan, Priscilla Robinson, James Tink, Chris Diakoulakis, and Elizabeth Wijaya. Chris, Elizabeth, and Louise Sheridan all read earlier drafts of parts of this book, providing invaluable feedback and encouragement, for which I remain extremely grateful.

At Palgrave Macmillan, I thank Paula Kennedy and Peter Cary in the UK office and Ryan Jenkins and Paloma Yannakakis in the US office for their great help, patience, and efficiency. My thanks also to Palgrave Macmillan's readers for their vital input. Parts of this book have been published previously. "Ghost Writing" and Chap. 2 "Mimes and Phantoms: Don DeLillo" are much-revised versions of "The Art of Everyday Haunting," part of the *where ghosts live* special issue of *Derrida Today* 5.2 (2012). Some of the material on Paul Auster appeared previously in "Paul Auster's *City of Glass*: The Graphic Novel" in *Modern Fiction Studies* 52.4 (2006) and "Paul Auster's Ghost Writers" in *Space, Haunting, Discourse* (2008), edited by Maria Holmgren Troy and Elisabeth Wennö. In all cases, I am grateful to the editors for permission to reprint.

Finally, my love and thanks go to Fiona, my inspiration, example, and other self. And they go also to the members of my family for their unwavering support and for prefacing every expression of concern with "We know we're not supposed to ask, but …" Somehow, that made all the difference.

Contents

1. Introduction: Of Spectrality

"A SPECTER IS HAUNTING THE WORLD—THE SPECTER OF CAPITALISM" (96): in Don DeLillo's *Cosmopolis* (2003), these words appear on the electronic display of the stock and currency tickers fronting a Times Square tower normally occupied by an investment bank but here temporarily controlled by masked protestors who bomb the bank, release rats into the surrounding buildings, smash the windows of nearby stores, spray graffiti across advertisements, drop from the towers, struggle with riot police, get punched and gassed and arrested, set fire to cars and barricades, and mass violently around the limousine in which Eric Packer, DeLillo's multibillionaire protagonist, rides untouched. The "head of Packer Capital" (92), he is one man in a sea of masked individuals who, like the crowds of DeLillo's *Mao II* (1991), are "one body now, an undifferentiated mass" (3), and are all "the same, young people from fifty countries, immunized against the language of self" (8). He's the other one, the different one, the named head to their faceless body, and yet "he'd like to be out there, mangling and smashing" (*Cosmopolis* 92), and then, somehow, he is. As he looks on, the words "A RAT BECAME THE UNIT OF CURRENCY" (96) appear on the ticker and Eric realizes that he and the protestors have been reading the same oppositional poetry, and can quote each other.[1] Suddenly, he's a part of them, and feeling exhilarated, invulnerable, immortal even, he borrows yen in amounts that will ruin him. He sacrifices himself to the total life of the crowd because, as DeLillo famously writes in *White Noise* (1984), "To

© The Editor(s) (if applicable) and The Author(s) 2016
D. Coughlan, *Ghost Writing in Contemporary American Fiction*,
DOI 10.1057/978-1-137-41024-5_1

become a crowd is to keep out death. To break off from the crowd is to risk death as an individual, to face dying alone" (73). And then there is death, something "happening. [...] There was a man on fire" (*Cosmopolis* 97). Everything is brought into question, and Eric wonders if any "culture is total" (90), any context total, when a thing so unassimilable, so "outside its reach" (100) can occur. His "chief of theory" (77) tells him that it's not truly outside, "not original [...]. It's an appropriation" (100); Eric would argue against this, and yet his counterargument also rests on the reproducibility of the dead man's experience: "Imagine him in bed, this morning, staring sideways at a wall, thinking his way toward the moment" (98–99), and "[i]magine the pain. Sit there and feel it" (100), rehearse it, and remember it, this other's unthinkable death, there outside and yet in you. This scene, therefore, presents an inside and outside, same and different, self and other, life and death, but the specter of each is haunting each. "There is no outside" (90) that isn't already inside, nothing present that isn't already unsettled by absence, no life without death, and therefore no life, in the sense of a total living, a fully lived and present life. This is what this book, *Ghost Writing in Contemporary American Fiction*, addresses—a world in which there is only posthumous life, life after death, life following death, a living on, as the dead living, as ghosts.

A Specter Is Haunting

"A specter is haunting [...]": DeLillo's revision of the first line from Friedrich Engels and Karl Marx's *The Manifesto of the Communist Party* (1848) connects his novel to the key theoretical text in *Ghost Writing in Contemporary American Fiction*—namely, Jacques Derrida's *Specters of Marx* (1994; *Spectres de Marx* [1993]). Derrida's text is widely acknowledged to be the harbinger of, even "the catalyst for" (Blanco and Peeren, "Introduction" 2), what very quickly came to be referred to as the "spectral turn" in critical theory (Luckhurst, "Contemporary London Gothic" 527; Weinstock 4). Yet, though very many works have since been published on ghosts, and very few of them fail to touch on Derrida, I would argue that fewer still look to embrace him.[2] He is widely quoted (*Specters of Marx* is a very quotable book), but selectively so, as if he might be invoked without consequence, and thus kept at a distance from the real business of ghost studies. The first aim of this book, therefore, is to attempt to grasp what the ghost is for Derrida and to follow where it leads. But this is not easily done; it soon becomes apparent that, for Derrida, the question of the ghost is wide-ranging.[3]

Illustrating this is the brief story that Derrida includes near the start of *Specters of Marx* (originally given as a two-part lecture), telling of how he arrived at its title. He says:

> More than a year ago, I had chosen to name the "specters" by their name starting with the title [...] when, very recently, I reread *The Manifesto of the Communist Party*. I confess it to my shame: I had not done so for decades [...]. Now, of course, I have just discovered, in truth I have just remembered what must have been haunting my memory: the *first noun* of the *Manifesto*, and this time in the singular, is "specter": "A specter is haunting Europe—the specter of communism." (4)

In this instance, Derrida is already staging something of the ghost for us. First, when he identifies the title that comes to him as something coming to him again, he recounts how the (word) "specter" always "*begins by coming back*" (11). This means it is difficult to speak of a true beginning or certain source, of the original title "Specters of Marx" (4), for example. There is no simple origin, therefore the name for the "specter" is always "specters."

Second, in the projected name that turns out to be an unrecalled citation, he shows that, where specters are concerned, time is not straightforward: "What seems to be [...] the future, comes back [...] from the past" (10). This actually follows from the observation that the specter begins by coming back, and from the realization that the specter therefore, as revenant, always "comes by *coming back*" (10), so that every future appearance is a reappearance, and every arrival is a return. For the ghost, the future will have been the past, and "[w]hat has not yet taken place therefore must have happened already" (Derrida, "Pa*ce Not*(s)" 59).[4] This remarkable statement is something to which we will come back.

Third, in this account, Derrida's "Specter's of Marx" is already the "specter" of Marx, and he is just repeating Marx's word, or rewriting Marx or writing in his place, in his stead. In a sense, he is ghostwriting, doing the creative work of naming the "specters," but then having to credit Marx as if the name were his.[5] Derrida tells what appears to be Marx's story. Or, alternatively, Marx is the ghostwriter, the one who secretly (because forgotten) does the work that the other would present as his own. Again, it is hard to identify the source of the "specter" that joins these two men separated by time and memory. But what this means is that my words are never mine alone but are always haunted by the other and open to being reworked by the other. This is why Derrida concludes *Specters of Marx* with a reference to "when one speaks there in a foreign language" (176) and why he says "[o]ne never writes either in one's own language or in a foreign language" ("Border Lines" 127). I can never write my own story but nor can I write the other's story, the foreigner's story.[6] This is the problem that faces all the writers, all the ghostwriters discussed in this book because the words they use to tell others' stories are never simply the other's words.

Fourth, and related to the consideration just raised, there is the question of one's responsibility to the other, and of doing justice to the other. Derrida's small admission that he has neglected his Marx—that to his shame, he has not been rereading him—may be about what he sees as a critical or intellectual lapse, but it also gestures to the larger issue of his duty to the person of Marx. What is forgotten along with the "specter"? To forget a word might mean to forget an individual, an idea, a culture, a politics, an ideology, an environment, a civilization, or communism, for example. But, as Derrida tells, these things haunt and can be remembered, recalled, mourned, or even revived. They can survive and live on. Later in *Specters of Marx*, therefore, he speaks of "a justice which, beyond right or law, rises up in the very respect owed to whoever *is not*, no longer or not yet, living, presently living" (97), a justice owed yet to the dead and the unborn.

But, fifth, when Derrida mentions that he has just remembered what must have been haunting his memory, he presents himself as someone not entirely present to himself. Until he has just remembered, he is haunted by something he remembers no longer or not yet, so that not present thing is somehow unsettling his comfortably inhabited present moment, his here and now which he realizes, too late, was a haunted home all along. This is the lesson that is least palatable to scholars, and especially scholars of ghosts: when Derrida speaks of "whoever *is not*," he does not speak only of the dead and unborn, he means you and me, and when he speaks of "whoever *is not* [...] presently living," he means you and me because we are, none of us, simply present, simply living. I am a "ghost whose expected return repeats itself, again and again" (*Specters of Marx* 10), and so are you. We are (all of us) ghosts.[7]

What Is a Ghost?

To speak to the ghost, therefore, is to speak to origins, time, others, justice, and the self. We have obviously moved away from what the *Oxford English Dictionary* identifies as the "prevailing sense" of the word ghost as the "soul of a deceased person, spoken of as appearing in a visible form, or otherwise manifesting its presence, to the living." In fact, this is one definition of ghosts that we should absolutely disregard, if we take it to mean the ghost is crossing from death to life, or returning from beyond this living world. There is no life after death that is not of this world. Nothing reaches the dead, or comes from the dead, and there is nowhere outside of this world, no other world where the dead can be. There is no other world but the world of the other that is lost, and lost utterly, when someone dies. His painful awareness of this is apparent in much of the work of Derrida who, as Nicholas Royle states, "doesn't believe in an afterlife: 'I do not believe that one lives on post-mortem',," he says (*Jacques Derrida* 7), and therefore he does not believe in ghosts as the literal return of the dead. Except, he does believe in ghosts as the literal return of the dead, if by that, we mean he believes in ghosts as the inscription or reinscription of the dead in the world, as a tracing of the remains of the dead in the world, or as a ghost writing (he believes in the return of spirit as "spirit"). And, in fact, he believes in another of the *OED*'s definitions of the ghost, "or spirit, as the principle of life," or of living.

To think of the ghost as the principle of life seems a strange definition of both life and the ghost. But perhaps what is becoming apparent is that the ghost is difficult to define because it has so much to do with definition, with identifying the limits of what something or someone is and is not, of when and where they are, of who they are. The ghost appears as something at odds with limits, this thing that is both living and dead, that is neither living nor dead, that is past and is not past but to come, that looks like a dead father, or husband, or daughter, and therefore the question of definition appears with it: "What art thou [...]?" (Shakespeare, *Hamlet* 1.1.45) asks the scholar Horatio of the ghost that he does not want to be a ghost. Because, a definition is also a conjuration, meaning that, as Derrida describes, it both brings "forth with the voice, [...] makes come, by definition, what *is not there* at the present moment" (*Specters of Marx* 41) and "means *also* to exorcise" (48), "to *conjure* (away) the ghosts" (47). In other words, the definition works exactly to unghost the ghost, to call forth the life from this living thing, to erase death from this not dead thing; or, from what is too easily considered the other side, to embrace the death of this dead thing, and smother the life of this not living thing. Calling to the ghost to identify it(self), we want only to exorcise its ghost-liness, to name it in relation to a certain life and a certain death. We want only to admit it as something that has crossed the line dividing death to life, crossed from outside to inside, when in truth, the ghost remains between. And, moreover, it is not settling in between the defined limits of life and death, not hunkering down between the absolute presence of life and the absolute absence of death; no, rather, it is the stubborn between-ness of the ghost which even gives us to speak of life as such, of death as such. Such things derive from the ghost, which is "[n]either in life nor in death *alone*. What happens between two, and between all the 'two's' one likes, such as between life and death, can only *maintain itself* with some ghost, can only *talk with or about* some ghost" (xviii).[8]

Conjuration, therefore, works to fix "all the 'two's'," like original and copy, or presence and absence, or life and death, or immediate and delayed, or speech and writing, or to fix what is and is not, so that speech is of the original, presence, life, the immediate, while "'writing' implies rep-etition, absence, risk of loss, death" (Bennington 49) and so must be cast out. But Derrida would like not to abide by this conjuration, this swearing together, but to attend to the "contradictory injunction" from "the one who orders 'swear'," the one who enjoins us to speak on what is to be or not to be, the ghost (Derrida, *Specters of Marx* 7). Derrida, therefore, is not an exorcist but a medium, letting the ghost speak of the medium, of the between which means the original is haunted by the copy, and the immediate haunted by the delay. After Derrida, for example, we cannot refer to the opposition of speech and writing outside the logic of supple-mentarity, within which we "are prey to the ghostly power of the supple-ment; it is the unlocatable site that gives rise to the *specter*" (Derrida, *Work of Mourning* 41).[9] We understand that "binary thought depends more or less secretly on the terms it subordinates in its foundational oppositions. [...] What one tries to keep outside inhabits the inside and there would be no inside without that fact. [...] We could say, for example, that the term excluded by the binary divide *returns* in some sense (let us also hear the ghost in this returning)" (Bennington 217), so that the one term "must be inhabited or haunted by the other, which is not outside" (221).[10] As a result, argues Derrida, "it is necessary to introduce haunting into the very construction of a concept. Of every concept, beginning with the concepts of being and time. That is what we would be calling here a hauntology. Ontology opposes it only in a movement of exorcism. Ontology is a conjuration" (*Specters of Marx* 161).

What is conjured up and what is conjured away by the concept of America? Does it need to be said that the American fiction of the title of this book is fiction of the USA and not fiction of the Americas, of South or Central or North America, of Mexico or Canada, or even of the territories of the USA? And yet, just the fact that one of these contemporary works of fiction is set in an America before the USA tells us that even as "[h]aunting would mark the very existence of Europe" (Derrida, *Specters of Marx* 4), so it marks the USA. A nation and a national identity form by force of definitions along geographical, political, ethnic, religious, or cultural lines, and by force itself, so that the very concept of the nation is haunted. As Martin Hägglund comments, the study of ghosts "concerns phantoms and specters as haunting reminders of the victims of historical violence, of those who have been excluded or extinguished from the formation of a society" (82). Those who are, by definition, excluded from the given present have been the focus of many of the studies on ghosts to date, which are concerned with "how conditions in the past banished certain individuals, things, or ideas, how circumstances rendered them marginal, excluded, or repressed" (Radway viii), so that "a ghost can be any person, living or dead, who figuratively haunts a culture or society in which they participate marginally" (Kröger and Anderson xi). Melanie Anderson, therefore, describes a process of "social ghosting" (13) where individuals are "ghostly because they are marginalized, silenced outcasts" (11). Similarly, for Esther Peeren, ghosts mean "a state of dispossession [...], certain marginalized groups of people" (4); for Peeren, "the ghost is a metaphor certain people (are made to) live *as*" (6), meaning ghostliness is the effaced visibility of others, their "*social invisibility*" (36). I suggest, however, that this emphasis on exclusion misses exactly the ghost's coming back, the ghost as the apparition of an absence, as the visibility of the invisible, or the ghost as a haunting, frightening, unsettling thing. In contrast to Peeren, Avery Gordon's important and influential *Ghostly Matters* (1997, new ed. 2008) therefore describes haunting as "an animated state in which a repressed or unresolved social violence is making itself known," and the ghost, she says, "is not the invisible or some ineffable excess. The whole essence, if you can use that word, of a ghost is that it has a real presence and demands its due, your attention" (xvi).[11] She says, "Haunting and the appearance of specters or ghosts is one way [...]

we are notified that what's been concealed is very much alive and present, interfering precisely with those always incomplete forms of containment and repression ceaselessly directed towards us" (xvi). The "past *always* haunts the present" (Radway viii), and the ghost is "the sign [...] that tells you a haunting is taking place" (Gordon 8).[12] Renée Bergland's *The National Uncanny* (2000) draws attention to these two ways of thinking about the ghost, either as a result of the exclusionary practices which would mark the other as dead, or as the unsettling return which means a realization that the dead remain inside. Discussing, in a more specifically American context, the "Indian ghost" as "the figure of the spectral" (1), she argues that "the practice of representing Indians as ghosts works both to establish American nationhood and to call it into question" (5). However, when she says that "[w]hen European Americans speak of Native Americans, they always use the language of ghostliness [...], they describe Indians as absent or dead" (1), it becomes clear that, in the first case, she is speaking about a conjuration, "a technique of removal" (4), which aims to define America as a present reality in contrast with the absent, unreal Indians who "are already gone" and "are so other that they are otherworldly" (5). But the ghost is not simply dead or absent, not simply marginalized or invisible, even if it is often presented in just those terms. Instead, as Bergland also recognizes, ghosts call things into question, they "present us with the possibility of vanishing ourselves" (5), because they speak also to our own ghostliness.

Therefore, rather than practicing a hauntology which would "introduce haunting into the very construction of a concept" (Derrida, *Specters of Marx* 161), many ghost scholars have attempted to "unghost" the ghost (Anderson 3) by accommodating it within existing categories.[13] Peeren, therefore, talks about "[g]hosts, literal [dead reappearing in some sort of perceptible form to the living (3)] or metaphorical" (12), again opposing the living to the dead, and the actual to the inactual. She is interested in "a concept—*spectrality*—adopted as an analytical tool" (9). Helen Sword, in *Ghostwriting Modernism* (2002), is interested in the way "spirits unsettle seemingly stable ontological—or, as Jacques Derrida would have it, 'hauntological'—boundaries" (xi), but ultimately she wants to rid ghostwriting of its ghostliness by incorporating marginalized figures into a defined history of Modernism, restoring their "real and visible presence" (165). And, even while Gordon laments "that radical scholars and intellectuals [...] insisted on distinctions—between subject and object of knowledge, between fact and fiction, between presence and absence, between past and present, between present and future, between knowing and not-knowing—whose tenuousness and manipulation seemed precisely to me in need of comprehension and articulation" (xvii), her desire is to look "for a language for identifying haunting and for writing with the ghosts" (7) or "to find a method of knowledge production" (xvii) where Derrida would argue that the untranslatable specter "no longer belongs to knowledge. At least no longer to that which one thinks one knows by the name of knowledge" (*Specters of Marx* 6). And, again, although Gordon urges that "we will have to learn to talk to and listen to ghosts, rather than banish them," she sees this "as the precondition for establishing our scientific or humanistic knowledge" (23) and concludes that "[f]ollowing the ghosts [...] is about putting the life back in" (22). But, any argument based on the idea that the social dead must be brought to life, that the invisible should be fully visible, or that the marginalized should be wholly incorporated within the centers of power, denies the ghost utterly. In other words, as Christopher Peterson puts it in his excellent *Kindred Specters* (2007), such an argument fails to ask, "What makes the ontology of the socially alive any more secure than that of the socially dead? Are not the socially alive themselves specters?" (9).

This ontological rather than hauntological approach is something that these scholars of ghosts share with Marx, who, says Derrida, "detests all ghosts, the good and the bad" (*Specters of Marx* 113) and wants only to "to denounce, chase away, or exorcise the specters [...] by means of critical analysis" (47). This is the crux of Derrida's philosophical disagreement with Marx, because for Derrida, these ghosts must live on. Believing that "the dividing line between the ghost and actuality ought to be crossed, like utopia itself, by a realization, that is, by a revolution" (39), Marx would conjure away the specter of capitalism and call forth the specter of communism and make it present, see it realized. For Derrida, however, revolution cannot occur without ghosts because a "revolution cannot be programmed" (Derrida and Roudinesco 83) but comes as something unseen, like the future. Here, we see how, as Peterson argues, "political and theoretical responses to the social death of racial and sexual others too often sustain the ontological presumptions through which the binary between social life and social death emerges" (12), and that any such revolution which aims "to 'raise the dead' reverses rather than displaces the logic through which dominant, white, heterosexual culture disavows and projects mortality onto racial and sexual minorities" (6). Hauntology, instead, "means to displace the binary opposition between presence and absence, being and nonbeing, life and death. Hauntology is thus another name for the spectrality that conditions all life" (10).

This conclusion, that "there is spectrality everywhere" (Derrida, "Following Theory" 18), is the one rejected by many ghost scholars. Peeren, for example, though recognizing Derrida's hauntology "as an alternative ontology [which] renders all being and meaning ghostly, and whose function and effects are difficult to distinguish from those of other deconstructive notions such as *différance*, trace and hymen" (11), deliberately steps back from this understanding, preferring to argue that "not everything is ghostly" (12).[14] But, as Hägglund argues, "What is important about the figure of the specter [...] is that it cannot be fully present: it has no being in itself but marks a relation to what is *no longer* or *not yet*. And since time—the disjointure between past and future—is a condition even for the slightest moment, spectrality is at work in everything that happens" (82). Any study that works to exorcise the ghost, even if it does so in traditionally positive terms by seeking to return it to full life, instead, closes the unghosted to the past, to the future, to the other, to anything that might happen, and therefore to life. Only ghosts survive:

> No doubt life protects itself by repetition, trace, *différance* (deferral). But we must be wary of this formulation: there is no life present *at first* which would *then* come to protect, postpone, or reserve itself in *différance*. The latter constitutes the essence of life. Or rather: as *différance* is not an essence, as it is not anything, it *is not* life [...]. Life must be thought of as trace before Being may be determined as presence. (Derrida, "Freud and the Scene of Writing" 203)

"Ghost writing" in this book, therefore, means something other than "ghost-writing" or "ghostwriting" (to give the more usual forms). Ghost writing means this trace of life, and the ways in which we write ourselves and others into the world, as ghosts.

To Be, or To Be Not?

Derrida's *Specters of Marx* is a chimerical animal, part explication of specters, part reading of *Hamlet*, and part response to the work of Marx. These parts can, and have, been addressed separately, but even then, it is as if they sit communing around a table, the specter key to Derrida's frequently critical reading of Marx, Marx telling of his love for Shakespeare, and *Hamlet* illuminating what the specter is. At this stage, I want to focus on this last angle, and the way in which Derrida draws on *Hamlet*, and specific lines from *Hamlet*, in order to think the ghost.

***

"I have seen nothing" (Shakespeare, *Hamlet* 1.1.21; Derrida, *Specters of Marx* 6); "'Do you see nothing there?'/'Nothing at all, yet all that is I see'" (Shakespeare, *Hamlet* 3.4.128–129): The word "specter" derives from the Latin *spectrum* from the verb *specere*, meaning "to see" or "to look at."[15] To see the specter is to see the body of the spirit, to see something that is not there. In this way, the ghost is always more: it is more material, like the "smallish and fine-bodied" (41) ghost in DeLillo's *The Body Artist* (2001) which illustrates that, as Derrida writes, "it is flesh and phenomenality that give to the spirit its spectral apparition" (*Specters of Marx* 6), "a supernatural and paradoxical phenomenality" (7); it is more than one, like Paul Auster's ghost writers; it is more than meets the eye, like Philip Roth's Coleman Silk, the man who spoke of spooks; it is more than expected, as in Marilynne Robinson's *Housekeeping* (1980); it is more visible and present, like Toni Morrison's *Beloved*; it is more alive. It is, as "the furtive and ungraspable visibility of the invisible, […] the tangible intangibility of a proper body without flesh" (7), more there. It is "nothing other than […] the visibility of nothing" ("Double Session" 218–219). Moreover, this "*nothing* visible" (*Specters of Marx* 6) looks at us in a "spectral asymmetry" (6) whereby this "thing meanwhile looks at us and sees us not see it even when it is there" (6). Derrida calls this "the *visor effect*: we do not see who looks at us" (7). In other words, we can never see the spirit as such, there is no spirit as such, there is only "spirit." Seeing "spirit," seeing the specter, we see nothing. Nothing is all there is to see, and we see it as "spirit," as something repeating, cited, as some "*thing* that is called spirit" (6). It is not the king that is seen but the "King," something "[i]n the same figure like the King that's dead. […] Looks 'a not like the King?" (Shakespeare, *Hamlet* 1.1.40–42). Who knows? This "being-there of an absent or departed one no longer belongs to knowledge" (Derrida, *Specters of Marx* 6). The visor effect—which, like *différance*, "de-synchronizes" (6)—means that we can never positively know what this thing is or is not, what it signifies. In this way, the ghost is always less: less present, less knowable, less identical, less than one, less there. It is the "invisibility of a visible X" (7), the ghost of writing. This is all there is in the absence of a certain origin, a transcendental spirit: "Since we do not see the one who orders 'sweare,' we cannot identify it in all certainty, we must fall back on its voice. The one who says 'I am thy Fathers Spirit' [sic] can only be taken at his word" (7). His word, his "spirit," is all we have to go on.

For Gordon, the idea of seeing nothing is important because, she says, haunting is "when the people who are meant to be invisible show up" (xvi). The ghost is "in the interstices of the visible and the invisible," and so she wants us "to consider a different way of seeing, one that is less mechanical, more willing to be surprised" (24). As a result, she takes DeLillo to task for being blind to the ghostly. Specifically, she is concerned with the "hypervisibility" (15) of his novel *White Noise* (1985) in which, as in the bright aisles of a supermarket, everything is there to be seen, brightly lit and consumable. In the novel, she says, "there are no ghostly haunts, or shadows" (15). She thinks DeLillo is blind for seeing too clearly, but DeLillo is, of course, here illustrating the blindness of a society that believes that everything is visible and therefore in control. In *Cosmopolis*, similarly, Packer believes everything can be charted; he can look "toward streams of numbers running in opposite directions" and think "[o]ur bodies and oceans were here, knowable and whole" (24). He sees the future as something wholly legible, programmable: "It charts. You'll see it" (37). But *Cosmopolis* tells us that the future could be looking right at us and we wouldn't recognize it. It tells us that visibility does not mean readability or translatability. Packer looked at "the shabby man at the ATM. There was something familiar about him. [...] But Eric didn't care whether this was someone he'd once known. [...] He was thinking about automated teller machines" (54). The man is his future murderer, but he is not to know that.

***

"Enter the ghost, exit the ghost, re-enter the ghost" (Derrida, *Specters of Marx* xx), "*Enter the Ghost, Exit the Ghost, Enter the Ghost, as before*" (11): "Revenant" comes from the French word meaning that which comes back.[16] The first time the ghost appears in *Hamlet*, Marcellus says, "Look where it comes again" (1.1.39). As Derrida says, "Repetition *and* first time: this is perhaps the question of the event as question of the ghost" (*Specters of Marx* 10). It does not matter that Marcellus is referring to the fact that he has seen the ghost twice before—the first appearance of the ghost is always an appearance again.[17] The ghost is always the ghost *of* something, so when the ghost first appears, it is as if that something, the dead father say, has come back. In this way, "a specter is always a *revenant* [...] because it *begins by coming back*" (11): the return of the dead father is the beginning of the ghost of the father. And then, when the ghost re-enters, "where it comes again" (Shakespeare, *Hamlet* 1.1.125), it enters as before; in other words, it is again a repetition and the first time. "Repetition *and* first time," says Derrida, "but also repetition *and* last time, since the singularity of any *first time* makes of it also a *last time*. Each time is the event itself" (*Specters of Marx* 10). Each appearance of the ghost is a repetition which cannot be repeated because it is happening for the first and last time. And this is the future, this survival of something from one moment to the next, this thing that "repeats itself, again and again" (10). So, "the specter is the future, it is always to come, it presents itself only as that which could come or come back; in the future" (39). The future is the ghost returning from the past.[18]

***

"To be, or not to be" (Shakespeare, *Hamlet* 3.1.55; Derrida, *Specters of Marx* 10, 11, 17): Hamlet, here, starkly opposes life to death. He is, like Horatio, a student, and as Derrida observes, "There has never been a scholar who, as such, does not believe in the sharp distinction between the real and the unreal, the actual and the inactual, the living and the non-living, being and non-being" (*Specters of Marx* 11). Hamlet sees his future existence in terms of these two options, and there really is no other possibility: "Beyond this opposition, there is, for the scholar, only the hypothesis of a school of thought, theatrical fiction, literature, and specu-lation" (11), a theory that to die would also be "perchance to dream" (Shakespeare, *Hamlet* 3.1.64). For the ghost, however, "to be" or "not to be," that is not the question. To be a ghost is to be not. "I am not dead," says the ghost, "I am not" (Morrison, *Beloved* 246). If "not to be" means to be dead, inactual, unreal, nonexistent, nonpresent, then "to be not" means to be "not," to actually be inactual, to really be unreal, to be existing nonexistence, to present nonpresence. As Derrida says, "This, the spectral, *is not* [...] is neither substance, nor essence, nor existence, *is never present as such*" (xviii). Because it is never present as such, it *is* this being-not-present, it *is* not. The ghost is not here, is not now. It haunts. Says Derrida, "Let us call it a *hauntology*. This logic of haunting" (10). It is not as strange as it sounds. How often have I said, "I am not here right now"? I do not even need to be present to say I am not present: "I am not here right now. Please leave a message, and I will get back to you." But, even when I return the call, do I ever do so there and then? The "traditional scholar" would say yes (Derrida, *Specters of Marx* 11). Unlike the hauntologist, the ontologist, proficient in exorcism and conjuration, would cast out the ghost and instate "the Being of beings, or [...] the essence of life or death" (51). But, for Derrida, the question remains if I can ever be present as such. Which means, is the question ever "to be" or "not to be," is it ever possible to be wholly and absolutely alive or dead, or is the answer always "to be not"?

***

"The time is out of joint" (Shakespeare, *Hamlet* 1.5.186; Derrida, *Specters of Marx* 1, 18–23 *passim*, 29, 49, 77–78 *passim*): To be present as such would require being in the present moment. And how could it be otherwise? I can't now be in the future, or now be in the past. But surely I will, at some point, be in a future "now," a future present, and I was, at some point, in a past "now," a past present? Perhaps not. What line does the future cross to become the present and the present cross to become the past? Derrida asks us to consider "a radically dis-jointed time, without certain conjunction" (17), which is to say without a certain order between future and present, present and past, the present and the nonpresent:

> If there is something like spectrality, there are reasons to doubt this reassuring order of presents and, especially, the border between the present, the actual or present reality of the present, and everything that can be opposed to it: absence, non-presence, non-effectivity, inactuality, virtuality, or even the simulacrum in general, and so forth. There is first of all the doubtful contemporaneity of the present to itself. Before knowing whether one can differentiate between the specter of the past and the specter of the future, of the past present and the future present, one must perhaps ask oneself whether the *spectrality effect* does not consist in undoing this opposition, or even this dialectic, between actual, effective presence and its other. (39–40)[19]

To be present as such is no longer a certain possibility because the present itself is not present as such: "The present is what passes [...] *between* what *goes* and what *comes*, [...] distributed in the two directions of absence, at the articulation of what is no longer and what is not yet" (25). Stepping between the past and future, time is out of step with itself, somehow dis-articulated or unhinged. It does not compute, it does not translate, like the passage itself—"The time is out of joint"—which "through the very effect of the specter" (18) appears in French translations which answer to "disparate demands" (18) when they variously state that "time is off its hinges," "time is broken down," "the world is upside down," or "this age is dishonoured" (19). The past is translated into the future, but then the past is also not translated into the future in the way that any translation is haunted by the unheard, the unsaid, the asserted presence, the yield to a demand. Translation's haunting means that all our futures to come must survive in a present which is not, therefore, only what is immediately legible or certainly understood, or only what might blithely be said to be, but must also be "not," be all that which is not but which will be once again.

Time is out of joint in DeLillo's *Cosmopolis*: "Time is changing [...]. We need a new theory of time" (86). Repeatedly, the screens in Eric Packer's limousine show him events that have not yet occurred: "He realized queerly that he'd just placed his thumb on his chinline, a second or two after he'd seen it on-screen" (22); "He saw his face on the screen, eyes closed [...]. He knew the spycam operated in real time, or was supposed to. How could he see himself if his eyes were closed?" (52); and "'You recoiled in shock.' 'On-screen.' 'Then the blast. And then.' 'Recoiled for real,' he said. 'Whatever that might possibly mean'" (95).[20] DeLillo here seems to be thinking along the same lines as Derrida, who believes that "ghosts are part of the future. And that the modern technology of images, like cinematography and telecommunication, enhances the power of ghosts and their ability to haunt us" (McMullen). Commenting on tele-technology, Derrida says:

> It obliges us more than ever to think the virtualization of space and time, the possibility of virtual events whose movement and speed prohibit us more than ever (more and otherwise than ever, for this is not absolutely and thoroughly new) from opposing presence to its representation, "real time" to "deferred time," effectivity to its simulacrum, the living to the non-living, in short, the living to the living-dead of its ghosts. (*Specters of Marx* 169)[21]

It is no wonder that such technologies, which allow us to communicate at a distance, to hear the voices of the dead, to watch ourselves now and then, are considered as haunted media by Jeffrey Sconce in his "cultural history of electronic presence" (6).[22]

But Eric still might well ask, "Why am I seeing things that haven't happened yet?" (DeLillo, *Cosmopolis* 22). This returns us to Derrida's argument that "[w]hat has not yet taken place therefore must have happened already" (Derrida, "Pace Not(s)" 59), meaning that things that haven't happened yet must have happened already, and that everything is a replaying of something prerecorded. Furthermore, we should not think that something recorded in the past remains in the past because, of course, there is no past present where it can be; and, for all that might happen in the future, there is no future present in which it can be: all that was and will be again must be in this present moment that "is not and has never been present" (Blanchot, *Step Not Beyond* 16).[23] The past that we think is no longer present, all the names and faces that have been erased, and all "who disappeared must have gotten inscribed someplace else" (Derrida, *Specters of Marx* 5); were something not inscribed, it would be lost to time, for all time. The inscribed past, therefore, remains with us and will return, though in forms we might or might not recognize: a woman might hear her deceased husband's voice coming from the mouth of a stranger; a father's silence might speak of a forgotten murder; a man passing as white might be betrayed by the color of his children; a man might dishonor his name; a beloved child might live again. In such ways, the past and the future, even our future death, haunt the "present," which is the only time given to us. At the end of *Cosmopolis*, therefore, when his timepiece gives him a vision of the world after his death, after his world has ended, Eric remarks, "This is not the end. He is dead inside the crystal of his watch but still alive in original space, waiting for the shot to sound" (209). As DeLillo writes, Eric survives, knowing and fearing "O shit I'm dead" (206), "I am already dead" (Derrida, *Glas* 19b and "Plato's Pharmacy" 146).

***

"Swear" (Shakespeare, *Hamlet* 1.5.149; Derrida, *Specters of Marx* 3, 7, 29–30, 41): The present is not a command executed by the program of the past. The past is not some code to be decrypted according to a key, uncrypted even, brought from the grave to full and unghostly life, the son the same as the father. "Guaranteed translatability, given homogeneity, systematic coherence in their *absolute forms*, this is surely […] what renders the injunction, the inheritance, and the future—in a word the other—*impossible*" (35). No, a "text lives only if it lives on [*sur-vit*], and it lives on only if it is *at once* translatable and untranslatable" ("Border Lines" 128), that is, haunted. So, this code passes secrets between its generations. In the disjunction between past, present, and future generations, an injunction is served by the ghost—"Swear"—that cannot be followed simply but instead calls for a response. It is the challenge of a difficult legacy. It is the challenge "to do and to decide (which is first of all, no doubt, the sense of the 'to be or not to be' of Hamlet—and of any inheritor who, let us say, comes to swear before a ghost)" (*Specters of Marx* 17):

> "One must" means *one must* filter, sift, criticize, one must sort out several different possibilities that inhabit the same injunction. And inhabit it in a contradictory fashion around a secret. If the readability of a legacy were given, natural, transparent, univocal, if it did not call for and at the same time defy interpretation, we would never have anything to inherit from it. We would be affected by it as by a cause—natural or genetic. One always inherits from a secret. (16)

The ghost enjoins you to decide between being and nonbeing, presentation and representation, uncle and murderer, faithfulness and betrayal, friend and enemy, host and guest, sanity and madness, fate and future.

CONTEMPORARY GHOSTS[24]

What follows are chapters on Don DeLillo, on Paul Auster, on Philip Roth, two on Marilynne Robinson, and on Toni Morrison, with each chapter asking why these contemporary authors write about ghosts, and why their ghosts are so often writers. The overall progression is from the smaller scale to the larger scale, from the person to the people, from the biography to the history, from individual mourning to national loss, from rooms to worlds, from the self to the other to God to the dead. But there are ideas which recur within the chapters also, including repetition itself, choice and destiny, and the future, because ghost writing does not manifest itself without these ideas making themselves known also. Between the chapters appear shorter pieces on Derrida, what I am calling interleaves, which focus on particular terms or texts from Derrida: "The Double Session" from *Dissemination*, the *pas*, the acolyte, *Of Spirit*, "Circumfession" from *Jacques Derrida*, hospitality, and mourning. Though these pieces follow on from what has been said in the chapters that precede them, by and large, they look ahead to what is to come in the next by considering what Derrida has to say on those questions and concerns that occupy the novels also. In each case, the part that the ghost plays in Derrida's understanding of, for example, beginnings or hospitality illuminates why these American authors might speak of ghosts.[25]

The first interleaf, "Ghost Writing," therefore sets the stage for a reading of DeLillo's novel *The Body Artist* by relating DeLillo's artist to the mime in Derrida's "The Double Session." Derrida's mime is a phantom that presents nothing and represents nothing, appearing as the double of no one, as a copy without model, as an allusion without source, or as a graft without root. I argue that Derrida here conceives of mimesis as a ghost writing which, as a writing both by and of the ghost, means nothing present presents nothing. The following chapter starts from DeLillo's line "I want to say something but what" (8) and argues that his novel is about how we inhabit and haunt ourselves and others. In his account of the relation between two people following the death of one, DeLillo details the structures of ghostly imitation, repetition, and allusion that enable us to love, to mourn, and in the end, to live on. In "Shadows,"

I consider Derrida's question, "What does it mean to follow a ghost?" (*Specters of Marx* 10) and argue that the question of following is always already the question of the ghost or shadow, and therefore unsettles any sense of an undivided present. This present divided between past and future is understood in terms of the *pas* (the step or pace that is also no pace) that Derrida tracks through the work of Maurice Blanchot, and which finds its way into the prose writing of Auster also. The accompanying chapter examines how Auster structures the relationship between self and other as an always-incomplete step toward the other. With reference to Auster's work over a 20-year period, the chapter shows how he represents his characters as specters, and how their survival between two deaths is predicated on an openness to another who, nevertheless, remains inaccessible. Auster's characteristic use of twinned figures who shadow each other allows him to confront the difficulties inherent in ghost writing, or in writing for another person. In "Haunts," I literally follow Daniel Quinn, the main character in Auster's *City of Glass*, through the streets of New York City, tracing the historical, biographical, cultural, and literary narratives inscribed in Quinn's passage, which takes him through many of Auster's old neighborhoods or haunts. Finding myself diverted from Quinn's story by a personal matter, however, I come to read my excursiveness in terms of Derrida's account of the acolyte, whose following is always interrupted, and which means that any following, or any relation between self and other, is a relation of faithfulness and betrayal. The next chapter reads Auster alongside Roth, focusing on Roth's primary ghost writer, Nathan Zuckerman, and examining the relation of a writer to his subject in terms of a responsibility to the dead, and a necessary betrayal of the dead. It argues that this inevitable interruption of the other's story is an interruption of the self's story also, which Roth illustrates by creating series of ghost writers who haunt the one story, the one name, the one face. For Roth, the ghost writer is not living, only writing, and there is always the possibility of betrayal, or of being displaced, effaced, or erased by another's story.

"Of 'Spirit'" outlines Derrida's discussion of Martin Heidegger's *Geist* while remarking on the ways in which Derrida's understanding of spirit does and does not relate to Robinson's. Derrida's opening line in *Of Spirit*, "I shall speak of ghost, of flame, and of ashes" (1), is a line that applies also to Robinson's *Housekeeping*, but Derrida's spirit is always spectral, whereas Robinson's spirit survives the ghost. Robinson would write of the spirit, where Derrida believes we are always writing "spirit." Robinson's first novel, therefore, attempts something remarkable in that it appears as if it were being told by someone after their death, so that its narrator is not so much a ghost writer as a spirit writer. Studying this spirit work, its transcendentalist influences, its use of analogy, and its references to water, darkness, fire, and the house, the chapter argues that Robinson presents her characters as transient ghosts, spirits housed in flesh which they must finally transcend. However, considering also her representation of time, it questions if a spirit writing is possible, or if, in writing, the spirit returns as spectral "spirit." "Death Sentence" considers *Jacques Derrida*, a remarkable book composed of two works, "Derridabase" by Geoffrey Bennington and "Circumfession" by Derrida, with whom it shares its name. It is this question of the name, as a ghost that one inherits and that survives one, that this interleaf addresses as it follows J.D. through issues of translation, citation, remembering, and time. Because in time, the secret ghost of one's own name returns, and so the future, life, and death happen. In conclusion, Derrida's approach is contrasted with Robinson's. Her God might cite one's secret name without one even knowing it, but Derrida's God is open to a future surprise. In the chapter, I argue that, together, Robinson's *Gilead* and *Home* are about the possibility of the survival of the spirit after death. Considering the repetition between *Gilead*, *Home*, and Robinson's *Lila* also, it's apparent that these works of generations and inheritances themselves share an inheritance, and that these repeating texts are, in turn, peopled by characters twinned in name and deed. At issue are questions of secrets, predestination, and surprises, but Robinson's conclusion can only be that the future holds no surprises for God, who names all possible futures, and brings all home. "Ghostpitality" provides a concise account of Derrida's interpretation of hospitality, detailing the aporetic relationship between conditional and unconditional hospitality. It argues against the idea that pure hospitality is an ethical ideal to aim for and posits that a conditional hospitality is necessary in order to survive the future. Considering the role of the ghost in Derrida's understanding of hospitality, this interleaf returns to DeLillo's *The Body Artist* which, posing the question "Who invites who in?" (118), shows that every host, and therefore every self, body, house, or inside, is haunted by returning guests. The concluding chapter begins with the word "spook," the originally American term for the ghost which returns as a primarily American racial slur, to examine the specter of race in the USA. Moving from Robinson's *Home* to Morrison's *Home*, by way of Morrison's *Paradise*, this chapter progresses from an idea of a community founded on the basis of an apparent covenant with God to the idea of the house, or, more specifically, from the idea of a spiritual paradise to a haunted home. As *Paradise* returns as spectral "Paradise," Morrison's novels themselves become haunted homes accommodating her ghost writing.

This book is intended to be, above all, a work of literary criticism rather than a work of philosophy or literary theory. Some of the interleaves are rather dense, admittedly, but they are also relatively short, while there is hardly a trace of Derrida in some of the chapters themselves. Have I, then, done something as obvious as invite Derrida to haunt this book on ghosts? I'm afraid I have.[26] And this is partly done also in order to follow at a respectful distance, to talk with Derrida but not have him answer for me, to be haunted by Derrida but not possessed by him.

NOTES

1. The line is from "Report from the Besieged City" by Zbigniew Herbert, the Polish poet who lived through Nazi occupation and Stalinist rule. Displaying poetry, the occupied building becomes the literary equivalent of the Nasdaq Center, whose "aq" is short for "automated quotations."
2. Referring to the growth in ghost studies, Sword comments, "When I first decided to write a book about modernist literature and popular spiritualism, it seemed I was venturing into unclaimed critical territory" (159), and "it was disconcerting to find that what I had initially considered a highly original, even unconventional, project had become, inadvertently, a trendy one instead" (160). The spectral trend makes it impossible to provide here even an adequate survey of the available literature, but a sample of works related to this project includes those by Anderson, Bergland, Brogan, Dell Villano, Downey, Garber, Gordon, Parham, Peterson, Thurston, and Weinstock's *Spectral America*. Blanco and Peeren have done valuable work in the area, writing *Ghost-Watching American Modernity* and *The Spectral Metaphor*, respectively, and jointly editing *Popular Ghosts* and *The Spectralities Reader*.
3. For more on Derrida and the question of the ghost, see Appelbaum, Buse and Stott's *Ghosts*, Castricano, Davis, De Boer, Royle's *The Uncanny*, Saghafi, Spivak, Sprinker, *The New International* special issue of *Parallax* 7.3 (2001), *Following Derrida: Legacies* issue of *Mosaic* 40.2 (2007), and *Romanticism and the Legacies of Jacques Derrida* special issue of *Studies in Romanticism* 46.2 (2007), among others.
4. Similarly, Blanchot says, "Everything will come again, everything already and forever has come again, on condition that it is not and has never been present," which is to say, is a ghost (*Step Not Beyond* 16).

5. We could just say that Derrida is ghosting, rather than ghostwriting. The *Oxford English Dictionary* describes how "to ghost" means to "write (something) as a ghost-writer," and details how the use of the word "ghost" for "[o]ne who secretly does artistic or literary work for another person, the latter taking the credit" predates the use of "ghostwriter" by over 40 years.

6. As Royle points out, this "upsets the very basis on which the foreign and the non-foreign might be thought" (*After Derrida* 152).

7. After I write this, I discover that I am citing Henrik Ibsen's *Ghosts* (1881).

8. This understanding of the ghost contrasts with, for example, Anderson's in *Spectrality in the Novels of Toni Morrison*, where she says, "Ghosts do not inhabit one state of being or another, life or death; rather, they inhabit the space between and serve as a conduit of knowledge from one to the other" (11), and she thereby leaves undisturbed the states of life and death.

9. In *Shakespeare's Ghost Writers*, Garber also observes, "Another useful analogue for the concept of a *ghost* as I am using it here can be found in what Jacques Derrida has called 'the logic of the supplement'" (19).

10. *Specters of Marx* is far from being the first time that Derrida writes on ghosts, therefore; he observes, "As for the logic of spectrality, [...] inseparable from the very motif (let us not say the 'idea') of deconstruction, it is at work, most often explicitly, in all the essays published over the last twenty years" (178n3). Buse and Stott state that ghosts "are the stock-in-trade of the Derridean enterprise" (10), while Saghafi shows that "a thought of ghosts, phantoms, and specters has been at work across the entirety or Derrida's corpus" (67) and provides a useful list of references in support (174n3).

11. The "undocumented migrants, servants or domestic workers, mediums and missing person" that Peeren discusses are explicitly "likened to ghosts [...] on the basis of their lack of social visibility, unobtrusiveness, enigmatic abilities or uncertain status between life and death" (5). As a result, she terms *living ghosts* (5) what others more accurately describe as the socially dead. Her expanded argument is closer to Gordon's starting position: "Subjects designated as ghostly in the dispossessing sense of being considered invisible and expendable are not restricted to the option of rejecting the association outright by insisting on their full visible materiality and social significance. They may also work *with* the metaphor, [...] to go from being overlooked to demanding attention by coming to haunt" (7–8) with "*spectral agency*" (16).

12. Gordon sees Derrida's *Specters of Marx* as "a moving and beautiful book [...] and a crucial political intervention" (210n7), but her "Marxist concept of haunting" (20) necessarily departs from Derrida's.

13. Conversely, Blanco seeks to re-ghost the ghost, "to completely forgo the use of any theoretical apparatus, [...] and strip our readings of any given set of preconceptions as a way of seeing the ghost afresh, bringing it back to the drama of its apparition" (20).

14. This choice, however, does not explain why Peeren then persists in critiquing Derrida on the basis of the very opposition between specters and "living, present beings" (14) that his hauntology questions. Her view that "not everything is ghostly" (12) is shared by Sword, who complains that "Derrida deploys the words 'specter' and 'spectral' so often, in so many different permutations and contexts, that they threaten to become verbal specters themselves: suggestive, thought-provoking, ethereal entities drained of all stable referential meaning" (163). And Luckhurst remarks that "it is the very generalized economy of haunting that makes me suspicious of this spectral turn" ("Contemporary London Gothic" 534) in which "to suggest an inevitably historicized mourning work that might actually seek to lay a ghost to rest would be the height of bad manners" (535). He concludes:

> The spectral turn reaches a limit if all it can describe is a repeated structure or generalized "spectral process"—perhaps most particularly when critics suggest the breaching of limits is itself somehow inherently political. [...] If, as Derrida constantly proclaims in "Marx & Sons," the whole thrust of *Specters of Marx* is to aim for a "repoliticization" then surely we have to risk the violence of reading the ghost, of cracking open its absent presence to answer the demand of its specific symptomatology and its specific locale. (542)

It is true that Derrida does not seek to banish the ghost: "The spectre's secret is a productive opening of meaning rather than a determinate content to be uncovered" (Davis 11), and "is not a puzzle to be solved; it is the structural openness or address directed towards the living by the voices of the past or the not-yet formulated possibilities of the future" (13). And, relatedly, for Derrida "the history and politics of a text can be properly found in its iteration and re-inscription, *not* in the imagined fecundity of origins. Historicism, however, seeks to close down these recontextualizations by artificially solidifying them into original contexts" (Buse and Stott 16). Therefore, although Derrida would likely agree with Luckhurst that reading is our only chance, the incalculable violence of that reading already means we cannot provide *the* answer to *the* demand of the ghost as such, here and now. Derrida himself concludes:

> Can one, in order to question it, address oneself to a ghost? [...] The question deserves perhaps to be put the other way: Could one *address oneself in general* if already some ghost did not come back? If he loves justice at least, the "scholar" of the future, the "intellectual" of tomorrow should learn it and from the ghost. He should learn to live by learning not how to make conversation with the ghost but how to talk with him, with her, how to let them speak or how to give them back speech,

> even if it is in oneself, in the other, in the other in oneself: they are always *there*, specters, even if they [...] give us to rethink the "there." (*Specters of Marx* 175–176)

15. According to the *Oxford English Dictionary*, the English form dates from 1605, after the appearance of *Hamlet*'s ghost which, therefore, "becomes, rather, some 'thing' that remains difficult to name" (Derrida, *Specters of Marx* 6).

16. *Revenant* dates from 1690. 1718 is the first time it means, in French, something coming back from the dead, which is its original meaning when it appears in English in 1823.

17. Ramadanovic notes that "the spelling of 'ghost' was not in wide use until the late 1500s, with Shakespeare among the first to use it to refer to a *manifested* 'apparition or specter' of the dead, rather than just the soul of the dead" (215n3). Indeed, the *Oxford English Dictionary* gives *Hamlet* as the first appearance of "ghost" as a visible spirit returned, which means "ghost" first appears when it "comes again" (Shakespeare, *Hamlet* 1.1.39).

18. In dialogue with Elisabeth Roudinesco, Derrida notes in respect of the key aspects of these two quotations, "I have come to insist more and more on this distinction between *specter* or *phantom* on the one hand, and *revenant* on the other. Like 'phantasm,' 'specter' and 'phantom' carry an etymological reference to visibility, to appearing in the light. To that extent, they seem to suppose a horizon on the basis of which, *seeing* what comes or comes back, one annihilates, masters, suspends, or deadens the surprise, the unforeseeability of the event. [...] The 'revenant,' however, comes and comes back (since singularity *as such* implies a repetition) like the 'who' or 'what' of an event without a horizon. Like death itself" (Derrida and Roudinesco 230–31n34).

19. This does not mean that "ideas of present and past merge into timelessness" (Anderson 10) but quite the opposite. The "spectral moment" only "no longer belongs to time, if one understands by this word the linking of modalized presents (past present, actual present: 'now,' future present)" (Derrida, *Specters of Marx* xx), and Derrida wants exactly to effect a change in our understanding of time.

20. Similar examples in DeLillo's *The Body Artist* center around the ghostly Mr. Tuttle: "'It rained very much.' 'It will rain. It is going to rain,' she said" (44); "She listened to him say, Don't touch it. I'll clean it up later. It is the thing you know nothing about. Then she said it herself, some days later. He'd been in there with her. It was her future, not his" (98). Di Prete argues that these examples should be read "within a temporal structure in which past and future converge—and flatten—in a static traumatic present, a dimension shaped by the compulsive repetition and surfacing of fragments of traumatic memories" (492).

21. See also Derrida and Stiegler, and Saghafi (65–82).

22. Keskinen notes that the "media in *The Body Artist* are haunted in the sense that they supernaturally provide Lauren with a live connection to the (at least potentially) dead or non-living. [...] Most of the conversations [...] are set in such a manner that both [participants] are sitting beside a table, with a tape recorder placed at the center. Formally, then, their interaction resembles a spiritualistic séance" (36).

23. In *The Body Artist*, Mr. Tuttle's "future is unnamed. It is simultaneous, somehow, with the present. Neither happens before or after the other and they are equally accessible, perhaps" (77).

24. This phrase is, of course, an oxymoron.

25. All of these writers have previously been discussed with reference to Derrida: for example, for DeLillo and Derrida, see Boxall and Kessel; for Auster and Derrida, see Brault, Dimovitz, McKean, Russell, Sorapure, Uchiyama, and Varvogli; for Roth and Derrida, see Loomis; for Robinson and Derrida, see Mattessich; for Morrison and Derrida, see Burr, Erickson, Loevlie, Luckhurst's "Impossible Mourning," Luszczynska, Page, and Peterson.

26. While writing this book, I discovered that Kelly's *American Fiction in Transition* employs a similar approach, beginning each of its chapters with a prologue which highlights a concept from Derrida's texts—in this case, secrecy, testimony, narcissism, and justice. Kelly explains that each chapter "then attempts to follow Derrida in treating literary criticism as an event of countersignature, a response to the singularity of the work that cannot be dominated by a pre-formulated set of laws" (23).

Ghost Writing

I want to say something in the following chapter about Don DeLillo's *The Body Artist*, a story about a mime and a phantom, but in order to set the stage, I begin here with Derrida's "The Double Session" from *Dissemination*, another account of mimes and phantoms. "The Double Session" is primarily a reading of Stéphane Mallarmé's short text *Mimique*, itself a response to the performer Paul Margueritte's mime piece *Pierrot Murderer of his Wife*, though Barbara Johnson notes that Mallarmé's piece is not so much about the mime artist as it is an imitation of "the very scheme of mimesis itself" (xxviii). Derrida's "The Double Session," therefore, would provide a context within which to consider not only the figure of the body artist as mime but the relation of DeLillo's novel to the scheme of mimesis also. Such a consideration finds that DeLillo's text, in some ways, even mimics Derrida's and Mallarmé's. For example, the editor's note to Derrida's essay remarks that, on the occasion of its oral delivery, "the room was lighted by a sumptuous, old-fashioned lustre" (qtd. in Derrida, "Double Session" 186), even as Derrida describes Mallarmé's work as lit by the "innumerable lustres that hang over the stage of his texts" (194), the light glittering off the many crystal facets perhaps like the face of the sun broken on the surface of a body of water, like the "streaks of running luster on the bay" the day after a storm, as DeLillo writes in the opening paragraph of *The Body Artist* (7), or like "the natural chestnut luster" (103) of the hair of the body artist.[1]

© The Editor(s) (if applicable) and The Author(s) 2016
D. Coughlan, *Ghost Writing in Contemporary American Fiction*,
DOI 10.1057/978-1-137-41024-5_2

When Derrida presented "The Double Session," he did so as something of a mime artist himself. While reading from his text, he would gesture to a blackboard on which a series of quotations was written in white chalk. As he explains, these quotations were to be "pointed to in silence" (192), so throughout his reading, Derrida is pointing to—mimes allusion to—these quotations which, white on black, are the negative image of the black on white text he reads, like their white shadow.[2] It is a question, as he says, of "writing in white" (192). Mallarmé's *Mimique* opens also in "silence" (qtd. in Derrida 189) before the appearance of Margueritte, the mime whose Pierrot will be described by Fernand Beissier as "white, long, emaciated, [...] with his cadaverous face" (qtd. in Derrida 210). Lauren Hartke, DeLillo's mime, will in turn be described as "wasted [...] rawboned and slightly bug-eyed" (*Body Artist* 103). Mallarmé writes that the mime is "white as a yet unwritten page" (qtd. in Derrida, "Double Session" 190), and when DeLillo writes of the body artist, it is also often in terms of whiteness or the uninscribed surface: "She is not pale-skinned so much as colorless, [...] ash white now, [...] albino" (103–104). "This was her work," he writes, "to become a blankness, a body slate" (84).

This blank page of the mime, which means that no words, spoken or written, have been prescribed to her or him so that she or he follows no script or order, leads Derrida to argue that there "is no imitation. The mime imitates nothing" ("Double Session" 208). This is not to say there is no mimicry, because "[t]here is mimicry" (216), but there is no imitation because there is nothing for the mime to imitate, there "is nothing prior to the writing of his gestures" (208). The mimicry cannot be understood as "a relation of resemblance or equality between a re-presentation and a thing," in which the "two faces are separated and set face to face: the imitator and the imitated" (206).

However, is it not the case here that Margueritte imitates Pierrot Murderer of his Wife and Mallarmé imitates *Pierrot Murderer of his Wife*? Because the unwritten drama of Margueritte's mime actually does have a source text—namely, the booklet *Pierrot Murderer of his Wife*—in response to which Mallarmé also writes *Mimique*. Except that Margueritte's booklet was printed in 1882 and then reprinted four years later (the first edition included a preface by Beissier which was replaced in the second edition by an author's note). The second edition is the one that Mallarmé read though it is possible he also saw the first and perhaps even the performance itself. It becomes difficult, therefore, to say what the "supposed 'referent'" of *Mimique* is, what it is responding to, or when that thing occurred

(Derrida, "Double Session" 211).[3] DeLillo reflects this in *The Body Artist* when, like Beissier who met with Margueritte the day after the performance, Lauren's friend Mariella Chapman interviews the mime after the event and then, like Mallarmé, writes in turn her response to something that is unidentifiable because, since Mariella sees "two of the three performances" given by Lauren (105), we cannot simply say to which of the performances her piece refers.

If Mallarmé's text is hardly face-to-face with Margueritte's, the same is true for the mime because both imitators would have read in the booklet, in the very face to be imitated, "a prescription that *effaces itself through its very existence*" (Derrida, "Double Session" 209) in the form of an order to the mime to ignore all orders, to "write upon a white page" (210), and therefore to imitate nothing, no act or word. Moreover, the booklet's prescription was written a year after the 1881 performance so that the late directions provided by the booklet for this past performance are to act as if these not-yet-written words will never have been written. This means that the booklet relates to the mime as a preface to its text because prefaces, written "after the fact" (Derrida, "Outwork" 6) and "in view of their own self-effacement" (7), direct the text to act as if the not-yet-written words of the preface will never have been written, as if the text were self-contained when written thus in white on white in the silence of a self-effacement. The mime therefore writes as he or she mimes, by and on his or her own body, so that the text is "composed and set down by himself" or herself (Mallarmé qtd. in Derrida, "Double Session" 190), the mime writing herself or "himself on the white page he" or she is, says Derrida, "[a]t once page and quill" (209). Margueritte, in his white greasepaint, mimes the killing by Pierrot of his wife by tickling her to death on their marital bed. Like Lauren's body, which "encompasses both sexes and a number of nameless states" (DeLillo, *Body Artist* 109), the white body of the mime plays all the parts, male and female, murderer and victim, his white figure writhing and writing on the white sheets of the bed, "white on white" (Derrida, "Double Session" 208), imitating nothing.

Not only does the mime, Margueritte, represent nothing, but he also is nothing present, is not "the presentation of the thing itself [...], its face" (Derrida, "Double Session" 206). When Margueritte mimes Pierrot miming the killing of his wife, the crime has already taken place. His wife is already dead, he has consulted with the undertaker, and now, "*under the false appearance of a present*" (Mallarmé qtd. in Derrida 190), he relates how he planned and committed the killing. The crime, therefore, is never in the present, "has never occupied the stage," says Derrida (212), and what is mimed is the remembered rehearsal of a future crime and the remembered committing of a past crime. The mime therefore appears to appear in the present, but "here anticipating, there recalling" (Mallarmé qtd. in Derrida 190), it is not present.

The mimes, therefore, do not present the thing itself but the thing already doubled, the thing anticipated or recalled and not "being-present" (Derrida, "Double Session" 204). The impossibility of the mime's self-presence is gestured to when Derrida quotes from "The Double Session" in "Outwork, prefacing," the first essay in *Dissemination*; as if on the threshold of the text, in this opening essay, the reader finds quoted, "Now—this question also announced itself, explicitly, as the question of the *liminal*" (13), but in the later essay, this appears as "But this question has also, explicitly, presented itself as the question *of the liminary*" (245) as if the reader is returned again to the "(pre)liminary question" (245) or the question of the prefatory.[4] Similarly, when Derrida quotes from Mallarmé in "The Double Session," saying "he mimes—'in the present'—'*under the false appearance of a present*'" (211), he returns to a silent allusion in "Outwork, prefacing" describing the preface, wherein it is as if "the text exists as something written—a past—which [...] a hidden omnipotent author (in full mastery of his product) is presenting to the reader as his future" and all "under the false appearance of a present" (6). There is no present face, only the pre-face: "the preface is everywhere" (42).

Mallarmé's mimesis means we are "faced then with mimicry imitating nothing; faced, so to speak, with a double that doubles no simple, a double that nothing anticipates, nothing at least that is not itself already double. There is no simple reference" (Derrida, "Double Session" 217). There is "the copy of the copy. With the exception that there is no longer any model, and hence, no copy" (217). By "imitating (expressing, describing, representing, illustrating)" (207), the mime alludes, "but alludes to nothing" (217). Mallarmé's *Mimique* even includes a quotation—"The scene illustrates but the idea, not any actual action, in a hymen [...], a pure medium, of fiction" (qtd. in Derrida 190)—that is "a simulacrum of a citation," "nowhere to be found," "a Mallarméan fiction," Derrida explains (290). But there are other allusions too, to Margueritte's booklet of course, which is, "for *Mimique*, both a sort of epigraph, an hors d'oeuvre, and a seed, a seminal infiltration: indeed both at once, which only the operation of the *graft* can no doubt represent," so that this text that writes itself is also "grafted onto the arborescence of another text" (214) and another, for the "whole mimodrama refers back one more step, [...] to another text. [...] An eye graft, a text extending far out of sight" (215), taking in Théophile Gautier's *Pierrot Posthume* (1847), or "Hoffmann or Edgar Allan Poe" (Margueritte qtd. in Derrida 292n22), or "an interminable network" of "threads provided by the *comedia dell'arte*," says Derrida (216). *The Body Artist* shares this allusiveness, with Mark Osteen identifying in it a series of "intertextual echoes: hints of the Gothic [...]; nods to the cinema of Ingmar Bergman [...]; a pinch of *Krapp's Last Tape* [...]; and even a dash of Harlequin romance," as well as references to James Joyce's *Ulysses*, to Euripides's *Alcestis*, and to Sophocles's *Ajax*, so that "*The Body Artist* haunts and is haunted" (65). Yet, as when Derrida mimes allusion in the presentation of "The Double Session," motioning to white-written quotations which are there on the white page before him, these are allusions to nothing. As Mallarmé describes it, the mime's "act is confined to a perpetual allusion without breaking the ice or the mirror: he thus sets up a medium, a pure medium, of fiction" (qtd. in Derrida, "Double Session" 190). In this medium of fiction, "this imitator having in the last instance no imitated, this signifier having in the last instance no signified, this sign having in the last instance no referent, their operation is no longer comprehended within the process of truth but on the contrary comprehends *it*" (Derrida 218).

The allusion to nothing is why Mallarmé can speak of the "ever original reappearance of Pierrot or of the [...] mime" (qtd. in Derrida, "Double Session" 189). "Original reappearance," Mallarmé writes, which reappears in Derrida's words as "[r]epetition *and* first time," which "is perhaps the question of the event as question of the ghost" (*Specters of Marx* 10). Yes, we have been waiting a long time, it seems, for the ghost to appear here. But, as Derrida writes, "[T]he specter is always a *revenant* [...] because it *begins by coming back*" (11), like the mime who, from the beginning, was described as "the phantom, white as a yet unwritten page" (Mallarmé qtd. in Derrida, "Double Session" 190); like Pierrots, who "are all, including Margueritte's, at once living and dead, living more dead than alive, *between* life and death" (Derrida, "Double Session" 293n23), and who wander about "like a phantom" (215); and like *Mimique*, which is "haunted by the ghost or grafted onto the arborescence of another text" (214).[5] The ghost has been here all along, both in Derrida's text of "mimes and phantoms" (217) and indeed in DeLillo's text of mimes and phantoms; when Lauren sees the ghost for the first time, she says, "You have been here" (*Body Artist* 43), always already. The body artist, therefore, who "worked her body hard," who put in the hard graft, whose "bodywork made everything transparent" (57), is haunted. DeLillo's mime and phantom are Lauren and Mr. Tuttle, as she calls him, but this mime is also like the phantom, and the phantom is like the mime because she imitates him, and he imitates her, so that it is as if they are mime and mime, or phantom and phantom. But this is just another way of saying that mimesis means a double that faces, so to speak, a double; or that ghost writing means a ghost (like the mime) is writing a haunted text (like *Mimique*) about a ghost (like Pierrot); or that Derrida conceives of mimesis as a ghost writing, which is writing both by and of the ghost. Ghost writing means nothing present represents nothing.

Notes

1. The same opening paragraph describes "a spider pressed to its web," this "wind-swayed web" (7) recalling the image of the text as "a web that envelops a web" at the beginning of Derrida's "Plato's Pharmacy" from *Dissemination* (69).
2. As Cowart notes (202), DeLillo's novel begins also with a silent allusion as the words "Time seems to pass" (7) recall the title of the middle part of Virginia Woolf's novel *To the Lighthouse*: "Time Passes." Woolf, like DeLillo, saw her novel as an architectural structure, as "two blocks joined by a corridor" (qtd. in Lee xiv). Lee describes Woolf's novel as "a ghost story" and argues that "this fiction is itself a 'haunted house'" (xxxiv).
3. *Mimique* is itself the final of three versions of Mallarmé's text, which appeared in 1886, 1891, and 1897.
4. My thanks to Chiara Alfano for drawing attention to the variant translations of this line.
5. In the original French, the words "haunted" and "grafted" in this final quotation rhyme: "*Mimique* est aussi hantée par le fantôme ou entée sur l'arborescence d'un autre texte" (Derrida, *La Dissémination* 230). My thanks to Forbes Morlock for drawing this to my attention.

2. Mimes and Phantoms: Don DeLillo

Don DeLillo's short novel *The Body Artist* opens on a beautiful morning, "a strong bright day after a storm" (7), as Lauren Hartke, the body artist, and her husband Rey Robles, the film director, are having breakfast together in the kitchen. They read the newspaper over coffee, they make toast, they move about the kitchen washing berries, getting the cereal or the orange juice, talking at times, and half-listening to the radio that plays in the background. They seem barely awake, muddled and forgetful, and they shamble "past each other to get things […], still a little puddled in dream melt" (7). The morning's "quickness of light" (7) is reflected in this opening chapter in DeLillo's own writing, which is like the dazzling brightness that leaves afterimages on the eye, or ghost impressions of what is not to be seen, like a memory of the sun. This is a novel about things seen out of the corner of the eye, about half-heard voices, about the noises in the walls, about half-unmade things. It is a ghost story about a haunted house, except that here the house means also the body, or the voice. For example, the first words spoken in the novel are "I want to say something but what" (8), Rey's words, and they echo throughout DeLillo's text, prompting questions about the origin and aim of the words we speak, about the relation between two individuals, about how one might speak for the other or in place of the other, and because these are words of forgetting, remembering, and repeating, about how any one of us can be truly present to herself or himself. In other words, DeLillo's ghost writing is about a way of being, a hauntology, or about how we inhabit and haunt ourselves and others.

© The Editor(s) (if applicable) and The Author(s) 2016
D. Coughlan, *Ghost Writing in Contemporary American Fiction*,
DOI 10.1057/978-1-137-41024-5_3

Under the False Appearance of a Present

Rey's "I want to say something but what" prompts many questions without appearing to be a question itself since there is no question mark at the end of his words. It is as if they are improperly addressed, or interrupted, or unfinished, even as they speak exactly of what is incomplete, of this lacking "what" that Rey desires to say. Even the fact that he says these words aloud seems an expression of their incomplete and supplementary state, as if, in externalizing his want, he manifests the distance by which his desire falls short of its object. Because he cannot get out the words he wants to say, he expresses only their absence, and in doing so he identifies something lacking in himself. The words he wants are not present to him, which means there is something he knows but has forgotten (and knows he has forgotten), which means he does not know himself completely at this time and is not fully present to himself as self. But Rey's phrase is just one of numerous instances in DeLillo's account of the breakfast scene where the self figuratively shambles past itself. Of Lauren, he writes, she had "noticed and forgotten" (*Body Artist* 8); she wonders "[w]hat's it called, the lever" (9); she "realized she had no spoon" (13); she "got up to get something. She looked at the kettle and realized that wasn't it" (16); she "took a bite of cereal and forgot to taste it" (19); she "read and drifted. She was here and there. The tea had no honey in it. She'd left the honey jar unopened" (23); a "voice reported the weather but she missed it. She didn't know it was the weather until it was gone" (24); and "[w]hen he walked out of the room, she realized there was something she wanted to tell him" (24). Of Rey, he writes, he "never remembered the juice until the toast was done" (10) and "he turned on the radio and remembered he'd just turned it off and he turned it off again" (15). The self tunes out, drifts out of step with itself, and so Rey's phrase speaks to this self which is not itself, or in itself.[1]

As Rey speaks out, it's not clear if he believes he can rely on what Plato might call his own "internal resources" (96) to remember. Perhaps Rey is addressing himself with these words, and if the distance from mouth to ear is like the distance between that self which knows that it wants to say something and that self which would know what that something is (which, ideally, would be no distance at all), he wants this nonquestion to close the gap between one self and the other, to catch one up to the other.[2] Except, there is also the understanding that what Rey wants cannot be thought without the other, either the other self or the other person. The transit of these words from mouth to ear will circle out, will take in Lauren too, and perhaps this is what Rey intended all along since he next remarks, "Something I meant to tell you" (DeLillo, *Body Artist* 8). His words, like writing, something far from self-contained, will prove "not a remedy for memory, but for reminding" (Plato qtd. in Derrida, "Plato's Pharmacy" 105) because Lauren, as the other half of the couple, might well be able to tell him what it is that he wants to say. His words may have strayed from him, but Lauren will trace them for him. Perhaps she has heard it all before, and that is how she will remind him now of his unremembered words, "echoing Rey, identifyingly" (DeLillo, *Body Artist* 9), and he will nod in affirmation and repeat them, with certainty. Or perhaps this is something unforeseen by her, but still he wants her to speak for him, to speak in his place, with her voice but his words, saying this something that he cannot, for whatever reason. The question then is whether she can ever say what it is, or if that which seems to lie on the other side of "what" will remain forever unspoken or unknown, at an "infinite remove" (Derrida, *Memoires* 6).

In this way, the "what" brings into play not only the (dis)connection with the self but also the (dis)connection between the self and other who "shambled past each other" (DeLillo, *Body Artist* 7) even as he "want[ed] to say something" (8) to her and "she realized there was something she wanted to tell him" (24). The sense of being discontinuous with ourselves, therefore, chimes with a discontinuous relation to the other that DeLillo also marks with the word "what," which forms the shaky grounds for shared communication. Rey, having told Lauren there is "Something I meant to tell you" (8), later declares, "I know what it is," to which she responds with "What?" meaning, writes DeLillo, "what did you say, not what did you want to tell me" (9). She is asking him to repeat, not to enlighten. What is it that Lauren and Rey talk about as DeLillo presents, in the space of just 19 pages, the following exchanges?

> "Yes exactly. I know what it is," he said. [...] She said, "What?" [...] realizing what it was he'd said that she hadn't heard. (9)
>
> He said, "Do you want some of this?" [...] She said, "What? Never drink the stuff." (10–11)
>
> "I always think this isn't supposed to happen here. I think anywhere but here." He said, "What?" (11)
>
> "I've seen you drink gallons of juice, tremendous, how can I tell you?" he said. [...] "What? I don't think so," she said. (12)
>
> "Cut yourself again." "What? [...] Just a nick." (13)

"Do you have to listen to the radio?" "No," she said and read the paper. "What?" (14)

"Not the young woman who eats and sleeps and lives forever." "What? Hey, Rey. Shut up." (15)

He said, "What?" "I didn't say anything." (16)

"Weren't you going to tell me something?" He said, "What?" (16)

"Just tell me okay. Because I know anyway." He said, "What? You insist you will drag this thing out of me." (18)

"All day yesterday I thought it was Friday." He said, "What?" (20)

"Have you seen my keys?" She said, "What?" He waited for the question to register. "Which keys?" she said. (25)[3]

In all but one of these instances, when Rey asks what it is that is not supposed to happen, the "what" means "what did you say?" And yet, repeatedly, a response follows the apparently unheard comment. Each time there seems to be a break in the communication, a message not received, but then the one responds to the other, responding not to the original utterance but—here anticipating, there recalling—responding instead to its expected repetition, or to a delayed form of it. Lauren says, "What?" and then, "She reached in for the milk, realizing what it was he'd said that she hadn't heard about eight seconds ago" (9).

These spoken words, therefore, are not heard in the present, and the word "what" marks a break in the here and now, a shift in the presence of the self and the other. The response is to a remark recollected or anticipated, not immediately apprehended, and therefore to something that has its source within the self and also in the other that lies without (but we've already seen how the words "I want to say something but what" disturb any proper sense of within and without). The question of self, therefore, is articulated around this "what" that places the other at an impossible distance and yet that also finds his or her tongue in my mouth: Rey "handed her what remained of his toast and she chewed it mingled with cereal and berries. Suddenly she knew what he'd meant to tell her" (DeLillo, *Body Artist* 17). Rey says, "I want to say something but what," but it is Lauren who gives voice to what he has yet to say, repeating his as-yet unheard words, planting his words in her mouth, saying, "The noise" (18). "The noises in the walls. Yes," says Rey, "You've read my mind" (18). She had read his mind, as if these words were "unspokenly, hers" (just before Rey says, "I want to say something but what," DeLillo writes, "They shared the newspaper but it was actually, unspokenly, hers" [8]).

Lauren's pronouncement of Rey's silent words, the words that were "unspokenly, hers," should remind us that she is also the mime, the one who "imitates nothing" (Derrida, "Double Session" 208), who "alludes to nothing" (217), who presents nothing that Rey has said. But we should not think that Lauren, in saying "The noise," can make Rey's "something" present, as if she could be identical to his self that wants to say this something. No, as Mallarmé tells us, the mime's mime, "here anticipating, there recalling," appears *under the false appearance of a present* (qtd. in Derrida 190), so that it is itself nothing present. This becomes even more apparent in the body artist's mime performances, which are present only as mimes of the future and as mimes of the past. For example, when Lauren's preparations are described, "the days she worked her body hard" (DeLillo, *Body Artist* 57), they include "slow-motion repetitions of everyday gestures, checking the time on your wrist or turning to hail a cab" (58). These mimed gestures are a rehearsal for those future performances which, when past, will be described by Lauren's friend and interviewer Mariella Chapman: "Here is a woman in executive attire, carrying a briefcase, who checks the time on her wristwatch and tries to hail a taxi. [...] She does this many times, countless times. Then she does it again, half-pirouetting in very slow motion" (106). Lauren's mime, therefore, is never present in the text and it presents nothing because the actions performed at every stage, checking the time and hailing a taxi, are described as "actions quoted by rote" (58), "the mechanical 'by-heart'" (Derrida, "Plato's Pharmacy" 111). Each action is the copy of a copy of no model, a copy without a copy.

Remarkably, therefore, when Lauren speaks for Rey, it is as if she is a mime artist imitating Rey. And, if the self imitates the other in this way (while still imitating nothing), each self seems also to imitate itself: following no script, but not giving immediate voice to their selves either, Lauren and Rey live on as perpetual allusions to no sure self in "a pure medium, of fiction" (Mallarmé qtd. in Derrida, "Double Session" 190), shambling past themselves as well as each other. This mimetic half-life, which is our life, is fictional exactly because it is not simple or simply present. And knowing this, we can understand also that when Derrida addresses mimesis, he too conceives of it in terms of a general "writing" or "text" which "comprises an effect of traces and remnants, marked by a ghostly logic of death and survival (or 'living on')" (Royle, *Jacques Derrida* 64). This ghost writing means a living on where always again "I want to say something but what."

White as a Yet Unwritten Page

The life described by the words "I want to say something but what" is incomplete, desiring, fallible, grafted to the other, taking a risk on the other, and therefore mortally exposed to the future. "I want to say something but what" conveys the terrible possibility of death's interruption, coming before even a question mark can be added to give the appearance at least of a proper end. So lacking, it addresses the distance between our living on, marked by death, and the idea of a life fully lived in the here and now, wholly present to itself, and speaking for itself. Yet, most importantly, DeLillo's novel tells us that if a self does speak for itself, or is one with its words and so does not speak the language of the other, this self speaks only to itself, in silence. If there is no distance between the self and its words, there is no room for the other, no chance for the other to listen in, to respond, chide, laugh, affirm, or echo, so the self is dead to the other. The self that is not marked by death (so that it is as if it were immortal) is dead.

And Rey is dead. Even on the first page of DeLillo's novel, the new day is also already identified as "this final morning" (*Body Artist* 7), the last morning Lauren and Rey will spend together. When it's over, Rey will say that he is going for a drive into town, and Lauren will think of a list of shopping to buy later on, some Ajax scouring powder, toilet cleanser, and a newspaper, but instead of just going for a drive, Rey will head to the New York apartment of his first wife and commit suicide, the cause of death being "a self-inflicted gunshot" (27). When Rey, therefore, says, "I want to say something but what," what he wants to say might be "I want to kill myself." Every "what," in this way, in marking the absence of the other, gives the "sense that death is already here, already with us at the breakfast table" (Boxall 218). But as long as Rey is saying, "I want to kill myself," which, in other words, is saying, "I want to say something but what" because it effects the distance of the want, then he is not dead but is living on.[4] It is only when, finally, he wants nothing, when there are no words to share, when there is only silence punctuated by a gunshot, that he is dead.

After Rey's death, the first words spoken in the novel ring out, again, "I want to say something but what," and seem to find a response, or an echo, a reflection, in a deferred anadiplosis in the second chapter, when Mariella calls to ask Lauren, "Are you all right?" and Lauren asks, "What am I supposed to say?" (DeLillo, *Body Artist* 39).[5] These two—"I want to say something but what" and "what am I supposed to say?"—may seem to work together to complete each other, for example in the way that Lauren provides Rey's words with their missing question mark as if she had full possession of these words. However, the shared though divided "what" at the center, which joins even as it separates these two lines, undoes any sense of a fully present meaning. Instead, the two parts, set face-to-face like imitator and imitated, pass the absent presence between them as they each look to the other on the question of what it is one wants or is expected to say. Each self calls to the other to finish things ("kill me," "love me"), only to be answered by the same call. The self and other, therefore, are folded together around a death (indeed, an obituary for Rey appears between the first and second chapters); they are unhinged by the "what" that will not let one complete the other's words, or fully translate the other, or answer the question never posed, or finish what the other never truly started.

The folding structure of "I want to say something but what," "what am I supposed to say," through which the impossible relation of the self and other plays out, is evident throughout DeLillo's novel. That first chapter, for example, opening on that "strong bright day after a storm" (*Body Artist* 7), doubles back upon itself, or pirouettes, so that it closes also "on a strong bright day after a storm" (25), as if effacing itself. Also, the last line of the novel describes how Lauren "wanted to feel the sea tang on her face and the flow of time in her body, to tell her who she was" (124); in its reference to time, this final line doubles back through Lauren's prepa-rations in the second chapter for her next performance and her plans "to organize time until she could live again" (37) and folds back on to the novel's first line, "Time seems to pass" (7). "Time seems to pass," but it seems to get us nowhere further than the first words again, so it is as if the book proper has not yet started; this (therefore) will not have been a novel, or, to put it another way, it will have been a novel that, like Rey, wants to say something but what. In this light, Rey's prefatory words haunt all that the novel is supposed to say, and what follows from them is repetition because everything has already been alluded to, unspokenly.[6]

The Body Artist, therefore, everywhere prefaced by the self-effacing "I want to say something but what," imitates the scheme of mimesis itself. "What" in the text marks, on the one hand, not being present and, on the other hand, the repetition of no present original, as when Lauren says, "'What?' [...] realizing what it was he'd said that she hadn't heard" (DeLillo, *Body Artist* 9). A complicated instance later in the novel illustrates this mimetic scheme wherein the double faces the double. It occurs in chapter 5, when part of Lauren's conversation with Rey on that last day is replayed for her: "'But where are you going?' He said, 'Just a little while into town.' [...]" (86). What this later repetition does is make explicit an earlier allusion occurring in the opening chapter; then, Lauren is seen to note "the Ajax she needs to buy" (25), but now it becomes apparent that she had remarked on this allusion to the hero of Greek mythology: "Ajax, son of Telamon, I think, if my Trojan War is still intact, and maybe we need a newspaper because the old one's pretty stale, and great brave warrior, and spear-thrower of mighty distances, and toilet cleanser too" (87). What Lauren does not say, however, is that Ajax also committed suicide. This unspoken allusion, therefore, anticipates Rey's future suicide, and the later replaying of these words (like the mime's mime) repeats the past rehearsal of a future death even as it recalls Rey's suicide under the false appearance of a present. Lauren thinks this is not just "remembering. It is happening now" (87), but what is happening now is not of the now. Rey's death is never present in the text but is alluded to as something in the future and in the past. The repeated allusion is to no simple reference, and the allusion itself is not simple because at what point does the reference to Ajax become an allusion to Rey's death? Is it at the point it appears, in the opening chapter, before he dies? Or is it perhaps at the point of the "what": "'I know what to get. We need some what's-it-called. Scouring powder.' He said, 'What?'" (86).

The mirroring structure of "I want to something but what," "what am I supposed to say," wherein nothing present represents nothing, is exemplified again by DeLillo in a passage from the first chapter when Lauren and Rey are still together in the kitchen. Lauren has been standing at the stove:

> When she started back she saw a blue jay perched atop the feeder. She stopped dead and held her breath. It stood large and polished and looked royally remote from the other birds busy feeding and she could nearly believe she'd never seen a jay before. It stood enormous, looking in at her, seeing whatever it saw, and she wanted to tell Rey to look up.
>   [...] But if Rey looked up, the bird would fly.
>   She tried to work past the details to the bird itself, nest thief and skilled mimic, to the fixed interest in those eyes, a kind of inquisitive chill that felt a little like a challenge.
>   When birds look into houses, what impossible worlds they see. Think.
> (*Body Artist* 21–22)

Either side of a windowpane, two mimes, the body artist and the jay, face each other, as one would face an image in a mirror. The bird looks inside from outside and impossibly sees, sees what is impossible to see, but without ever breaking the glass.[7] In the same way, each complicated self can see—even think—the complicated other but can never immediately possess them; they may be "never so close" (22), and still they are not close enough. But in the end (and Lauren "knew it was ending already" [22]), it is this very distance which means they are not closed to others: if they were simply themselves, as if outside, then they would be dead to the other; if others could simply be them, as if inside, then those others would not be themselves. In this scene, see how the jay and Rey are joined and separated by the rhyming of their names and by the series of actions in which Rey's looking up leads in to the line of flight of the bird, in a strange echo. This scene never appears exactly as Lauren wants it to, with herself and Rey and the jay all present, but for this, she should be grateful. It is only because no context is complete that anything survives from one moment to the next. It is only because no self is complete that Lauren can ask, when Rey is dead, "What am I supposed to say?" and still give the echo of an answer, an allusion to nothing. Lauren, mourning Rey, must want to say something of, to, for the one who is now so very absent. But was Rey ever properly present? Is the other ever wholly there? Osteen remarks that "it is scarcely surprising that Rey haunts Lauren, because in some sense he was already a ghost when alive" (69). *The Body Artist* tells us that death is always already here and that is why something can survive it. Perhaps, therefore, the answer to "what am I supposed to say?" is the same as the answer to "I want to say something but what," is "noise" (18), the word that Lauren impossibly speaks when she repeats what Rey has not yet said.[8] As Royle observes, *The Body Artist* is concerned "with the ways in which a loved one doesn't die when he (or she) dies" ("Clipping"), and this original reappearance of words, this ghost writing, is what finally survives Rey.

THE EVER ORIGINAL REAPPEARANCE

There is something ghostly about both Lauren and the jay in the above scene: the one stopped dead and holding its breath, and the other appearing as if for the first time even though it has been there before. In fact, it will always have been here before, as a nest thief, with this house as its haunt. Similarly (and soon after she asks, "What am I supposed to say?"), when Lauren finds the ghost, DeLillo writes, "In the first seconds she

thought he was inevitable. She felt her way back in time to the earlier indications that there was someone in the house and she arrived at this instant,
unerringly" (*Body Artist* 41). She is perhaps thinking of the noises in the
house, the "noises in the walls" (18) as Rey describes them, so when Rey
says, "I want to say something but what" (8), it is a question of ghosts.

The ghost is a small, boyish figure of a man, and Lauren will call him
Mr. Tuttle. She finds him "sat on the edge of the bed" (DeLillo, *Body
Artist* 41), exactly where one might find the mime Margueritte's mimed
Pierrot also, that white figure writ(h)ing on the white sheets of the bed. It
is a scene that Mallarmé might be describing when he concludes *Mimique*
with the line that "between the sheets and the eye there reigns a silence still,
the condition and delight of reading" (qtd. in Derrida, "Double Session"
190). The ghostly figure is between the eye that reads (in French, *lit*) and
the bed (in French, *lit*), whose sheets double now as sheets of paper, their
surfaces warped by his slight appearance. He has been here all along but
barely here, for where is the "here" of the "between"? "Because," as he
says himself, "nothing comes between me" (DeLillo, *Body Artist* 74). The
ghost is "in the walls" (18), between an inside and outside, between here
and there, between now and then, between the present and the nonpresent, between distance and nondistance, between the sun and the luster,
"outside the easy sway of either/or" (69), and therefore giving rise to the
very structures within which we understand an inside and outside, self and
other, truth and appearance, presence and absence, life and death.[9] Mr.
Tuttle takes place in-between, like the never-present "what" of "I want
to say something but what," "what am I supposed to say?" which enfolds
Rey and Lauren and is the medium through which they communicate
even as they find they cannot speak immediately to each other. He is in-
between Rey and Lauren, taken under Lauren's wing, and, from his first
words, brought into the fold of the anadiplosis: Mr. Tuttle "said something. She said, 'What?'" (43).[10]

The scene of ghost writing, which structures the relations between
eye and page, involves the "necessity of folding," says Mallarmé (qtd. in
Derrida, "Double Session" 237). The stage is set as in a cave of mirrors with the "blankness" of those virgin sheets and of the mime
(DeLillo, *Body Artist* 84), with the fold in the fabric or the material,
and with the silence and the ghost.[11] In this space, the mime "mimes
a kind of writing (hymen) and is himself written in a kind of writing. Everything is reflected in the medium or speculum of reading-
writing, '*without breaking the mirror*'" (Derrida, "Double Session"

232). What could such a medium look like, this medium which, "illustrating nothing—neither word nor deed—beyond itself, illustrates nothing
[…] but the many-faceted multiplicity of a lustre which itself is nothing
beyond its own fragmented light" (218)? If we are on "that side of the
lustre where the 'medium' is shining" (221), there will be, no doubt, "a
quickness of light and a sense of things outlined precisely and streaks of
running luster on the bay" (DeLillo, *Body Artist* 7). Indeed, as regards the
"origin […] of appearing beings, it is not possible to speak simply" because
"it is no more possible to look them in the face than to sta[r]e at the sun"
(Derrida, "Plato's Pharmacy" 87), so we find ourselves "only looking at
the image […] reflected in the water" (Plato qtd. in Derrida 89). The light
streaks off the surface of the water, reflects, refracts, and disperses across the
medium, like drops of water threaded on a spider's web, or like "how water
from the tap […] ran silvery and clear and then in seconds turned opaque"
(DeLillo, *Body Artist* 8). The light diffracts, illuminating things that are
glimpsed as if out of the corner of an eye or even snatched from half-heard
sounds because the light is scattering words and meaning.[12] We've seen
it already in the way the name Rey echoes in "jay" (21) and echoes on in
"bay" (7), "day" (7), "swayed" (7), "radio" (10), "say" (16), "ashtray"
(23), and "stray" (108).[13] You might even hear it in Mallarmé.[14] You can
find it also in the words "reality" (12), "everything" (17), "retroactively"
(20), "clearly" (21), "memory" (24), "yesterday" (25), or prefatory.[15] And
Rey echoes in Lauren's name, also, which comes from the Bay Laurel (while
Robles comes from the Spanish for "oaks"). Mark Osteen takes this aural
grafting further when he draws attention to Lauren's description of soya as
having "a faint wheaty stink with feet mixed in" (13) and "notes here how
'feet' itself 'mixes' the sounds of the words 'faint' and 'wheaty'" (68). Also,
in the scene between Lauren and the bird, the word "jay" seems to move
through being "royally remote" to appear as "Rey" (21); the jay is a mimic,
and the word "jay" is a mimic.[16] Osteen observes too how words "change
shape, sometimes merely eluding capture and at other times transmigrating
from noun to verb, from blade to body" (68) when Lauren "had to sort
of jackknife away from the counter when he approached to get the butter
knife" (DeLillo, *Body Artist* 12). When Lauren says to Mr. Tuttle, "Do
Rey. Make me hear him" (71), Osteen says "an attentive listener may hear
behind her exhortations the syllables of an ascending and descending major
scale in solfeggio ('Do, re, mi …')" (73), so her "words flutter and dart,
seldom landing on a precise definition" (67). Philip Nel also traces pat-
terns of sound and look and shows "how carefully shaped language appears
to bind words to things but all the while radiates implications elsewhere"

(748). Ghost writing is not single-minded but wanders, obliging, giving itself freely, democratically, taking offers. It is open to finding itself in different places, in different mouths, home to different understandings, housed in different hearts.

Plato calls "written discourse only a kind of ghost" (qtd. in Derrida, "Plato's Pharmacy" 148), not living, or true, or present, or real, but DeLillo's text shows that the ghost is not outside of speech, or life, or the self; rather, it has been here all along.[17] Beyond the opening chapter, DeLillo continues to represent the ghostliness of life. He describes how the "dead squirrel you see in the driveway, dead and decapitated, turns out to be a strip of curled burlap, but you look at it, you walk past it, even so, with a mixed tinge of terror and pity" (*Body Artist* 111). He describes how "you drop something. Only you don't know it. […] But once you know you've dropped something, you hear it hit the floor, belatedly. […] Now that you know you dropped it, you remember how it happened, or half remember, or sort of see it maybe, or something else […], but when you bend to pick it up, it isn't there" (89–90). He describes how Lauren "thought she saw a bird. Out of the corner of her eye she saw something rise past the window, eerie and bird-like but maybe not a bird. […] She saw it mostly in retrospect because she didn't know what she was seeing at first and had to re-create the ghostly moment, write it like a line in a piece of fiction" (91). He describes how Lauren felt that she "saw a man sitting on his porch, ahead of her, through trees and shrubs, arms spread, a broad-faced blondish man, lounging […], that she saw him complete. His life flew open to her passing glance. […] When the car moved past the house, in the pull of the full second, she understood that she was not looking at a seated man but at a paint can placed on a board" (70). He describes how things "seemed doubtful—not doubtful but ever changing, plunged into metamorphosis, something that is also something else, but what, and what" (36). What is described here is not something less than what happens in the mimetic art of the body artist. Lauren sees "a white-haired woman, Japanese, alone on a stone path in front of her house" (35), and she metamorphoses in the performance into "an ancient Japanese woman on a bare stage, gesturing in the stylized manner of Noh drama" (105); Mr. Tuttle is presented as "the naked man" who "wants to tell us something" (107). In art as in life, the "thing is communicated somehow" (83), but art is not afraid to foreground the "[s]omehow. The weakest word in the language" (92), and to speculate on how it plays out in the world. DeLillo's art in the unreal, fictional world of this novel is to ask if somehow life appears as if real, as if present: "It was always as if. He did this or that as if " (45), "as if, as if" (78), as if "[e]verything is reflected in the medium or speculum of reading-writing" (Derrida, "Double Session" 232).[18] In this medium, Mr. Tuttle can say, "The word for moonlight is moonlight" and it can be "beautiful and true" (DeLillo, *Body Artist* 82). But it is true because Mr. Tuttle, this "strange quasiperson," is not claiming, as Calvin Thomas suggests, "that the word moonlight *really is moonlight*" (56), thereby contradicting "the impossibility of a word's meaning merging with its real being" (57); rather, he is pointing to the moonlight's unreal being and to the truth that the word for moonlight is a double that faces no simple reference, that the word in fact reflects a mirror because the sun is the real source of a moon's reflected light. So, what really is moonlight? Mr. Tuttle's statement is true "because every image in every mirror is only virtual, even when you expect to see yourself" (DeLillo, *Body Artist* 113). "*There is nothing outside of the text* [*il n'y a pas de hors-texte*]" (Derrida, *Of Grammatology* 158), there is no "not-as-if of things" (DeLillo, *Body Artist* 90), no "as such" of things, and everything is instead reflecting rays of light, like Rey's light. In this world, it is as if the ghost is alive, this something which is the appearance of nothing, which represents what is not present, which gives voice to what is unheard, which is the caress of no touch, which is "a ghost that is the phantom of no flesh" (Derrida, "Double Session" 217).

It Was Always as If

Mr. Tuttle, in the flesh, is described by Lauren as "smallish and fine-bodied and at first she thought he was a kid, sandy-haired and roused from deep sleep" (DeLillo, *Body Artist* 41). From this description, it might seem that Mr. Tuttle is rather too solid to be a ghost, too physical or bodily, but the ghost is always that nothing which is more there, more present, than one might expect. It is the nothing that is written into the world, as when Lauren names the ghost Mr. Tuttle because she "thought it would make him easier to see" (48), this "almost unnameable thing" (Derrida, *Specters of Marx* 6).

This instance of ghost writing is key to understanding Mr. Tuttle's appearance in the novel, which occurs at a point where Lauren is at risk of disappearing herself, like Rey. Mariella calls, asks Lauren, "Are you all right?" (DeLillo, *Body Artist* 39), and continues, "God. But you don't want to fold up into yourself. [...] But you have to direct yourself out of this thing, not into it. Don't fold up" (39). The very structure of the novel seems to invite Lauren to fold up into herself in the way that the body of the narrative (from Chap. 2 to Chap. 6) is separated from the opening and concluding chapters by Rey's obituary ("Rey Robles, 64, Cinema's Poet of Lonely Places") and Mariella's interview ("Body Art in Extremis: Slow, Spare and Painful"), respectively. If, in the first chapter, Lauren "stopped dead and held her breath" (21), if, in the second chapter, she hears from "New York, where she lived" (36) but where she is not, and if she must perform "breathing exercises" (37) that will continue until the final page of the book sees her "breathing completely" (124), then Lauren is entombed within the narrative's central chapters, or "lives in limbo" (Osteen 70), effectively cut off from and dead to the world. When Mariella then asks, "Are you all right?" and Lauren replies, "What am I supposed to say?" and is told "you don't want to fold up into yourself," we understand that she is being told to live on and is meant therefore to direct herself toward the other or to fold herself around the other because only the fold of the anadiplosis will open her to what is outside herself, in the distant first chapter, in "I want to say something but what."[19] In the fold of "I want to say something but what," "what am I supposed to say," the outside haunts the inside. It is this outside other which haunts Lauren in the form of Mr. Tuttle, who appears shortly after her conversation with Mariella and means she will not disappear into herself. As Derrida writes, "Ghosts: the concept of the other in the same, [...] the completely other, dead, living in me" (*Work of Mourning* 41–42).

Lauren and Mr. Tuttle are a mime and a phantom, which is to say a mime and a mime, or a phantom and a phantom, the same but different. He is the "what" that ensures the same is different and distanced from self and other, as in "I want to say something but what," "what am I supposed to say." The distance is there in what Osteen terms the "echo-lalia" (70) of his speech, such as when he repeats Lauren's "The white ones" and "beyond the trees" (DeLillo, *Body Artist* 44) or responds to her "Talk to me" with "Talk to me" and "Say some words" with "Say some words" (46). Later, however, their positions are reversed, and Lauren now responds to Mr. Tuttle's "Say some words" with "Say some words" and "In when it comes" with "In when it comes. What?" (81). As well as this repetition, there is a more pronounced form of imitation when Mr. Tuttle speaks, and it "wasn't outright impersonation but she heard elements of her own voice [...]. She wasn't sure it was her voice. Then she was [...], and she began to realize she'd said these things to Rey, here in the house [...]. She remembered, she recalled" these other moments (50–51). It is through an appeal to technology first that Lauren attempts to explain Mr. Tuttle's ability to repeat her words: he'd "heard her voice on the tape recorder" (56) she tries to convince herself, so that his repetitions are no more than a replication of technical means of reproduction, something to do with a reminding rather than a remembering. She is trying to identify the source of her own words, feeling they have strayed from her, and they have, for the hand gesture that Mr. Tuttle makes as he speaks, she realizes, is "unmistakably Rey's, two fingers joined and wagging" (51), so that these are her words as heard by Rey, or drawn from the distance between her mouth and his ear. These words have returned to her only because they were distanced from her and were never immediately present to her alone.

Mr. Tuttle, therefore, is what survives the present that threatens to become for Lauren a tomb or a grave. As a result, she recognizes in him a disordering of the present, or of the here and now, observing that "[m]aybe this man experiences another kind of reality where he is here and there, before and after [...]. She thought maybe he lived in a kind of time that had no narrative quality" (DeLillo, *Body Artist* 64–65). "His future is unnamed. It is simultaneous, somehow, with the present" (77), he "remembers the future" (100) and rehearses the future, repeating it in advance. Lauren is disconcerted by Mr. Tuttle's double-time because initially, she conceives of temporality in terms of a conventional series of past present, present, and future present moments: "Something is happening. It has happened. It will happen" (98–99). This conception of "time existing in reassuring sequence, passing, flowing, happening" (77) is a comforting vision because it "stretches events and makes it possible for us to suffer and come out of it and see death happen and come out of it" (92). In other words, belief in a definite past, present, and future brings with it the happy possibility that she might at least move on and leave suffering and death in the past, behind her. "Time is the only narrative that matters" (92), she thinks, looking forward to when the "future comes into being" (99) as a present moment cleansed of the past. Alternatively, the other happy possibility is that Mr. Tuttle might make the past itself present, returning Rey to her; when Mr. Tuttle imitates the past, as when he recites Rey's last words back to her, she wants to set this in the here and now: it "was Rey's voice alright [...], but she didn't think the man was remembering. It is happening now. This is what she thought. [...] Rey is alive now in this man's mind, in his mouth and body and cock" (87). What has happened is happening and is the same, she thinks. Identifying these ambivalent positions, Osteen writes that, "On the one hand she seeks to scour away the past [...]. Yet she also desires to recapture the past through Tuttle" (74) or, as Rachel Smith says, "Lauren looks to this possibility of stopping time, of living perpetually in a group of always-present and palpable simultaneous moments, as a way of life that could allow her to avoid leaving the dead behind" (100). Sadly for Lauren, however, even in those moments when she is convinced that Mr. Tuttle represents "not some communication with the dead. It was Rey alive in the course of a talk he'd had with her" (61), still DeLillo writes also that "she realized [Mr. Tuttle] was talking to her. But it was Rey's voice she was hearing" (60), so there is no simple present but rather one doubled between Mr. Tuttle and Rey. Lauren must finally conclude that "Rey is not alive in this man's consciousness" (91) and come to terms instead with the way one (time) haunts another. In this sense, time only *seems* to pass; time is out of joint and doesn't really pass from a past present to a now to a future present.[20] Lauren may think of Mr. Tuttle that, "The future comes into being. But not for him" (98), but the truth is that the future doesn't come into being for any of us. The future is always coming but never *is*. And time is passing; it is going and coming.

Mr. Tuttle "laps and seeps, somehow, into other reaches of being, other time-lives, and this is an aspect of his bewilderment and pain" (DeLillo, *Body Artist* 92) even as it is an aspect of Lauren's pain and of the hurt of all who are in mourning. Lauren's mime performance, *Body Time*, when you "feel time go by, viscerally, even painfully" (104), emerges from her contact with Mr. Tuttle. It is a "repetitious" (106) effort "to think of time differently, [...] open it up" (107). It's "a still life that's living" (107), or still living, surviving, through repetitions and citations, but imitating nothing. "How simple it would be," she says to Mariella, "if I could say this is a piece that comes directly out of what happened to Rey. But I can't" (108). It's more complicated than that, representing "an undertaking of the dead that must remain incomplete [...] by permitting them to live again as echoes" (Osteen 65).[21] Mr. Tuttle, as phantom mime, has illustrated for Lauren the "mimetic interiorization" (Derrida, *Memoires* 34) that lets a dead man speak, those repetitions that "let him speak within oneself, to make him present and faithfully to represent him" (Derrida, *Work of Mourning* 38), and that Derrida describes as "at once a duty [...] and the worst of temptations, the most indecent and most murderous" (38), as we risk either betraying the dead completely by erasing others in words that are more our own, or remaining too faithfully true to others, desiring to be consumed by them, possessed utterly. Though Mr. Tuttle may have brought Rey and Lauren close again, he has also shown her that "it would be unfaithful to delude oneself into believing that the other living *in us* is living *in himself*" (Derrida, *Memoires* 21). The other always remains at the distance of the "what," and the self always speaks impossibly for the other. This is why, soon after Rey's death, when Lauren begins to pick up the phone, she uses "a soft voice at first, not quite her own, a twisted tentative other's voice, to say help, who is this, yes" (DeLillo, *Body Artist* 36). It is after this that she hears her own voice coming from Mr. Tuttle, almost unrecognizable, and then she hears the voice of her absent husband from this same mouth. This is why, when Mr. Tuttle is gone, "[a]t first the voice she used on the telephone was nobody's, a generic neutered human, but then she started using his. It was his voice, a dry piping sound, hollow-bodied, like a bird humming on her tongue" (101).[22] She cannot speak as Rey, but she can speak as the ghost of Rey, the ghost of the other, alluding to nothing.

At the end of her interview with Mariella, Lauren excuses herself for a moment, "but she doesn't come back" (DeLillo, *Body Artist* 110). Then she does, in the last chapter, like a ghost shambling past herself. Things are the same but different: "She threw off the sweater and hit her hand on the hanging lamp, which she always forgot was there"; "She knew it was five-thirty and looked at her watch" (112); "She sat down to eat the food on the plate and thought I'm not hungry" (113). There are folds within folds and a distorted echo of the anadiplosis as a man arrives at the house and she says to him, "And there is something you want to discuss" (118), and follows it with, "This is not what he was supposed to say" (119). She mimes killing herself with "the spray-gun bottle, [...] the pistol-grip bottle of tile-and-grout cleaner, [...] the muzzle to her head" (114). Then, it is as if what has happened is happening again because, before, "[i]n the morning she heard the noise" (40) and Mr. Tuttle appeared and, now, after, "[i]n the morning she heard the noise" (120) and she imagines him "sat on the edge of the bed in his underwear, lighting the last cigarette of the day" (122), but is this Mr. Tuttle on the bed or Rey lighting his cigarette? She's at the threshold of her room but "stopped at the edge of the doorway, [...] stopped at room's edge, facing back into the hall" (123), and looking back at her final morning with Rey, trying to rewrite it in fact, so she "takes his car keys and hides them, hammers them, beats them, eats them, buries them in the bone soil on a strong bright day in late summer, after a roaring storm" (123). Smith draws attention here to the way "the novel begins to produce two Laurens, one who is physically present with Rey in the room, [...] and the other who narrates the scene without looking" (107). Lauren wants only for the two to become one, to sync, as if she were "fitting herself to a body in the process of becoming hers" (DeLillo, *Body Artist* 121) so that "[o]nce she steps into the room, she will already have been there" (122), and she's now only "catching up" (124). But instead, she finds herself, like a ghost, between the first and third floors, between new and used, between the last light of the day and the morning light, between the hall and the room, between the "oh" of grief and the "ha" of pleasure, between her mother's and her husband's deaths, between two real bodies and the empty bed that she knew and felt was empty all along. She is between life and death, as I am and you are too, surviving a life haunted by death.

DeLillo writes that she "walked into the room and went to the window. She opened it. She threw the window open. She didn't know why she did this. Then she knew. She wanted to feel the sea tang on her face and the flow of time in her body, to tell her who she was" (*Body Artist* 124). Haunted but, as Osteen observes, "[n]o longer possessed, [...] Lauren has, at last, undertaken herself" (78) by opening herself to the coming, as-yet-unwritten future. Because, despite Mariella's assertion that Lauren's body writing "is about who we are when we are not rehearsing who we are" (DeLillo, *Body Artist* 110), when are we not rehearsing who we are?[23] I am a perpetual allusion to myself, writing in white, alluding to nothing, never breaking the glass, asking the other to tell me who I am, asking, "What am I supposed to say?"

Notes

1. Derrida writes, in *Memoires: for Paul de Man*, that "*we* are never *ourselves*, and between us, identical to us, a 'self' is never in itself or identical to itself" (28).
2. See also Chiara Alfano's discussion of "Nancy's and Derrida's accounts of how the self listens and relates to itself," where she argues that, for "Derrida, the voice of the relationship to self can never be purely idealised, it can never be properly muffled. Similarly for Nancy, voice never just sounds, it *re*-sounds" (221).
3. There are many similar examples to be found also in DeLillo's *Cosmopolis*: "'You do this what.' 'What. Every day'" (43–44); "'Dead.' 'No. What. Can't be'" (131).
4. Derrida writes, "'I want to kill myself' is a sentence of mine, me all over, but known to me alone, the mise en scène of a suicide and the fictive but

oh how motivated, convinced, serious decision to put an end to my days, a decision constantly relaunched, a rehearsal which occupies the entire time of my internal theater, the show I put on for myself without a break, before a crowd of ghosts" ("Circumfession" 38). The "I" here is not Derrida alone.

5. Anadiplosis, from the Greek, means "doubling back" or "folding" and is defined by the *Oxford English Dictionary* as "the beginning of a sentence, line, or clause with the concluding, or any prominent, word of the one preceding."

6. As Derrida details, the declared logic of the preface, which is "preceding what ought to be able to present itself on its own," is that "this residue of writing remains anterior and exterior to the development of the content it announces" ("Outwork" 8). Derrida insists, however, that despite its apparent logic, and like Rey's phrase, the preface "belongs both to the inside and to the outside" (10).

7. Speaking of the *i* in Mallarmé's "Crisis of verse" ("Crise de vers" from *Divagations* [1897]), which "continually pricks and rips through—or almost—the veil," Derrida assigns it "its quill or its wing, its penna," but the *i* is also the eye of the bird above the beak ("Double Session" 246).

8. Derrida writes after Paul de Man's death that, "Speaking is impossible, but so too would be silence or absence" (*Memoires* xvi).

9. Mallarmé marks this being "between" with the word "hymen" (qtd. in Derrida, "Double Session" 190). Between the inside and outside (of a body), between virginity and consummation, between desire ("I want") and fulfillment, the hymen, writes Derrida, "produces the effect of a medium (a medium as element enveloping both terms at once; a medium located between the two terms)" (222). It is "the undecidable" (222), "the threshold never crossed" (224), "at the edge of being" (225), and "it never *is*" (238). Derrida notes also that the "eyelid ([…] in some birds is called a hymen)" (225), which would mean that the blinking eye of Lauren's blue jay sees the bird's hymen unfold and fold between "impossible worlds" (DeLillo, *Body Artist* 22).

10. And the ghost says, "So art thou to revenge when thou shalt hear," to which Hamlet responds, "What?" (Shakespeare 1.5.7–8). Similarly, in Gautier's *Pierrot Posthume*, Pierrot describes himself as "a ghost who is dying," prompting Columbine's response, "Say that again?" (qtd. in Derrida, "Double Session" 215). It is as if the appearance of the ghost always coincides with "what." As Derrida asks (if it is a question), "*What is* a ghost?" (*Specters of Marx* 10).

11. As Derrida describes it, "[I]t is within the folds and the blankness of a certain hymen that the very textuality of the text is re-marked" ("Double

Session" 254), and the "polysemy of 'blanks' and 'folds' both fans out and snaps shut, ceaselessly" (259), like the plumage of a bird.

12. For Wood, too, "[t]here is archived light in texts: the glimmer of light itself, rather than light hidden by what we can see thanks to it" (174).

13. This writing, the "phantom, the phantasm, the simulacrum [...] is like all ghosts: errant" and wanders and strays (Derrida, "Plato's Pharmacy" 144). During their interview, Mariella reminds Lauren of a time, "in Rome, when Rey showed up for dinner with a stray cat on his shoulder" (DeLillo, *Body Artist* 108). Mallarmé lived in an apartment on the rue de Rome in Paris, where he owned a cat "whose name, almost needless to say, was Blanche" (Weinberger 22).

14. Commenting on the Mallarméan "play of *rhyme*" ("Double Session" 264), Derrida remarks that "[r]hyme—which is the general law of textual effects—is the folding-together of an identity and a difference" (278).

15. Another text bewitched by Derrida's *Dissemination* and particularly "Plato's Pharmacy," with its "yarns of suns and sons" (89), is Nicholas Royle's novel *Quilt*. Rey is here ray, the sting ray to which Socrates is compared (see Derrida, "Plato's Pharmacy" 120), and Royle in his text traces "the way the ray leaves its mark in everyday language," creating a "dictionaray": "Airy, Awry, Anniversary, Anteriority [...]" (121).

16. In an extended reading of this passage, Nel similarly observes, "Even as his language pushes the vision into precise, poetic diction, DeLillo reminds us that mimesis is easily bent by the mimicry upon which the writer's art depends—because that art inevitably drifts away from the signified, revealing associations behind and beyond the moment" (744).

17. As a result, says Derrida, the "*ghost* can no longer be distinguished, with the same assurance, from truth, reality, living flesh, etc. One must accept the fact that here, for once, to leave a ghost behind will in a sense be to salvage nothing" ("Plato's Pharmacy" 106).

18. Saghafi shows how "the coming of the other is always *like* the apparition of a ghost. Every time the other comes to me, it is *as if* I were encountering a ghost" (60).

19. Though Osteen interprets Mariella's admonition differently, saying "this involution is precisely what [Lauren] needs: to fold up," still his conclusion is the same, that Lauren must "then spring out like [...] a bird taking wing" and "stand outside of herself" (70).

20. Commenting on the novel's first words, Bonca also says that "time doesn't really pass at all" and that our perception of this "reveals ourselves to ourselves as beings who are bound to our own negation, to nothingness and death" (61). Otherwise, Bonca reads the novel in ontological rather than hauntological terms, discussing Mr. Tuttle "as if he were Being itself" (65).

21. Longmuir, too, argues that "*The Body Artist* presents Lauren Hartke's performance art as a means of actually re-embodying [...] self-erasing artistic voices" like Rey, who "finds his only means of resistance or escape is through silence—in his case the silence of suicide" (533). However, Longmuir goes on to state that "Lauren's bodily performances also succeed in restoring Rey himself for an instant" (533) whereas Osteen and I would believe that Rey himself is never present as such.

22. Keskinen remarks that Lauren is possibly hallucinating Mr. Tuttle, in which case "if there is imitation in Lauren's discourse, it is a reproduction of Mr Tuttle's voice that she had already produced" (35), so that when she incorporates her taped conversations with Mr. Tuttle into her mime piece, she "most likely lip-syncs to her own articulation of Mr Tuttle's voice, representing a recording that is already a representation of a presumably non-existent original" (40).

23. Osteen agrees that "the novel implies that such a condition may not exist" (64) and that both Lauren's "work and DeLillo's imply that there is no 'who' who is not also performing [...]. We are only 'ourselves,' it seems, when we are somebody else, the echo of an echo" (76).

.

Shadows

"What does it mean to follow a ghost?" Derrida asks. "And what if this came down to being followed by it, always, persecuted perhaps by the very chase we are leading? Here again, what seems to be out front, the future, comes back in advance: from the past, from the back" (*Specters of Marx* 10).[1] To follow a ghost might mean to follow behind the ghost, to track it, to watch its every advancing movement. But, at the same time, to follow a ghost might mean to arrive once the ghost is gone, as the night follows the day, to come after the ghost, and to leave the ghost following behind, trailing behind me in the past. In this way, following the ghost, I am followed by the ghost. In this way, from those who have gone before, I inherit the past. What does this mean for me? "This above all," says *Hamlet*'s Polonius, "to thine own self be true/And it must follow as the night the day/Thou canst not then be false to any man" (Shakespeare 1.3.77–79). But aren't all of Polonius's certain oppositions—day and night, true and false, self and other—unsettled by what it means to follow? Because the question of following, of shadowing, is always already the question of the ghost, the "shadow" that is the "spectral form, phantom" (relating to "shade" meaning the "visible but impalpable form of a dead person, a ghost") and also the "detective who follows a person in order to keep watch upon his movements," as the *Oxford English Dictionary* defines it. To follow a ghost is to shadow a shadow, is to be the shadow of a shadow, the ghost of a ghost. The ghost follows the ghost, and the ghost

© The Editor(s) (if applicable) and The Author(s) 2016
D. Coughlan, *Ghost Writing in Contemporary American Fiction*,
DOI 10.1057/978-1-137-41024-5_4

is followed by the ghost, the one seemingly overtaking the other, and the one seemingly overtaken by the other, each striding past the other, one step after the other.

So where am I in all this? As it happens, I am [*je suis*] only because I am following [*je suis*].[2] Therefore, "'I am' would mean 'I am haunted': I am haunted by myself who am (haunted by myself who am haunted by myself who am ... and so forth)" (Derrida, *Specters of Marx* 133). I am only because I am a followed and following ghost; I am a memory of what has gone before and a projection of what has happened, so I "appear to myself only by holding on to myself [...] and anticipating myself" (Hägglund 70), as one divided between disappearing and reappearing. Where I am not to be found, by this understanding, is at the heart of all this, as a true self lodged at the very center, as an identity properly present in a here and now and simply flanked by the ghosts of the past and the ghosts of the future. If I were bound to the present like this, I could not even move in to the future. It would be as if I were buried alive, entombed within my selfsame self, and dead to the world beyond, to which I would be entirely other because I could not be anything other than myself. No, in order for my self to have a future, it must be open to something that is not me, to what is no longer and not yet me. I emerge from my world only as I diverge from my world. Or, in other words, because I am a creature in time, I will be something other than what I am; as Hägglund puts it, "[W]hat makes it *possible* for anything to be at the same time makes it *impossible* for anything to be in itself" (81), and as Royle remarks, "[T]his 'same' of 'the same time' is ghostly" (*Jacques Derrida* 74).

So, instead of something bound to the present, I am something bound(ing) to happen, something stepping lively between past and future, in a between haunted by the past and future, which is perhaps all that the "present" is. As Derrida describes:

> each so-called "present" element, each element appearing on the scene of presence, is related to something other than itself, thereby keeping within itself the mark of the past element, and already letting itself be vitiated by the mark of its relation to the future element, this trace being related no less to what is called the future than to what is called the past, and constituting what is called the present by means of this very relation to what it is not: what it absolutely is not, not even a past or a future as a modified present. ("Différance" 13)

There was and will be no undivided present, no past present and present present and future present, and instead, the "being of any moment is nothing but its own becoming past and becoming related to the future" (Hägglund 60). Instead of the ordered three parts of past, present, and future, there is the switching, doubling disorder of a becoming-past relative to the future and a becoming-future relative to the past. This holds for me too: "The living present is always already a trace. [...] The self of the living present is originally a trace" (Derrida qtd. in Hägglund 71). So I do not hop from a certain past to a certain present to a certain future set out like stepping stones, but like a bridge without supports, I am a ghostly span, stepping between a past that was not and a future that will not be present. I am a series of ghosts, always stepping away from my (delayed) past self and always stepping toward, and never gaining on, my (deferred) future self, just that step beyond.

Every step I take is incomplete, is not a step in itself. Every leading leg is the following leg of the next step; every following leg is the leading leg of the step before. Each step must be divided, must refer to other steps, and "must be inhabited or haunted by the other, which is not outside" (Bennington 221) but there in the movement of the scissoring step. "In Derrida," therefore, as Hägglund explains, "'the other' does not primarily designate another human being. On the contrary, alterity is indissociable from the spacing of time" (75), so the other is that which intervenes in my "present," is that "temporal distance that prevents me from ever coinciding with myself" (Hägglund 70), that prevents my past self from being one with my future self, that has me somehow out of step with myself. It is this lack of unity, this distortion of the ideal self, that will lead some to think that, in "the disjointure of the present time" (Derrida, *Specters of Marx* 25), there is something wrong with me, I have gone astray, I am fallen and must "set it right" (Shakespeare, *Hamlet* 1.5.187). But, for Derrida, the self that will admit of no other and that is therefore wholly the same cannot be said to have set foot in this world.

The self, therefore, cannot be thought without the other, yet the other is always without the self, is a part of it while set apart from it, at a distance. If we think of "the other" here as the other person, then this becomes apparent because, "[i]f the other could appear for me as him- or herself, from his or her own perspective, he or she would not be an other" (Hägglund 88). Hägglund concludes, "Derrida articulates a double argument concerning the relation between self and other. On the one hand, he emphasizes that the subject cannot go outside of itself. The openness to the other is mediated through one's own experience and thus necessarily limited. On the other hand, the subject can never be in itself but is always exposed to an alterity that exceeds it" (88). I can no more step outside of my self, therefore, and into the world of the other than I can step beyond my "present" and be in my future. Uncannily, therefore, I relate to the other as to my past or future self, the self that I remember or imagine as an other I. After all, a "gap in time always separates me from my past, since the one who remembers cannot coincide with the one who is being remembered. In the same way, I cannot have a direct access to the consciousness of the other" (64). And it is through remembering or imagining my own alter egos that I recognize that the alter, the other, is also an ego, an I, because "[w]ithout the awareness that I am an other for the other, there would be no way of recognizing the other as an I for itself" (64) and of recognizing that "there is no '*the other*' *as such*" (Saghafi 124). A distance remains, however, even between mutually recognized alter egos. The other advances toward me like the future, always coming but never here, like a death.

The step, therefore, is a way to think the disjointure of the present, my distance from my self, and the inaccessibility of the world of the other. If I am only because I am not properly present but am instead following and followed by my self at a certain distance, the step (in French, *le pas*) is a way of thinking this being not (in French, *pas*). This double *pas*, this step/not, is considered at length in Derrida's "Pas," one of four essays in *Parages* which read or, as Saghafi puts it, "skirt around the edges of [Maurice] Blanchot's oeuvre" (103).[3] Derrida argues, "In every *récit* of Blanchot, this *pas* is at stake" ("*Pace Not(s)*" 21), this step of steps, the "two *pas*'s, the double *pas* disunited and allied with itself nonetheless, one passing the other immediately" (46).[4] All that I have written above, therefore, is a retracing of the *pas*: I follow a ghost like the "*pas* extra—the other *pas*—works (over) silently its homonym, haunts or parasitizes it" (45); I am following because "I do(es) not exist before *come*" (66), before the call to follow; the "present" element, like the "presence of the present (*récit*) is that presence, impossible, of this strange '*pas*' of distancing, this strange no/pace of distancing" (20); the self that cannot be thought without the other is the self with(out) the other in "the with-drawal [*re-trait*] of the (non)pace" (77), the "pace/not toward the other [*Le pas vers l'autre*]" (83), which Saghafi translates as the "step (not) taken toward the other" (116); the self cannot go outside itself because "[p]as does not (*pas*) pace beyond, does not surpass" ("*Pace Not(s)*" 98), because there is "[p]as *d'au-delà*, no beyond" (33), writes Derrida in a reference to Blanchot's *The Step Not Beyond* (*Le pas au-delà* [1973]); and, finally, Derrida describes the distance between self and other as "the relation near-far" (25) because there is no simple "opposition of near and far" (17) in "this '*pas*'—that can immediately be placed [...] within quotation marks— since it will never be present to itself, close by self, near self in some self-return [...] in the disjointed time of the *récit*" (20), because in "its double *pas* (pace, not), the other dislocates the opposition of the near and the far, without however confusing them" (26).[5] The step not beyond, therefore, is a step without step in the sense that the self with(out) the other is a "self without self [*moi sans moi*]" (78). This "altogether singular syntax of *without (sans)*" (24) is the other fascinating aspect that Derrida identifies in Blanchot's writing. The without "deprives [the same] of nothing save its identity to self, of what would prevent it from distancing itself from self" (78); the without is "'without' without *without*, *less*-less '-less'" ("Living On" 132). You can see this in the way the word "without" interrupts the appearance of the same word, sets it at the near-far distance of a step from itself, the distance that is the step, the "step without step," the *pas*.

Perhaps I follow Derrida too closely in that last paragraph. It is, as Saghafi identifies, the issue of "[h]ow to approach the text of the other or the other's work" or, "more generally, how not only to take on the other's work but also to broach the topic or the subject of *the other* while writing on the texts of another" (101). I am following Saghafi approaching Derrida approaching Blanchot (Derrida declares, "I would say that never have I imagined him so far in front of us as I have today" ["*Pace* Not(*s*)" 43]). And where is all this leading? And what does it have to do with Paul Auster, whose work is discussed in the coming chapter? Well, as it happens, we know that Auster has been reading Blanchot for quite some time now. He says, for example, "I first discovered Joubert's work in 1971, through an essay written by Maurice Blanchot" ("Invisible Joubert" 726), and in her translator's introduction to Blanchot's *The Gaze of Orpheus* (1981), Lydia Davis writes, "Paul Auster deserves special thanks for his constant encouragement and thoughtful advice, and for first pointing the way to the works of Maurice Blanchot" (qtd. in Nealon 108n6). In 1985, Auster himself was the translator of Blanchot's *Vicious Circles: Two Fictions & "After the Fact"* (the two fictions in question, "The Idyll" and "The Last Word," are among the early *récits* in which Saghafi identifies the beginnings of "a sustained treatment of and engagement with the other" [105]). Whether or not Auster has been reading Derrida is another question. Early on, he twice quoted Derrida's observation that "in the last ten years nothing has been written in France that does not have its precedent somewhere in the texts of Jabès," in the 1976 essay "Book of the Dead" (183) and the 1981 preface "Twentieth-Century French Poetry" (230), but this indicates a shared interest in Edmond Jabès rather than Auster's interest in Derrida. Adam Kelly notes that "Auster claimed in a 1993 interview never to have read Derrida, but to 'know who he is and basically what he writes about,' professing himself 'astonished' that their work could be seen to have anything in common" (126n2), and yet, studies of Auster's work are rarely likely to reference Blanchot without also bringing in Derrida.[6] But perhaps this is only fitting when Auster and Derrida are both so fascinated by Blanchot, as if following him in step with each other.

In *Awaiting Oblivion* (*L'attente l'oubli* [1963]), Blanchot writes, "I sense that you are following me, you who are nevertheless in front of me" (qtd. in Derrida, "*Pace* Not(*s*)" 47), or that you are shadowing me, you who are shadowed by me. Saghafi observes:

> In Blanchot's *récits*, the undecidable, neutral—spectral—step/not toward the other is taken toward an other that is itself strangely spectral. Nothing but a shade (*une ombre*), a pure reflection without consistency, a void or a gap (*une vide*), a double, the double of the thing, the thing doubled [...], belonging to the zone of shadows, neither real nor unreal, this ghostly "neutral" figure, this phantomatic "image," is the exemplary *figure* of Blanchot's *récits*. (121)

I would suggest that the same is true of Auster's narratives, as in *City of Glass*, for example, the account of Daniel Quinn's step/not toward Peter Stillman, of Quinn with(out) Stillman, of Quinn without Quinn, in the city, the labyrinth, and the room, Auster's spaces, or (s)*pace*(*s*).[7] Quinn follows Stillman as a detective, as his shadow, and Auster's novel is concerned with "how the other is implicated in the self-constitution of the investigator" (Alford 19), of the private eye, or "I." For Auster, the "I" cannot be thought without the other that it follows at a distance. And the "I" cannot be thought without the distancing step (not) toward the other, that distance to the other which haunts the "I."

It is not a coincidence that Quinn also follows Stillman as a writer. For Auster, the step by which the "I" moves along between past and future, between what lies behind and what lies ahead, relates to the written word, which preserves the passing present for the coming future; the pace toward the other is the spacing of the "I" in the world in the way that "a sentence remains solely as a trace of its own movement towards the other" (Clark 98).

But this means that the step is not just a way of thinking the word but that, as I am stepping into the world, I am inscribing myself in the world, I am an "*inscription* that enables repetition across the gap in time" (Hägglund 71), so that I am written into the world, I am the trace of life: "Life is a text" (Derrida, "Following Theory" 27). Auster's work means "to go write-on-living," to use Derrida's phrase ("Living On" 105), both in the sense of intending to write on or about living and in the sense of continuing to write, to write on, and therefore to live, to go right on living. As such, Auster's work addresses also the questions posed by Derrida: "And to go write-on-living? If that were possible, would the writer have to be dead already, or be living on?" (105). For Derrida, "writing, mark, trace […] neither lives nor dies; it lives on" ("Border Lines" 129) and "living on can mean a reprieve or an afterlife, 'life after life' or life after death, *more* life *still* or *more than* life, *and better*" ("Living On" 104–105). Life as a living on is a part of the following ghost, of the divided present, and of the haunting other that complicate ideas of the self and other and of presence and absence; in turn, living on is "a complication of the opposition life/death" (Derrida, "Learning to Live Finally" 51). Derrida speaks of "[s]urvival and *revenance*, living on and returning from the dead: living on goes beyond both living and dying" ("Living On" 134); "living on [*survivance*] is also phantom *revenance* (the one who lives on is always a ghost)" (159). The following chapter, therefore, is about living on and returning from the dead in Auster's work, about what he calls "a posthumous life, an interval between two deaths" (*Timbuktu* 14), which is the interval of the pace, of the "present" beyond which lies the future and the past: "*The void of the future: there death has our future. The void of the past: there death has its tomb*" (Blanchot, *Step Not Beyond* 15). And in this interval is posthumous life, or life after death, life following death. In this way, following Auster, ghost writing in contemporary American fiction appears differently as the ghost writer (who writes on living) becomes a ghost writing (who writes on, living). After Auster, "I" am a ghost writer, "I" am my own ghost writer, and what I write is my living on.

Notes

1. On the question of what it means to follow, see also Derrida's essay "The Animal That Therefore I Am (More to Follow)" in *The Animal That Therefore I Am*. As translator David Wills notes, "[T]he *je suis* of Derrida's French title—'L'animal que donc je suis (à suivre)'—plays on the shared first person singular present form of *être* ('to be') and *suivre* ('to follow')" (162n).

2. Derrida writes that "before the question of (the) *being* as such, of *esse* and *sum*, of *ego sum*, there is the question of following, of the persecution and seduction of the other, what/that I am (following) or who is following me, who is following me while I am (following) it, him, or her" (*The Animal That Therefore I Am* 65).

3. The essay "Pas" has been translated into English by John P. Leavey as "*Pace* Not(*s*)." In a note on his translation, Leavey comments, "Derrida's text explores the various interrelations, intimations, suggestions, allusions, and limits of this French word with itself, its double in its 'supposed' two functions, its singular/plural (*le pas, les pas*), and the word *pas* itself (its graphic and sonic forms). [...] *Pas* is rendered by pace/no, no/pace, (non)pace, pace (not), and so forth" (251n1).

4. Blanchot calls his fictions *récits*, which can be translated as "accounts" or "narratives" though, as Derrida comments, "it will be better to leave the 'French' word" ("Border Lines" 113).

5. As Lauren asks Mr. Tuttle in DeLillo's *The Body Artist*, "'Why do I think I'm standing closer to you than you are to me?' She wasn't trying to be funny. It was true, a paradox of the spectral sort" (85–86).

6. Studies which cite both Derrida and Blanchot include Kelly and Nealon, as well as Boulter, Cohen's "Desertions," Eastman, Herzogenrath, Little, Segal, and Shiloh. Blanchot appears alone in Nicol, Tabbi, and Wirth.

7. As Moraru notes, Quinn is Peter Stillman's "shadow" and Stillman's "name recalls Adelbert von Chamisso's shadowless vagrant from the 1814 novella *Peter Schlemihl's wundersame Geschichte*" (71). *The Wonderful Story of Peter Schlemihl* is referenced in Nathaniel Hawthorne's "The Intelligence Office" (1844), as well as in Karl Marx's *Eighteenth Brumaire of Louis Bonaparte* (1852) and in turn, in Derrida's *Specters of Marx* (117).

3. One Pace After the Other: Paul Auster

The Invention of Solitude (1982), Paul Auster's first major prose work, was written in response to the death of his father. It is divided into two parts, each with its own title, epigraph, and date of composition: "Portrait of an Invisible Man" (1979) and "The Book of Memory" (1980–1981). Toward the end of the first part, Auster writes:

> For the past two weeks, these lines from Maurice Blanchot echoing in my head: "One thing must be understood: I have said nothing extraordinary or even surprising. What is extraordinary begins at the moment I stop. But I am no longer able to speak of it."
> To begin with death. To work my way back into life, and then, finally, to return to death.
> Or else: the vanity of trying to say anything about anyone. (63)

The lines quoted are from Blanchot's *Death Sentence* (*L'Arrêt de mort* [1948]) and close the first of that work's two parts, in one of which an "I" narrator tells the story of J., and in the other of which an "I" narrator (apparently the same man) tells the story of Nathalie.[1] In J.'s story, the narrator tells us that the woman's "doctor had told me that from 1936 on he had considered her dead" (Blanchot, *Death Sentence* 134); then, she does die, but she is "returned to life" at the narrator's "bidding" (151) when he calls her name. She is returned to life, but we understand from the final lines of the first part that, now, of course, death is coming

© The Editor(s) (if applicable) and The Author(s) 2016
D. Coughlan, *Ghost Writing in Contemporary American Fiction*,
DOI 10.1057/978-1-137-41024-5_5

for J. again. She is coming to an end, coming to a stop: "[L]ife stops. And it can stop at any moment" (Auster, *Invention of Solitude* 5). There is, as Derrida describes it, "J.'s life after the death sentence, then death, then life-after-death, then death" ("Living On" 163).[2] But, as he also asks, "[W]ill we ever know whether she died, whether death came for her?" (136). This woman's death, that extraordinary thing, is not something that can be written; her death is beyond the narrator's words, beyond even her words, because "[i]n order to write one must already be writing" (Blanchot, "Gaze of Orpheus" 442), or "as long as you go on speaking, you will not die" (Auster, *Locked Room* 149).

J.'s life-after-death is a writing again, a repetition, so "that what had happened the night before [...] was beginning all over again" (Blanchot, *Death Sentence* 148), so that the night before her pulse "scattered like sand" (143) "and 'scattered like sand'" (151) again the night after. But of course, a return to life is a return to writing's citations. Isn't this all that life is to begin with, a self repeating itself in the face of death? The event of life is marked for and by reinscription from the start, and death is the failure to recite. Death begins the moment I stop (*je m'arrête*) writing, and all the while I'm writing, death is coming (and all the while, I'm writing death is coming).

And all the while the narrator is writing, J.'s death is coming. Such is the terrible responsibility of writing for another. It's the narrator, absent when J. first died, who cannot countenance her ending, and so he "called to her by her first name; and immediately" she was alive again (Blanchot, *Death Sentence* 144). But of course, J. is not simply returned to life; she is alive again and dying again. Named, she goes write-on-living, sentenced to death by language. Because, as Blanchot explains:

> Of course my language does not kill anyone. And yet: when I say, "This woman," real death has been announced and is already present in my language; my language means that this person, who is here right now, can be detached from herself, removed from her existence and her presence [...]. My language does not kill anyone. But if this woman were not really capable of dying, if she were not threatened by death at every moment of her life, bound and joined to death by an essential bond, I would not be able to carry out that ideal negation, that deferred assassination which is what my language is. ("Literature and the Right to Death" 380)[3]

As her deferred assassination, *Death Sentence* is the surviving repetition of her death sentence.[4] The *arrêt de mort* under which J. remains "is a sentence that condemns someone to death" (Derrida, "Living On" 135) but "also arrests death by suspending it, interrupting it, deferring it with a 'start' [*sursaut*], the startling starting over, and starting on, of living on" (139). "Living on is the survival of the death sentence; as long as I am condemned to die, I survive" (Couglan et al. 2), and so J. lives on through this surviving *Death Sentence*, this *arrêt de mort* that will see her die again by her writer's hand.[5] "Come, please come, J. is dying" (Blanchot, *Death Sentence* 142), the narrator is urged, and he comes in the end like death comes, which is why J. says, in life-after-death, "'Now then, take a good look at death,' and pointed her finger at" the narrator (149). At the same time, J. can say to the narrator, "If you don't kill me, then you're a murderer" (141), meaning that if he does not kill her by naming her himself, then he forgets her and lets her die, again. This is perhaps what Auster means by the vanity of trying to say anything about anyone; for all that we might desire to give them back their life, all we can grant them is a return to death.

To Begin with Death

Auster's characters, like J., so often live a "posthumous life, an interval between two deaths" (Auster, *Timbuktu* 14). When we join them, they are close to death, or as good as dead.[6] The first part of *The Invention of Solitude* is entitled "Portrait of an Invisible Man" because Auster can say this of his father: "Even before his death he had been absent" (6). In *City of Glass*, the first tale in *The New York Trilogy* (1987), it is said of Daniel Quinn that a "part of him had died" (4), so that it were "as if he had managed to outlive himself, as if he were somehow living a posthumous life" (5). In *Moon Palace* (1989), Marco Stanley Fogg is reduced to "[j]ust a lot of bones" (45) in a bare room that's like "a coffin" (44), while Thomas Effing, when known as Julian Barber, is twice described as "already dead" (155, 164). In *The Music of Chance* (1990), "little by little [Jim Nashe] had turned himself into a ghost" (4), so that "he could just as well have been invisible" (6).[7] In *Mr Vertigo* (1994), Walt Rawley is told, "You're [...] a piece of human nothingness. [...] If you stay where you are, you'll be dead before winter is out" (3). In *Timbuktu* (1999), the opening line is "Mr. Bones knew that Willy wasn't long for this world" (3).[8] In *The Book of Illusions* (2002), David Zimmer says of himself, "I wasn't really alive. I was just someone who pretended to be alive" (102). Sidney Orr, in

Oracle Night (2004), says, "I had been sick for a long time. [...] They had given me up for dead" (1), while in the story that Orr writes, his character Nick Bowen is "walking around in a dead man's clothes. Now [...] he has ceased to exist" (82). In *The Brooklyn Follies* (2005), the narrator, Nathan Glass, says he "had given [himself] up for dead" (3) and was "looking for a quiet place to die" (1).

These men either do not have or do not want a future. To have a future means to see death coming, to risk death or violent erasure, but these men feel as if death has already arrived for them, is here and now. The future is all but closed to them, so they do without it, impassively—perhaps even gratefully—because they have already risked and lost too much, whether it is their health or, worse, loved ones: Quinn's wife and son have died; Fogg writes, "My uncle simply dropped dead one fine afternoon in the middle of April, and at that point my life began to change, I began to vanish into another world" (Auster, *Moon Palace* 3); Nashe's wife walks out on him, and he can no longer be there for his daughter; and Zimmer's wife and sons are also dead. Quinn declares that a "part of him had died [...] and he did not want it coming back to haunt him" (*City of Glass* 4), and therefore he seals his so-called life against the future, preferring to be overtaken by the past: "It had been more than five years now. [...] Every once in a while, he would feel what it had been like to hold the three-year-old boy in his arms—but that was not exactly thinking, nor was it even remembering. It was a physical sensation, an imprint of the past that had been left in his body, and he had no control over it" (5). This possession by the past is mirrored by Zimmer's attempts to walk in his sons' shoes: "I wasn't able to think about them directly or summon them up in any conscious way, but [...] I felt that I was temporarily inhabiting them again—carrying on their little phantom lives for them by repeating the gestures they had made when they still had bodies" (*Book of Illusions* 7–8). Zimmer is not looking to call his sons to life but instead to inhabit them, to close that impossible divide and be the same as the other, to annihilate the self and in this way know death. He is "a dead man who spent his days translating a dead man's book" (102), and it is the death that he desires to translate.

Such possessions by the past also recur in the novels in the very form of possessions or money passed on as an inheritance, in *The Music of Chance*, for example, or *Timbuktu*. It is in *Moon Palace* that we see most clearly how the inheritance can lay claim to a life. When Fogg is given the gift of "one thousand four hundred and ninety-two volumes" (Auster, *Moon Palace* 12) by his uncle, he converts "the boxes [of books] into several pieces of 'imaginary furniture'" (2), living in this room of books. After his uncle's death, he says, "was when I started reading Uncle Victor's books. [...] Each time I opened a box, I was able to enter another segment of my uncle's life, [...] and it consoled me to feel I was occupying the same mental space that Victor had once occupied" (21), just as it consoled Zimmer to occupy the lives of his boys. As he read the books, he sold them, and as "I divested myself of my inheritance" (22), he says, and lost yet another piece of furniture, "it produced a physical result, an effect in the real world. [...] Piece by piece, I could watch myself disappear" (24). These men are in mourning for what will not have a future. They stand before the tomb of Lazarus, and rather than call "come out" (John 11.43), they want to join him in death.

In a strange way, all of these men are Auster's father, that invisible man who "left no traces" (Auster, *Invention of Solitude* 6).[9] Like him, as Fogg puts it, they "did not believe there would ever be a future" (*Moon Palace* 1), and so they seek to erase themselves, to unhouse themselves from their lives. The Fogg who ends up "living on the streets" (1) is the same as the Nashe who takes to the road, who "walked out, climbed into his car, and was gone" (*Music of Chance* 11), is the same as the Quinn who takes to walking to feel "[l]ost, not only in the city, but within himself as well" (*City of Glass* 4). For him, "New York was an inexhaustible space, a labyrinth of endless steps" (3) that allows him "to be nowhere. New York was the nowhere he had built around himself" (4). Similarly, Orr in *Oracle Night* cannot see his way ahead, and instead, as he says, "I had trouble telling where my body stopped and the rest of the world began" (1). The city's network of streets gives access to any number of paths, allowing these men to stray in any direction, aimlessly, without regard for what lies ahead, in a world of head-spinning motion which serves only to turn their heads and leave them nowhere. But then something happens.

To Work My Way Back into Life

What happens is that chance intervenes. Anyone familiar with Auster's writing will know the part that chance plays in his work. As early as on the first page of *City of Glass*, the reader is being told that Quinn's feeling was that "nothing was real except chance" (3); Fogg sees his story as a "series of lost chances" (*Moon Palace* 243); and in *Oracle Night*, Orr is reworking an episode from a Dashiell Hammett story that shows how "the world is governed by chance" (12).[10] The New York streets, therefore, which are a labyrinth of endless steps, are also the streets that—in their gridlike structure, in their crossroads and intersections, in the vertical planes of their buildings and skyscrapers, in their traffic lanes and files of pedestrians, in their radiating telegraph wires, in this multitude of potential lines of intersection—produce everywhere the points of possible coincidence where chance, strange and unhinging, might intervene. Nashe, wondering if "he had just committed himself to the wrong road" when he misses his turn, is wrong to decide that "there was no difference, that both ramps were finally the same" (*Music of Chance* 6), because all roads do not lead straight and unerringly to the same destination. If they did, "one of those random, accidental encounters" (1), like his meeting Jack Pozzi (Jackpot), or Glass's "Unexpected Encounter" (12) in *The Brooklyn Follies* with his nephew, or the "coincidence" (180) of a chosen name in *Moon Palace*, could never happen, the future could not happen, and therefore life could not happen. We see this in *Oracle Night*, in the story that Orr writes, when Bowen is walking down a street and

> eleven stories above him, the head of a small limestone gargoyle attached to the façade of an apartment building is slowly breaking loose from the rest of its body [...]. Nick takes another step, and then another step, and at the moment the gargoyle head is finally dislodged, he walks straight into the trajectory of the falling object. (22)

Moments before, Bowen is thinking that "something inside him has been broken [...] that his marriage has failed, that his life has come to a dead end" (21–22). After this event, however, when "he should be dead," since the "stone was meant to kill him," he realizes that "a new life has been given to him" (22). And, in *Leviathan* (1992), Benjamin Sachs falls from the arms of Maria, "the reigning spirit of chance" (102); realizes, as he puts it, that "I was a dead man falling through the air, and even though I was technically still alive, I was dead" (117); and resolves after the accident to "change my life" (122). It is not for nothing that Nathan Glass used to work for Mid-Atlantic Accident and Life, for this is the pattern in Auster's work: the accident, or chance, or coincidence, or fateful event, and then life.

In this way, life and death hinge on the unhinged moment, or death and then life. For all that these men seek to put themselves into an early grave, to close the context of their existence to the world, chance pries it open. These men desire so much to erase themselves, to leave no traces, but again and again they are written into existence. Auster's father, for example, though he absents himself from the world, still leaves a legacy—his son—who, on hearing of his father's death, says, "I knew that I would have to write about my father. [...] I thought: my father is gone. If I do not act quickly, his entire life will vanish along with him" (*Invention of Solitude* 6). Like Blanchot's J., therefore, Auster's near-dead are opened to life in an encounter with a same-but-different other, the double who seems to repeat that which they would see erased, who bids them to return to life. In *The Locked Room* (1986), the third book in *The New York Trilogy*, the narrator is Fanshawe's double to the extent that, as Fanshawe's mother observes, "You even look like him, you know. You always did, the two of you—like brothers, almost like twins" (261); Nash and Pozzi in *The Music of Chance* are affected by "the curious correspondence [...] found between their two lives" (49); in *Timbuktu*, "William Gurevitch concluded his business on this earth, and from his flesh a new man named Willy G. Christmas was born" (22) after the "specters" (20) "set his life on an entirely different course" (17); Zimmer connects with the "woman with the strange double face" (*Book of Illusions* 108) and later realizes that "she had brought [him] back from the dead" (316); and in *Moon Palace*, Fogg says, "If not for a girl named Kitty Wu, I probably would have starved to death" (1)—he's "wearing the same shirt she is" in a "weird coincidence," as if he were "Kitty's twin brother" (34)—but instead, he says, he remembers those days "as the beginning of my life" (1), "my return to the land of the living" (94).

The chance moment, however, does not oppose death to life, or switch Auster's characters from a condition of pure death to pure life. It does not provide a direct path from death to life. The unhinged moment steps between death and life and death again and, like the step, is a twinned and twinning thing. After these chance occurrences, Auster's dead become ghosts, shadowing and shadowed by their doubles, calling the other to life and called to life by the other: Auster and his father in *The Invention of Solitude*; Quinn and Peter Stillman in *City of Glass*; Blue and Black in *Ghosts* (1986), the second book in *The New York Trilogy*; the narrator and Fanshawe in *The Locked Room*; Fogg and Effing, and Effing and Barber, in *Moon Palace*; Nashe and Pozzi in *The Music of Chance*, who are so close that, as Pozzi tells Nashe, "You were breathing life into me" (138), so much so that, in Nashe's absence, Pozzi "was turning into a corpse" (99); Peter Aaron and Sachs in *Leviathan*; Master Yehudi and Walt in *Mr Vertigo*; Mr. Bones and Willy in *Timbuktu*; Zimmer and Hector Mann in

The Book of Illusions; John Trause and Orr, and Orr and Bowen, in *Oracle Night*; and so on.[11] These pairs of characters do not together form a whole. The two men in each case do not represent parts of one man, or are not past and future versions that, combined, give rise to a present identity. Instead, one is the self and one is the other, and the distance between them means they are not the same. These twinned figures, therefore, these shadows, speak to the ghostliness of life, to the self near-far from the other, to the self taking a step (not) toward the inaccessible other, to the self interrupted by the other, to the self that does not coincide with itself, to the self with one foot to the past and one foot to the future, to the self that seems forever to follow and be followed by itself, to the self without self. After all, "[n]o one can live without other people" (*Book of Illusions* 65).

For Auster's ghosts, their living on is always (as) writing, to the extent that the body and the corpus are almost indistinguishable. In *Moon Palace*, for example, we are told "[e]very man is the author of his own life" (7); in *Leviathan*, Sachs plans for Reed Dimaggio "a memorial in the shape of a book [...] keeping him alive" (225); in *Timbuktu*, Willy is concerned for "his life's work [...]. If the words vanished, it would be as if he had never lived" (8–9); in *Ghosts*, a writer called Black hires a detective called Blue to observe, trail, and report on him "to prove he's alive" (181); and in *The Locked Room*, the narrator, the literary executor of his old friend Fanshawe, carries the load of unpublished manuscripts away from the apartment Fanshawe shared with his wife Sophie in two large suitcases that "together [...] were as heavy as a man" (208). Auster's ghosts are ghost writers: "'In some sense, a writer has no life of his own. Even when he's there, he's not really there.' 'Another ghost'" (Auster, *Ghosts* 175). Just as the narrator writes for J. in Blanchot's *Death Sentence*, so Auster writes for his father in *The Invention of Solitude*, Quinn for Stillman in *City of Glass*, Blue for Black in *Ghosts*, the narrator for Fanshawe in *The Locked Room*, Fogg for Effing in *Moon Palace*, Aaron for Sachs in *Leviathan*. In *Death Sentence*, the narrator calls to J., deceased, and she speaks again. In Auster, when the narrator in *The Locked Room* attempts to write a biography of Fanshawe, Sophie, now the narrator's wife, urges him to stop because she fears he is "bringing him back to life" (285), and of course, Fanshawe is still alive, just as, in the first line of *The Book of Illusions*, Zimmer says of Mann that "everyone thought he was dead" (1), but once Zimmer has written his book, *The Silent World of Hector Mann*, he turns up alive.

For the self and other self, following and followed, one is like Lazarus or Eurydice, dead already, forever rising from the underworld, and the other is like Jesus or Orpheus, forever saying "come out," with a pace between them. One speaks from the grave, while the other looks up to the skies. One is placed in a room, while the other wanders the world.[12] One writes, while the other walks, the double *pas*, because, as Derrida asks, "And to go write-on-living? If that were possible, would the writer have to be dead already, or be living on?" ("Living On" 105). The entombed writers include Quinn in "one of the rooms at the back of the apartment, a small space" (Auster, *City of Glass* 126); Sachs "writing the book in prison" (*Leviathan* 19); Fogg in "a windowless room" (*Moon Palace* 179); Orr, who works in a room "hardly bigger than a closet" (*Oracle Night* 9) and is so much the ghost that his wife protests, "I opened the door and peeked inside. But you weren't there. [...] I didn't see you" (23); and in *The Book of Illusions*, François-René de Chateaubriand, who writes in *Memoirs from Beyond the Grave* (*Mémoires d'outre-tombe* [1849–1850]), translated by Zimmer ("which in German means *room*" [*Invention of Solitude* 99]) as *Memoirs of a Dead Man*, "*I pre-fer to speak from the depths of my tomb. My narrative will thus be accompanied by those voices which have something sacred about them because they come from the sepulchre*" (67).[13] But, time and again, it is made clear that these writers remain one step (not) ahead of death. All the while they are writing, death is coming, but they are not dead yet: Fanshawe, in the titular locked room, lives to say "I'm already dead. I took poison hours ago" (312); Zimmer, living on, says, "If and when this book is published, dear reader, you can be certain that the man who wrote it is long dead" (*Book of Illusions* 318); and Glass gives the impression, too, that he's a dead man, writing, "[M]y own life was coming to an end [...] and a moment later I was gone" (*Brooklyn Follies* 294–295), before admitting, "I didn't die" (296). All of these writers feel how intimately writing is related to death, how writing announces my coming death even as the writing that is my death sentence also stays my execution, is a "deferred assassination," a death without death (Blanchot, "Literature and the Right to Death" 380).[14] I read my death in my writing, but I am also like Effing, who says, "I was dead, or at least they thought I was dead [...], and after it got written up in the papers, I was able to stay dead" (Auster, *Moon Palace* 125), stay death.

As noted in "Shadows," therefore, Auster's work means "to go write-on-living" (Derrida, "Living On" 105), both in the sense of intending to write on the living and in the sense of continuing to write on, or to go right on living. The clearest illustration of this is the character of M.S. Fogg, whose "initials stood for *manuscript*" (Auster, *Moon Palace* 7) and therefore for "a life as work-in-progress" (Barone 5); at the same time, his name identifies three wanderers: Marco Polo, Henry Morton Stanley, and Phileas Fogg. As such, his name identifies the unhinged self that exists in the pace (not) between past and future, in the becoming-past relative to the future that Auster aligns with writing and the becoming-future relative to the past that he aligns with walking even as he acknowledges the disorder of the step. That this self without self is, for Auster also, a self with(out) other is evident in the way that Fogg steps (not) beyond his name, as the writer to his uncle first and then Effing, for whom he writes in a room "no larger than a monk's cell" (Auster, *Moon Palace* 104). Then, one steps past the other, the one following becomes the one followed, and after Effing has died and after Fogg has also "buried [his] father in the grave that had been destined for [him]" (291), he finally finds himself "walking [...], borne along by a growing sense of happiness" (297), leading him to declare, again, "This is where I start, [...] this is where my life begins" (298).

To be so close to death and yet not dead is remarkable. To be mortal, to be alive, is a cause for boundless happiness. Indeed, the narrator in Blanchot's *Death Sentence* sees that, "in absence, in unhappiness, in the inevitability of dead things," there is also a delight in survival, one that leads him to declare, "I take this unhappiness on myself and I am immeasurably glad of it" (186). This same marriage of death and joy reappears in Auster's work also: in *The Invention of Solitude*, Auster relates how his grandmother, Anna Auster, having been found innocent of the murder of her husband, states, "Now I regret that he had to die by my hand. I am as happy now as I ever expect to be" (47); in *Moon Palace*, Effing "had been ready to die. Now, he was trembling with happiness" (163); Nashe, in his final minutes, "was happy, he realized, happier than he had been in a long time" (*Music of Chance* 214); Mr. Bones "felt stronger and happier than he had felt in months," even as he runs toward his death (*Timbuktu* 186); and in *Oracle Night*, Orr can say, "[E]ven as the tears poured out of me, I was happy, happier to be alive than I had ever been before" (207).[15] This happiness is perhaps what Blanchot describes as "the happiness of not being immortal or eternal," a happiness born of the knowledge that only the dead can't die: "Dead—immortal" ("Instant of My Death" 5). To live is not to triumph over death but to be "bound to death by a surreptitious friendship" (5).

At the end of Auster's *The Brooklyn Follies*, Nathan Glass, having just been discharged from the hospital after his near-death experience, declares, "I felt so glad to be alive [...]. I was happy, my friends, as happy as any man who had ever lived" (303–304). He has had an idea: "Eventually, we would all die. [...] No books would be written about us. [...] Most lives vanish. A person dies, and little by little all traces of that life disappear. [...] My idea was this: to form a company that would publish books about the forgotten ones. [...] I would resurrect that person in words [...] that would outlive us all" (300–302). It is the morning of September 11, 2001, just hours before "the smoke of three thousand incinerated bodies would drift over toward Brooklyn and come pouring down on us in a white cloud of ashes and death" (304). The white cloud, here of ashes but more commonly of snow, recurs often in Auster's writings, with Carsten Springer observing that it "is almost always associated with death—a ending [sic] which is also a beginning" (13–14). In *The Invention of Solitude*, it is "[w]inter in the country: a world of [...] whiteness" (6) the morning Auster learns of his father's death; in *Timbuktu*, Mr. Bones's "body was covered with snow [...]. There was something eerie about the whiteness of snow" (183); and in *The Music of Chance*, Nashe imagines "the immensity of the white field, and the snow continuing to fall until even the mountains of stones were covered, until everything disappeared under an avalanche of whiteness" (215). Both Mr. Bones and Nashe are about to die, and the snow-covered world is for them "a blank page of death" (*Moon Palace* 150). These final pages recall how, at the end of *City of Glass*, the "city was entirely white now" (132), yet turn the page and *Ghosts* is really only beginning when "snow is falling on the quiet street, and everything has turned white," so that "Black's shoes have made a perfect set of tracks on the white pavement," like words on a new page, and "Blue follows the tracks" (140), one pace after the other. "Most lives vanish," says Glass, and leave no trace. Auster is urging us to follow, therefore, and to write on this ash-white page after those whose lives have been erased from this world.[16]

But is it possible to tell the story of the other's life, to extend the life of the other, or extend life to the other, as Auster would for his absent father? If *The Invention of Solitude* is "an exploration of how one might begin to speak about another person, and whether or not it is even possible" (Auster and Mallia 276), Auster's fiction in general confronts the reality that what makes it possible for the "I" to survive at the same time makes it impossible for the "I" to have life without death; and what makes it possible for the other to survive at the same time makes it impossible for the "I" to write the other itself. The other, like death, is not something that can be written even as it is all I write about. The other is always coming and begins at the moment I stop. As a result, it is no wonder that Auster has said, "At bottom, I think my work has come out of a position of intense personal despair, a very deep nihilism and hopelessness about the world, the fact of our own transience and mortality, the inadequacy of language, the isolation of one person from another" (qtd. in Barone 12). Auster's fiction never steps beyond that isolation, never claims that any one of us has immediate access to any other. Instead, it admits death—of the self or the other—and welcomes what lives on. The fiction itself lives on. His characters are very aware that they cannot write forever, that the time will come when "the entire notebook has almost been filled" (Auster, *Country of Last Things* 183) and then "there are no more pages" (*City of Glass* 131), yet they believe also that "[y]ou stop, but that does not mean you have come to the end" (*Country of Last Things* 183). In the way that J.'s life stops and yet she does not come to an end, Auster's fictions effect a stop without ending, repeating from one novel to the other. Speaking of "The Book of Memory," Auster has said, "In retrospect I can see that everything I have done has come out of that book. The problems and questions and experiences that are examined there have been the meat of the things I have done since" (qtd. in Varvogli 12). Again, Auster is following Blanchot here, who "often re-cites and rereads certain terms and motifs from his previous work" (Saghafi 108), but he is also following Edmond Jabès (and Blanchot was "a recurrent point of reference for both Jabès and Auster" [Cohen, "Desertions" 97]). In a 1978 interview with Auster, Jabès says:

> You are always at the beginning ... and each of my books in some way is the beginning of another book that is never written. That is why when the second book prolongs the first, it also cancels out part of the reading you have already made. [...] The book that would have a chance to survive, I think, is the book that destroys itself. That destroys itself in favor of another book that will prolong it. (Auster, "Book of the Dead" 206)

The aim, as Josh Cohen describes in the context of Auster's Jewishness, is not "the apocalyptic end which completes history, but the spectral end which keeps it open" ("Desertions" 106). The evident repetitions that this chapter identifies in Auster's different, successive texts are finally to do with what survives the end without end of the other: writing and writing again and again, Auster is saying to the other and to death "eternally, 'Come,' and eternally it is there" (Blanchot, *Death Sentence* 186). These are the words with which Blanchot concludes the second part of his *Death Sentence*.

Finally, to Return to Death

Having traced Auster's ghosts through this series of books that spans 20 years, I want now to return to the work that they all follow—to *City of Glass*—to look more closely at the way in which the relation to the self and the other is, from the very beginning, an experience of ghost writing. *City of Glass* introduces us to Auster's first shadow, Daniel Quinn, who writes detective stories featuring Max Work under the pseudonym William Wilson.[17] The book's opening clause, "It was a wrong number that started it" (3), seems pretty straightforward but immediately signals the work's concern with improper communication, with the failure of the number to work. The number which connects to the wrong person is equivalent to the sign that no longer corresponds with its referent in a nonarbitrary way, or to the word that no longer names its essential object. But it is only a wrong number that could have started it. In order for writing to happen, in order for anything to be, something does not work well or goes askew, something is out of joint, something breaks with itself or is divided from itself, interrupted by the gap of the other. The right number would start nothing (or finish everything, it's hard to know), and yet it appears to be what we desire or think ought to happen. Quinn, it turns out, likes words to work, and so do I, apparently, as when I say that these words are "straightforward" and "immediately" signal that they are diverted and untimely.[18]

It is as a result of this wrong number, "the telephone ringing three times in the dead of night, and the voice on the other end asking for someone he was not" (Auster, *City of Glass* 3), that Quinn, the writer of detective stories, becomes involved in a real-life investigative case.[19] The "someone he was not" is Paul Auster, detective, and this is the person that Quinn plays at being as he undertakes his case. The case itself involves protecting one Peter Stillman from his father, Peter Stillman Sr, who was confined to a hospital for the insane for keeping his young son imprisoned for nine years from the age of two, has recently been released, and now, again, could pose a threat to his safety. So Quinn intercepts Stillman at Grand Central Station and becomes his shadow:

> The next morning, and for many mornings to follow, Quinn posted himself on a bench in the middle of the traffic island at Broadway and 99th Street. [...] By eight o'clock Stillman would come out, always in his long brown overcoat, carrying a large, old-fashioned carpet bag. For two weeks this routine did not vary. The old man would wander through the streets of

> the neighbourhood, advancing slowly, sometimes by the merest increments, pausing, moving on again, pausing once more, as though each step had to be weighed and measured before it could take its place among the sum total of steps. (58)[20]

Quinn monitors his every movement, trailing him through the labyrinthine steps of New York. It all seems rather pointless, however. Stillman does not attempt to approach Peter, but instead, each day, simply leaves his hotel, walks through the city by seemingly random and arbitrary routes, picks broken and useless items off the streets and places them in his bag, lunches in the Riverside Park, dines at the Apollo Coffee Shop on 97th Street and Broadway, and then returns to his hotel.

Eventually, to stave off boredom, Quinn begins to take a careful note in a red notebook of what Stillman does and where that he goes, devising a method of carrying notebook and pen which meant that "Quinn was now able to divide his attention almost equally between Stillman and his writing, glancing now up at the one, now down at the other, seeing the thing and writing about it in the same fluid gesture" (Auster, *City of Glass* 63). After Quinn has been following Stillman through the streets of New York for some days but has yet achieved nothing, no insight into Stillman's motives, and no advancement of the case, "for no particular reason" (67), he looks over his notes and begins to map out Stillman's journey for each day. The first resulting diagram resembles a rectangle though "it might also have been a zero or the letter 'O'" (68). The second is "a bird of prey perhaps, with its wings spread," or it is the letter 'W' (68). It is followed by the letter 'E', then "a shape that resembled the letter 'R' [...] a lopsided 'O' [...] a tidy 'F' [...] a 'B' that looked like two boxes haphazardly placed on top of one another [...] a tottering 'A' [...] a second 'B': precariously tilted on a perverse single point" (70). From these nine letters, so far spelling out OWEROFBAB, Quinn realizes that the entire series will read THE TOWER OF BABEL, inferring from his knowledge that Stillman had previously written a book entitled *The Garden and the Tower: Early Visions of the New World*.

Stillman's book relates the biblical Tower of Babel to the Garden of Eden, where Adam, given the task of naming all the things of the world, spoke words that grasped the essential heart of their objects; as Auster writes, "A thing and its name were interchangeable. After the fall, this was no longer true. Names became detached from things" and "language had been severed from God" (*City of Glass* 43).[21] The story of the Garden of Eden, then, is not only the story of "the fall of man, but the fall of language" (43). However,

Stillman's project is to restore the language of man to a prelapsarian state, to undo the effects of the fall that saw the word divided from the thing it named. He had tried to use his son to access the prelapsarian language, incarcerating him in that room so that "he would forget everything he knew" and emerge "speaking God's language" (49). Now, collecting broken things, Stillman instead creates a new language by renaming what has lost its original function, so that the word is again a part of the true thing, so that the word works. In this, Stillman is attempting to return to a world of myth, which, as understood by Blanchot, "supposes no separation of sign and referent; meaning cannot be disembodied from the agents of the mythical narrative. It is as if the myth would ideally return the reader to a primitive state in which thought had not learnt the trick of abstracting from physical things" (Clark 77). "Primitive man knows that the possession of words gives him mastery over things," says Blanchot, because "the name has not emerged from the thing" ("Literature and the Right to Death" 379).

If Stillman has been writing his way across the surface of the city, his steps tracing a literal passage as he makes his way through the streets, this seems also a part of his naming project because it renames New York as the new Tower of Babel, the construction of which will herald the return of the language from before the fall, meaning it would "be possible for the whole earth to be of one language and one speech" (Auster, *City of Glass* 48). In this naming, the word seems again a part of the thing, for Stillman's writing is a language of the earth, or of the city; his steps have taken place in the streets of New York. Stillman's text, then, stands in relation to Auster's own in *City of Glass* as both of them write on and about the New York streets, working within the same space but interpreting the results of their actions in opposing ways. Though Auster's New York, true to Stillman's renaming, is interchangeable with the words that produce it, it is not, as Stillman believes, because the words are one with the city. THE TOWER OF BABEL is not the city's essential name in this world, the mark of its true presence. Rather, for Auster, there is no city outside the text, and the world is produced by it, not simply represented within it. We cannot access Auster's New York except through Auster's text, but there is nothing to that New York but its text, to the extent that when Quinn walks through the city, an account of his path is given by naming: "He walked down Broadway to 72nd Street, turned east to Central Park West, and followed it to 59th Street and the statue of Columbus. There he turned east once again, moving along Central Park South until Madison Avenue, and then cut right, walking downtown to Grand Central Station" (106). This New York is formed of words alone.

It is the difference between Stillman's and Auster's interpretation of the world that causes Quinn difficulties. Quinn is a rational protagonist who believes in the power of reason, who believes that the apparent randomness of the world around him need only be viewed in the right way, or read in the right way, before the order that surely is inherent in the world can be perceived: "[T]he key to good detective work was a close observation of details. [...] The implication was that human behaviour could be understood, that beneath the infinite facade of gestures, tics, and silences, there was finally a coherence, an order, a source of motivation" (Auster, *City of Glass* 67). As Jeffrey Nealon notes, "[T]he work of the detective mirrors not only the work of reading [...], but also—and more importantly for Quinn—the work of writing" (92–93), so that "the writer and the detective are interchangeable" (Auster, *City of Glass* 8). "In the good mystery," Quinn believes, "there is nothing wasted, no sentence, no word that is not significant. [...] Everything becomes essence; the centre of the book shifts with each event that propels it forward. The centre, then, is everywhere, and no circumference can be drawn until the book has come to its end" (8), but once the end arrives, then the center that has been driving it, the organizing principle, is revealed (the idea of a center that would hold the whole together would naturally appeal to a man whose own life has been decentered by the loss of his wife and son). The center is the present voice of the author, the *logos* which speaks to meaning and truth. Quinn is like that other detective, Blue in *Ghosts*, who shares Stillman's view of what language should achieve: "Words are transparent for him, great windows that stand between him and the world" (146).[22] In his city of glass, Quinn is seeking exactly this world of transparency where there is a direct correspondence between the signifier and the signified, between the word and its object. Quinn's detective, Max Work, therefore becomes for him the embodiment of the detective's rational belief in purposeful observation, in linearity, causality, and closure; he "allows Quinn's texts to accomplish an end, to create order" (Nealon 94) so that "Work (as a character) allows Quinn's writing to perform work (as a concept)" (93).

Nealon is here referring to the concept of work as explained by Blanchot: "For example, my project might be to get warm. As long as this project is only a desire, I can turn it over every possible way and still it will not make me warm. But now I build a stove: [...] I had in front of me stones and cast iron; now I no longer have either stones or cast iron, but instead the product of the transformation of these elements—that is, their denial and destruction—by work" ("Literature and the Right to Death" 370–371).

Therefore, "If," as Auster writes, "the object was to understand Stillman, to get to know him well enough to be able to anticipate what he would do next" (*City of Glass* 65), then this would appear to be job done. Without even having to witness it, Quinn knows what Stillman will do next because he knows of the EL to come, he knows what is to be written in the future.

And yet, Quinn cannot trust the evidence of his own eyes. It is said, "It seemed to him that he was looking for a sign. He was ransacking the chaos of Stillman's movements for some glimmer of cogency" (Auster, *City of Glass* 69), and as a result, "He had imagined the whole thing. [...] It was all an accident" (69). Quinn feels he is "no closer to Stillman than when he first started following him. He had lived Stillman's life, walked at his pace, seen what he had seen, and the only thing he felt now was the man's impenetrability" (67).[23] Why is it so difficult for Quinn to believe in the proper existence of these letters, to read the words of THE TOWER OF BABEL? Blanchot would say that the reason is that writing is different, that it does not work but rather "plays at working in the world" ("Literature and the Right to Death" 395); "For Blanchot, the literary work is characterized not by its negation of words before the inevitable ends and limits of meaning, but rather by the work's inability to be limited, to mean something univocally" (Nealon 98). Stillman wants to close the gap between his words and their object so that they say only one thing—in fact, are the same thing. He limits their meaning by limiting their context to a page "bounded on the north by 110th Street, on the south by 72nd Street, on the west by Riverside Park, and on the east by Amsterdam Avenue" (Auster, *City of Glass* 58) and to a day for each letter. And it almost works. His writing is so singular that it barely lasts the instant of its production, barely survives its here and now. Quinn notes, "Stillman had not left his message anywhere. True, he had created the letters by the movement of his steps, but they had not been written down. It was like drawing a picture in the air with your finger. The image vanishes as you are making it. There is no result, no trace to mark what you have done" (71). But then he continues, "And yet, the pictures did exist—not in the streets where they had been drawn, but in Quinn's red notebook" (71).[24] Words, therefore, are uneconomic, wasteful, and will not work for the writer alone, and in the text of Auster's New York City, Stillman's writing, meant for one thing only, is necessarily marked by its iterability, is opened to recontextualization, removed from its author, and set to play.[25]

If, in this scene, Quinn is analogous to Auster and Stillman to his father, a man who left no trace to mark his passing, then the play of *différance* which opens the father to his son, which allows communication between them, is also that which makes proper communication—in the sense of a right, straight, and direct address—impossible. In his unauthorized rein-scriptions, Quinn is uncertain whether a rectangle or zero, a bird of prey or "only two abstract shapes" (Auster, *City of Glass* 68), a doughnut, two boxes, a ladder, and an upside-down pyramid are really to be read as let-ters. And if they are, are these letters to be read then in the context of Stillman's life and works, to arrive at the words THE TOWER OF BABEL?[26] Though Stillman may think his words one with the city, a gap remains, even as it does between Stillman and the man who shadows him and between the father and the man who writes about his. However closely they follow, one from the other, they remain apart. Auster finds that his father remains inaccessible, that essences evade expression:

> Never before have I been so aware of the rift between thinking and writ-ing. [...] I have begun to feel that the story I am trying to tell is somehow incompatible with language, that the degree to which it resists language is an exact measure of how closely I have come to saying something impor-tant, and that when the moment arrives for me to say the one truly impor-tant thing (assuming it exists), I will not be able to say it. (*Invention of Solitude* 32)[27]

Furthermore, with the discovery in *The Invention of Solitude* that Auster's paternal grandfather had been murdered by his wife, the absence of a cer-tain origin, and with it a sense of the proper order of things, is dramatized for Auster in the most personal terms as he experiences an absence of the father which extends back in series along the line for generations.[28] Auster places Quinn in the same unsettling situation, for the text he is working on, THE TOWER OF BABEL, lacks both a beginning and an end, an origin and a purpose. It was only on the fifth day that he started to take note of Stillman's steps, and so those first four days are missing: "[T]he mystery of those four days was irretrievable," writes Auster (*City of Glass* 69–70). And Quinn does not see what will be written in the future. He knows it only as the further deferral of full communication, so that the end that would draw the circumference that would fix the shifting center never comes.[29] That absent EL leaves Quinn struggling with the possibility that the "letters were not letters at all" (71). Considering the "E" and "L" that he anticipates are yet to come, Quinn remembers that El was "the ancient Hebrew for God" (72), the Father, the ultimate figure of the *logos*, the nonpresent author of meaning. There is no god in Babel, it seems, and what Quinn has amounts to no more than "a mountain of rubbish" (72), the waste of words.

After days of shadowing, "Quinn felt no closer to Stillman than when he first started following him" (Auster, *City of Glass* 67), but how close was he when he first started following him? Maybe a distance of one step? How much closer could he be? Auster writes that Quinn "had lived Stillman's life" (67) just one step behind, which is to say, one word behind because Auster repeatedly relates the step to the word, for example when he describes writing about his father as having "to invent the road with each step" (*Invention of Solitude* 32), or when Quinn is "seeing the thing and writing about it in the same fluid gesture" (*City of Glass* 63), or when Quinn reads Stillman's steps as words, or when Quinn, telling his own story to the character called Auster, "began at the beginning and went through the entire story, step by step" (94). But Quinn cannot close an impossible distance, cannot step Stillman's steps, cannot write Stillman's writing. Quinn's is a restepping, a rewriting, going astray. The structure of the *pas*, the step/not, the step without step means this—that there is an order and disorder in the step. Like the movement of signification, this literal movement is possible only if the no-longer-present, passing footfall is related to the same but different, not-yet-present, coming footfall. The step goes nowhere, means nothing, except that it is coming from somewhere and going toward somewhere through the disarticulation of a past and a future element, both of which are necessary for a step to be a step at all. There are Quinn and Stillman, at a distance of one step; the foot of one is not yet fallen where the foot of the other is no longer, and the foot of one is no longer where the foot of the other is not yet, their steps falling together, trailing and advancing, and perhaps we can say that these are the steps that matter, these steps between them that together they take and make and that mean we can no longer speak of just "one step" "behind or ahead." Because, what is the order between the two of them? Is Quinn in the past and Stillman in the present, or is Quinn in the present and Stillman in the future? Do we say that Quinn is in the past and comes after or that Stillman is in the future and goes ahead? What if following Stillman came down to being followed by Stillman? Stillman seems to be out front, the future, but he is overtaken in Quinn's anticipation of the EL, an anticipation that then comes back to haunt Quinn like an absent origin. Quinn follows Stillman, and Stillman follows Quinn, and neither one is closer to the other.

Nevertheless, Quinn is such a good follower of Stillman that when he does finally fail in his investigation, he goes on to recreate the circumstances of Stillman's first experiment to use his son to recover the prelapsarian language, removing himself to a room in Peter and Virginia Stillman's empty flat. After writing in solitude for some time, Quinn "felt that his words had been severed from him, that now they were a part of the world at large, as real and specific as a stone, or a lake, or a flower" (Auster, *City of Glass* 130).[30] "Here," says Norma Rowen, "are words that turn into things, images of such force and clarity that they seem able to take their place in the world of objects, to become matter" (232), and so, she asks, "Has Quinn found the prelapsarian tongue?" (231). I would argue that he has not. Quinn may feel that the words are a part of the world, but he does not say that they turn into things. And though Rowen argues that here, "Quinn again laid hold on his vocation as a poet" (232), Quinn himself observes that his words "no longer had anything to do with him" (Auster, *City of Glass* 130); they have been "severed from him" (130) as words were "severed from God" (43) after the Fall. In this room, it is not that words exist as things but that things exist as words. This is the room that Auster returns to time and again in the later novels—such as in the form of the room of books in *Moon Palace*—and that he first describes in *The Invention of Solitude*, for example, when he remembers standing in Emily Dickinson's room and feeling that "if words are a way of being in the world, [...] it was the room that was present in the poems and not the reverse" (123). For Blanchot, therefore, words are a kind of nature; for Auster, they are a way of being in the world; and Quinn's story "is not a story, after all. It is a fact, something happening in the world" (*City of Glass* 40), with all the possibilities and risks that entails.

As Carl Malmgren comments, "Quinn tried to pretend to be a Work, but he was condemned to be a Text" (197).[31] Because, of course, it is not Quinn who follows Stillman but Quinn playing at being Paul Auster, the detective. In the same way, it is not Quinn but William Wilson who writes the novels following the exploits of the detective Max Work. Quinn thinks, "If he lived now in the world at all, it was only at one remove, through the imaginary person of Max Work" (Auster, *City of Glass* 9), so he lives vicariously in the world, a distance of a step from the absent other. Quinn is one of a series of his own ghosts, calling himself Auster, Wilson, or Work, and then Henry Dark and Peter Stillman. Stillman is not wrong when he says to him, "I like your name enormously, Mr Quinn. It flies off in so many little directions at once" (74). If Quinn's name connects to distant parts, so do the words he writes and the words in which he is written. When Auster notes of Quinn, "What interested him about the stories he wrote was not their relation to the world but their relation to other stories" (7), it is not only to affirm that Auster himself fosters such relations, his text invoking the works of Poe and Cervantes to foreground the themes of identity and authorship and connecting to the other stories in *The New York Trilogy* and to more, to the works of Marco Polo, Robert Louis Stevenson, Charles Dickens, Walt Whitman, Henry David Thoreau, Herman Melville, and Hawthorne through a complex web of namings, citations, and references. Looking at Quinn's place in the text, it seems possible to isolate him from anything nontextual. Certainly, Quinn himself had "long ago stopped thinking of himself as real" (9); he presents himself to the world as Wilson, who, though "an invention, [...] now led an independent life" (4) (Quinn is tempted but fails to introduce himself as Wilson to a young woman at a train station when he sees her reading one of his novels, and the woman who has moved into his apartment knows only that a writer, William Wilson, lived there); he has a literary agent whom he never meets; the people he encounters on his case include a deaf mute and a counterman "whose name he did not know" (37); Stillman commits suicide, and when Quinn learns of his death, he is told it was "all over the papers" (122); Quinn knew that Peter and his wife Virginia were gone too when "the line went dead" (123). The only characters who encounter Quinn and remain are the writer Paul Auster, his wife, and their son Daniel.

Following Stillman, Quinn comes to an understanding of the shadowy nature of his existence, of the way he writes himself into the world. "Language is not truth," writes Auster, "It is the way we exist in the world" (*Invention of Solitude* 161). When Quinn writes the initials DQ on the first page of the red notebook, which "was the first time in more than five years that he had put his own name in one of his notebooks" (*City of Glass* 39), he inscribes within the text his own adherence to the text and names his mortal existence. Quinn exists because, "[m]aterializing the signs, the notebook *creates* them" (Malmgren 197), which means also that "with the dwindling of pages in the red notebook [...], Quinn was coming to the end" (Auster, *City of Glass* 130), his end. And he was happy: "He remembered the infinite kindness of the world and all the people he had ever loved. Nothing mattered now but the beauty of all this" (130–131). He wonders if he could survive the end, "if he could learn to speak instead, filling the darkness with his voice" (131), to be as a spirit and not as a ghost. We cannot say. "The last sentence of the red notebook reads: 'What will happen when there are no more pages in the red notebook?'" (131), but the only certainty is that what follows will be that extraordinary thing—death—which, all the while he is writing, is coming.

All that remains of Quinn in the end, all his remains are, is that red notebook in which he kept his notes on Stillman and which, in conjunction with the character Paul Auster's witness, allows the unnamed narrator to tell Quinn's story. There is no proper conclusion; this text, too, lacks an EL because what life is ever more than OWEROFBAB, ever more than "half the story" (Auster, *City of Glass* 132) as it steps between an absent origin and absent end? Instead, the unnamed narrator can say of Quinn only that "it is impossible for me to say where he is now" (132). But this is an impossible text throughout, in the detail of the narrative, in the disparity between the content of the narrative and what is quoted directly from the red notebook, and in the reporting of Quinn's dreams "which he later forgot" (106). This text, which is wrong in so many ways, is the anticipated and remembered EL of the one who follows the other, of the son who loses his father and fears "his entire life will vanish along with him" (*Invention of Solitude* 6). This text is the impossible rewriting of the vanishing world of the other. After Quinn, at the end, snow is falling, erasing everything, so that the "city was entirely white now" (*City of Glass* 132), like an empty page, a new page, a new beginning, a writing again that will "never end" (132).[32]

NOTES

1. In the "I" that lies between them, the two women are "joined: separated," as Blanchot puts it (qtd. in Derrida, "Living On" 179), or "[s]eparated: joined," as Derrida puts it (181), thus drawing attention to the disorder between the parts. Because once the "Christ parallel" (151) of *Death Sentence* is acknowledged, "we can always wonder [...] whether the time of the 'second' *récit* does not come, will not have come, before that of the 'first.' [...] J.'s life [...], then death, seem in fact to be succeeded by the long-awaited entrance of Nathalie—a first name that refers to the Nativity with the resonance of good news" (163). The given order is "J. and 'I': 'I' and N." when the "proper" order is "N. and 'I': 'I' and J.," and suddenly the two parts "are ahead of or lag behind one another" (139), following or followed by one another, one pace after the other.

2. Derrida writes at length on *Death Sentence* in his essay "Living On" in terms that will be familiar after the discussion in the previous chapter on DeLillo's *The Body Artist*. He comments, for example, on the figure of the "I" as "the unreadable hymen between the two women" (186), like the "what" that comes between Lauren and Rey. And if "it's as if the narrator desired [...] one thing: that the two women should love one another, should meet, [...] should be the same [...]: this is what he desires, what he would die of" (188), then he is like Mr. Tuttle, desiring to bring Lauren and Rey close but ensuring they are not the same, that the past is not one with the present and therefore dead to the future.

3. Similarly, Castricano comments that "writing is necessarily marked by departure, by leave-taking, and by death. To write, thus, is *to anticipate the memory of one's other,* one's departed" (41).

4. And *Death Sentence* is also the surviving repetition of an earlier effort at telling the story that the narrator "reread [...] and destroyed" (Blanchot, *Death Sentence* 131).

5. As Boulter argues of Auster's *Travels in the Scriptorium* (2006), "[T]he novel argues that the very act of imagination is guilty in that it conjures subjectivities against their wills" (57).

6. In Blanchot's *Death Sentence*, the narrator in the first *récit* tells us that the doctor "had just given me six months to live and that was seven years ago" (134); in the second *récit*, the narrator says that others "thought I was nearing my end, [...] was dying" (163), "had been on the point of dying" (165).

7. "Ghost" in this instance is a synonym for "invisible man." In a previously published version of this material, I described all these characters as "ghosts before their time, alive but not living" (142), but now I would suggest they are not living exactly because they are no longer—or not yet—ghosts.

8. Might the initials of Mr. Bones and of Mr. Blank in *Travels in the Scriptorium* stand for the M.B. of Maurice Blanchot?

9. As in *Hamlet*, in *City of Glass* the "spirit of the father is going to come back" (Derrida, *Specters of Marx* 4).

10. Chance plays an important part in Derrida's work also. He comments, for example, that the play of *différance* introduces "the unity of chance and necessity in calculations without end" ("Différance" 7). See especially "My Chances/*Mes Chances*: A Rendezvous with Some Epicurean Stereophonies."

11. And what of Auster's women, who so often come between the two men: Virginia Stillman in *City of Glass*, Sophie Fanshawe in *The Locked Room*, Tiffany in *The Music of Chance*, Fanny and Maria in *Leviathan*, the "spectral" Alma Grund in *The Book of Illusions* (288), Grace in *Oracle Night*? If, in Blanchot's *Death Sentence*, we have "the narrator: *the hymen between the two women*" (Derrida, "Living On" 185), Auster has the woman as the hymen between the two men, but he denies her the "I" of the narrator (Anna Blume in *In the Country of Last Things* is the exception). This suggests that, for Auster, the primary issue is between father and son. In this context, see Fredman, who argues that in *The Invention of Solitude* "women are rendered as void and men are imagined as self-generating" (23), so that the "woman's role in this fantasy of masculine self-generation is 'effaced'" (27).

12. "[T]he labyrinth, room," says Derrida, "so many structures of the *pas*" ("*Pa*ce Not(*s*)" 61).

13. Roth puts a similar emphasis on Zuckerman's isolation, on the fact that he had "spent half his life sealed off in rooms" (*Anatomy Lesson* 9), had "chosen monasticism and retreat" (180), "the sternest form of incarceration" (180), so that he was like "some certified madman groaning over a table in his little cell" (36), writing. He is "in lonely rooms/country recluse/ anonymous expatriate/garreted monk" (*Operation Shylock* 87).

14. Derrida describes it as a "deathless death" or "[d]eath's *faux pas*," its false step ("*Pace* Not(*s*)" 85).

15. Similarly, in Edgar Allan Poe's "The Man of the Crowd" (1840), the narrator describes how he "had been ill in health, but was now convalescent, and, with returning strength, found myself in one of those happy moods [...] of the keenest appetency" (84). In each case, to be happy to be alive, to be happy to be living on, is to be happy not to be dead, so that this happiness is indissociable from the possibility of dying. As Derrida puts it, "I am never more haunted by the necessity of dying than in moments of happiness and joy. To feel joy and to weep over the death that awaits are for me the same thing" (*Learning to Live Finally* 52).

16. "Effaced before being written. If the word trace can be admitted, it is as the mark that would indicate as erased what was, however, never traced. All our writing—for everyone and if it were ever writing of everyone—would be this: the anxious search for what was never written in the present, but in a past to come" (Blanchot, *The Step Not Beyond* 17).

17. "William Wilson" is also, of course, the title of a short story by Poe about a character of the same name, though it is not his real name, and a doppelgänger who shares that name, his date of birth, and his appearance. *City of Glass* also contains references to the baseball player Mookie Wilson, whose "real name was William Wilson" (128).

18. Derrida observes, "The perversion of that which, out of joint, does not work well, does not walk straight, or goes askew (*de travers*, then, rather than *à l'envers*) can easily be seen to oppose itself as does the oblique, twisted, wrong, and crooked to the good direction of that which goes right, straight, to the spirit of that which orients or founds the law [*le droit*]—and sets off directly, without detour, toward the right address, and so forth" (*Specters of Marx* 20).

19. This wrong number connects Auster's novel with Blanchot's *The One Who Was Standing Apart From Me*, the opening line of which—"I sought, this time, to approach him" (263)—means it "begins with this false beginning or this *faux-pas* of beginning" (Derrida, "*Pace* Not(*s*)" 82). Anyone beginning without beginning in this way, with a beginning that "has not purely and simply missed its destination," might ask, "What are my chances of reaching my addressees [...]?" (Derrida, "My Chances" 345). The telephone connects also with Blanchot's *Death Sentence*, in which, Derrida

argues, the "narrator is always away, distanced (at a distance, *tele-*)" ("Living On" 157) and the two women "telephone each other ('Come') across the infinite distance of a no-connection" ("Living On" 186).

20. Reading Blanchot, Derrida comments, "Rather than accompanying such a text with a commentary it does without [*dont il se passe*] (as completely other) as surely as it requires it, I will read it slowly, underlining here of there a word [*mot*], a passage, a *moment*, a *movement*. Another reading, another time, will underline otherwise" ("*Pace* Not(*s*)" 62).

21. The severing of language from God is both an example of violence and also the very "possibility of violence" which, in metaphysics, "can thus only be accounted for in terms of a Fall, that is, in terms of a fatal corruption of a pure origin" (Hägglund 75). In the context of Auster's work, it is important to note that Derrida, in a discussion that takes in Poe also, reads the fall in general in terms of "luck or chance": "what falls is not seen in advance" ("My Chances" 348).

22. This transparency, of course, relates directly to the concept of a City of Glass (the title is a play on Augustine's *The City of God*, which suggests that an eternal order exists outside the realm of sense). In Blanchot, however, the glass relates to the inaccessibility of the other, that "place that was very near and infinitely separated from me, as if it were behind a window" (*Death Sentence* 172), so that the "truth is that after I had been fortunate enough to see her once through a pane of glass, the only thing I wanted, during the whole time I knew her, was [...] to break the glass" (161). In Poe's "The Man of the Crowd," the narrator spots his man while sitting "at the large bow window" (84) of a coffee-house, with his "brow to the glass" (87), and it is as if the man remains behind glass when the narrator, at the end of the story, "wearied unto death, and, stopping fully in front of the wanderer, gazed at him steadfastly in the face. He noticed me not" (91).

23. The account of his shadowing recalls that of Poe's "The Man of the Crowd" where the narrator, after following the old man "close at his elbow" as he "crossed and re-crossed the way repeatedly without apparent aim" (89), concludes that, "It will be in vain to follow; for I shall learn no more of him, nor of his deeds" (91) for he is like that book which "does not permit itself to be read" (84).

24. Stillman's writing remains writing, and, as Derrida reminds us, a written sign is "a mark which remains, which is not exhausted in the present of its inscription" and "a written sign carries with it a force of breaking with its context, that is, the set of presences which organize the moment of its inscription" ("Signature Event Context" 317).

25. As Dimovitz argues, "[T]he novel implies that if a primal language of God exists—which the novel never really believes—that language would remain

completely solipsistic, incommunicable, and probably not meaningful at all" (617).

26. Here, Derrida would point out to Quinn that "a context is never sufficiently determined to prohibit all random deviation" ("My Chances" 347) and that "no meaning can be determined out of context, but no context permits saturation" ("Living On" 108).

27. Similarly, in Blanchot's *Death Sentence*, the narrator comments, "If I have written novels, they have come into being just as the words began to shrink back from the truth" (131). Boulter comments that Blanchot "suggests that what defines the author's relation to the work at the moment of its completion is the author's radical failure to know the work, to read the work, to interpret the work" (53).

28. *Différance* puts into question "precisely the quest for a rightful beginning, an absolute point of departure, a principal responsibility" (Derrida, "Différance" 6). *City of Glass*, accordingly, draws attention to the uncertain authorship of a number of its embedded narratives, including the Max Work novels written by William Wilson; Henry Dark's *The New Babel*, which is summarized in Stillman's *The Garden and the Tower: Early Visions of the New World*, though of course, "there never was any such person as Henry Dark" (Auster, *City of Glass* 80); and Cervantes's *Don Quixote*, which Cervantes claims was written in Arabic by Cid Hamete Benengeli, while Cervantes then simply had it translated into Spanish.

29. Quinn stands in a field that "is in effect that of *play*, that is to say, a field of infinite substitutions only because it is finite, that is to say, because instead of being an inexhaustible field, as in the classical hypothesis, instead of being too large, there is something missing from it: a center which arrests and grounds the play of substitutions" (Derrida, "Structure, Sign, and Play" 289).

30. The rooms and objects of Auster's *The New York Trilogy* are often drawn from Blanchot's work, work which "always leads back to the water" (Derrida, "*Pace* Not(s)" 81). In Blanchot's *Death Sentence*, we find the "notebook" (133) and the "lamp" and "bed" (146) that will appear in Auster's *Ghosts*: "It will not do to call the lamp a bed [...] or the bed a lamp" (148). Blanchot uses the example "I say a flower!" a number of times, as Derrida notes ("*Pace* Not(s)" 85), so Auster's flower not only recalls the "perfect rose" (147) in *Death Sentence* but also his stone and flower relate to the "the pebble" and "*a flower*" (383) from Blanchot's "Literature and the Right to Death" ("Littérature et le droit à la mort" [1949]). In the same paragraph in which they appear, Blanchot writes, "My hope lies in the materiality of language, in the fact that words are things, too, are a kind of nature" (383). Flower and Stone are also the names of characters in *The Music of Chance*, whose "wall also figures prominently in Maurice Blanchot's story 'The Idyll'" (Shiloh 513).

31. Nicol comments that the "act of writing [...] for Blanchot, is tantamount to confronting one's own non-existence" (182), so that "[a]s he becomes lost in the labyrinthine plot of his case Quinn resembles the writer surrendering to the force of the Blanchotian 'work'. He is never sure of where his writing will take him" (182–183).

32. And Quinn doesn't end. "He's somewhere" (Auster, *Locked Room* 307). Dimovitz insists that "Quinn has not melted or ceased to exist. He has only disappeared" (621), and Zilcosky observes that "Quinn does not die; his red notebook is read and related to us by the Narrator, allowing Quinn to live on through fiction" (203). So he lives on. In *The Locked Room*, a man named Quinn is hired to find Fanshawe; in Auster's *In the Country of Last Things*, you can find "the passport of a man named Quinn" (36); there's Walt's "nephew, Daniel Quinn" (276), in *Mr Vertigo*; and in *Travels in the Scriptorium*, a man says, "I'm Quinn, Mr. Blank [...]. Daniel Quinn. Your first operative" (120). Mr. Blank, here the author of all Auster's returning characters, refers to them as the "damned specters [...]. My victims. All the people I've made suffer over the years" (80–81). Boulter notes, "Auster is careful [in *Travels in the Scriptorium*] to figure these characters from previous novels as phantoms, ghosts, as fully spectral" (53) so that "the work cannot end, but maintains itself in a constant, spectral real" (53), and "Blank is haunted, in other words, by the infinite work" (54). Blank is haunted also by "the crushing sense of guilt" (Auster, *Travels in the Scriptorium* 28). "Please forgive me, he says" (120).

Haunts

The first time I was in New York, on my first full day in the city, I planned to spend it on my feet, following in the footsteps of Daniel Quinn, the main character in Paul Auster's *City of Glass* from *The New York Trilogy*. My intention was to recreate a long walk that Quinn takes in the novel, lasting an entire day (or about two pages, depending on which way you look at it). Previously, and probably like many others, I'd plotted his walk on a map of the city, tracing his movements through the grid of Manhattan's streets, to see if his day's passage would deliver some message, some meaning, some revelation. The story practically requires you to do this: before embarking on his own long walk, the writer and now detective Quinn discovers that the aimless wanderings of Stillman, the man he has been tailing, actually seem to spell out the words THE TOWER OF BABEL, so when he then wonders "what the map would look like of all the steps he had taken in his life and what word it would spell" (129), the chances seem good that something significant will appear.[1] But there's nothing.

So, instead, I decided to walk it and use it as my introduction to the city. Because, as it turns out, it serves that purpose rather well.[2] I started on West 107th Street (where Quinn lives and Auster did from 1965 to 1970), between Riverside Drive (where the character Paul Auster lives and Auster did from 1974 to 1977) and West End Avenue, and I headed east before turning right onto Broadway and walking from Straus Park down to Verdi Square on 72nd Street (having breakfast on the way). Turning left, I walked to Central Park West and the entrance to the park adjoining

© The Editor(s) (if applicable) and The Author(s) 2016
D. Coughlan, *Ghost Writing in Contemporary American Fiction*,
DOI 10.1057/978-1-137-41024-5_6

Strawberry Fields, named in memory of John Lennon in the year that *City of Glass* was published (The Dakota apartment building, outside of which he was murdered, is just across the road). Following the edge of the park and passing within a block or so of Dante Park and the Lincoln Center for the Performing Arts, at 59th Street, I discovered the statue of Columbus. If it hadn't already been apparent to me, it would have been made clear here that this walk was not about tracing a word across the city but was about retracing the web of historical, biographical, cultural, and literary narratives that weave their way through the streets. As I strolled along Central Park South, down Madison Avenue, east on 45th Street, down Lexington Avenue, west on 42nd Street, and down 5th Avenue, I walked behind St Patrick's Cathedral, saw the wonderful Chrysler Building, and took in Grand Central Station (scene of a significant decision in *City of Glass*), the New York Public Library (where the Paul Auster archive is housed in the Berg Collection of English and American Literature and where, at this very moment, writing these words, here I am, seeing my ghost pass outside), and the Empire State Building (the world's tallest building from 1931 until the first World Trade Center surpassed it in 1970). Following Quinn, I saw the Flatiron Building at Madison Square (one of New York City's first skyscrapers), Christopher Park (and its statue of Philip Henry Sheridan, the Union general whose infamous words Auster paraphrases in *City of Glass*: "[T]he only good Indian was a dead Indian" [42]; the park is flanked by Grove Street, where Thomas Paine once lived, and by Christopher Street, which saw some of the worst fighting during the Draft Riots of 1863 and witnessed also the 1969 Stonewall Riots, which are often marked as the beginning of the gay liberation movement in the USA), Washington Square (which gives its name to the novel by Henry James), New York University, and Varick Street (which meant I had arrived in another neighborhood in which Auster had once lived, another one of his old haunts).

Finally, I arrived at the site of the World Trade Center, where Quinn has lunch. That wasn't an option for me. It was after September 11, 2001, when the Twin Towers had fallen, and the place that since that day had been known as Ground Zero was a vast construction site on which a new World Trade Center rose amid reflecting glass surfaces, and a roof's steel arches curved out of the ground like the ridged backbone of some great Leviathan. Coming after Quinn, I arrived there late, in a different era, some might say, post-9/11. But, at the same time, I could still have been following his story of skyscrapers and falls, of beginnings and endings, as if 9/11 were the anticipated conclusion to *City of Glass*, like Quinn's foreseen "EL," or as if 9/11 were the erasure of a proper ending to an American story, like Quinn's foreseen "EL." Stillman wanted New York City to work as the new Tower of Babel, to work as a place in which every man and woman would be "speaking God's language, prepared to inhabit the second, everlasting paradise" (Auster, *City of Glass* 49). God had objected to the original Tower of Babel because it "contradicted a command that had appeared earlier in Genesis: 'Be fertile and increase, fill the earth and master it'" (44), but with the entire continent now settled, Stillman believed the time was right for America to achieve its destiny as "a second Garden of Eden" (41), "a veritable City of God" (42). What did 9/11 mean in this context: the time was wrong; "God's punishment" (44); the persecution of "God's newly chosen people" (48); a fall from innocence; when "heaven and earth were joined at last" (48); the loss of a paradise; Eden's deferral; the one language is mortal grief; when "[h]istory would be written in reverse" (48); when man "would forget everything he knew" (49)? Did it mean that every step begins and ends, that "it was only after the fall that human life as we know it came into being" (42), and that "the Tower of Babel stands as the last image before the true beginning of the world" (43)? Could I say anything about 9/11 without contributing to "the numerous misreadings that had grown up around it" (43)? I would still be wondering about this on a later visit to the city when, late one evening, I stood at the South Pool of the 9/11 Memorial, before the names of the dead, close to the first fall of water, looking beyond to the other fall of water further into darkness, seeming impossibly distant, as if a world away.

After lunch, and depending on how you interpret things beyond this point, Quinn's walk will take you into the financial district, across Wall Street, past the New York Stock Exchange and the New York City Opera, to the Charging Bull at Bowling Green (where the Dutch colonists bought Manhattan from the Native Americans for approximately $24), close to the Staten Island Ferry (always to be recommended because it's free and affords great views of the skyline), and then back up through the city, past St Paul's Chapel (the oldest surviving church in Manhattan), City Hall, and the approach to Brooklyn Bridge (the story of which is told in *Ghosts*), and beyond to Chinatown, the Bowery (the oldest route in Manhattan), Cooper Square, Union Square (regularly the scene of protests and rallies, even to the present day), and all the way to the United Nations. It's a proper New York City story, and yet it's not just one story. It is, of course, a ghost story, of the lives, the losses, the violence, the victory, the discriminations, the migrations, the protests, the revolutions, the power, the propaganda, the history that haunts those streets and is inscribed in those streets. So Quinn "concentrated on the things he had seen while walking," and then he tells the unauthorized, haunting story of "the tramps, the down-and-outs, the shopping-bag ladies, the drifters and drunks. They range from the merely destitute to the wretchedly broken" (Auster, *City of Glass* 108). To speak of these broken women and men, of the unhoused, of those whose lives may have gone awry, is to speak of the ghosts of words, of the wasteful play that sees them tell more than the one, fixed story. In this way, Quinn and I can follow the same path and yet live in different worlds.

As it happens, though, I didn't even make it to the United Nations. Trying to navigate my way around the construction work at Ground Zero, I ended up going west on Vesey Street, in the direction of the Hudson River. As I neared the water, I saw something which seemed utterly out of place and yet undeniably familiar. It looked like a field from home, from Ireland, complete with stone walls and a derelict cottage, except the grass didn't seem quite the right shade of green, and the walls were like new. There was a man standing in this small strip of a hillside field in Manhattan, and then he turned and disappeared into the building. Where the field sloped down to meet me there was a fence, so I walked around to the raised back of what I now discovered was the Irish Hunger Memorial, commemorating the Great Famine of the mid-nineteenth century which saw a million people emigrate from Ireland and a million more die. Three sides of the memorial displayed texts from the period, and I found a reference to a Father Lyons from Mayo, my mother's maiden name and home county. Passing from the entrance, through the cottage, I took the path up through the field, where stones bore the names of the different counties in Ireland, and I looked for and found my own, Cork, and by the time I reached the top, I was in welcome tears and feeling strangely, humbly grateful. And that's when I looked out across the water and saw, for the first time, the Statue of Liberty.[3]

Having strayed so far from Quinn's course, I still couldn't help but think we were "like two twins cleaving together" (Milton qtd. in Auster, *City of Glass* 42), given "the paradox of the word 'cleave,' which means both 'to join together' and 'to break apart'" (Auster 43), like the order and disorder of the step. Because in *City of Glass*, Auster writes, "Quinn was now able to *divide* his attention almost equally *between Stillman and his writing,*

glancing now up at *the one*, now down at *the other*, seeing the thing
and writing about it in *the same* fluid gesture" (63, my emphasis). The
one gesture, the same gesture, is, from the beginning, divided, between
Stillman and Quinn, between the one and the other. So, when Quinn
writes about Stillman, following in his wake, surely his notes are not so
much a proper record of Stillman's movements as of Quinn's experience
of them, or a record not so much of Stillman's writing but of Quinn's
witnessing of this writing. In this sense, Quinn's act of following is a
reading which is already a rewriting, a repetition delayed from "now" to
"now." His later mapping of Stillman's passage, therefore, is a retracing
of his own path and not a representation of the equivalent but not identical path taken by Stillman. In the end, when Quinn discovers the text in
the city, he is reading what he himself has already written, his own story,
as do I. Quinn and I are joined together exactly because we break apart,
because we break from those we are following.

There is, therefore, an impossible relation between the self and other.
Following after Stillman, Quinn is what I, following Derrida, would call "an
acolyte, that is, someone who accompanies" ("Le Parjure" 181). Derrida
continues, "[T]he acolyte accompanies with an eye to following and assist-
ing. He is an attached subject, who follows the other, listens to him, and
is joined to him like his shadow" (181) as Quinn shadows Stillman in
his role as detective. Yet, Derrida remarks that the acolyte "accompanies,
but without accompanying altogether, in any event, at a certain distance"
(181), perhaps, though Derrida does not say, at a distance of a step. As a
result, he says, we can "associate the figure of the *acolyte*, which accompanies, with its negative, the *anacoluthon*, which does not accompany"
(182) but designates "an interruption in the sequence itself, [...] or in an
order in general" (181).[4] The acolyte haunts the other "since the acolyte
assists without being absolutely identical or in agreement, therefore not
fully present to the person" (181). However, he suggests that "there is no
simple opposition between the acolyte, or the 'acoluthon' and the '*ana*co-
luthon'. That is a problem, because to accompany, or to follow in the most
demanding and authentic way, implies the '*ana*col,' the 'not-following,'
the break in the following, in the company so to speak," which means
that "what appears as a necessity is that, in order to follow in a consistent
way, to be true to what you follow, you have to interrupt the following"
("Following Theory" 7). Following is, therefore, "a relation of fidelity
and betrayal" (9).

We have to break with those we follow. Quinn cannot faithfully read Stillman's text without betraying him because, as Bennington describes, "[T]here could be no reading absolutely respectful of a text, for a total respect would forbid one from even touching the text, opening the book" (165). As Derrida explains, "*Within* the experience of following [...] there is something other, something new, or something different which occurs and which I sign. That's what I call a 'counter-sign', a counter-signature" ("Following Theory" 10). If we did not betray those we follow, if we were absolutely faithful to them, so faithful as to occupy their very here and now, so faithful as to think their thoughts and breathe their air, then we would be the same and would no longer "respect the alterity of the other" (10). There would be no alter ego, which is to say, there would be no past or future ego either. Says Derrida, "[T]he anacoluthon interrupts forever the relation to self, the possibility of a relation to self" ("Le Parjure" 196), but even as it prevents me from saying "I am the same" ("Following Theory" 25), it means I can say "I am" because in order for my self to be, I must break with the "present," betray my absolute allegiance to what I am "here" and "now," make of me my own "missing companion" ("Le Parjure" 182). Every moment of living on is a betrayal of life and a recommitment to it, "the product of the oath" ("Following Theory" 25). All the while I am writing my life, death is coming and life comes back to haunt me. And so, following 9/11, I found myself, uncannily, back in an Irish field in New York City, and I, who had pursued the study of American literature in part (it cannot be denied) to distance myself from my Irish roots, instead felt closer to them than I ever had. And I could not have been happier.[5]

NOTES

1. In Auster's *Moon Palace*, Fogg says, "I had no idea what that question was, but the answer had already been formed in my steps" (297). In *The Invention of Solitude*, Auster writes, "It sometimes seems to A. that his son's mental perambulations while at play are an exact image of his own progress through the labyrinth of his book. He has even thought that if he could somehow make a diagram of his son at play [...] and then make a similar diagram of his book (elaborating what takes place in the gaps between words, the interstices of the syntax, the blanks between sections—in other words, unravelling the spool of connections), the two diagrams would be the same" (165). See also the "[d]iagram from the manuscript of Paul Auster's 'The Book of Memory'" (Auster and Contat 174).

2. A guided *City of Glass* tour, narrated by Auster, is not such an absurd idea when you consider that "Auster has narrated a walking tour and history of the neighbourhood around what is now Ground Zero"; *Manhattan, Ground Zero: A Sonic Memorial Soundwalk* (2005) "has the same geographical exactness as Quinn's plotting of Stillman's footsteps (and his own) around the Upper West Side" (Brown 193).

3. The memorial's rebuilt cottage, brought from Mayo, reminds me, of course, of the stones of the castle transported from Cork with which Nashe and Pozzi must build a "monument in the shape of a wall" (86) in Auster's *The Music of Chance*.

4. Both "anacoluthon" and "acolyte" come from the Greek word *akolouthos*, meaning "following."

5. The uncanny and unexpected return of and to the familiar reoccurs in Auster also. In the opening lines of *The Brooklyn Follies*, for example, Glass says, "I was looking for a quiet place to die. Someone recommended Brooklyn [...]. I hadn't been back in fifty-six years, and I remembered nothing [...], but I instinctively found myself returning to the neighborhood where we had lived" (1). Similarly, in *Timbuktu*, when Willy and Mr. Bones end up in "Poe-land" (46), Mr. Bones remarks, "They'd come here looking for one thing and had found another [...]. Willy had managed to get himself home again" (47). In the same way, the subject of the next chapter, Philip Roth, writes of his first visit to Prague, "Within the first few hours of walking in these streets between the river and the Old Town Square, I understood that a connection of sorts existed between myself and this place [...]. Looking for Kafka's landmarks, I had, to my surprise, come upon some landmarks that felt to me like my own" (qtd. in Gooblar 61–62). The idea of (the other's) death in which is found my self, identifies exactly the betrayal at the heart of ghost writing.

4. Exit Ghost Writer: Philip Roth

Who is the ghost writer in Philip Roth's *The Ghost Writer* (1979)? Is it the author, E.I. Lonoff, or the acolyte, Nathan Zuckerman, or "Roth himself" (Budick 122)? Lonoff is a likely candidate, living as he is between two deaths since, for many of his readers, he has "supposedly died" by 1956 (Roth, *Ghost Writer* 10), the year in which the book is set, but won't actually die until 1961. And, more accurately, he is not living between two deaths because, as his aggrieved wife Hope puts it, "*Not* living is what he makes his beautiful fiction *out* of!" (174–175). Indeed, he says to Zuckerman, "Nothing happens to me" (16). Immediately after he says this, however, Zuckerman writes, "It was here that the striking girl-woman appeared" (16), this woman being none other than the ghost of Anne Frank, the no-thing that happens and another ghost writer. Zuckerman, the "worshipful young acolyte" (*Exit Ghost* 21), in turn, writes about both these ghosts, and so we have a series of ghost writers, all of whom could perhaps be the author of Lonoff's *It's Your Funeral* (1927), addressing the dead, or the ghost. This chapter, therefore, reads the author alongside the acolyte, reads the graveside alongside the deathbed, reads the self alongside the other self, and does so by reading Roth alongside Auster, suggesting that Roth, as with Auster, begins with death, works his way back into life, and, finally, returns to death.

© The Editor(s) (if applicable) and The Author(s) 2016
D. Coughlan, *Ghost Writing in Contemporary American Fiction*,
DOI 10.1057/978-1-137-41024-5_7

To Begin with Death

The writing of Nathan Zuckerman, Roth's original ghost writer, always begins with death: the death of Zuckerman's spiritual father E.I. Lonoff in *The Ghost Writer*, of Zuckerman's actual father in *Zuckerman Unbound* (1981), of his mother in *The Anatomy Lesson* (1983), of Zdenek Sisovsky's father in *The Prague Orgy* (1985), of Zuckerman's brother in *The Counterlife* (1986), of Swede Levov's father and the Swede himself in *American Pastoral* (1997), of Ira Ringold in *I Married a Communist* (1998), and of Zuckerman's friend Coleman Silk in *The Human Stain* (2000). The writing ends with the final scene that Zuckerman composes in *Exit Ghost* (2007) and that concludes with him "[g]*one for good*" (Roth, *Exit Ghost* 292). The novels are directly concerned with the responsibility of the writer to the dead and with the writer's seemingly inevitable betrayal of those for whom he writes. The conclusion of *The Ghost Writer* provides a fitting image for this relationship between the writer and his subject. After a fraught breakfast scene, Amy Bellette, Lonoff's former student and assumed current lover, has departed, followed by Hope, who has packed a bag to leave her husband, followed in turn by Lonoff himself, making his way across the snow-covered driveway after her while behind him Zuckerman is left to make his "feverish notes" on what he has witnessed (*Ghost Writer* 180). In this novel, it seems a writer's life really is "reading and writing and looking at the snow" (30); so the words will appear on the paper like tracks in the snow, but how closely will Zuckerman follow in Lonoff's footsteps? Is it possible, or even desirable, to follow wholly and faithfully the passage of another?

In *Zuckerman Unbound*, the impending death of Dr Victor Zuckerman haunts the novel, and all the more so because, in writing *Carnovsky* (his *Portnoy's Complaint* [1969]), Zuckerman will have proven himself a betrayer of his Jewish heritage and, as he puts it, a "[c]oldhearted betrayer of the most intimate confessions, cutthroat caricaturist of your own loving parents, graphic reporter of encounters with women to whom you have been deeply bound by trust, by sex, by love" (Roth, *Zuckerman Unbound* 54). In other words, in his writing, he breaks with those to whom he is closest. But as he sits by his father's deathbed, unaware that his ailing father has had *Carnovsky* read to him, Zuckerman still believes that he can write faithfully of and for his dying father, as when, "in his own hand, he signed 'Dr. Victor Zuckerman'" (181) to the letter he believes his father might have in mind. In his last words to his father, he describes to him "the creation of the universe and [...] the origin of everything" (184–185) as if he could tell his father's story in its totality, the whole of his life, as if it were possible to "[f]inish the story" (190) of a "universe being reborn and reborn and reborn, without end" (192). But in response to his son, Dr Zuckerman's very last word is "Bastard" (193), speaking exactly to a betrayal, an interruption between origin and end, and an illegitimacy in the authorized line. The father's death, far from securing his son's identity by creating an intimate closeness between the two, seems instead to erase everything, telling Zuckerman, "You are no longer any man's son, you are no longer some good woman's husband, you are no longer your brother's brother, and you don't come from anywhere anymore, either" (224–225). His brother details Zuckerman's error, telling him, "The origin of the universe! When all he was waiting to hear was 'I love you!' 'Dad, I love you'—that was all that was required!" (219). In other words, rather than making an absolute statement on life and death, a statement of absolute faithfulness, Zuckerman needed to face his father's mortality, to promise himself to his father, and, in the face of his own unending betrayal, to recommit again and again to the surviving life of the other who will die.

The self-defeating nature of utter faithfulness to the other and the need continually to break with and recommit ourselves to those we love become very apparent in *The Anatomy Lesson*, in which Zuckerman loses his mother. The night before her funeral, Zuckerman sleeps in his mother's bed, and it is as if until "that night Zuckerman hasn't known who the dead were or just how far away. [...] An inch separated them, nothing separated them, they were indivisible—yet no message could make it through" (Roth, *Anatomy Lesson* 45). His dead mother is just a step beyond, "a nearby object at a dreadful distance" (45), so close and yet uncontactable, communicating nothing. Here, Roth anticipates a cemetery scene in Paul Auster's *The Locked Room* which places Fanshawe and his father side-by-side on the page, one in a grave and the other on his deathbed. Fanshawe has climbed down into a freshly dug grave and is lying at the bottom, staring at the sky above. The narrator remarks, "Fanshawe was alone down there, thinking his thoughts, living through those moments by himself, and though I was present, the event was sealed off from me, as though I was not really there at all" (Auster, *Locked Room* 220–221). Standing there, "trying to imagine what he was thinking," the narrator "understood that this was Fanshawe's way of imagining his father's death" (221). Fanshawe's father, who had always been "a cipher" (218), is, at that very moment, dying in his room in the family's house, and once the narrator comments that "the snow was coming down heavily, and the ground was turning white" (220)—the sign in Auster of a coming death—it is not a surprise that he has passed away by the time the boys return. The scene, therefore, presents us with a series of characters—the narrator, Fanshawe, the father—trying to imagine the other. In the course of the narrative, this means imagining the other, imagining the other dead, and imagining the dead other, that is, Fanshawe, Fanshawe's father's death, and Fanshawe's father who has died. Fanshawe, sealed off, seems unknowable, and his father, a cipher, seems unknowable, so that "it would seem impossible to say anything about a man until he is dead" (253), when the end of a life determines what was at the heart of it.

Except, the end as such never comes: "In the end, each life is no more than [...] a chronicle of chance intersections [...] that divulge nothing but their own lack of purpose" (Auster, *Locked Room* 217), their own lack of an end. It is this lack of an end that means it is as impossible to say anything about a dead person as a living person; but to put it another way, it is this lack of an end that makes possible this thing that "would seem impossible." It is the lack of an end that leaves things open, like the grave in which Fanshawe lies, like the locked room in which he dies, and allows the narrator to understand a mind that he is sealed off from. As Fanshawe lay there and "looked up at the sky, his eyes blinking furiously as the snow fell onto his face," the narrator describes how he also "turned [his] head up to the darkening winter sky—and everything was a chaos of snow, rushing down on top of [him]" (221). The displaced repetition of the narrator's understanding, like the imagined death of Fanshawe's father, is possible only because of this chaos of chance, the oblique fall of events. In contrast, it would be impossible for the narrator to say anything of Fanshawe if the grave in which he lay, or the distance between him and his father, were properly closed. If death determined his life, if the end coincided with the center, if he existed thus timelessly, then he would be beyond writing. He would be entirely the same (as himself) or entirely other (to himself). It would be as if the snow were falling straight down, directly down, so that, to one looking up, the snow's origin, center, and end would seem one and the same, and there would be no trace of its passing. It would fall straight into the grave.

What this scene demonstrates is that the self, the other, and the dead other relate impossibly to each other. And, it is neither more nor less impossible to relate to the other or to the dead other. The dead are at an impossible distance from me, but I should not think that the one who sits across

from me, who speaks to me and looks at me, is necessarily more immediately accessible for being within touching distance. The self never has
direct access to the other; it always touches on the limit of the self. This is
true even of the other self, the past self or the future self, whom one can
remember or imagine but never be (which means also that both Fanshawe
and his father are imagining the latter's death in the same way). It is always
as if one has stepped away, snow has fallen, and the other looks to follow
in those absent footsteps. We stand together, and each and every one of us
is present and "not really there" (Auster, *Locked Room* 221).

Admittedly, it would be a poor consolation for Zuckerman to hear that
his mother, even when alive, was always already a step beyond, "a nearby
object at a dreadful distance" (Roth, *Anatomy Lesson* 45). He had been
following his parents and writing about them like Auster's Quinn following Stillman, and therefore, he sees the future disappear with them. They
are no longer the ones forging ahead, and instead he is at the head of the
line, facing a future that has become a blank page on which he must write
(but that always was a blank page on which he retraced steps of no simple
origin). Following her funeral, he observes:

> The burial had taken no time at all. He was thinking that they *ought* to do
> these things twice: the first time you could just stand there not knowing
> what's happening, while the second time you could look around, see who
> was in tears, hear the words being said, understand at least a little of what
> was going on; sentiments uttered over a grave can sometimes alter a life, and
> he'd heard nothing. (237)

He'd heard nothing, and now what he needs to do to survive is repeat
this nothing. In other words, he needs to write. Except that, after his
mother's death, his writing has been replaced by a physical pain; he is
suffering from an "untreatable phantom disease" (28) that is surely
inseparable from the emotional pain of losing her. Writing and pain are
the one and the same mark of his survival, and so he does not write
because he does not want to live with the ache of her death, or live on
with her ghost: "A first-generation American father possessed by the
Jewish demons, a second-generation American son possessed by their
exorcism: that was his whole story" (40). To live with, which is to say
to write about, "his mother's ghost" (228), who was "[c]lose, [...] but
not too close" (229), seems unbearable. He realizes "that his mother
had been his only love" (239), and he would ideally commit himself

utterly to her so that, like Auster's writers possessed, he becomes one with his dead, becomes dead himself, feeling "a pain in his head the size of a lemon. It was her brain tumor" (45).

This feeling that he has one foot in the grave and might as well be "[g]one" (Roth, *Anatomy Lesson* 68) with all the others is intimately connected with the critic Milton Appel's negative reappraisal in "The Case of Nathan Zuckerman" of his life's work, echoing Irving Howe's "Philip Roth Reconsidered" (1972). Howe's judgment that "[t]he cruelest thing anyone can do with *Portnoy's Complaint* is to read it twice" (74) effectively declares that Roth's work, and by extension Zuckerman's, does not deserve to survive into the future but is better off forgotten. Zuckerman's writings belong to the past, and Zuckerman does too.

The alternative is to start anew. Rather than allow himself to be consumed by the past so that, as he declares in the graveyard, "*We* are the dead! These bones in boxes are the Jewish living! These are the people running the show!" (Roth, *Anatomy Lesson* 262), he will make a break for the future. He tries, therefore, to leap from death to life, from *thanatos* to *eros*: if Appel wants to bury his most seminal work, then Zuckerman will pose as the uncensored "pornographer Milton Appel" (183), defending anyone's right to be sexually unfaithful; if he is finished as a writer, then he will become a doctor instead and have "a second life" (195) as one who gives life. Everyone and everything else may be "[g]one. Mother, father, brother, birthplace, subject, health, hair [...], his talent too" (68), but what if the ghosts have gone too and still he remains? Convincing himself that the past is truly and irrevocably past, he comes to believe that his "exorcism's done. Why *not* this as a second life?" (109), this life as a doctor that is all about preserving life for the future, instead of a writer's half-life preserving loss.

Except, this "burning to begin *again*" (Roth, *Anatomy Lesson* 206), as Zuckerman puts it, is no different to a "burning to end" (206). This desire to throw himself into a future of pure life is, at root, no different from the fear of falling into a dead past. At the end of the novel, accompanying a friend's father to the cemetery to visit the grave of the man's wife before the coming snows "bury her anew every night" (237), it's as if Zuckerman "had ended too" (258) because "[h]is parents were gone and he was next" (254). Falling headfirst against a gravestone in the "white snow whirling" (262), Zuckerman wakes in hospital to find "he himself had become his mouth. [...] In that hole was his being" (266), as if he himself had been swallowed by the grave and obscured by the blanketing snow.

All that saves him from extinction is writing, making marks on the white page as if painfully identifying graves lost once again beneath the falling snow. "Write for me, Zuck. You know how to do that" (266), his doctor friend says to him in his hospital bed, and "Zuckerman wrote on a clean notebook page: WHEN HE IS SICK EVERY MAN NEEDS A MOTHER" (270), the same but different words with which the novel begins: "When he is sick, every man wants his mother" (3). This repetition between the beginning and the end of the novel goes hand in hand with the repetition of the scene of Zuckerman standing again by a mother's grave, doing this thing twice because, after all, "they *ought* to do these things twice" (237).[1] This repetition does not only characterize the life of the writer that Zuckerman would rather renounce—"My life as cud [...]. Swallow as experience, then up from the gut for a second go as art" (196)—but living on in general, which is a ghost writing, a "present" divided between "seeing the thing and writing about it" (Auster, *City of Glass* 63). Zuckerman will always have been writing on a blank page, following the other. This delayed return to the beginning, therefore, is a return to writing, is time resuming, and is Zuckerman resigning himself to a future with(out) his mother: he will never "unchain himself from a future as a man apart and escape the corpus that was his" (Roth, *Anatomy Lesson* 291), forever remaining the haunted ghost writer.

All of this relates also to a cemetery scene in Roth's *The Human Stain* where, following Coleman Silk's death, Zuckerman describes how, "standing in the falling darkness beside the uneven earth mound roughly heaped over Coleman's coffin, I was completely seized by his story, by its end and by its beginning, and, then and there, I began this book" (337). Zuckerman relates to Silk as Fanshawe does to his father, therefore, or the narrator does to Fanshawe, which means that he writes of Silk without any surety that he will finally comprehend him; he displays what Adam Kelly describes as "a willed belief in the vocation of the writer to testify through imagination to what cannot ever be known or proven" (74). He knows that the fact of a death doesn't then make it possible to say something final about a man, and so the paragraph that ends with Zuckerman beginning his book starts with Silk's sister Ernestine's statement that "[o]ne can do only so much to control one's life" (Roth, *Human Stain* 337), from which it can be taken also that "one can do only so much to control the other's life." Indeed, following the revelation of Silk's secret that he was a black man who had been passing as white for 45 years, Zuckerman admits, "I couldn't imagine anything that could have made Coleman more of a mystery to me than this unmasking. Now that I knew everything, it was as though I knew nothing, and instead of what I'd learned [...] unifying my idea of him, he became not just an unknown but an uncohesive person" (333). "Everyone knows" (38), and yet they don't know. Roth, however, in having Zuckerman "completely seized" by an incomplete story, shows that this failure to tell the whole story is a necessary betrayal. To identify completely with the dead other, to reduce your life to the life of another or possess their life completely, or to believe that you might faithfully relate, even continue, the life of the other in an uninterrupted way, as if it were your own, would be to sacrifice true living to a sense of life so immutably fixed that it would effectively be the death of the other. This absolute faithfulness would be an absolute betrayal: "Faithfulness is unfaithful" (Derrida and Roudinesco 160).[2]

As in Auster, therefore, Roth's ghosts' writing is a following that is also an inevitable and necessary not-following, a rewriting at a "creative remove" (Roth, *Human Stain* 19), a displaced repetition. Zuckerman thinks of Silk, "You'd written the book—the book was your life" (345), but this life's chaos of secrecy is reimagined first as the book *Spooks* by Silk, then by the anonymous and vitriolic online poster who "was writing *Spooks* now" (291), and then by Zuckerman as *The Human Stain*, so that Silk's story becomes (also) Zuckerman's story.[3] Therefore, the writer is unfaithful to the other with the writer's self and, of course, exists only because of this unfaithfulness. Zuckerman, in the five years prior to meeting Silk, has lived as if in the grave, in "rigorous reclusion" without "even a life of [his] own to care about, let alone somebody else's" (43), having been left incontinent and impotent after surgery for prostate cancer. Keeping to himself, he doesn't seek society but finds "sustenance [...] in the wisdom of the brilliant deceased" (44) until, as he puts it, "Coleman Silk danced me right back into life. [...] And made the proper presentation of his secret my problem to solve" (45). In this way, as in Auster's work, the writer steps between death and life by unfaithfully shadowing the other; as Zuckerman describes, "[H]e led, and, as best I could, I followed" (25). And, in this way, each of us, writing the book that is our life, steps between death and life by being unfaithful to our other selves with our self, presenting our secret time and again, writing "spooks," "spooks," "spooks."

To Work My Way Back into Life

This life-giving ghost writing is evident in Auster's *The Locked Room* too, where the narrator believes that becoming an acolyte of his presumed-dead friend represents the chance, as he says, "that I could one day be resurrected in my own eyes" (208). Writing Fanshawe's biography, it is no surprise that he is told that it "could be as much about you as about him" (246) because the narrator himself admits in the opening lines, "It seems to me now that Fanshawe was always there. He is the place where everything begins for me, and without him I would hardly know who I am" (199). The narrator is in pursuit of his shadow, therefore, following behind the one who is always already there, behind everything. And so, writing about Fanshawe, the narrator becomes the one to be written about as Fanshawe proves himself to be equally adept at "ghost writing" (204). Fanshawe writes in a letter that the narrator should "say nothing to Sophie. Make her divorce me, and then marry her as soon as you can" (237), and this is exactly what the narrator does, so that "Fanshawe's writings—his manuscripts and letters—become a meta-writing that scripts the course of the narrator's existence" (Bernstein 91). Indeed, the narrator faithfully betrays his friend by living his interrupted life, by living this half-life; he could grant Fanshawe that "you who are now no one now run my existence" (Roth, *Human Stain* 344).[4] Moreover, at the end of the story, through the door of the locked room, the narrator communicates with his "already dead" double (Auster, *Locked Room* 312), who speaks "so close," says the narrator, "that I felt as if the words were being poured into my head" (304). Trying to visualize Fanshawe, all he can see is "the door of a locked room. [...] Fanshawe alone in that room, condemned to a mythical solitude [...]. This room," he says, "I now discovered, was located inside my skull" (293); he places what are two parts of himself, the ghost writer and the ghost writer, either side of a locked door, but communing. Any effort to contact the uncontactable other, through the snow or the locked door, returns the writer only to himself but to a self haunted by the otherness of the other. This is what Auster's narrator concludes: "Every life is inexplicable [...]. No one can cross the boundary into another—for the simple reason that no one can gain access to himself" (247). Or, as Roth writes, "One's truth is known to no one, and frequently [...] to oneself least of all" (*Human Stain* 330).

In *The Ghost Writer*, the ghostly relationship between Zuckerman and Silk, or *The Locked Room*'s narrator and Fanshawe, has three near-analogs in Lonoff and Bellette, Zuckerman and Bellette as Anne Frank, and Bellette and Frank, with the outcome of the relationship again framed as a second life. This life after death hinges on the scene where Zuckerman, on the bed in Lonoff's downstairs study, reads Henry James's "The Middle Years" (1893), in which a writer realizes that at "the end of his life" (Roth, *Ghost Writer* 113), finally, his "genius has flowered" (113), but he would need "a second existence" (113) to see it fulfilled, and as James writes, "A second chance—*that's* the delusion. There never was to be but one," never was to be but "what passes" (qtd. in Roth, *Ghost Writer* 116).[5] Immediately following this, Roth moves from what passes to what passes on. In the room above, Lonoff and Bellette begin to talk, and Zuckerman, listening from beneath "the old floorboards" (Roth, *Ghost Writer* 118) like *Hamlet*'s ghost "*under the stage*" (Shakespeare 1.5.149), hears Bellette offer exactly the life that Lonoff had identified when he was asked by Zuckerman earlier in the evening, "How would you live now, if you had your way?" (Roth, *Ghost Writer* 68). Lonoff, it seems, is being granted what James's writer never had: a second chance, not at writing but at life, and a second existence, not as a writer who "happens not to exist in the everyday sense of the word" (41) but as someone to whom life happens, "living like everybody else" (160).

In turn, Zuckerman, suffering writer's block in "the cell" (Roth, *Ghost Writer* 76) of Lonoff's study as he tries to compose a letter to his father and then hardly enjoying a little masturbatory death, is reinvigorated after this scene and inspired to write the "true" story of Amy Bellette, who "can't *live*" (118) but is "the great survivor" (118), who is, Zuckerman imagines, none other than Anne Frank. In this "sideshadowing," to use Rachael McLennan's term, which "presents an alternative to the known historical outcome (Frank's death in Bergen-Belsen)" (700), Zuckerman imagines their love for each other, their marriage, their unborn children, and how his relationship with the thought-lost woman would see him resurrected in his father's eyes and would redeem the "inexplicable betrayal" of Zuckerman's story "Higher Education" (Roth, *Ghost Writer* 96): "*Anne? Oh, how I have misunderstood my son. How mistaken we have been!*" (159).[6] Even as Zuckerman writes a new life for Anne Frank, he revises and redeems his own, therefore, only belatedly realizing that this writing itself represents "a desecration even more vile than" his original story (171) and so a further betrayal.

Meanwhile, Anne remains inaccessibly within Amy, like Fanshawe in his locked room, ensuring that she will never have (a) full life. As Zuckerman tells it, her great "secret" (Roth, *Ghost Writer* 123) is that Frank, another confined writer, like Fanshawe "is really alive [...], she survived" (123). The tragedy is that, for her supposed death to mean anything, she still has "to be dead to everyone" (124), she has to be "believed to be dead" (145), a living "corpse" (119) sacrificed to her writing: "she has had to make herself ghostly" (O'Donnell 373). Recalling Glass's determination to "resurrect that [forgotten] person in words" (Auster, *Brooklyn Follies* 302), Frank's "responsibility was to the dead [...]: to restore in print their status as flesh and blood" (Roth, *Ghost Writer* 147). The negation of the self and the death that is in every writing are made explicit here as there is no survival for Frank except in her writing, which is "her survival itself. *Van Anne Frank*. Her book. Hers" (134), and yet the very same writing sentences her to continuing death. The only way for her to be faithful to Anne Frank is to betray Anne Frank, the only way for her to live is "to forget her life" (125), the only way for her to be herself is to be other than herself, to be Amy Bellette. Bellette is Frank's acolyte, therefore, living the other half of her interrupted life. In this way, Amy betrays "the *Anne*" (159), but of course, there never was *the* Anne, never is any one who is not haunted by the writing of the self. That is why Roth very deliberately quotes *the* Anne Frank's remark that "*I have an odd way of sometimes, as it were, being able to see myself through someone else's eyes. Then I view the affairs of a certain 'Anne' at my ease, and browse through the pages of her life as if she were a stranger*" (135).[7] Here is the historical Frank, author of *Het Achterhuis*, already shadowing herself, already rewriting *the* Anne as "Anne," already revising her life for publication, already drafting the diaries of one Anne Robin, already ghosts in series, writing Frank, "Anne," Robin, Bellette, writing "spooks," "spooks," "spooks."[8]

FINALLY, TO RETURN TO DEATH

Auster writes in *The Invention of Solitude* that "faces rhyme" (161). They do so famously in *City of Glass* when Quinn first catches sight of Stillman and "[w]hat happened then defied explanation. Directly behind Stillman, heaving into view just inches behind his right shoulder, another man stopped, took a lighter out of his pocket, and lit a cigarette. His face was the exact twin of Stillman's" (55–56). As the "first turned right, the second turned left," and Quinn has to choose to follow one or the other, knowing that the choice "would be arbitrary, a submission to chance. Uncertainty would haunt him to the end" (56). Auster writes that "Quinn craved an amoeba's body, wanting to cut himself in half and run off in two directions at once" (56), so that he might follow both men instead and trace not only THE TOWER OF BABEL through the streets of New York City but perhaps some other message also. In *The Ghost Writer*, Zuckerman uses Bellette's resemblance to Frank to project another life for her, and then he imagines further alternatives, takes her life in a different direction, so that Amy was never Anne but "had chosen to become Anne Frank" (Roth, *Ghost Writer* 155). Auster suggests that such an attentiveness to that other, alternative narrative is a responsibility of the writer and, "in the event that a thought should engender more than a single thought [...], it will be necessary not only to follow the first thought to its conclusion, but also to backtrack to the original position of that thought in order to follow the second thought to its conclusion" (*Invention of Solitude* 122). This should remind us that time does not consist of a secure present fitting neatly into a future present (simply the same but further down the line) and that it is as if the writer provides an alternative translation of the so-called present into a future that will always remain haunted by what could not also be (read). The survival of such haunting histories is evident when, for example, Zuckerman's ill mother "took the pen from his hand and instead of [her name] 'Selma' wrote the word 'Holocaust,' perfectly spelled. [...] Zuckerman was pretty sure that before that morning she'd never even spoken the word aloud" (Roth, *Anatomy Lesson* 41).

Debra Shostak has explored at length the ways in which "Roth's compulsion to contradict and counterimagine drives the logic within each narrative as well as the juxtaposition of one novel to the next or to some previous work" (4). *The Counterlife* is an excellent example as it works its way through various possible scenarios in chapters that fold back upon and into each other: "What if instead of the brother whose obverse existence mine inferred—and who himself untwinnishly inferred me—*I* had been the Zuckerman boy in that agony?" (46). When Roth is asked, "[H]ow did the structure of the book come about? 'I wrote one section and then I thought, "What if the opposite happened?"' he says" (Pierpont 145). Roth the author has the amoeba's body that Quinn craves. Discussing these opposites and twins, Cohen draws attention to the way in which Roth's "fictive doubles are means of dramatizing the fundamental predicament of selfhood [...]— the means through which the self divides and multiplies itself" ("Roth's Doubles" 82–83). In *The Counterlife*, therefore, Zuckerman insists that "I, for one, have no self" (Roth, *Counterlife* 324) and, moreover, "[t]here is no you, [...] any more than there's a me. [...] It's *all* impersonation—in the absence of a self, one impersonates selves, and after a while impersonates best the self that best gets one through" (324). If Quinn is haunted by uncertainty, Roth "will dwell in the house of Ambiguity" (*Operation Shylock* 307), in the haunted house of the self. Cohen concludes, "What we are reading is not an assortment of fictional counterlives to set against the truth of a real life, but a meditation on life as always and necessarily counterlife—always, that is, doubled, haunted by the specter of the 'someone else' leading it alongside the self" ("Roth's Doubles" 88).

The example from Roth's fiction that is most strikingly similar to the manifestation of the two Stillmans in Grand Central Station is the appearance of Roth's own twin in *Operation Shylock: A Confession* (1993). In this remarkable novel, Roth is not a Quinn faced by twin Stillmans but a Stillman himself who, looking over his right shoulder, suddenly finds another Stillman beside him, "the other Philip Roth" (17), a detective, of course, and a "shadow" (56), "a vaporous ghost" (70), "terminally ill" (79), who has assumed his identity.[9] The uncanny effect of *Operation Shylock* is exacerbated by a paratextual frame within which Roth either attests to its factuality or its fictionality, including a "Preface," "Note to the Reader," and an article in the *New York Times Book Review* called "A Bit of Jewish Mischief," in which Roth recounts the claimed true events that inspired the novel:

> In January 1989 I was caught up in a Middle East crisis all my own [...]. A man of my age, bearing an uncanny resemblance to me and calling himself Philip Roth, turned up in Jerusalem shortly before I did and set about proselytizing for "Diasporism," a political program he'd devised advocating that the Jews of Israel return to their European countries of origin in order to avert "a second Holocaust," this one at the hands of the Arabs. (1)[10]

As David Brauner shows, this approach has been interpreted by critics "in directly contradictory ways" (91) as either making fiction seem real or reality seem fictional, but in Roth's house of ambiguity, fiction and reality haunt each other like Roth's doubles, so that the real is never itself. Roth underlines this not only through the counter-reality of "A Bit of Jewish Mischief" but also through the uncertain relations between Philip Roth (the author of *Operation Shylock*), Philip Roth (the author in *Operation Shylock*), and Philip Roth (the other in *Operation Shylock*, called Moishe Pipik by the author). These relations reflect in many ways the equally uncertain though real-world relations between the men at the center of the Israeli trial that features in the novel: the Ukrainian-born Ivan Demjanjuk, the

Americanized John Demjanjuk, and Ivan the Terrible from the Treblinka camp in Nazi-occupied Poland. Pipik passes as Roth with an American passport in which, Roth admits, the "photograph was one taken of me some ten years ago. And the signature was my signature" (*Operation Shylock* 78); and "*his* picture, *his* signature" (97) on an identity card provide evidence that Ivan the Terrible is, it seems, passing as Demjanjuk.[11] These specific examples of the difficulty in establishing identity relate to the general impossibility of securing identity, so that "misunderstanding becomes the paradoxical essence of the human being" (Cohen, "Roth's Doubles" 89). I am (*je suis*) only as I follow (*je suis*) myself, and "[*w*]*ithin* the experience of following [...] there is something other, something new, or something different which occurs and which I sign. That's what I call a 'counter-sign', a counter-signature" (Derrida, "Following Theory" 10). I sign for and betray my impersonating, playing, deceiving, joking, repressed, secret, guilty, possible, desiring, haunting self.

The impossibility of immediately putting the right name to the right face, and the right face to the right story, reflects the way in which no one's story is one's story alone. Zuckerman is forever being told that his (fictional) story is someone else's (real) story, so to the series of spooks we can add Nathan Zuckerman, Gilbert Carnovsky, and Alvin Pepler, who tells Zuckerman that *Carnovsky* is "the story of my life no less than yours. [...] What I mean is that if I ever had the talent to write a novel, well, *Carnovsky* would have been it" (Roth, *Zuckerman Unbound* 148). In *The Anatomy Lesson*, Zuckerman hears from his accountant that *Carnovsky* "was his own life story" (118), and in *Operation Shylock*, the fictional Roth hears from Gal Metzler that the relationship he has with his father is "exactly like the one Nathan Zuckerman had with *his* father" in *The Ghost Writer* (168). And now Pipik's face cites the face of Roth like each story cites another and each self cites the other, so that we can no longer speak of the true origin of the story or of the true source of the self. This leads Cohen to argue that the "double's doubling is at the same time an annihilation of the self. As the novels attest, however, this is a profoundly generative annihilation; the loss of one's self is infinitely rich in creative possibilities" ("Roth's Doubles" 92). In part, this is true, and it is implied by Lonoff's comment to Zuckerman, "You're not so nice and polite in your fiction [...]. You're a different person" (Roth, *Ghost Writer* 180). But, terrifyingly, at the beginning of *Operation Shylock*, Roth feels like someone who is entirely not himself: "Where is Philip Roth? [...] Where did he go?" he asks (22). "Halcion, the pill [...] driving people crazy" (24) is to blame, but the experience is repeated later in the novel, which "narrates Roth's increasing possession by his double's words and desires" (Cohen, "Roth's Doubles" 91), so that "the more he strives to differentiate himself from his false counterpart, the more undifferentiated they become" (92): "I am Philip Roth and you are Philip Roth, I am like you and you are like me, in name and not only in name" (Roth, *Operation Shylock* 320). This loss of the self's oneness speaks to the terrible realities of ghost writing: we inhabit but do not possess our selves, and we are haunted by an other who will one day lay claim to our lives. But it is not the same as the loss of one's self. The one self must be risked, to death and the other, in order that it might survive, but the absolute loss of one's self, or one's story, to the other would not be a creative possibility but a final death. For creation, for life, for an afterlife, something of the self must remain, even if it is something recreated, regenerated, rewritten, mistranslated, illegible, effaced, or erased by the self and story of the other; we see this in the way that Lonoff, "the man making up the stories all his life, winds up, after death, remembered, if at all, for a story made up about him" (*Exit Ghost* 275).[12] Roth's ghost writing, therefore, unsettles definitions of other and self, which to a degree, in *Operation Shylock* and *The Counterlife*, he maps onto Diasporism and a militant Zionism. The former relates to "the diffusion of his presence" in the other (Cohen, "Roth's Doubles" 92) and the latter relates to a unity of the self, to "the promise of integrating the scattered parts of his selfhood" (88), to "the escapist fantasy of the undivided self" (90). As seen in "Shadows," such a self, the self that does not follow another, is not of this world.

The ghost writer, Zuckerman, is close to death. In *Exit Ghost*, it is as if he is dead because he has "ceased to inhabit not just the great world but the present moment" (Roth, *Exit Ghost* 1). Then, returning to New York as "a revenant" (31), he finds he is "the virile man called back to life" (104) by the "resuscitating breath" (103) of his desire for a young woman and his faithfulness to Amy Bellette and E.I. Lonoff and his legacy. But his memory is failing him, so much so that he's become increasingly reliant on his notes to self. It is not for nothing that he quotes Keats: "I have an habitual feeling of my real life having past [...] and that I am leading a posthumous existence" (qtd. in Roth, *Exit Ghost* 221). Even as, in *Operation Shylock*, Roth's "mind began to disintegrate" (20), at the end of *Exit Ghost*, Zuckerman "*disintegrates*" (292). His last act is to write a conclusion. Like Quinn in Auster's *City of Glass*, he becomes only the words on the page, the HE that he represents in the text. "If I lost touch with my pages, if I could neither write a book nor read one, what would become of me? Without my work, what would be left of me?" (106), he thinks, as if he doesn't already know the answer. There is nothing outside the work. The last we'll see of him are these words. Exit ghost writer.

NOTES

1. The novel is replete with repetitions: beds reoccur, as in Zuckerman's parents' honeymoon bed in the Hotel Riviera, his mother's deathbed, and Zuckerman's bedding, including the orthopedic pillow provided by a Dr. Kotler who once had his office in The Riviera; Milton Appel is impersonated; and Zuckerman returns at 40 years of age to the University of Chicago, where he had studied as a young man.

2. In contrast to Zuckerman, in *Exit Ghost* Richard Kliman wants, actually, to conjure up Lonoff by uncovering his secrets in his proposed biography. He wants to see the ghost exited and exorcised and Lonoff returned to life: "He wants to resurrect a writer" (Roth, *Exit Ghost* 108), and he will excuse this betrayal by saying he is "just trying to be responsible" (50).

3. As Kelly makes clear, "Like an event or a decision, a written text will go on to offer itself endlessly to future contexts, as testimony to the mysterious processes of agency and temporality, processes which transcend the control of any origin, any source" (75).

4. Dimovitz cleverly maps the three stories of *The New York Trilogy* onto each other: "*City of Glass* narrator reconstructs Quinn who watched Stillman at the request of Stillman"; "*Ghosts* narrator reconstructs Blue who watched Black [who is actually White] at the request of White"; "*Locked Room* narrator reconstructs Fanshawe who watched X at the request of Y" (623). An attempt to complete the last line, thinking in terms of following rather than watching, provides us with an insight into the nature of the acolyte: *Locked Room* narrator reconstructs Fanshawe *and* his ("resurrected" [Auster, *Locked Room* 208]) self who followed Fanshawe ("it could lead me to Fanshawe" [268]) *and* was followed by Fanshawe ("I watched you" [309]) at the request of Fanshawe ("he tells his wife what to do" [239]) *and* in defiance of Fanshawe ("I beg you not to look for me" [237]). Dimovitz concludes that *The Locked Room* "effects a critique" of Derrida (629). And yet, the final page of the story describes a "book that had been written for" the narrator but in which "everything remained open, unfinished, to be started again. I lost my way after the first word," says the narrator, "and from then on I could only grope ahead, faltering in the darkness, blinded by the book" (Auster, *Locked Room* 314); we can read this in terms of the acolyte and the faltering *anacoluthon*, following's counter-signature, and that replacing of the book written for me (like Fanshawe's red notebook)

by a book written by me (like *The Locked Room*) through a rewriting which takes place on a white page as blank and blinding as the snow.

5. Fittingly, in this context, *The Middle Years* (1917) is also the title of an incomplete, posthumously published autobiography by James.

6. McLennan here is discussing the importance of Frank not in Roth's but in Auster's work, particularly *The Invention of Solitude*. Her conclusion, that "first and foremost, Anne Frank is a figure for Auster's father—but his father as a suffering child" (704), supports the previous chapter's observation that Auster's female characters are always subsumed within the father-and-son relationship.

7. McLennan notes that "Frank imagines a future in America, as an actress (putting on different faces? imagining herself as other?)" (706), and Wilson reminds us that in "the *Zuckerman Bound* series, this 'ghost' of Anne Frank makes two more appearances, both times embodied by women who are actresses" (106), namely Caesara O'Shea in *Zuckerman Unbound* and Eva Kalinova in *The Prague Orgy*,

8. O'Donnell comments, "The effect is to put into question the very act of writing: self-denial and self-estrangement 'generate' it; its product, the text, only appears as the sign of the loss of self" (374).

9. And, to return to Auster, in *Leviathan*, Aaron "discovered that someone had been impersonating me—answering letters in my name, walking into bookstores and autographing my books, hovering like some malignant shadow" (4). Sachs is the one impersonating Aaron. And when Aaron then observes, "I have given my book the same title that Sachs was planning to use for his: *Leviathan*" (142), this means that Sachs is effectively signing in advance the book that will be written in his name. Aaron and Sachs, the self and other self, sign and countersign in a relation of mutual betrayal; "Auster's narrative technique involves Aaron telling another author's story, trying to do him justice, but ultimately betraying him, metaphorically because he cannot write about someone else without writing about himself, and literally because he unwittingly helps the FBI to identify Sachs's body" (Varvogli 146). In his excellent reading of both Roth and Auster in terms of secrecy, testimony, and truth, Kelly details "the complexity of relations between testimony, story-telling, and knowledge of self and other" in *Leviathan*, and he argues that "the impossibility of knowing the *other*, which is the central insight of *The Human Stain*, is merely the starting point in *Leviathan*, which is further concerned with the vexing impossibility of *self*-knowledge outside of or prior to narrative conventions" (64).

10. Similarly, Auster claims that the novel *City of Glass*, in which it was "a wrong number that started it" (3), was "inspired by a wrong number" (*Red Notebook* 377). Auster, of course, is well known for including auto-

biographical elements within his work. Springer details autobiographical material in the novels up to *Timbuktu*, and Brown notes that the behavior of Trause's son Jacob in *Oracle Night* is based "in part on problems Auster's own son Daniel had with drugs and the law" (96). The same material features in Auster's wife Siri Hustvedt's novel *What I Loved* (2003).

11. The 1988 sessions of the Jerusalem District Court that Roth describes in the novel found Demjanjuk guilty of crimes against humanity and sentenced him to death, but as Roth's "Preface" details, an appeal in the Israeli Supreme Court heard "the surname of Treblinka's Ivan the Terrible to have been Marchenko and not Demjanjuk" (*Operation Shylock* 14), and in 1993 (and after the publication of the novel), the verdict was overturned. On his death in 2012, however, Demjanjuk was again appealing a conviction, this time as an accessory to murder as a guard at the Sobibor death camp in Poland.

12. Budick comments, "Roth understands ghostwriting as our condition in language. How we place ourselves in relation to that condition—whether we will facilitate or oppose other ghostwriters or ghost writers ghostwriting through us—is our choice" (134–135).

Of "Spirit"

"I shall speak of ghost [*revenant*], of flame, and of ashes" (1), begins Derrida in *Of Spirit*. In *Housekeeping*, Marilynne Robinson, too, writes of "ghost" (96), of "flame" (212), and of "ashes" (202) in a novel that, above all, is of spirit. But it's not easy to translate between Derrida's and Robinson's spirits, and as Derrida immediately signals, when it comes to spirit, translation matters.[1] He is writing about Martin Heidegger's warnings to avoid the terms "spirit" or "spiritual" as "non-things [which] in general one claims to oppose to the thing" (*Of Spirit* 16), but Derrida specifies that the question is of "not spirit or the spiritual but *Geist, geistig, geistlich*" (1), the German spirit. The warning against *Geist* appears in 1927, the warning against *geistig* in 1953 (and, as Derrida notes, "this was not just any quarter-century" [1]), but between these two warnings, Heidegger continues to mention and make use of this vocabulary. First, he uses it without using it by having "*Geist*" in place of *Geist*, and then, in 1933, he drops the quotation marks, and *Geist* proper "makes its appearance. It presents itself. Spirit *itself*" (31). Heidegger seems now to believe that *Geist* can translate into a "'non-metaphysical' *spirit*" (Lucy 109), into a spiritual history, a spiritual world of a people, a spiritual unity that would be "a true *unity*, for what is *proper* to spirit is, precisely, to unify" (Derrida, *Of Spirit* 65). This is the spirit Derrida would avoid because, as Niall Lucy makes clear, "[d]econstruction is opposed to anything that claims to gather up, to unite, to bring

© The Editor(s) (if applicable) and The Author(s) 2016
D. Coughlan, *Ghost Writing in Contemporary American Fiction*,
DOI 10.1057/978-1-137-41024-5_8

together as one—whether in the form of an 'accord' within Being or as the 'spirit' of a nation. For whatever gathers up also closes off. [...] Such a [present] gathering cannot admit the ghosts of the past (*specters*) and the others yet to come (*arrivants*)" (78). Deconstruction, instead, admits the ghosts, even the ghosts of spirit. Derrida writes, "*Geist* is always haunted by its *Geist* [...]. Metaphysics always returns, I mean in the sense of a *revenant* [ghost] [...]. Of the double which can never be separated from the single. Is this [...] the unavoidable itself—spirit's double, *Geist* as the *Geist* of *Geist*, spirit as spirit of the spirit which always comes with its double? Spirit is its double" (*Of Spirit* 40–41). Nothing is simple.

Therefore, when Derrida begins *Of Spirit* with the words "I shall speak of ghost [*revenant*]" rather than "I shall speak of spirit [*Geist*]," he is speaking of the return of metaphysics, of the spirit of metaphysics or the metaphysical spirit, as a ghost. This is the spirit that "always returns," is always a returned spirit, meaning spirit is always "spirit" in quotation marks. "Spirit returns" (Derrida, *Of Spirit* 23) and so is always spied through "a sort of drape, a veil or curtain" (31) suspended between its marks, like the white sheet of a ghost. Derrida will reiterate this in *Specters of Marx* when he comments on "the essential contamination of spirit (*Geist*) by specter (*Gespenst*)" (113).

This is how the spirit first appears in Robinson's *Housekeeping*, also. A bereaved woman is hanging "a sodden sheet" on the clothesline when it begins "to billow and leap in her hands, to flutter and tremble, and to glare with the light, [...] as if a spirit were dancing in its cerements" (16). But Robinson does not believe in Derrida's ghosts but in "soul, consciousness, spirit, person. Spirit is not the thing, spirit is not the body" (Derrida, *Of Spirit* 15) but is for her opposed to ordinary matter seen in an ordinary light: "Everything that falls upon the eye is apparition, a sheet," she says (*Housekeeping* 116), and "[e]very spirit passing through the world fingers the tangible and mars the mutable, and finally has come to look and not to buy [...] and the spirit passes on, just as the wind" (73). Spirit as wind joins Robinson to the tradition of *pneuma* and *spiritus* and "the Platonic-Christian, metaphysical or onto-theological determination of the spiritual" (Derrida, *Of Spirit* 12), and as part of that tradition, *Housekeeping* seeks finally to transcend the material house, to see it consumed by the fire of the spirit. "Spirit is flame," agrees Derrida (84), but "[f]lame writes, writes itself, right in the flame" (104), meaning spirit writes itself also, as "spirit." The challenge for Robinson, therefore, is to get a sodden sheet to burn, to unhouse the "spirit" of its marks, to write without writing of spirit.[2]

NOTES

1. Mattessich has provided one such translation, successfully I think. It is important at this point just to note his observation "that even Robinson might not be in control of her subject, which is precisely the impossibility of such control, and even when its name is spirit" (65).
2. If, like Derrida, and as Mattessich argues, Robinson "*thinks the metaphysics that persist in every denial of metaphysics*" (61), my sense is that her heart still lies with the metaphysical. Mattessich rightly identifies that the novel's "spirituality, linked to the idea of a 'whole' or transcendent plan that governs all things, carries over into something more sceptical, more radically unsettling" (64), but I suggest that this is despite Robinson's best efforts.

5. Passing Through: Marilynne Robinson

Housekeeping, Marilynne Robinson's first novel, takes in three generations of a family living in the town of Fingerbone, Idaho. The story tells of Sylvia Foster and her husband, Edmund; their three daughters, Molly, Helen, and Sylvia (known as Sylvie); and Helen's two daughters, Lucille and her older sister Ruth (or Ruthie), the novel's narrator. It's very much a story of the women in the family: when Molly is just sixteen, Helen fifteen, and Sylvie thirteen, Edmund dies when, for some unknown and unknowable reason, the train on which he is travelling crashes off the bridge over Lake Fingerbone in the dead of night and disappears into the waters; later, both Helen's husband, Reginald Stone, and Sylvie's husband, Fisher, abandon their wives and similarly vanish. This is a story, then, of women raised by women, or, as happens, a series of women. Ruth and Lucille are not yet seven years old when their mother returns with them from Seattle to Fingerbone, leaves them on the porch of her mother's house, and then commits suicide by driving her borrowed Ford into the lake, joining her father in "the blackest depth of the lake" (Robinson, *Housekeeping* 22). For five years until her death, the girls' grandmother cares for them in a strange reprise of that past time when she reared her own daughters but, forgetfully, "had never taught them to be kind to her" (19). When she passes, her sisters-in-law, Nona and Lily, come from Spokane to look after the girls, but the raising of children does not suit these two who, now in their mid-sixties, "enjoyed nothing except habit and familiarity" (32). So,

© The Editor(s) (if applicable) and The Author(s) 2016
D. Coughlan, *Ghost Writing in Contemporary American Fiction*,
DOI 10.1057/978-1-137-41024-5_9

they reach out to the daughter Sylvie, "'An itinerant.' 'A migrant worker.' 'A drifter'" (31), who comes home to find her mother lost to her, and Ruth and Lucille in place of her absent sisters. The novel then charts the growing closeness between Sylvie and Ruth, who comes to see life in a way that Lucille will not.[1]

SPIRIT WRITING

After *Housekeeping*, almost 25 years passed before Robinson published another novel, and in that time, her first, understandably and productively, invited a large number of feminist readings. These see its woman-centered narrative testing or even exceeding the limits of a patriarchal world; those limits set the lines along which patriarchy defines its proper self by opposing man to woman, outside to inside, the public political to the private domestic, town to house, sociocultural to natural, and so on.[2] It is argued that *Housekeeping* reflects a world more accommodating of women as the transient Sylvie looks to "what lies beyond opposition" (Friedman 242) and unsettles what seems established by crossing over or breaking down all of the identified borders, even those between human and natural and between life and death. For example, Robinson writes that not only Sylvie but all "the transients wandered through Fingerbone like ghosts, terrifying as ghosts are because they were not very different from us" (*Housekeeping* 178). Yet, though this has led to the observations that the hobos and wanderers are "linked to death" (Hall 45) and that the novel "presents Ruth and Sylvie's decision to become drifters as a kind of death" (Foster 86), it is nevertheless the transiency of those who "haunted the town" (Robinson, *Housekeeping* 179), and not their ghostliness, that attracts attention. In place of the ghost, critics focus on "the novel's central metaphor of transience" (Burke 717). But, I would suggest, this view doesn't get to the nub of the question of transients and ghosts because it doesn't recognize that Sylvie is a transient exactly because she is a ghost. Transients are like ghosts because the ghost is transient, it is "spirit passing through the world" (Robinson, *Housekeeping* 73), it is spectral.[3] The transients, like the ghosts, are terrifying because they remind us souls of our mortality, they tell us that we are the ghosts and that "every soul is put out of house" (179) in the end, that every spirit sheds its ghostly garment of flesh and moves on. It is no doubt an unspoken awareness of this that leads Ruth to confess, in the middle chapter of the novel, to a "feeling of ghostliness" (106), admitting that she "often seemed invisible—incompletely and minimally existent, in fact" (105), and wondering if Sylvie also "felt ghostly" (106). But ghostliness in the novel, therefore, is not something to which Sylvie and Ruth are "doomed" (Geyh 119), is not a lesser mode of existence indicating some lack or deficiency, but is a reflection of their sensitivity to, and part in, the spiritual in the world.

The novel, therefore, is above all concerned with "that ultimate border crossing from life to death" (Burke 724) and with the belief that death is not death, after all. This sense of a final crossing is most apparent at the conclusion of the novel where Sylvie and Ruth leave Fingerbone by walking across the bridge over the lake, a route so dangerous that they are assumed to have died in its waters. This is a "crossing of a threshold into another state of being" (Rubenstein 225). As Ruth's "disembodied voice" (Schaub 314) says, "we are dead" (Robinson, *Housekeeping* 217), and Sylvie carries a newspaper clipping which tells as much. There is something wonderfully spooky about Robinson's description of Ruth's afterlife, working as a waitress, for example, who puts "a chill on the coffee by serving it" (214) and is encouraged by the customers to eat "to put meat on [her] bones" (214). In fact, such descriptions have led some critics to wonder if Ruth and Sylvie are actually, rather than figuratively, dead. If they are, and if "the narrative can be understood as a communication from the dead" (Burke 723), then, as William Burke observes, "The story that Ruth narrates may be coming from and may constitute a verification of the mysterious realm of ghosts, spirits, and the place of the perished of the earth" (724). If Ruth is narrating her story many years after her actual, as opposed to apparent, death, then she is no ghost writer but a spirit writer, her words issuing not so much from the cold waters of the lake but from a here and now that is not of this world.

The indeterminate ending has proven unsettling for scholars because, as Burke again notes, "The implication that the dead are but a perceptual leap away is alien enough to conventional literary discussion as to skew our critical judgments" (719n2).[4] For example, even as Joan Kirkby perceives the spirit, she takes a critical step back. Describing Ruth's writing after her death as "a voice speaking from another dimension" (106), she says, "There is a breaking down of the barriers between the human and the natural, the dead and the non-dead, the mortal and the fairy, and a recognition that the two states are not in opposition but may be co-extensive" (103). But when she concludes, "Whether dead or alive, they [...] are ghosts and forever lost to the social world" (106), it becomes apparent that, for her, the key point is that Sylvie and Ruth have "become one with nature's forces" (106); she continues, therefore, to oppose the human to the natural so that she can locate Sylvie and Ruth on one side or the other of an indivisible boundary, moving them from inside to "outside the house and into the watery world of nature" (107).[5] For Robinson, this chapter argues, the spirit is harder to accommodate and sees exactly the inside coextensive with the outside, with darkness and water throughout. The significant limits in the novel are not set by culture, or society, or gender, and they do not coincide with the walls of the house but are determined by the limits of one's reflection or one's "attention," as Ruth observes (Robinson, *Housekeeping* 154). The limit is a blindness to the spiritual world, meaning "*Housekeeping* spills over convenient and culturally-conditioned critical enclosures to challenge both our perceptions and our conventional and taming critical terminology" (Burke 717). Burke and Thomas Schaub were unusual, therefore, in reading *Housekeeping* in a spiritual context from early on, but since the publication of her second novel *Gilead* and the subsequent appearance of *Home* and *Lila*, Robinson's work is now more likely to be read in the context of her religious faith and her religious experience than her understanding of "femaleness" (Schaub and Robinson 233).[6] This chapter, too, attempts a reading that would be true to the spirit of the novel by taking it on its own terms, which is to say, in terms of spirit. And yet, critically, it is also argued that it is finally "spirit," and not spirit, that is essential to *Housekeeping*.

SPIRITUAL ELEMENTS

Describing herself as an American liberal Protestant in the Calvinist tradition, Robinson believes in a universe created according to God's plan, so that "we live in a vast, ordered cosmos that inspires awe and gratitude" (Shy 256); she believes that God has a plan and vision also for humanity, that "we are the wonder of the universe, incomparably complex, brilliant, poignant—and perverse" (Painter and Robinson 490), and that the nature of this plan does not exclude what she calls a "softened predestinarianism. God alone judges" (Robinson, "Onward, Christian Liberals" 216); she believes, therefore, in what she sees as Calvin's "sense of majesty of the human person (tempered always by a sense of our fallenness)" (Painter and Robinson 491), which means believing both in humankind's inherent holiness and its total depravity, meaning here being "warped or distorted" (Robinson, "Onward, Christian Liberals" 219); and she believes that the fallen state of humankind demands "a robust sense of human fallibility, in particular forbidding the idea that human beings can set any limits to God's grace" (215). She applies this sense of fallibility to her own work also, so that *Housekeeping* for her is about "trying to be beyond [her] own grasp or outside [her] own expectations" (Schaub and Robinson 241) and is concerned with "the limits of [her] ability to comprehend or articulate" (Hedrick and Robinson 6). The novel, like the theology she admires, is an "imagination of the nature of reality itself" (Painter and Robinson 487) that, as a work of Christian metaphysics, sees the spiritual and material worlds haunting each other and sees every individual as a ghost just passing through, briefly housed in this world. For Robinson, therefore, an experience of God is possible in this world but only for those who regard reality as something more than meets the eye and who are sensitive to that which has pried through the seams of "the most modest and ordinary aspects of life" and has "elevated them and revealed mysteries in them" (Painter and Robinson 485). "To put the matter another way," says Robinson, "we baffled creatures are immersed in an overwhelming truth. What is plainly before our eyes we know only in glimpses and through disciplined attention" ("Onward, Christians Liberals" 211). *Housekeeping*, therefore, is about the existence and perception of something out of the ordinary.

This "openness to the perception of the holy in existence itself and, above all, in one another" (Robinson, "Onward, Christians Liberals" 211) is what Robinson defines as personal holiness. And it is this high regard she holds for a humankind possessed of such holiness that leads Todd Shy to argue that Robinson's faith "is, if it is Calvinist at all, a Calvinism stretched and molded to humanist purposes" (253).[7] As a humanist Calvinist, it is no wonder that Robinson has consistently "identified the transcendentalist writers of the nineteenth century as her guiding influences" (Schaub and Robinson 231), given Transcendentalism's indebtedness to Unitarianism, which distinguished itself from orthodox Calvinism by its liberal view of human nature.[8] For Robinson, "experience is meaningful, which is what Emerson was so eager to insist on" (Hedrick and Robinson 4), and she is following Dickinson, Melville, and Thoreau in seeing where this idea can lead.[9] "I am an Emersonian," she declares ("Let's Not Talk Down" 11).[10]

Transcendentalism's, and particularly Thoreau's, influence is very apparent in *Housekeeping* as Robinson uses analogy, the lake, and the house to structure Ruth's spiritual growth.[11] In relation to the first of these, Robinson directly references Thoreau when she argues that "reality must somehow be describable as linked through analogue," so that one small insight might expand to a larger truth, like "a genetic strand that opens a whole genealogy" (Schaub and Robinson 239) or like the seed that puts forth the mighty tree: thinks Ruth, "I, the nub, the sleeping germ, should swell and expand [...], my skull would bulge preposterously and my back would hunch against the sky" (Robinson, *Housekeeping* 162).[12] In *Housekeeping*, the idea of the vortex provides Robinson with a central analogy of scale. On the smallest scale, out on the lake, "Sylvie's oars set off vortices. She swamped some leaves and spun a feather on its curl" (149) while, on a far larger scale, in the heavens, the stars are "pulled through the dark along the whorls of an enormous vortex" (211). The clever nature of this analogy is such that it does not only establish levels of scale but enables transmission between them, with God himself pulled from the heavens, "pulled after us into the vortex we made when we fell, or so the story goes" (194), while out on the surface of the lake, Sylvie and Ruth, "if there were a vortex, [...] would be drawn down into the darker world" (149–150). The strata of the novel's world build up like layers of paint on old furniture, the windows of the submerged train lying parallel to the bottom of the lake below, parallel to the surface of the lake above, and parallel again to the heavens above, and the layers bleed into each other, so if the women were drawn down into the dark, then, thinks Ruth, her grandfather "might see us and think he was dreaming again of flushed but weightless spirits in a painted sky, buoyant in an impalpable element" (150). These analogies hold out the promise that, one day, every little thing, every individual, would rise to its place in a higher order, brought from "just under the surface" into "the rarer light" (91). This final resurrection, thinks Ruth, "would put an end to all anomaly" (91) and ensure that "time and error and accident were undone, and the world became comprehensible and whole" (92). After all, "[a]scension seemed at such times a natural law. [...] What are all these fragments for, if not to be knit up finally?" (92).

The lake is the second element in Robinson's vision of the spiritual. The novel, very much like the town of Fingerbone, is set on the lake and seeped in the lake. The lake seems to be there on every page, even as it suffuses the land and air around it, so that "one is always aware of the lake in Fingerbone, or the deeps of the lake, the lightless, airless waters below. When the ground is plowed in the spring, cut and laid open, what exhales from the furrows but that same, sharp, watery smell. The wind is watery" (Robinson, *Housekeeping* 9), so much so that the drafts in the house would come "sweeping down the polished steps in torrents, flooding the parlor, eddying into the kitchen" (48). More than anything else in the novel, the lake is used to provide the sense of a layered and permeable reality: "At the foundation is the old lake [...]. Then there is Fingerbone, the lake of charts and photographs [...]. And above that, the lake that rises in the spring [...]. And above that the water suspended in sunlight" (9). Robinson's descriptions, as Mattessich observes, "so commingle the elements of earth, water, and air that they seem more like gradations of a single element [...] permeating the world" (65). For Robinson, this element is spirit. Water is in the land and the air just as spirit is, and Robinson is using the lake as that which mediates between the mundane and the spiritual.[13] Ruth makes clear this connection between water and spirit and the idea that ordinary reality floats in a more profound world:

> I dreamed that I was walking across the ice on the lake, which was breaking up as it does in the spring, softening and shifting and pulling itself apart. But in the dream the surface that I walked on proved to be knit up of hands and arms and upturned faces that shifted and quickened as I stepped, sinking only for a moment into lower relief under my weight. The dream and the obituary together created in my mind the conviction that my grandmother had entered into some other element upon which our lives floated as weightless, intangible, immiscible, and inseparable as reflections in water. (Robinson, *Housekeeping* 41)

Her dead grandmother, therefore, is seen as if existing in the same element that holds both her grandfather and her mother, body and soul, but it is clear that the lake gestures to a more general haunting: "[T]he waters were full of people" (172). Moreover, these are people who might one day return in that final, general resurrection. The lake's "puzzling margins" (4) suggest that movement through these layers is as easy as ice melting into water and water floating into steam, so that water speaks to that seemingly inevitable ascension.

The idea that our lives float "as reflections in water" in a more profound element shows that the lake lends itself to a further analogy between the ice on its surface, reflections on water, and mirrors and windows, all of which relate to the general appearance of things, in the world, in our thoughts and memories, and in our dreams. Robinson's use of this analogy recalls Paul's First Epistle to the Corinthians, in which he comments, "We see in a mirror dimly" (qtd. in Robinson, "Onward, Christian Liberals" 219), meaning we have only a superficial grasp of a deeper knowledge and that a greater truth eludes us. For Robinson, our images of the world effectively blind us to what is truly there: "Everything that falls upon the eye is apparition, a sheet dropped over the world's true workings" (*Housekeeping* 116). Images have no substance and cannot bear the weight of things, cannot record their impact. A train crashes into the water and disappears because "[f]ragments of transparent ice wobbled on the waves [...] and, when the water was calm again, knitted themselves up like bits of a reflection" (7); a father crashes into the water and disappears because the "disaster had fallen out of sight, like the train itself, and [...] the dear ordinary had healed as seamlessly as an image on water" (15). The world offered up to the eyes, therefore, is only a pale reflection of a spiritual reality, as seen when the lake floods shortly after Sylvie's arrival and the town of Fingerbone is submerged:

> Fingerbone was strangely transformed. If one should be shown odd fragments arranged on a silver tray and be told, "That is a splinter from the True Cross, and that is a nail paring dropped by Barabbas, and that is a bit of lint from under the bed where Pilate's wife dreamed her dream," the very ordinariness of the things would recommend them. [...] So Fingerbone, or such relics of it as showed above the mirroring waters, seemed fragments of the quotidian held up as proof of their significance. But then suddenly the lake and the river broke open and the water slid away from the land, and Fingerbone was left stripped and blackened and warped and awash in mud. (73–74)

In this analogy, the parts of Fingerbone visible above the mirroring waters seem as miraculous as the holy relics on the silver tray, but in truth, all these relics mean nothing compared to what lies beneath the surface, and "the ordinary is no more than a relic, cut off from what matters" (Gardner 18); in the absence of spirit, the world is as dull and mean as Fingerbone when the water is gone. The tragedy, therefore, would be to exist in a world without spirit, to have only the remains of the cross without access to the salvation it represents. The tragedy, Robinson feels, would be for you to know nothing of the dark depths, to know only the mirror that reflects you and your world back to you, like the woman travelling in the brightly lit carriage of the train who cannot see Ruth and her sister running alongside in the dark outside: "[t]he woman looked at the window very often, clearly absorbed by what she saw, which was not but merely seemed to be Lucille and me" (Robinson, *Housekeeping* 54). Such people know only "their own depthless images on the black glass" (54). Or, from the other side, for the spirits of the dead the saddest thing would be to be lost in the waters and see the surface of the world heal behind you like the ice and know that you cannot be seen and cannot break through:

The images are the worst of it. It would be terrible to stand outside in the dark and watch a woman in a lighted room studying her face in a window, and to throw a stone at her, shattering the glass, and then to watch the window knit itself up again and the bright bits of lip and throat and hair piece themselves seamlessly again into that unknown, indifferent woman. It would be terrible to see a shattered mirror heal to show a dreaming woman tucking up her hair. And here we find our great affinity with water, for like reflections on water our thoughts will suffer no changing shock, no permanent displacement. (162–163)

The brightly lit room set against darkness, "light associated with appearance and darkness with reality" (Burke 720), relates to Robinson's use of the house. Sylvie's receptiveness to the spiritual reality is seen in the way she opens the house to the water and to the darkness, letting the watery air in through the doors and windows and showing the same disregard for margins as the lake does. As Ruth puts it, "Sylvie in a house was more or less like a mermaid in a ship's cabin. She preferred it sunk in the very element it was meant to exclude" (Robinson, *Housekeeping* 99). The flood, occurring only a week after the appearance of her "conjured [...] presence" (61) and ensuring that "water poured over the thresholds" (61) until the "house flowed around" (64) its occupants, seems to provide her natural element.[14] In the kitchen, she prefers "the light off" (49) so that the room sits submerged in the outside darkness, its "window luminous and cool as aquarium glass and warped as water" (86). Ruth comes to appreciate the dark, thinking "it seemed to me that there need not be relic, remnant, margin, residue, memento, bequest, memory, thought, track, or trace, if only the darkness could be perfect and permanent" (116). It is in the darkness under the bridge, out on the lake in a boat with Sylvie, that Ruth imagines, for a moment, that "the faceless shape" in front of her (166) is not Sylvie but Helen, her mother, ascended bodily from the waters. "I expected—an arrival" (166), she says, and it is as if her mother's spirit appears then, and not just her phantasm, another image or relic.

An Unhoused Ghost

Housekeeping is, as Burke identifies, "an unconventional primer on the mystical life" (717), for both Ruth and the reader. Having established that the spirit is only temporarily housed in this world, the novel conveys Ruth's spiritual journey through the analogy of the unhousing. Burke characterizes this as an "expansion of consciousness through a process of border crossings—social, geographic, and perceptual" (717),[15] but Robinson's analogies of scale complicate any sense of defined border crossings through their nested repetitions which house a house within a house within a house. But Burke sees this also, pointing out, "In a less conventional sense the title also suggests that the material universe is a house or body. [...] The lake is house, nature is house. This house, moreover, is inhabited by spirit" (719). As Mattessich observes, "'[O]utside' is where [the novel's] protagonists always are" (60) as they ascend into what Robinson imagines is "a world that is whole and complete" (Burke 717), God the Father's promised house of many rooms.

As Sylvie educates her niece "in the hard disciplines of instability, loneliness, uncertainty, and change—the necessary conditions for seeing the hidden but real workings of the world" (Burke 721), her growing influence on Ruth, and in turn, Ruth's growing distance from Lucille, develops through three scenes structured around an experience of a house and the lake wherein Ruth comes to understand that "the house and other physical structures are merely temporary containers for the eternal but insubstantial soul" (Rubenstein 219). On the first occasion, Lucille and Ruth, having walked for miles along the shore of the lake, leave it too late to return home and decide instead to spend the night outdoors in a makeshift shelter they build of driftwood and branches. The scene is marked by the erasure of differences, by a state of "equilibrium" (Robinson, *Housekeeping* 114) when the "sky and the water were one luminous gray" (114), and later, by "absolute darkness" (115) inside and outside. Ruth and Lucille both outgrow their small abode and break through its roof, as if now existing on a larger scale. But one difference remains between Lucille, who cannot accept that "all [...] human boundaries were overrun" (115), and Ruth, who "simply let the darkness in the sky become coextensive with the darkness in [her] skull and bowels and bones" (116).

On the second occasion, it is Sylvie who brings Ruth out on the lake in a stolen boat to visit a ruined house in the woods. When Sylvie then disappears, Ruth is left alone by the house with only the ghosts of children for company. Ruth imagines that she could ignore the teasing sensation of the unseen, "cold, solitary" children at her back if Lucille were still with her then because "[h]aving a sister or a friend is like sitting at night in a lighted house. Those outside can watch if they want, but you need not see them. You simply say, 'Here are the perimeters of our attention'" (Robinson, *Housekeeping* 154). But lonely, without Lucille or Sylvie, Ruth gains a different perspective on the lighted house, thinking, "When one looks from inside at a lighted window, or looks from above at the lake, one sees the image of oneself in a lighted room [...]. When one looks from the darkness into the light, however, one sees all the difference between here and there, this and that" (157–158), so that, "[a]lthough darkness places one on the outside [...], it compensates by erasing the deceptive images of the visible world" (Burke 721).[16] And in the darkness, Ruth sees "her own body as a house that confines her spirit" (719) and would rather be rid of her body completely to have the company of spirits: "Let them come unhouse me of this flesh, and pry this house apart" (Robinson, *Housekeeping* 159), she puts it, beautifully. Unhoused, she might even find herself in the company of her mother, "lost to all sense, but not perished, not perished" (160).

On the third and final occasion, Ruth's attunement to the spiritual world, nurtured in her by Sylvie, is presented as her conversion into something that seems coextensive with that world and its elements, something "fleshed in air and clothed in nakedness and mantled in cold, and her very bones were only slender things, like shafts of ice" (Robinson, *Housekeeping* 204), something that "could walk into the lake without ripple or displacement and sail up the air as invisibly as heat" (204). This description appears during a scene where Ruth hides from Sylvie in the trees around the house, not fully knowing why but, perhaps, in return for being left alone at the ruined house. Now, in the trees, hiding from Sylvie, Ruth has become one of those ghost children, and she makes this clear by narrating a contrasting story of a rehousing, a projected return to the world of flesh which would mean the loss of her connection to the dead:

> The house stood out beyond the orchard with every one of its windows lighted. [...] I could not imagine going into it. Once there was a young girl strolling at night in an orchard. She came to a house she had never seen before, all alight [...]. A door stood open, so she walked inside. [...] She would be transformed by the gross light into a mortal child. And when she stood at the bright window, she would find that the world was gone, the orchard was gone, her mother and grandmother and aunts were gone. [...] And now, lost to her kind, she would almost forget them, and she would feed coarse food to her coarse flesh, and be almost satisfied. (203–204)

Ruth's time in the woods is interrupted by the arrival of the sheriff because, where she fears she will be lost to her kind, he fears she will be lost to society. "Come on home with me," he says (Robinson, *Housekeeping* 206), but Ruth refuses. Realizing now that Ruth will likely be taken away from Sylvie, the two of them decide to take flight and, as a first step, to burn the house down. Just as each of the three houses that structure Ruth's spiritual development must be breached so that Ruth might outstrip it, this house too must be ruined. The fire represents, therefore, the final step in the process of transfiguration. To leave the house, which is like a body or "like a brain" (209), to the "equal light of disinterested scrutiny" (209) would be to see it "transformed into pure object" (209), pure materiality. Burning it would see it transformed into pure spirit. Except that the house will not burn; it is too damp. And so, instead of an unimaginable return to the house, Ruth, while undertaking the dangerous crossing of the bridge, instead imagines the house burning:

> I thought of the house behind me, all turned to fire, and the fire leaping and whirling in its own fierce winds. Imagine the spirit of the house breaking out the windows and knocking down the doors, and all the neighbors astonished at the sovereign ease with which it burst its tomb, broke up its grave. Bang! [...] Every last thing would turn to flame and ascend, so cleanly would the soul of the house escape. (211–212)

This imagined burning of the house follows soon after Sylvie and Ruth's burning of magazines, newspapers, and books in the orchard. Then, it was on the page that there was "fiery transfiguration" (200), as if the words were allies to the flames, and it was the words that began "finally to ascend" (199); the words are of the spirit, just as "the bureau mirror fell in shivers the shape of flame and had nothing to show but fire" (212). Now, it is Ruth's words, or this fire of words, that consume without burning, that see the house go up in flames.

The house both does not burn, because it is so dank, and still does, because Ruth imagines it. The final state of the house, in fact, is never confirmed because Ruth does not revisit it. All we know is that a house survives on the site· and that "[s]omeone is living there" (Robinson, *Housekeeping* 216), but we cannot say if it is the old house or a new one, the old body or a new structure. "The only true birth would be a final one, which would free us from watery darkness and the thought of watery darkness, but could such a birth be imagined?" (162), Ruth asks, and perhaps Robinson is here addressing the limits of comprehension by presenting an ascension that both exceeds and does not exceed the material world and that speaks to both a state of wholly spiritual existence and a bodily resurrection, one that cannot be conceived of without recourse to the word and, specifically, the consuming fire of words.

Both Ruth and Sylvie exist in the same ontological state as the consumed house. They effectively emerge from it, their souls escape from it, because Ruth has already "dreamed that the bridge was the frame of a charred house" (Robinson, *Housekeeping* 174). And, like the house, they have been transfigured by a word, as Ruth recalls when thinking back to the bridge crossing: "[D]id we really hear some sound too loud to be heard, some word so true we did not understand it, but merely felt it pour through our nerves like darkness or water?" (215), she wonders. But perhaps it would be more accurate to say that they have been transfigured into words, that their "being is now the being of words" (Schaub 313), and that the end of the novel sees their spirits held in words like souls held in water. Dead, Ruth is not a ghost who writes but is a ghost because she is figured as writing, is the ghost that is writing, is ghost writing. It is what she is.

Derrida would say also that this is all she is and that there can never be a spirit that is not a specter, which is to say a spirit of writing, a "spirit." That's why the word heard on the bridge is felt as water pouring through and not as a fire burning and why it does not see Sylvie and Ruth ascend like flames into the rare light but dampens them down instead. But is it also really the case that Robinson cannot conceive of the spirit outside of immanence? No, I think rather that, for Robinson, the ghost never leaves off passing through, and the specter remains with the spirit, but the spirit also transcends this world and extends to "an existence beyond this one, [...] a reality embracing this one but exceeding it" (Robinson, *Gilead* 162–163). But comprehending this means learning, as Ruth does, "that transience involves a movement away from chronological time" (Burke 721).[17]

"SPIRIT" TIME

Future surprises are key to Robinson's conception of time. Those characters who see only what is ordinary in the world look to avoid them, including Ruth's grandmother and her sisters-in-law, Nona and Lily, who desire "the precise replication of one day in the next" (Robinson, *Housekeeping* 32). Of Lucille, it is said, "Time that had not come yet— an anomaly in itself—had the fiercest reality for her. [...] Lucille saw in everything its potential for invidious change" (93) and so she plans to be prepared for the future and all eventualities. As if to master in retrospect the unexpected loss of her mother, she looks to determine what is coming, and she does not wish for that which she cannot foresee. In contrast, Sylvie is said to have "inhabited a millennial present. To her the deteriorations of things were always a fresh surprise" (94) because she cannot conceive of a future at all and lives as if in an everlasting present. As one transfigured, she anticipates a time after the general ascension, which "would put an end to all anomaly" (91), including time that had not yet come. She anticipates an end to anticipation and is therefore surprised when the future still happens.

Ruth is between Lucille and Sylvie, and her perception of time allows us to see that Robinson's conception of temporality appears also to work on the basis of analogies of scale, as if time were a fractal in which the structure of every small moment copied the structure of time, specifically biblical time, as a whole. Ruth's awareness of the discrete structure of temporal moments is apparent as she watches Sylvie attempt to row a boat to shore, against the wind and the current, and observes that "the motion was always the same, and was necessary, and arduous, and without issue, and repeated, not as one motion in a series, but as the same motion repeated because here was the mystery, if one could find it" (Robinson, *Housekeeping* 169–170). Each motion, and therefore each moment, is "without issue" and therefore generates nothing, no momentum, and so there is nothing left but to start again. Each moment starts again and is also the start, the one and the same start, again, as if every moment has the same beginning, the same creation.[18] The story of one moment is the story of every passing moment and of all time, and it is exactly the story of creation, of Genesis. Ruth writes, "The force behind the movement of time is a mourning that will not be comforted. That is why the first event is known to have been an expulsion, and the last is hoped to be a reconciliation and return" (192). When asked about this idea that "what drives time and any story forward, what makes time what it is, is mourning" (Hedrick and Robinson 3), Robinson reinforces Ruth's insights with reference to her own source, replying:

> [Jonathan Edwards in *The Doctrine of Original Sin Defended*] talks about the world being continuously renewed so that if the energy of creation ceased, it would all collapse—there is no intrinsic momentum behind being, there is simply the continuous recreation of being. I think that's an interesting model: if you think that the inner workings of things are actually sustaining them, no, that's not true. (3)

Like Adam and Eve expelled from the Garden of Eden, each instance of creation is expelled from the present presence of God and, remembering and mourning this lost wholeness, looks forward to its return: "So memory pulls us forward, so prophecy is only brilliant memory—there will be a garden where all of us as one child will sleep in our mother Eve" (Robinson, *Housekeeping* 192). At every level, the force behind the movement of the novel is a mourning, for Lucille, for the mother, for generations, for a present God. And what is hoped for is a return.

Out on the lake, just before she speaks to Sylvie as if she were the ghost of her mother, and before she observes that every moment is the repetition of the same moment, Ruth says:

> I hated waiting. If I had one particular complaint, it was that my life seemed composed entirely of expectation. I expected—an arrival, an explanation, an apology. [...] That most moments were substantially the same did not detract at all from the possibility that the next moment might be utterly different. And so the ordinary demanded unblinking attention. Any tedious hour might be the last of its kind. (Robinson, *Housekeeping* 166)

Ruth is waiting for the return and reconciliation that follows the last hour of its kind, and perhaps of any kind. What follows this arrival and reconciliation? A sense of what Robinson might envisage can be garnered from the novel's imagined resurrections, like the one that sees the train "leap out of the water, caboose foremost, as if in a movie run backward, and then [...] continue across the bridge. The passengers would arrive" (96), she imagines, and not just her grandfather but her grandmother and mother, too, would be among them. This reference to "a movie run backward" (96) is not the only occasion that the train is described with reference to film or motion pictures. Earlier, Ruth imagines Sylvie, Lucille, and herself "posed in all the open doors of an endless train of freight cars—innumerable, rapid, identical images that produced a flickering illusion of both movement and stasis, as the pictures in a kinetoscope do" (50). The kinetoscope was a precursor to the film projector that, instead of throwing out its image for general viewing, allowed an individual to see a film through a window at the top of the device. In Ruth's image, therefore, each car of the train becomes a frame of the film, with the figures of the three women occupying every frame and given the flickering illusion of movement as the successive images flash before the eye of the viewer. The train, as time, passes, and people are born and live and die in the frame of light that is the passing moment. But, simultaneously, both the train and the filmstrip present a spatialized conception of time where, in the darkness outside of the brightly lit window, all created instances, past and to come, are copresent, all the fragments of time knit up finally.

Housekeeping is concerned with communicating a sense of the world after the awaited resurrection, in which every instance of creation would return to the present presence of God, so long mourned for and yearned for. Anthony Domestico, discussing "Ruthie's use of imperatives to instruct her reader to imagine certain hypothetical events or situations" (94)—those times when we are instructed to "Imagine" (Robinson, *Housekeeping* 152, 211, 218) or "Say" (16, 96, 162)—convincingly argues that they "serve as the creedal statement, the strongest truth-claims imaginable, for Ruthie's vision of the world" (Domestico 94–95). These "creedal moments, Ruthie's imperative hypotheses, enable Ruthie and the reader to occupy a similarly millennial present [...], making present what has come before and what will come to be" (102), so that "Ruthie's moments of visionary memory are intimations of eternity, hinting at the divine perspective and the existence of a realm in which past, present, and future are simultaneously present" (104). The effect of Ruth's mode of narration is complemented also by the geography of the novel because, as Paula Geyh observes, the "haunted house in the woods represents the future of the house on the edge of town, and so the two houses are in effect coextensive, linked and transposable across time" (114) and, moreover, "if the house in the woods might be the future of the house on the edge of town, it might also be its past" (115) because, as Ruth notes, "It might have been this house that peopled all these mountains" (Robinson, *Housekeeping* 157). The space of the novel, therefore, synchronically relates the past, present, and future of the house. And it becomes apparent now, the narrative achieves the same thing, if not something more; it appears to end ambiguously with the house either burned down or not burned down, but it ends, in truth, comprehensively with the house both burned down and also not burned down, both the same house altered and also a new house on the old site, both occupied and also not occupied by Lucille, as if every iteration of the house existed at once. And Sylvie and Ruth are alive and dead and are born again, are ghosts and spirits. In this way, the novel imagines "the world will be made whole" (152).[19] And this is time as God sees it.

And yet, toward the end of *Housekeeping*, Robinson has Ruth present an extraordinary portrait of the God of the Book of Genesis; she declares, "In the newness of the world God was a young man, and grew indignant over the slightest things. In the newness of the world God had perhaps not Himself realized the ramifications of certain of His laws, for example, that shock will spend itself in waves; that our images will mimic every gesture"

(192–193). What is striking here is that this is a God in time, who does not know what will happen, or who sees something coming without seeing it coming. But of course, in a narrative that must see every iteration of a thing realized, there must be a housed God who needs to unhouse himself, surprise himself, before he is that which houses all things, even the future. Seeing all, God sees a time when he did not see all. But how can it be that, at one and the same time, God both sees and does not see all? And, "[i]f the world was created good, how did the fall occur in the first place?" (Latz 294). Andrew Brower Latz argues that "*Housekeeping* can be read as an exposition of the doctrine of the fall, problematising and complicating any facile appropriation of religious ideas" (294), but what are the results of Robinson's willingness to engage with the idea of a spirit that falls into spectralizing time before returning to spirit? As Stefan Mattessich rightly argues, this is the Hegelian spirit that "'falls' into a temporal order construed as a pure becoming and […] effects […], through the crisis of its own otherness (and of others), its 'return to itself' at a level of representation and knowledge" (62). And this is the Hegelian spirit that, as Derrida details, Heidegger denounces. As Derrida describes:

> If, as Hegel says, "history, which is essentially history of spirit, unfolds 'in time'," if therefore "the development of history falls (*fällt*) into time," how can spirit thus fall into time, into this pure sensible order […]? For such a fall to be possible, the essence of time and the essence of spirit must have been interpreted in a certain fashion by Hegel. Heidegger says […] the idea of a fall of spirit into time presupposes a vulgar concept of time. (*Of Spirit* 25–26)

For Derrida and Heidegger, there is no spirit outside of space and time, no spirit as such, only "spirit" or ghost. For Robinson, I think, there is no spirit that is not also of space and time, of the specter, so that she "folds the desire for transcendence back into a world that is always *this* world of passage" (Mattessich 79). But I would suggest that she believes also in something beyond the specter, yet which, housed in *Housekeeping*, can only ever appear as the specter. Mattessich therefore recognizes that "Robinson never leaves the 'real' world" (63) and that her writing "gives to the spiritual a spectral function of reserve or trace undoing position, perhaps even that of spirit, since as a specter or a ghost it is suspended between worlds, or rather in between the world" (69). As a writing of the ghost, the world of her novel is "a finitude that *lacks any transcendence*," he says (62), which is true but perhaps not what Robinson wanted.

Either way, for Robinson the wholeness of the world cannot be grasped without attending to the ghost. Because the arrival is the future return of a remembered and mourned past, it appears as a revenant, like Sylvie and Ruth. Lucille does not see them "stood outside her window" (Robinson, *Housekeeping* 218), these specters looking, like "[n]o one watching this woman" (219), but they are not there, all around her. Robinson writes, and I emphasize, that Sylvie and Ruth "*do* not sit down at the table next to" Lucille (218) and that her "mother, likewise, *is* not there" (218) and her grandmother and grandfather, they all "*are* nowhere in Boston" (218). Ruth was always waiting for the revenant, but now Lucille "*does* not watch, *does* not listen, *does* not wait, *does* not hope, and *always* for [Ruth] and Sylvie" (219). She sits in a restaurant, and her "water glass has left two-thirds of a ring on the table, and she works at completing the circle with her thumbnail" (218), but Ruth would have her leave an opening for the ghost, expect what cannot be foreseen, nudge the circle into a vortex, and ascend to be restored to her family.

NOTES

1. Most of the women's names are significant: Hartshorne remarks that "Ruth" "is both 'friend, companion' and 'be satisfied (with water)' or 'water abundantly'" (57n10), while Ruth's Biblical namesake, as Barrett notes, "voluntarily abandons her native home" (95); Sylvia, as her surname implies, becomes a foster-mother to the two girls; Sylvie Fisher's name underlines the links to the woods and the waters of this woman who sometimes "came home with fish in her pockets" (Robinson, *Housekeeping* 147), in contrast with her sister Molly, intent on being one of Christ's "*fishers of men*" (91); and the names Helen and Lucille both refer to light, while the surname Stone suggests either Helen's fall into the water or a reference to Lot's wife who was turned to salt and to whom Ruth imagines building a statue in the woods, so that the ghosts of children might "forgive her, eagerly and lavishly, for turning away, though she never asked to be forgiven" (153).

2. For examples of such readings, see Foster, Friedman, Geyh, Hall, Hedrick, Kirkby, Meese, Rubenstein, Tigchelaar, and Walker. Despite such readings providing necessary insights into the novel and into our conception and construction of gender roles and social systems, as Esteve observes, they can "too often overstate claims about its critique of patriarchal order" (227). Indeed, it is exactly such critical responses which prompt Schaub, in an interview with Robinson, to begin by asking her about the tendency to read the novel simply as one confirming and conforming to "the social and

political narratives within the critical community" (Schaub and Robinson 232). In a later essay, Schaub again targets critics "quick to appropriate the novel's story for the work of social reform" (309), but he is far more critical of Robinson's own politics, of her "nationalist rhetoric" (300) and "universalizing idealism" (318). Schaub appreciates the novel, but he concludes, as I do, that "Robinson's novel denies the very usefulness its critics wish to find in it" (317).

3. "[T]he ghost is just passing through," says Derrida (*Specters of Marx* 136).

4. "As theoreticians or witnesses, spectators, observers, and intellectuals, scholars believe that looking is sufficient. Therefore, they are not always in the most competent position to do what is necessary: speak to the specter" (Derrida, *Specters of Marx* 11).

5. "There has never been a scholar who, as such, does not believe in the sharp distinction between the real and the unreal, the actual and the inactual, the living and the non-living, being and non-being" (Derrida, *Specters of Marx* 11).

6. See Domestico, Hungerford, and Mattessich for examples of spiritual or religious readings of *Housekeeping* after the publication of *Gilead*. The journal *Christianity & Literature* published a special issue on Robinson in 2010.

7. See Shy's discussion of Calvin as a guiding, but also unravelling, thread in Robinson's work (256). However, see also Leise, who suggests that "this is where Shy misses the point" and who argues that "Robinson is consciously reading the Puritan tradition against itself" (350).

8. When Robinson writes of the holy in each individual, what comes to mind is the Unitarian William Ellery Channing's argument that, "[t]o understand a great and good being, we must have the seeds of the same excellence" (147). It may even be possible to describe Robinson as a radical Transcendentalist, using the term "radical" both in the implied sense of "the root and its presumed unity," which gives Derrida reason to be uncomfortable with the word (*Specters of Marx* 184n9), and in Hägglund's sense that "the root uproots itself and the ground undermines itself" (207n1).

9. In her introduction to her collection *When I Was a Child I Read Books*, Robinson praises Whitman and Dickinson, as well as William James and Wallace Stevens, for their "vision of the soul" (xiii).

10. Robinson's continuing conversation with nineteenth-century writers is often instead presented as a feminist revision of a masculinist movement. See Aldrich (130), Hedrick and Robinson (2), Kirkby, Ravits, and Hartshorne for the claim that Robinson has "revised, reinvented, and feminized the 'traditional' canon of American literature" (50). For Schaub, however, it is straightforwardly "a brilliant, meditative resurrection of American romanticism" (310).

11. Robinson goes so far as to say that *Housekeeping* is "commenting on *Walden*" (Hedrick and Robinson 4). For *Housekeeping* and *Walden*, see also Kirkby (94, 101–102).

12. Preferring to describe the novel in Emersonian terms, Schaub observes, "Ruth's world is the image of the transparent eyeball, and it is transformed by her into allegories of spiritual facts.[...] Through Ruth's habit of analogy, Robinson reproduces the logic of Emerson's correspondence between natural and spiritual fact" (311).

13. In her interviews and non-fiction, too, Robinson will often use an allusion to water to communicate an experience or vision of spirit. Speaking of nineteenth-century writers, she says they "declare the senses bathed in vision" ("The Hum Inside the Skull" 30), and elsewhere she says, "It is vision that floods the soul" ("Onward, Christian Liberals" 220).

14. The novel often references the song "Goodnight, Irene" (Robinson, *Housekeeping* 20, 88, 165, 196), in which a transient man sings, "Sometimes I live in the country. Sometimes I live in town. Sometimes I take a great notion to jump in the river and drown."

15. Ruth's spiritual growth can be contrasted with the limited perception by other characters of their world. For example, Lucille's growing dissatisfaction with Sylvie and her desire for a more conventional life are illustrated by her preference for "the lighted kitchen with its blind black window" (Robinson, *Housekeeping* 102). Similarly, Grandmother Foster knows only "the ordinary light" (10) and "the resurrection of the ordinary" (18); because "she distrusted the idea of transfiguration" (10) and doubted that the things of her world would be "substantially changed" (10) in an afterlife, Ruth imagines that her resurrected grandmother's first instinct would be to look "to see how nearly the state of grace resembled the state of Idaho" (165). Sylvia should be contrasted with her husband Edmund because, as Burke shows, the "impulse to cross conventional frontiers is fathered by Grandfather Foster" (717). His death in the train accident reflects the fact that the train plays an unusual role in the text because it does not simply represent but effectively provides passage from one state of existence to another, from a time before life to life, to death, and then to an afterlife.

16. Robinson comments, "[L]oneliness is the encounter with oneself—who can be great or terrible company, but who does ask all the essential questions. [...] I sometimes think it is the one great prerequisite for depth, and for truthfulness" (Painter and Robinson 492).

17. As the Reverend John Ames observes in Robinson's *Gilead*, "I can't believe that, when we have all been changed and put on incorruptibility, we will forget our fantastic condition of mortality and impermanence" (65).

18. "'[A] Creation every moment.' That is George Herbert," notes Ames in *Gilead* (126). Later, he comments, "[I]t has all been one day, that first day" (239), meaning that "Ames regards every day as the first day of creation" (Latz 286).

19. Schaub says that "the reader decides that whether or not the ghostly pair have jumped, fallen, or crossed over the bridge, in either sense, is beside the point" (313), and Meese argues that "in the novel's concluding pages, it is not whether the old house is there or not there, whether Lucille lives in it or sits in a Boston restaurant, or whether she even thinks of Ruth and Sylvie that matters. Rather, […] all of these things are true and not true, the only reality being the fact of how the narrative's own discourse is interpreted" (68), but I am trying to suggest that it does matter for Robinson as she tries to communicate that, for God, reality doesn't require interpretation but is all true as he sees it, and he sees all.

Death Sentence

The name is the specter of a certain "spirit" of writing, the apparition of the trace. My name is the ghost that I inherit and that outlives me, as I pass through, here one moment, gone the next. My name survives me, and Jacques Derrida's name survives, identifying him as the author of *Specters of Marx*, for example, but also providing the title of a remarkable book by Derrida and Geoffrey Bennington.[1] *Jacques Derrida* is composed of two works, "Derridabase" by Bennington and "Circumfession" by Derrida. The former's 31 parts occupy the top two-thirds of each page, while at the bottom of the page the latter extends through 59 periods and periphrases, one for each year of Derrida's life to that point.[2] The hierarchical aspect of this arrangement is fully intended because the stated aim of Bennington's text is to provide an overview of Derrida's work so as to describe "the general system of that thought" (Bennington and Derrida 1). The result of a "friendly bet" (1), this is Jacques Derrida "[t]ranslated by Geoffrey Bennington" as the title page states, with Bennington attempting "to systematize J. D.'s thought to the point of turning it into an interactive program" (one "named after the software dBase" [Hägglund 152]), presenting this system clearly and, importantly, without ever quoting Derrida (1). Derrida, in turn, "having read G. B.'s text, would write something escaping the proposed systematization, surprising it" (1) and, typically, while not seeking to overturn the established hierarchy, certainly shaking it to its foundations. Derrida's revolutionary, vertiginous writing aims to elude Bennington and to show that

© The Editor(s) (if applicable) and The Author(s) 2016
D. Coughlan, *Ghost Writing in Contemporary American Fiction*,
DOI 10.1057/978-1-137-41024-5_10

"this undertaking was doomed to failure from the start" (1). Or, in other words, Derrida's writing will prove a bug in the program, both in the sense of a computer fault and in the sense that Hamlet intends when he speaks of "such bugs and goblins in my life" (Shakespeare, *Hamlet* 5.2.22), or of such imaginary and terrifying things as ghosts.[3]

Bennington's "Derridabase" and Derrida's "Circumfession" are twinned texts, the one looking to find in the other only its own mirror image, or at least foreseeing a future text in which it would recognize nothing that it had not already accounted for. Above the line, therefore, Bennington's text is clear and illuminating, an invaluable commentary on Derrida's work. Below the line (you might almost say, below the surface), the circumlocutory passages of "Circumfession" are intensely personal pieces of autobiography telling the story of Jacques Derrida; of the Derrida of 1976–1981 and of 1989–1990; of Derrida and his mother Sultana Esther Georgette Safar Derrida who, suffering from Alzheimer's disease, was close to death when Derrida was writing "Circumfession"; of Saint Augustine and his mother Saint Monica; and, in a way, of Bennington too. Though Bennington does not quote Derrida, Derrida mines both Augustine's *Confessions* and his younger self's notes toward an unwritten book on circumcision, to be called *The Book of Elie*. The 59 periods of "Circumfession" pass between other texts, therefore, and Derrida describes them as "written in a sort of internal margin, between Geoffrey Bennington's book and work in preparation" (Bennington and Derrida np). They occupy a present moment divided between Bennington's past work (which aims to account for all of Derrida's work, past, present, and future) and Derrida's future work. And these transient periods bear witness also to a transient Derrida, seemingly always on the move, in body or mind, between California, Nice, Paris, Algiers, Spain, Prague, London, New York, or Moscow. These passages and periods emerge from particular places and times of writing, then, even as other locations and moments thread through them like veins.[4]

In contrast with this felt transience, Derrida complains that Bennington would present his work as something knowable within a permanent and infinite program. Bennington, says Derrida, "remains very close to God, for he knows everything about the 'logic' of what I might have written in the past but also of what I might think or write in the future" and for all time ("Circumfession" 16). The logic of this program means that Bennington can do without Derrida, can do "without quoting any singular sentences that may have come to" Derrida (16), because no name need be attached to these eternal words. Derrida might be forgotten altogether, as his mother has forgotten him; Bennington does not quote Derrida "like my mother doesn't speak my name" (28), he says. The sourceless words are one with the unnamed son, and it is as if Derrida is effaced and unacknowledged, disowned by those he addresses, left "periphrasing here for whomever no longer recognizes me" (25). He is writing for Bennington and, he says, "I am writing *for* my mother" (25), but they will not put a face to his words. Instead, Derrida's writing is in a duel, he says, with what Bennington "will have written [...] *for* me" (26). Bennington will have written for Derrida writing for his mother, so that Bennington is writing *for* Derrida's mother, meaning perhaps both that he is writing in her place, in order not to name Derrida, and that he is writing to have her, to lay claim to her heart. Bennington takes the place of Derrida with the woman he loves, "to love in my stead," Derrida fears (34).

Derrida's is not the only name cut throughout *Jacques Derrida*, as can be seen in the pruning of the titles of texts by Derrida to which Bennington refers. For example, he will (even as, tongue in cheek, he will not) cite:

> the practice of quotation (LI, 40ff.; SI, 126-8), the relationship between commentary and interpretation (AT, 10; GR, 159; SP, 31, 53), the identification and delimitation of a corpus or a work (GR, 99, 161-2), the respect (GL, 216a; NM, 37-8; WD, 121) owed to the singularity (PS, 560; WD, 22, 169ff.) or the event (PC, 304; TW, 146) of a work in its idiom (GL, 1496; SI, 24), its signature (GL, 3ff.; M, 230-1; SI passim). (Bennington 9)

This abbreviating seeps down into Derrida's text also in references to individuals, so that it becomes hard to identify such people as the (unpunctuated) SA who is Saint Augustine but can refer also to *"Savoir Absolu"* ("Circumfession" 54) or absolute knowledge, or the J.-C. in period 29 who is Jean-Claude Lebensztejn. How can J.D. turn the tables on mother-loving Bennington, who is G. for Geoff and God? Or Geoff who is Djef and D. for Dieu, a God even in French?

But Derrida is also D. for Dieu, and Jacques is J. for Jehovah, and Elie (Derrida's "secret name" ["Circumfession" 87]) is E. for Elohim. And Geoff is not God, only "very close to God" (16), more like an acolyte, the one who follows and accompanies. If anyone is playing God here, it is Derrida, in this account of his own genesis. Because Genesis is, of course, another twinned text, a tale with two beginnings, the same but different origin twice told. First there is "The Beginning," which says, "In the beginning God created the heavens and the earth" (Gen. 1.1), and then there is "Adam and Eve," which says, "This is the account of the heavens and the earth when they were created" (Gen. 2.4). It's a familiar story, but it's one that's barely recognizable in "Circumfession." The Lord of the Old Testament forbids man to eat of the tree of the knowledge of good and evil, but Derrida laments that Geoff will not eat what is offered, will "do without my body" ("Circumfession" 28) as Derrida says. In the Garden, man and woman find themselves ashamed of their nakedness and cover themselves, but Derrida's mother willfully exposes her nakedness, "Because I'm attractive," she says (24). God gives man the task of naming all the animals of the earth, but Geoff on high makes like he is out to reverse all of that, like a negative poet, stripping things of names as if everything were the same, identical, as if the proper name of Jacques Derrida, like "God," named all: a text, a person, a corpus, a program, an eternity. Geoff would have Jacques room within God's house, but Jacques prefers to be in the garden, knowing that in Genesis, in the beginning, it is identity above all that Jehovah guards against. God says, "The man has now become like one of us, knowing good and evil. He must not be allowed to reach out his hand and take also from the tree of life and eat, and live for ever" (Gen. 3.22),[5] because what difference would there be between God and a man who knew good and evil and would have eternal life? Jacques doesn't want to be one with God, or to have eternal life.

Because, what could ever happen if there was only ever God? What could the future hold if it were no different to any other period? It is the future which is at stake in this duel with Geoff's machine, or, as Derrida says, "[N]ow future is the problem since if G. [...] has made this theologic program capable of the absolute knowledge of a nonfinite series of events properly, [...] here I am deprived of a future, no more event to come from me" ("Circumfession" 30). That is why Derrida turns to Genesis, where we are given the peculiar portrait of God as a young man, a God in time, open to the event to come. In *The Animal That Therefore I Am*, Derrida describes how this God looks to Adam (Ish) to name the animals in the Garden of Eden:

> God thus lets Ish do the calling all alone; he accords him the right to give them names in his own name—but just in order to see. This "in order to see" marks *at the same time* the infinite right of inspection of an all-powerful God *and* the finitude of a God who doesn't know what is going to happen to him with language. And with names. In short, God doesn't yet know what he really wants: this is the finitude of a God who [...] sees something coming without seeing it coming. (17)

This "in order to see" marks "God's exposure to surprise" (17), and this surprise, this unforeseen future happening, is bound up with an exposure to the name and to language. When Geoff can do without quoting, then Derrida fears that he "should have nothing left to say that might surprise him" ("Circumfession" 16). The surprise will be what does not break but escapes the machine, as that which is unprogrammable or incalculable. Derrida will write "improbable things which destabilize, disconcert, surprise in their turn G.'s program, things that in short he, G., any more than my mother or the grammar of his theologic program, will not have been able to recognize, name, foresee, produce, predict, *unpredictable things* to survive him" (30–31).

Derrida will write things to surprise and to survive his God. He writes, quoting his younger self, "'*I still address, you are a mortal god, that's why I write, I write you my god*' (9-4-81), to save you from your own immortality" ("Circumfession" 264). Reading this, it becomes clear why, for Hägglund, "The decisive question, then, is what the love of 'my God' refers to in Augustine's and Derrida's respective confessions" (146). For Augustine, according to Hägglund, the answer is a love for "God's eternal Word," which "transcends the love for anything that is spatial and temporal" (147). But "Derrida answers the question of what he loves in the opposite way [...] as a love for the mortal. The beloved 'you' that Derrida addresses throughout *Circumfession* has a number of shifting references—himself, his mother, Geoffrey Bennington, and others—but [...] whoever is addressed as my god, as the one I love above all, is mortal" (147). Therefore, "[i]mmortality is not the end that one desires and hopes for but the end that one fears and struggles against, since it would put an end to mortal life" (147). Says Derrida, "The point is that it belongs to life not necessarily to be immortal but to have a future" (*Death Penalty* 256). For there to be a future, there needs to be the possibility to be surprised by death.

And there will be a future, if there is a name. The name as trace "enables the past to be retained, since it is characterized by the ability to remain in spite of temporal succession. The trace is thus the minimal condition for life to resist death in a movement of survival" (Hägglund 1). The name, therefore, inscribing me in time, preserves me for a possible future; at the same time, it speaks to my death because it can remain in spite of my absence. It can outlive me. As Derrida writes, "[E]very case of naming involves announcing a death to come in the surviving of a ghost, the longevity of a name that survives whoever carries that name. Whoever receives a name feels mortal or dying precisely because the name seeks to save him, to call him and thus assure his survival" (*The Animal That Therefore I Am* 20). But, again, without this future death, there would be no future at all: "[t]he trace can only live on, however, by being left for a future that may erase it" (Hägglund 1).

Time enters with the name and its generations of comings and goings. Therefore, as Bennington points out, "[T]here is no proper name. [...] For there to be a truly proper name, there would have to be only one proper name, which would then not even be a name" (105). And "if one wishes to call this origin by the name of God, the best proper name, the most proper name [...], then one draws God into the violence of differ- ence" (106), he says, because "[w]e are already in writing with proper names" (105), which means we are already in "a system of differences: this or that proper name rather than another designates this or that indi- vidual rather than another and thus is marked by the trace of these others" (105).⁶ I mean, what should Derrida properly be called? Derrida, Jacques Derrida, J.D., Jackie, or his secret name—Elie—which he bore "*without bearing, without its ever being written*" (Derrida, "Circumfession" 96), like an effaced face? The way in which Elie haunts Jacques marks the traces of these other names and individuals that pass through his own: his brother Paul Moïse, "his double" (138), who died a year before the birth of Derrida, "the twin brother of a dead one" (277) and "the one whose ghost lives on in him" (Hägglund 149); his brother Norbert Pinhas, who died when Derrida was ten; his friend Elie Carrive, who committed suicide in 1955; the prophet Élie, or Elijah; or his uncle Eugène Eliahou, who was called Elie for a "secret reason" (Derrida, "Circumfession" 185), named after an uncle "that no one ever mentioned again in the family from the day he abandoned his wife and children to make a new life" (185). In this way, the ghost of a secret twin, the unknown uncle of an uncle, returns in the name that both does and does not name him, that survives him and forgets him. And in this way, the secret ghost of his own name returns to surprise Derrida.

Even as these absent others, and he says, all the "heavy secrets I inherit unbeknownst to myself" ("Circumfession" 187), haunt Derrida, can Bennington ever be without Derrida either, or ever not speak his name? Can *Jacques Derrida* ever not also name the unwritten "novel" *The Book of Elie* (274)? A secret name can be unknowingly cited, the secret name which is not one truly proper name wholly belonging to one individual but is a name in writing and therefore always already incomplete, cut, abbreviated even, in French (L. I.) and English (L. E.): "*eh! lis, et lie, élit, et lit, et l'I, elle y, L. I., l'Y*" (Derrida, "Double Session" qtd. in "Circumfession" 182). Can Bennington ever have avoided quoting Elie, the bug in the program, for example in reference to "the questions to which this type of book must habitu*ally* presuppose replies, around for example the practice of quotation" (Bennington 9, my emphasis)? Can Augustine be read without Derrida: "Tolle, lege!" ['Take up and read', 'Prends *et lis*'] (*Confessions* 8.12.29, my emphasis)? Can we ever not inherit ghosts?

For this reason, says Derrida, "[I]t's enough to recount the 'present' to throw G.'s theologic program off course" ("Circumfession" 311). Because to account for the present (and the future), you need to account for the past, but the "past" is not an open book, and so we have, instead, a "present" haunted by inherited ghosts which will surprise us when they make their return appearance in the "future." The last words of "Circumfession"—"you the crossing between these two phantoms of witnesses who will never come down to the same" (315)—place you, the mortal god, between the ghost of the past and the ghost of the future who will never coincide, even as they place you, the last words, between the ghost of the writer and the ghost of the reader. These last words might always be the words of a ghost, the words of someone lost to death, that "incalculable interruption" (207), that "interruption of an ability to sign" (Bennington 157). As Bennington states, "Circumfession" confronts that "certainty underlying any encounter, namely that one of us will die before the other, will in some sense see the other die, will survive the other" (166). Derrida's mother is so unwell while he is writing "Circumfession" that it is not clear that she won't die before the text is written. He dreads "the imminent but unpredictable coming of an event, the death of my mother" (Derrida, "Circumfession" 206); it "haunts Derrida's confession from beginning to end" (Hägglund 149), and, sadly, she did die soon after its publication, on 5 December 1991. And Derrida is further reminded of his own mortality during this period when he contracts Lyme's disease, which paralyses one side of his face and seems to leave him shaken. It is this necessary mortality, which, to use Derrida's words, "cannot be quoted, only incorporated" ("Circumfession" 197), that the text enacts, in its own way, at the conclusion. On the last page of "Derridabase," Bennington refers to the "so humble signature, so low, effaced, of Jacques Derrida, here below, now, here" (316). But where? There is no sign of it. The last words are overleaf.

Signing words in the face of death; secret names and secret twins; ghosts, inheritance, and generations; surprises: Derrida and Robinson have all of these in common, and more.[7] When I read of the dissymmetry of Derrida's paralyzed face and "the cruel specter of this left eye that no longer blinks" (Derrida, "Circumfession" 100), I think of, in Robinson's work, the grandfather's loss of his right eye in the Civil War, a blinded eye which lets him see God.[8] Vision, or seeing things again in a new way, is important to both. When Derrida writes, during his illness, that "this conversion ought to be the surprise of an event happening to 'myself,' who am therefore no longer myself, [...] but the fact that it is not decipherable here on the page does not signify in any way the illegibility of the said 'conversion'" (124–125), it seems to me that he is urging us to turn the page, not over, but with him, physically 90 degrees, so we can no longer read but can now see Bennington's and his twin texts as a dissymmetrical face, its blind eye with visions of God and its unblinking eye staring straight at death. It is "the dissymmetry of a life in caricature" (123).

You might recognize something of Robinson and Derrida in this face also, of the one who writes that "God is a sphere whose center is everywhere and whose circumference is nowhere" (Robinson, "My Western Roots" 166) and the other who writes of "the lack or absence of a center" (Derrida, "Structure, Sign, and Play" 289), of the one who is one with spirit and the other who speaks to ghosts. For Robinson, the ghost is only ever the temporary housing of the spirit, but for Derrida, there is nothing outside of the ghost. Both speak of transience, but for one, this is a passing through into eternity, and for the other, it is a true passing, a stark and sorrowful reality that is also profoundly meaningful, perhaps granting beauty. At times, nevertheless, Robinson seems haunted by the transience of the ghost, or fearful that if she lets her characters die, then they will simply be dead. These novels look dedicated to the life of the "spirit." But, as I will argue, when read together the novels attest again to a spirit life, a living on with God. Robinson finds a comfort in this that others will not. For example, Bennington in the end says, "[W]e have betrayed him" because "we have absorbed Derrida, his singularity and his signature, the event we were so keen to tell you about, into a textuality in which he may well have quite simply disappeared" (316). But Robinson would reject any idea that she has betrayed Lila by returning her to God, the One, even if she thereby repeats what Bennington laments by absorbing Lila, the singularity of Lila, into God's book, presenting her as a citation of God's word and not as a woman to be cited. For Robinson, all are recorded within God's program, a program so complete that he might cite our secret name without us even knowing it. Derrida's God, on the other hand, might cite our secret name without his knowing and leave himself open to a future surprise.

NOTES

1. In his wonderful reading, Hägglund describes the book as a staging of the "desire for survival" (146).

2. As Hägglund details, "Each section runs as one long sentence [...]. The termination of the sentence is not decided by Derrida but rather by the computer program in which he writes his sentence. [...] Hence, Derrida writes in relation to a death over which he has no command" (151). In fact, there is one section, 21, that is interrupted by a period appearing other than at the end; it comes near the beginning, after the phrase "the origin of evil" (Derrida, "Circumfession" 106). For Derrida, this commanded termination, this death sentence, would indeed be an evil. Arguing against the death penalty, he says, "The insult, the injury, the fundamental injustice done to the life in me, to the principle of life in me, is not death itself, from this point of view; it is rather the interruption of the principle of indetermination, the ending imposed on the opening of the incalculable chance whereby a living being has a relation to what comes, to the to-come and thus to some other as event, as guest, as *arrivant*" (*Death Penalty* 256).

3. My thanks to Jim Kennedy for the connection between Derrida and bugs. In this context, we might also consider computer viruses and, as Derrida describes them, "all the dead-alive viruses, undecidably between life and death, between animal and vegetal, that come back from everywhere to haunt and obsess my writing" (*The Animal That Therefore I Am* 38).

4. It is as if "Circumfession" is about the shift from the "Derridabase" to the "Derrid(h)app," a program of (h)appenstance and of (h)appening (my thanks to Chiara Alfano for the (h), and my apologies for the pun).

5. Auster notes that there is a "conscious echo" (*City of Glass* 44) of these words in the story of the Tower of Babel: "But the Lord came down [in order] to see the city and the tower that the men were building. The Lord said, 'If as one people speaking the same language they have begun to do this, then nothing they plan to do will be impossible for them. Come, let us go down and confuse their language so they will not understand each other'" (Gen. 11.5–7).

6. In contrast, the Reverend John Ames in Robinson's *Gilead* believes that "God is set apart—He is One [...]. His name is set apart" (158).

7. A small confession: it was the idea of pairing Bennington's and Derrida's twinned texts with Robinson's twinned novels, *Gilead* and *Home*, that first got me started on this path. The (surprising?) later publication of *Lila* leaves things fittingly lopsided.

8. And when I read that Derrida's discourses "grind up everything including the mute ash whose name alone one then retains, scarcely mine, all that turning around nothing, a Nothing in which God reminds me of him, that's my only memory" (Derrida, "Circumfession" 273), I think of how Ames received a "biscuit ashy from [his] father's charred hand" (Robinson, *Gilead* 130) and of how Ames remembers "that day as if [his] father had given [him] communion" (117). As one from an Irish Catholic background, it's interesting for me to think of the relationship between Derrida and Robinson, or Derrida and Bennington (remarking on the body unknowingly, consuming the body unknowingly), in terms of communion, which means different things to us even as its meaning is "common." When Derrida uses the word, noting that "*among the Algerian Jews, one scarcely ever said* [...] *Bar Mitzvah but 'communion'*" ("Circumfession" 72), he not only registers the dissonance of Jewish life in French Algeria but also links communion back through *Bar Mitzvah* to another set of twins, the 13-year-old sons of Isaac, Esau and Jacob, also common to both Robinson's and Derrida's texts (as well as Roth's *The Counterlife* [86] and *The Human Stain* [61]).

6. Gone Sometime. Home to Stay: Marilynne Robinson

Marilynne Robinson's second novel, *Gilead*, begins with the words "I told you last night that I might be gone sometime" (3). Her third, *Home*, begins with "Home to stay, Glory! Yes!" (3). These two beginnings do not reflect but rather speak to each other as signature and countersignature because, while every signature promises to outlive its author as the mark of that which is presently here but will be gone sometime, the countersignature can be evidence of a return home, of survival and not yet death. It is this ability to sign, this writing which attests to living on in the face of inevitable death, that gives *Gilead* so much of its force. The novel is a letter, or it is a series of letters, with interruptions in the writing marked by a blank line or, on one occasion, a blank page, as if each white space were to be read as an invisible signature, each one threatening to be the final signature of a now-absent author. Its narrator is Reverend John Ames, who, in 1956, at the age of 76, knowing that he is a "dying man" (Robinson, *Gilead* 6), begins this letter to his son, at that point not yet seven years old. The aim, he says, "is to tell you things I would have told you if you had grown up with me, things I believe it becomes me as a father to teach you" (152).[1] He intends his son to read the letter as a grown man, by which time Ames will "have been gone a long time" (4), as he says, and will "know most of what there is to know about being dead,

© The Editor(s) (if applicable) and The Author(s) 2016
D. Coughlan, *Ghost Writing in Contemporary American Fiction*,
DOI 10.1057/978-1-137-41024-5_11

but I'll probably keep it to myself" (4). *Gilead*, then, is a letter addressed from beyond the grave, but unlike *Housekeeping*, it is not presented as a spirit's communication. This letter's writer is now only playing at being a spirit, for example when he pretends his writing is contemporaneous with the reading of the letter—"I pray all the time. I did while I lived, and I do now, too, if that is how things are in the next life" (5)—but he has not yet crossed that bridge, to put it in the terms of the earlier novel. Nevertheless, this is a ghost writing, the words appearing in a spectral time out of joint. Written for a now-absent reader it "might never reach" (22), as Christopher Leise observes, "[T]he epistle has the strange effect both of looking back as well as looking forward" (348), facing both in the direction of a father's past writing that is no longer and a son's future reading that is not yet. Ames is already the ghostly father who returns to educate his son who will know what will have happened, and this spectral novel is somehow noncontemporaneous with itself, existing in no present moment but rather between generations.

"It really is a matter of generations," says Robinson (Painter and Robinson 486), and so, in his letter, John Ames, "son of John Ames and Martha Turner Ames, grandson of John Ames and Margaret Todd Ames" (Robinson, *Gilead* 10), tells his son about his father and mother, about his older brother Edward, about the two sisters and the brother lost to diphtheria, about his fearsome grandfather, about how he met and married his wife Lila, and about the town of Gilead, Iowa.[2] He tells him also about his good friend of many years, the Reverend Robert Boughton, and about his four girls and four boys, and especially his daughter Glory and his son Jack. Jack, for so long a troublemaker creating heartache for his father, has been gone from Gilead for some time but is home now, whether to stay or not no one knows. His story recalls the parable of the prodigal son, but Robinson marks also some important differences:

> I really see this as a parable about grace, not forgiveness, since the father runs to meet his son and embraces him before the son can even ask to be forgiven. Or it is about love, which is probably a synonym for grace. The prodigal can leave his old life behind him. Jack brings his to Gilead—in the form of loss and loneliness and also hope, and a painful and precious secret. Again, for me the issue between him and his father is not one of forgiveness. His father cannot absolve him of the pain and difficulty of his life, and Jack does not expect him to. He comes home seeking help in restoring a good life he had made, which has been destroyed by the pressures of law and social custom. (Painter and Robinson 488)

Jack's return home derails Ames, who becomes increasingly preoccupied with his presence, as evidenced by this letter to his son where he confides things about Jack's past that he withholds from Lila, repeats conversations he has with Jack, and shares revelations. The overall effect is strangely unbalancing. It becomes hard to say whose story this is and whether it is Ames's, or Jack's, or Gilead's, or the story of a son's unknowable future. It suggests that it is hard to circumscribe a life so as to tell it as just one story, complete in itself, and uninterrupted by the stories of others.

In fact, it is the interruption that provides Ames's most important lesson. He plans to tell his son things he believes it becomes him as a father to teach, as if he could pass on his legacy as a program of action, something to be put into effect when necessary (and this is, above all, a program of ethical action). But Jack is the bug in his system, and it is Ames's reaction to this friction that will ultimately prove more instructive to his son, if his son lets the ghost speak. It is what does not compute in Ames's world, what requires interpretation, that provides his son with an inheritance. If Ames's letter affected his son as if by a cause, depriving him of a future because he need only repeat what Ames had done in the past, then there would be nothing for him to inherit from the letter because you always inherit from a secret, from the unsaid or unacknowledged, from the ghost.

In this novel of generations and inheritances, therefore, it is hard to tell Ames's story from Jack's. In the same way, it is hard to tell *Gilead* from *Home* because the story of *Gilead* is also the story of *Home*, the same but different story of Reverend Robert Boughton, and of his daughter Glory and his son Jack, and of the visits of Reverend John Ames and his wife Lila and son Robby. These, therefore, are twinned texts, sharing an inheritance, the second repeating the first but with a shift from Ames's first-person narration to a third-person narration largely told from Glory's point of view. These twinned, parallel stories are, in turn, peopled by characters twinned in name. Edward was named after his uncle Edwards, and Reverend Robert Boughton shares his name with Ames's young son Robert "Robby" Boughton Ames, probably because Reverend John Ames shares his name with John "Jack" Ames Boughton. As Ames puts it, Boughton "was always naming his sons after other people" (Robinson, *Home* 193). In Jack's case, Ames performed the baptism himself, understanding that the child's name was to be Theodore Dwight Weld. Instead, as he describes it, "[W]hen I asked Boughton, 'By what name do you wish this child to be called?' he said, 'John Ames.' I was so surprised," Ames says, "that he said the name again, with the tears running down his face"

(*Gilead* 214). Ames is so surprised to be put in this position that his first thought is, "This is *not* my child," and he admits, "It took me a while to forgive him for that. I'm just telling you the truth" (214). Ames and Jack, "that man, my namesake" (215), get off on the wrong foot, therefore, and Ames continues to struggle with forgiving the son for that original sin of the father. "I have never been able to warm to him, never" (215), he says, and yet then he will avow that "John Ames Boughton is my son. If there is any truth at all in anything I believe, that is true also. By 'my son' I mean another self, a more cherished self" (215).

The novels present, therefore, four generations of John Ameses—the grandfather, father, son, and the namesake—and what is at issue is what does not translate between the one John Ames and the next. Because what emerges is that it is not just the relationship between Ames and Boughton's son that is strained but that each generation has been at odds with the next and each generation has had its secrets. As Robinson's novel proceeds, it moves also backward, further into the past, from the arguments to their roots, as if Ames is uncovering memories that he hasn't ever forgotten and is slowly revealing to his son a secret that he already knows. Very early in *Gilead*, therefore, Ames and his father visit his grandfather's grave in Kansas, and we learn that "[i]t grieved [his] father bitterly that the last words he said to his father were very angry words" (Robinson, *Gilead* 11). Before the visit to the grave, they find and dispose of some bloodied shirts and a pistol that the grandfather had left behind when he departed their home for Kansas. Ames admits, "I was predisposed to believe that my grandfather had done something pretty terrible and my father was concealing the evidence and I was in on the secret, too—implicated without knowing what I was implicated in" (93); only a couple of pages later, he further admits, "I did know a little about the shirts and the gun" (95), and then he acknowledges that "my grandfather was involved pretty deeply in the violence in Kansas before the war" (97), fighting for "the cause of abolition" and all those "bound in chains" (56), as the Lord was when he had come to the grandfather in a vision. It is this arguably legitimate violence that leads Ames's father to oppose his own: "I remember when you walked to the pulpit in that shot-up, bloody shirt with that pistol in your belt. And I had a thought as powerful and clear as any revelation. And it was," he declares, "This has *nothing* to do with Jesus" (96). These are the last, angry words he will later regret. And the violence and its secret live on from father to son, so that Ames will say, "I felt certain that he should hide the guilt of his father, and that I should also hide the guilt of mine" (97).[3]

This communication between generations is presented by Robinson along familiar lines. If, in *Housekeeping*, we saw the word of the spirit emerge from the body consumed in fire, then here, fire marks the ghost that passes from generation to generation.[4] Between grandfather and father, there are the words "'The Lord Our God Is a Purifying Fire' [...], those incendiary words" (Robinson, *Gilead* 113) that drive the younger man from his father's church after the Civil War, and there are the bloodied shirts he looks to burn, for "the garments rolled in blood, shall be for burning, for fuel of fire" (Isaiah 9:5 qtd. in 92). Between the grandfather who proudly fought in the Union Army and the grandson, there is the younger man's sermon against the First World War "burned the night before" it was to be preached (47). Between father and son, there are the words "'the tongue is a fire'—that's the truth. When my father was old he told me that very thing in a letter he sent me. Which, as it happens, I burned" (7). And between the three generations, there is the story of when the grandfather's church "burned. Lightning struck the steeple, and then the steeple fell into the building" (107). Says Ames, "I remember my father down on his heels in the rain, water dripping from his hat, feeding me biscuit from his scorched hand, with that blackened wreck of a church behind him [...]. I remember it as communion, and I believe that's what it was" (109). This fire burns up to the present, and Ames seeks to transmit "some version of that same memory" (118) to his son: "I broke the bread and fed a bit of it to you from my hand, just the way my father would not have done except in my memory" (118), he says, his words echoing those of Jesus at the Last Supper. This communication coming from the blackened church relates to Ruth's communication from the charred house and retrospectively casts that as communion also, with Ruth's spirit present in those words like Christ is believed to be present with the Eucharistic bread and wine. In the same way now, the spirit of Ames's communion with his father is passed on to his son as memory taken in the mouth, a memory impossible without those words also: "I broke the bread [...] in my memory."[5]

Between Ames and his other "son," his other self, John Ames Boughton, there is also a secret. In fact, it will turn out to be the same secret, the one relating to the unspeakable violence done to and by the individual, the family, and the community in the USA in the name of race. Jack's sympathy with Ames's grandfather's convictions are evident in his quiet observation that "during the Civil War Iowa had a colored regiment" (Robinson, *Gilead* 193), for example, but Ames doesn't recognize the significance of such comments. He is, however, aware of other parallels between his and Jack's lives. In fact, the two are almost impossibly alike while being in every way different; they are negative images of each other. Both find themselves in opposition to their father; both receive a letter which describes a loss of faith, either in God or in the man; and both have lost a woman and child in the past. Ames had previously had a wife, Louisa, who died giving birth to their daughter, who died herself shortly after. During her short life, Boughton baptized her Angeline (20), but she was to have been named Rebecca, and that remains Ames's secret name for her. Jack didn't have a wife, but as Ames tells it, "while he was still in college at any rate, he became involved with a young girl, and the involvement produced a child" (177). Jack refused to marry the young girl, "never acknowledged the child, to make any provision for it at all" (178), and it was left to his father, his sister, and Ames to make the best of a bad situation, until the child died when she was three years old with no name to put on the gravestone but "Baby [...] (her mother had never really settled on a name)" (181). Jack's story here seems almost a betrayal of Ames's, and this is what Ames struggles with. He says: "That one man should lose his child and the next man should just squander his fatherhood as if it were nothing—well, that does not mean that the second man has transgressed against the first," but "I don't forgive him. I wouldn't know where to begin" (187). And, "If young Boughton is my son, then by the same reasoning that child of his was also my daughter, and it was just terrible what happened to her, and that's a fact" (216). Ames seems both sinned against and sinning, as if the shared name involves a transmission of both blame and guilt. No doubt he also feels that the girl with no name had a claim on one of his daughter's two.

It is these parallels between Ames and Jack that feed into his later discomfort because, once Jack comes home, Ames cannot help but notice the understanding that develops between him and Lila. It is clear that Ames's fear is that Jack will take his place in Ames's home when he is gone, be husband to Ames's wife, be father to Ames's child, be John Ames in flesh and deed as well as word. He fears "leaving my wife and child unknowingly in the sway of a man of extremely questionable character" (Robinson, *Gilead* 160). Jack will love Ames's wife and, what is worse, Ames "might well be leaving her to a greater happiness" (238). Love, thinks Ames, "is the eternal breaking in on the temporal" (272), love is a sharing in eternity, and is shared eternally. This is what Ames dreads, that Jack will share his eternal life with the woman that Ames loves. Jack will take the place of John with the woman he loves, to love in his stead, and she will be like a stranger to him, or a mother who does not know her own son's name.[6]

What follows, therefore, is a surprise, something that in *Housekeeping* might be termed unexpected or unforeseen or unprogrammable. In *Gilead* and *Home*, these ideas are more closely tied to the issue of predestination, described as a concept "put to crude uses" (Robinson, *Gilead* 171), and a discussion of which takes place in both books (*Gilead* 170–175; *Home* 229–238). It is Jack who instigates the debate, and understandably so, since his past behavior seems to mark him out as one of those "irretrievably consigned to perdition" (*Gilead* 170).[7] Even Ames has passed judgment on him, viewing him as a dishonorable man, and as he says, "[T]hose who are dishonorable never really repent and never really reform" (178). Jack wonders, however, "how the mystery of predestination could be reconciled with the mystery of salvation" (173), and he finds an ally in Lila, who states, "A person can change. Everything can change" (174). The conclusion of the novel bears her out and demonstrates to Ames that he should not think that the future is knowable and can be read so easily. Instead, after a single blank line has separated each entry in Ames's letter from the next, suddenly, late in the novel, a blank page appears. And then Ames writes, "Jack Boughton has a wife and child. [...] That did surprise me" (247).

Ames and Jack, therefore, which is to say Ames and his "more cherished self," are like "those who are born as twins [...] Esau and Jacob. But, the same events did not befall both men" (Augustine qtd. in Derrida, "Circumfession" 280–281).[8] Despite their lives taking parallel paths, they have arrived at different destinations. The woman that this John Ames loves has a different name; Jack's Della is not Ames's Lila, and because Ames cannot imagine himself not loving Lila, and because here now is a part of himself that loves another, this is the surprise. Or, as Jack puts it, "I've interrupted you" (Robinson, *Gilead* 253). Who can say, then, what is destined for either of them in the afterlife? Why should Jack's damnation be guaranteed when what also seemed inevitable, his loving Lila, has and will not come to pass?[9]

For Robinson, of course, God can say what the future holds. The future holds no surprises for Robinson's God, for whom the reconciliation of predestination with salvation presents no mystery, and who, therefore, cannot surprise Himself. Explaining her position in a way that should remind us of her motion toward eternity at the end of *Housekeeping*, she says, "I really feel that there has to be something we don't understand about being, time, causality, something that would allow us a richer sense of alternatives than is offered by free will and predestination, both of which are very problematic notions from a theological point of view" (Painter and Robinson 489). God's mastery over the future is signaled by his mastery over names as the author of Creation, as the final Word. Robinson reveals this through her twinned texts, her tale with two beginnings (like her John Ames, born in 1879 and 1880), in *Gilead* and in *Home*. It is toward the end of *Gilead* that we learn that Jack's son is Robert Boughton Miles. But it is not until *Home* that we learn that Ames's son is also Robert Boughton. These boys are secret twins, or doubles, negative images of each other, ghosts of each other. But Robinson's point is that, though "we are such secrets from each other" (*Gilead* 224), we are not secrets to God. Ames's son's secret name is secretly cited in the naming of Jack's son, but the revelation is a surprise to the reader, not to God. This is not a God who can be surprised by secret names but a God who surprises by knowing the names even of those without names. For example, the implication is that God knows the name of Jack's unchristened daughter when Ames and Glory witness a quasi-baptismal scene of the mother playing with her baby in the river: "[H]er mother cupped her hands and poured water on the baby's belly, and the baby laughed [...]. And the sun was shining as well as it could onto that shadowy river" (186–187; see also *Home* 159).

The future is as legible to God as names are, but more than this, and returning to the question of predestination, Robinson implies that God names all futures, or all possibilities. For example, Ames's final blessing of Jack, which reads as a repeated and more truthful baptism, also names the different aspects of the man, or the different parts that make up the whole: "Lord, bless John Ames Boughton, this beloved son and brother and husband and father" (Robinson, *Gilead* 276). In other words, even as at the end of *Housekeeping* Sylvie and Ruth are alive and dead, are born again, and are ghosts and spirits, here Robinson moves toward a Godly vision that does not exclude anything. It might be that, as God sees all versions of one thing, so Robinson gives us *Gilead* and *Home*, the same but different stories of the same but different John Ames and his same but different son Robert Boughton. *Gilead* and *Home*, then, work together to replicate the effect of *Housekeeping*'s "spirits." Ames begins his letter "dreading interruption" (247), which is to say dreading death, and any signature might be his last, to be answered only by the countersignature of his son as reader: "This is another thing you know and I don't—how this ends," Ames writes to him (83). And as readers, we think we know how this ends also, but once Ames writes that "I think I'll put an end to all this writing. [...] The expectation of death I began with reads like a kind of youthfulness, it seems to me now" (272), then we can no longer know if the end of the novel coincides with his death. Instead, death remains in the future, as an event to come. "I'll pray," Ames writes, "and then I'll sleep" (282), and the novel ends.

But I would suggest that this is not the end of Ames's story. *Housekeeping* is remarkable for letting the dead speak as "spirits," but perhaps *Gilead* and *Home* do also. We just need to rethink the story told by the twin beginnings of these two novels: "gone sometime" and "Home to stay." Ultimately, these novels are about finding a home both in this world and the next. Ames tells his son, "I don't know how many times people have asked me what death is like [...]. I used to say it was like going home. We have no home in this world, I used to say, and then I'd walk back up the road to this old place" (Robinson, *Gilead* 4). Ames, despite what he used to say, does find a home in this world with Lila and Robbie—"I didn't feel very much at home in the world, that was a fact. Now I do" (4)—but the two novels together are about his journey to that other home. Whether he lives or dies at the end of *Gilead* is undecidable, but he will be gone sometime, gone home, and literally so, if we understand that the beginning of *Home* does not serve as a countersignature marking Ames's survival but as a countersignature signed by God after his death and his return "Home to stay, [in the] Glory [of God]! Yes!" The blank line means an interruption in writing, the blank page means an interruption in self, there is the blankness that is death's interruption of life, and then God takes up his writing again, and the afterlife afforded to Sylvie and Ruth is Ames's also in the bridging of two novels.

... AND *LILA*

Like the same-but-repeated motion of Sylvie's rowing in *Housekeeping*, *Lila* steps again into the same river as *Gilead* and *Home*, telling now the story of Ames's wife. Lila, like Jack, and like Sylvie and Ruth before him, is a transient, given to walking "out at night, because then you can see into people's houses" (Robinson, *Lila* 196). As such, she is a creature of spirit, with Robinson observing that "[t]here is a way in which her destitution has made her purely soul, unaccommodated, as King Lear might say, though reduced not to animal but to essence" (qtd. in "Interview"). The reference is to Act 3, Scene 4 of *King Lear*, the same scene from which Robinson takes Ames's final words, "I'll pray, and then I'll sleep," a sentence which, as Sarah Churchwell observes, "marks Lear's great shift into a moral accountability based on care" as he finally realizes his neglect of the "houseless poverty" (Shakespeare, *King Lear* 3.4.26).[10] If *Housekeeping*, therefore, is about unhousing the spirit of its spectral flesh and lodging it in eternity, *Lila* is about housing the spirit, this pure soul, in this world. And, again, this housing involves names.

Robinson's approach to the character of Lila can be traced back to an earlier observation in her interview with Schaub, that is, "I think that one of the primary mistakes people make is to take people's spoken language to be equivalent to the level of their thinking" (Schaub and Robinson 237). Taken, or rescued, from her family at an early age by the itinerant worker Doll, Lila receives only limited schooling, but her lack of education should not be confused with a lack of insight into the mysteries of this world and God's ways. Lila is initially wary of the concept of God because, first, "[i]f there was a Good Lord [...] Doll had never mentioned Him" (Robinson, *Lila* 17), and second, "she understood that Doll was not, as Boughton said, among the elect" (97), which meant that, although "[f]or a while Lila had liked the thought of resurrection because it would mean seeing Doll" (100), she later fears that being saved would mean losing Doll for eternity. In the end, however, "Lila comes to an ingenious conclusion. Because no concept of paradise could accommodate knowledge that our loved ones suffer eternal torment, Lila decides that the unsaved must get a free pass from the saved who love them" (Churchwell). Therefore, if Lila is saved, so is Doll; or, if Ames is saved, so is Lila, and then so is Doll.

Lila's doubts and hesitations over whether or not she wants to believe in God are marked by her relation to Robinson's spiritual element, water, as Lila experiences a series of baptisms, unbaptisms, and rebaptisms (which means, like the house in *Housekeeping*, that she exists in the novel as something simultaneously built, unbuilt, and rebuilt). So, "she had been born a second time, the night Doll took her up from the stoop and put her shawl around her and carried her off through the rain" (Robinson, *Lila* 12); the first time she ever saw Ames, "she wandered into the church dripping rain. [...] He baptized two babies that morning" (11); later, after Ames baptized her in the river, Lila "went to the river and washed herself in the water of death and loss and whatever else was not regeneration" (103) and "unbaptized herself" (105); and finally, "when the Reverend had baptized their infant at the church that day and put him into her arms, he touched the water to her head, too, three times" (257). Ames, as John the Baptist, baptizes in water but, Lila is told, Jesus "shall baptize you in the Holy Spirit and in fire" (87).

These baptisms and namings accord with Robinson's treatment of water and words as spiritual housings. Lila's realization of her faith is inseparable from her growing knowledge of the words to describe it, which is not to say that her spiritual life does not exist before she can name it, but rather that it seems confirmed by the right words. To put it another way, she discovers there are words for the things she has experience of. This begins, in fact, with more mundane things—"There was a long time when Lila didn't know that words had letters, or that there were other names for seasons than planting and haying. Walk south ahead of the weather, walk north in time for the crops. They lived in the United States of America. She brought that home from school. Doll said, 'Well, I spose they had to call it something'" (Robinson, *Lila* 10–11)—and expands from there— "She knew a little bit about existence. That was pretty well the only thing she knew about, and she had learned the word for it from him. It was like the United States of America—they had to call it something" (74). And though she knew about existence before she knew about the word "existence," still, she wonders, "Could she have these thoughts if she had never learned the word?" (178). Therefore, when, alongside the words "the United States of America" and "existence," she is given new words to name herself, this also allows for different thoughts: "Lila Dahl. The teacher had misunderstood somehow and made up that name for her. [...] That was the first time she ever thought about names. Turns out she was missing one all that time and hadn't even noticed" (46).

What the teacher misunderstands is the name Doll, which she appends to Lila's own as her surname, so that Doll becomes the ghost that haunts Lila's name, the inherited secret.[11] When Ames baptizes her, therefore, Lila protests that Lila Dahl "ain't my name," but Ames replies, "If I christen you with it, then it *is* your name" (Robinson, *Lila* 87). The sacrament of baptism couples her with another, as her marriage does also—"I am baptized, I am married, I am Lila Dahl, and Lila Ames" (94)—and, as with Ames and Jack, these twinned souls speak to the mysteries of salvation. Lila's fear was that, "If there was a stone on [Doll's] grave, there was no name on it" (97), but because God knows the secret names, the ghost is saved alongside the soul. God reads Doll inscribed in Lila Dahl, just as Lila sees a correspondence between her name and Ames's: "Lila Dahl. She had four letters in each of her names, and he had four letters in each of his. She had a silent *h* in her last name, and he had one in his first" (68). She continues, "There were graves in Gilead with his name written out on them, and there was no one anywhere alive or dead with her name" (68), but Robinson's point is that, even though Lila may not be able to tell of her "begats" in the way that her husband can identify generations of John Ameses, God knows her story. This is what Lila discovers when, as part of her self-education, she transcribes verses of the Bible, only to find herself inscribed within them. As Robinson explains, "[W]hen she reads the passage in Ezekiel about the baby inexplicably cast out and by chance taken up by a passing stranger, she sees herself and her circumstance even further acknowledged. This is the parable of her own life" (qtd. in "Interview"). Or, as Lila observes, "[S]he came straight out of the Bible" (Robinson, *Lila* 227). Lila finds, therefore, that God has names for all things and words to house all spirits.

On the face of it, this appears like a positive thing. The homeless Doll and Lila lead such limited lives that they can hardly have a sense of the shape of their society, never mind have a voice in it, but God, it appears, recognizes their existence and their value: "In those days it seemed to Lila that they were nothing at all, the two of them, but here they were, right here in the Bible" (Robinson, *Lila* 126). This connects with what Robinson is doing in *Housekeeping* also, with its focus on the Bible's nameless women, Lot's wife and Noah's wife, and its concern for the "nameless woman, and [...] all those who were never found and never missed, who were uncommemorated, whose deaths were not remarked, nor their begettings" (*Housekeeping* 172; see also Ravits 657). Robinson is ensuring that these women have their stories told also.

Unfortunately, she does this by effectively declaring that these women have already had their stories told, by God: Lila's story is told in Ezekiel, just as Ruth's story is told as much in the book of the Bible which bears her name as it is in *Housekeeping*. There, Ruth says to her mother-in-law, "Where you go I will go, and where you stay I will stay. Your people will be my people and your God my God. Where you die I will die, and there I will be buried. May the Lord deal with me, be it ever so severely, if anything but death separates you and me" (1.16–17). This passage sheds light on the deep relationship between Ruth and Sylvie ("we were almost a single person," says Ruth [Robinson, *Housekeeping* 209; see also 133, 145]), but in addition, by underlining the extent to which Ruth is committed now to her mother-in-law rather than her mother, it illustrates the way in which Sylvie might be considered not just to have taken the place of Ruth's mother, Helen (see 41, 53), but effectively to have become her ("the faceless shape in front of me," says Ruth, "could as well be Helen herself as Sylvie" [166–167]).[12] The series of women who raise Ruth and Lucille

becomes a series of interchangeable women, and the circle completes itself
when Sylvie comments that Ruth is "her mother all over again" (182).
This is the reading that Laura Tanner wants rejected when she criticizes
those who argue that "*Housekeeping* authorizes a typological rendering
that collapses the distinction not merely between biological and surrogate
mothers but between one character and the next" (96), and yet again
and again, Robinson presents characters who are the same but repeated.
Lila gives us yet another John Ames, the brother "John Ames who died
as a boy" (Robinson, *Lila* 40), and it tells us that one sister was named
Martha, after her mother, and the other Margaret, after her grandmother.
And though Lila may have sole claim to her name, the names Doll,
Lila, and Della also seem linked. Amy Hungerford, in addition, argues,
"Robinson imagines Della [...] as an analog for Jack—the daughter of
a powerful minister, part of a large, close family dignified by its religious
commitments, flawed in the prejudices that naturally arise from its otherwise valued insularity" (171n16), an argument which reminds us that
analogy is, for the Transcendentalist Robinson, what links the fragments
of the world. Each of these characters, therefore, is analogous to another,
each cites another, each haunting the other in its return.[13] Except, the
biblical sources for Ruth, Lila, and Jack (as the prodigal son) suggest that
each series is collapsible into the one original individual or, rather, should
not be seen as collapsing in upon itself but rising above itself, transcend-
ing the material world, because each finds his or her analogy in the word
of God, citing God and not the other. Each character in this world is the
falling point of a vortex, cast down from his or her corresponding figure
in the spiritual world. This means that there is not a series of characters as
such because each character is the start again, the one and same start, as
if each character, even each novel, has the same beginning, and each is a
first-generation ghost expelled from the presence of God.

In so many ways, Lila is the exemplary specter. In love, she is Ames's
wife come back to him; in aspect, she is his daughter Rebecca (Angeline)
returned (see Robinson, *Gilead* 23); in Robbie, he knows again fatherhood. She is a revenant, her arrival at the church that first time unforeseen and surprising.[14] She is the ghost as event, the unexpected future,
and, as such, will be "always surprising" (*Lila* 84; see also 35, 128, 187).
She is surprising and singular because, as Ames notes, "Any human face
is a claim on you, [...] the singularity of it" (*Gilead* 75) and "When
you encounter another person, [...] it is as if a question is being put to

you" (141). It is as if the question "What is a ghost?" is being put to you, which is to say "What is not here now?" or "What is your other name?" or "What will happen?" and this is a question asked again and again, and each time for the first time and the last.[15]

"What will happen?" you were asked, and of course, you "knew what would really happen next. One day [Lila] and the child would watch them lower John Ames into his grave" (Robinson, *Lila* 251), because death will happen, even if you cannot say when. But for Robinson, God can say when, and that is why Lila does not ask, "What will happen?" but about "why things happen the way they do" (29), allowing Ames to reply, "Things happen for reasons that are hidden from us, [...] coming to us from a future that God in his freedom offers to us" (222). There is no future for Robinson except as it comes from God. When Ames, therefore, writes a sermon with Lila in mind (a sermon she doesn't come to hear), it is "about welcoming the stranger because you might be welcoming 'an angel unawares'" (*Gilead* 234), recasting the ghost as God's messenger, a bearer of God's original word.[16] God becomes the source of all words because it turns out that it is the angel Lila who is responsible for Ames's writing, telling him, "You might as well be writing things down" (*Lila* 252). For Robinson, God has already accounted for someone like you or me, each one of us cites his word, and each specter is the "spirit" of God's spirit, a repetition of the first time and therefore no longer a singular individual. There is no name that he might cite without his knowing, surprising him; instead, his program might cite our secret name without us even knowing, readying our return to him. As Ames observes, "Our experience is fragmentary. Its parts don't add up. They don't even belong in the same calculation" (223), but for God nothing is incalculable, nothing anomalous, because "[w]hat are all these fragments for, if not to be knit up finally?" (*Housekeeping* 92). The answer to "What is a ghost?" is then, for Robinson, always what is no longer and not yet God. Her understanding of the future is a messianism with Messiah, a return of and to God's all-encompassing presence, an accommodation in his house, in an "Eternity [that] had more of every kind of room in it than this world did" (*Lila* 260). There can be no other way. If there were, and if transience were not a passing through into eternity but rather just a passing through, then Ames would not live on beyond his ghost writing and that final period could mean only that he was "dead, after all" (261).

NOTES

1. Time seems to be somewhat out of joint in Robinson's *Gilead*. Ames states that he was born in 1880 (10), that he "was sixty-seven, to be exact" (184) in June 1947, and that he is 76 years old when he starts his letter during "a fine spring" (9). That would all be fine, and would put the year of composition at 1956, except that his 77th birthday comes later in that same year "with the first yellow leaves" (212), which both suggests that he is writing his letter in 1957 and means he can't yet have been 67 in June 1947. However, Ames also says, "If I live, I'll vote for Eisenhower" (107), clearly referring to the presidential election of 1956. That, I would suggest, is the year in which Robinson intends the novel to be set, but it means that Ames's stated year of birth is wrong; he needs to have been born in 1879 for all of the other given dates to work.

2. The town of Gilead is "modeled on Tabor, in rural southwest Iowa" (Kirch 22).

3. Grandfather Ames, who, as Churchwell notes, "could be called a terrorist," is guilty of killing a soldier in his efforts to aid the insurrectionist abolitionist John Brown, 100 years before his grandson starts his letter. But his son and grandson could also be considered guilty, as the one "declares the struggles of the civil war best forgotten, and betrays his heritage," and the other "remains wilfully innocent about the civil rights movement, although it is the direct consequence of the story he is recounting" (Churchwell).

4. There are other similarities also. Like *Housekeeping*, *Gilead* also takes in transients, notably Lila and Jack, who "used to look in people's windows at night and wonder what it was like" (228). Water retains its essential aspect, though it is more explicitly presented in this novel in the context of baptism: "luminous water [...] was made primarily for blessing" (32; see also 27, 72, 186, 231). And, there is again the insistence on the need for vision: "Wherever you turn your eyes the world can shine like transfiguration. You don't have to bring a thing to it except a little willingness to see. Only, who could have the courage to see it?" (280).

5. The sense of communion that exists between his father and Ames, who receives "[t]hat biscuit ashy from my father's charred hand" (Robinson, *Gilead* 130), exists also between Ames and Lila, at the first sight of whom Ames's "sermon was like ashes on my tongue" (24).

6. Fascinatingly, prior to the publication of *Lila*, Kohn speculated that "the secret [Ames] is keeping from his son" is that "his wife, Lila, as she now calls herself, had been the fifteen-year-old Annie who gave birth to Jack Boughton's baby more than twenty-two years earlier" (7), in which case, if Jack were to replace John, this would simply restore things to the way they were before John replaced Jack.

7. Robinson's interpretation, however, is that "whom God loves he loves […]. Seen from that side, predestination is grace in a very radical form. Jack sees it from the other side, of course" (Painter and Robinson 489).

8. In *Home*, when Boughton quotes Isaac speaking to his son Jacob just after he has been deceived into giving him his blessing, and Jack responds with a quotation from Esau—"Bless me, even me also" (155)—Boughton will tell Jack, "You're confusing Esau and Jacob," and Jack will observe, "Yes, I am the smooth man [Jacob]. How could I forget? I'm the one who has to steal the blessing [from his father]" (155). In fact, Jack is like both: he is like Esau in that he believes the woman he marries will displease his father, but he is like Jacob in that he usurps another's birthright. As he explains to Ames, when he meets Della's father, Reverend Miles says, "'I understand you are descended from John Ames, of Kansas.' Of course anyone else would have put that right, but I thought there might be some advantage in letting him believe it—he was referring to your grandfather, of course" (*Gilead* 259).

9. Ames is a fitting name for these twinned spirits, given that *âmes* in French means "souls." On the question of the chosen soul, Derrida comments in a conversation with Roudinesco on Judaism on the "*political* use of the very serious theme of election (so difficult to interpret), and more precisely of the 'chosen people'" (Derrida and Roudinesco 189). He says, "I have a great deal of trouble with the 'doctrine' of election," preferring to speak of a "structure" of election in which predestination gives way to what we might call indestination: "I am irreplaceable in the place of this decision, in being obliged to respond: 'It is me,' 'I am here,' etc. This *election of each* seems to me to give to all responsibility […] its chance and its condition" (193).

10. My thanks to Roy Sellars for first bringing this allusion to my attention.

11. Doll haunts Lila even as a voice from beyond the grave. At a low point in her life, when Lila is going through a personal "hell" (Robinson, *Lila* 198) and working in a brothel, she imagines leaving this world behind, imagines that "the whole damn house would burn down" (198) and she would be "all fire like that" (198), all spirit. But Doll's ghost admonishes her, declaring, "If I was still living I wouldn't waste it standing around in no cellar wishing I was dead. You never learned that from me" (199).

12. Therefore, while Ravits sees that Ruth "recognizes in her mother's sister Sylvia her Naomi-figure or mother-substitute" (652), Schaub goes further, arguing that "Sylvie, after all, is less another person than she is the medium of Ruth's memory and then of her self-image" (316).

13. At this point, my argument diverges somewhat from Hungerford's. Recognizing that "the narrative is designed to knit up a broken world in to a whole, through simile and analogy" (Hungerford 120), but starting

from Ginsberg's declamation that "'Like' means *is not*," she argues, "If metaphor is the language of collapse, simile is the language that maintains difference within the embrace of kinship" (120), so that "[d]ifference, then, is encompassed by the family sphere; radical unlikeness is comprehended by 'home'" (120). But, for Robinson, and for the God who *is* that home, is there a final "difference between the living daughter and her dead mother" (120)? The failed reconciliation of grandfather Ames and father Ames would seem to undermine Hungerford's argument that difference can be accommodated within the earthly home, while at the same time the twinned selves of Ames and Jack, the two-in-one who are aligned with the father and grandfather respectively, show that in God's book the same story can account for the one and the other, so that there is no unlikeness in that heavenly home.

14. "Repetition *and* first time: this is perhaps the question of the event as question of the ghost" (Derrida, *Specters of Marx* 10).

15. "Repetition *and* first time, but also repetition *and* last time, since the singularity of any *first time* makes of it also a *last time*. Each time it is the event itself, a first time is a last time. Altogether other" (Derrida, *Specters of Marx* 10). On the question of the name, see Derrida's *Of Hospitality*: "Does hospitality consist in interrogating the new arrival? Does it begin with the question addressed to the newcomer [...]: what is your name?" (27).

16. In the same way, "Doll had come to [Lila] like an angel in the wilderness" (Robinson, *Lila* 30).

Ghostpitality

In the final chapter of DeLillo's *The Body Artist*, when Lauren has returned to the house she shared with Rey, a man visits "[t]o talk about the house" because, as he says, "It seems this is my house, still. My wife's and mine" (117). As they stand outside, looking at the house, Lauren asks him, "Who invites who in?" (118). It is a question of hospitality, or of the laws of hospitality. As detailed by Judith Still, "this sense of 'laws' denotes both the political domain of laws and rights, and also a socially situated moral code [...] which covers a physical (embodied) practice made up of a series of gestures, and [...] will also explicitly or implicitly refer to an affective structure" (5). "Welcome," you might say, motioning me in. "It's good to see you." These laws are not trivial because, as Still comments:

> At first glance then, hospitality may seem to be a matter of inviting friends or relatives into your home, but it is critical also to consider the traditional question of the stranger-guest, and then, beyond moral and social relations between individuals, to recognise that hospitality can be, and *is*, evoked with respect to relations between different nations or between nations and individuals of a different nationality. (2)

In Derrida, there exists a paradox between this conditional hospitality ("a *hospitality of invitation*") and the absolute or unconditional hospitality ("a *hospitality of visitation*" [Derrida and Roudinesco 59]) that one would like to offer to the foreigner, a hospitality offered "without asking

© The Editor(s) (if applicable) and The Author(s) 2016   169
D. Coughlan, *Ghost Writing in Contemporary American Fiction*,
DOI 10.1057/978-1-137-41024-5_12

of them either reciprocity," he says, "or even their names" (Derrida and Dufourmantelle 25). In contrast to the laws of conditional hospitality, therefore, there is "[t]he law of unlimited hospitality" (77):

> Let us say yes *to who or what turns up*, before any determination, before any anticipation, before any *identification*, whether or not it has to do with a foreigner, an immigrant, an invited guest, or an unexpected visitor, whether or not the new arrival is the citizen of another country, a human, animal, or divine creature, a living or dead thing, male or female. (77)

But, what if someone was to turn up at your house, at this very moment, unanticipated and without identifying themselves? How would you give this new arrival an unconditional welcome? What should you say to this person? Because, is it not your duty to receive them? Yet, even if you were to say nothing, even if you just motioned them to sit, this would already be a conditional welcome as you would thereby affirm "the law of hospitality" as "the law of a place," your home, and "the law of identity," where you are the host and the stranger is a guest ("Hostipitality" 4). As Derrida explains, the conditions attached to the law of hospitality draw a line through "the double sense that the French *hôte* has of *guest* and *host*" (*Aporias* 8), placing guest and host either side of a threshold that ensures the master of the house "maintains his own authority *in his own home*" when he invites the stranger in ("Hostipitality" 4). Hospitality is offered, but only on the condition that the host "remains master in his house" (4).

This one of many laws of hospitality, therefore, opposes itself to the law of unconditional hospitality because, as Derrida says, it "violently imposes a contradiction on the very concept of hospitality in fixing a limit to it" ("Hostipitality" 4), meaning that hospitality "is a self-contradictory concept and experience" (5). Derrida expands on this in *On Hospitality*[1]:

> It is as though hospitality were the impossible: as though the law of hospitality defined this very impossibility, as if it were only possible to transgress it, as though *the* law of absolute, unconditional, hyperbolical hospitality, as though the categorical imperative of hospitality commanded that we transgress all the laws (in plural) of hospitality, namely, the conditions, the norms, the rights and the duties that are imposed on hosts and hostesses, on the men and women who give a welcome as well as the men or women who receive it. And vice versa, it is as though the laws (plural) of hospitality, in marking limits, powers, rights, and duties, consisted in challenging and transgressing *the* law of hospitality, the one that would command that the "new arrival" be offered an unconditional welcome. (75, 77)

Still observes also that it is Derrida's absolute law of hospitality "which has caught his readers' imagination" (10), but she is concerned that the "distinction between this unconditional hospitality and the laws of hospitality is too easily assumed as an absolute fixed opposition with insufficient attention paid to the *ways in which* each interrupts the other" (15). Despite what some might believe, "what Derrida calls unconditional hospitality," as Hägglund explains, "is not an ethical ideal that we unfortunately have to compromise due to political realities" (103), and conditional hospitality is not a corrupted form that must be set right.[2]

Instead, Derrida warns that "[p]ure hospitality consists in leaving one's house open to the unforeseeable arrival, which can be an intrusion, even a dangerous intrusion, liable eventually to cause harm" (Derrida and Roudinesco 59). He cautions, therefore, that "pure or unconditional hospitality is not a political or juridical concept. Indeed, for an organized society that upholds its laws […], it is indeed necessary to limit and to condition hospitality" (59). Instead, "exposure to the other one *who* or which comes […] has a role in ordinary life: when someone arrives, when love arrives, for example, one takes a risk, one is exposed" (60). Therefore, though unconditional hospitality seems, on the face of it, to be that to which we should aspire, it would, for example, be ecologically and environmentally irresponsible on a planet of limited resources when, as Still reminds us, hospitality is effectively unsustainable as it means "giving more than you know you have" (3). Nor would you, as an individual, offer unlimited hospitality, say, to disease or infection, or throw down the welcome mat for death. But isn't this what a pure hospitality would mean, in the end: "the violent alteration of time" (Hägglund 104)? Which would mean also that conditional hospitality is necessary to ensure that what "is" is not only the other and that something of the self survives the future that is visited upon us.[3]

If "*nothing happens* without the unconditional hospitality of visitation" (Hägglund 104), perhaps nothing survives without the conditional hospitality of invitation. Derrida, anyway, is clear that, in relation to the contradiction between the laws and the law of hospitality, "this necessary aporia is not negative" ("Hostipitality" 13). He writes that

> even while keeping itself above the laws of hospitality, *the* unconditional law of hospitality needs the laws, it *requires* them. This demand is constitutive. It wouldn't be effectively unconditional, the law, if it didn't *have to become* effective, concrete, determined […]. And vice versa, conditional laws would cease to be laws of hospitality if they were not guided, given inspiration, given aspiration, required, even, by the law of unconditional hospitality. (Derrida and Dufourmantelle 79)

The law and laws need and pervert each other, and "hospitality limits itself at its very beginning, it remains forever on the threshold of itself" (Derrida, "Hostipitality" 14). Even the word remains on the threshold of its own meaning (even as *hôte*, meaning both "guest" and "host," does) because, as Derrida reminds us, hospitality is a word of Latin origin, "a Latin word that allows itself to be parasitized by its opposite, 'hostility,' the undesirable guest" (3), so that we have "the foreigner (*hostis*) welcomed as guest or as enemy. Hospitality, hostility, *hostpitality*" (Derrida and Dufourmantelle 45). But also, as Still shows, "[h]ospitality in theory and practice relates to crossing boundaries […] or thresholds […], including those between self and other, private and public, inside and outside, individual and collective, personal and political, emotional and rational, generous and economic" (4). "Who invites who in?" asks Lauren, awaiting an answer that will conjure away the ghost of the *hôte* between host and guest.

What brings us "from the host/guest to the ghost" (Derrida, *Aporias* 60)?[4] We need only remember that the hospitality of visitation of the future must also be a hospitality of *re*visitation, a first time *and* repetition. We are "awaiting what one does not expect yet or any longer, hospitality without reserve, welcoming salutation accorded in advance to the absolute surprise of the *arrivant*" (*Specters of Marx* 65), but nor can we distinguish between "the figures of the *arrivant*, the dead, and the *revenant* (the ghost, he, she, or that which returns)" (*Aporias* 35). In this way, ghostpitality names the return of the *hôte* as *hôte*; it names the haunting of every inside (every self, body, house, "present") by the outside, every interior by the anterior and exterior.[5] It is, to use Rey's words, "About the house. This is what it is" (DeLillo, *Body Artist* 8). For example, Lauren thinks of Mr. Tuttle as someone "found in someone else's house" (45), and she thinks, "I don't want someone in my house" (46), forgetting that it is not her house. For one, Mr. Tuttle was likely there before her, going by "the earlier indications that there was someone in the house" (41). She is thinking of the noises in the walls, but also, as Michael Naas points out, she should be thinking of a hair that she picked "out of her mouth" at breakfast time on the final day, "a short pale strand that wasn't hers and wasn't his" (DeLillo, *Body Artist* 10). Naas writes, "Just as Rey and Lauren sense that something else is living in their house, Lauren fears that someone else has infiltrated her body" (94), so that the novel is "not exactly about a haunted house but about a haunted mouth, a possession or ventriloquism of the voice" (99). *The Body Artist*, therefore, asks, "Whose house, whose body, and whose voice *is* this anyway?" (93) and what are "the boundaries between one self, body, or house and another" (90). And the answer is that the present house of the self is haunted by another, and the "novel thus concludes with Lauren imaging Rey, remembering him, [...] in a time and a body that are hers but not only" (106).[6] "You're my happy home" (DeLillo, *Body Artist* 17), Rey says to Lauren, his happy, haunted home.

Who else haunts this home? Because, as Naas points out, "If the story of *The Body Artist* is thus able to pose questions about the limits of dwelling in a house, or living in a body separate from others, or speaking with a voice that is one's own, it does so only by posing the limits of the *body of the text*" (104). Which is why, at the threshold of the text haunted by the ghost, before "they" appear, before "she" appears, before "he" appears, before "I" appear, "you" are there as the (g)host: "Time seems to pass. [...] You know more surely who you are" (DeLillo, *Body Artist* 7). Who invites who in?

NOTES

1. The seminar's title is "*Pas d'hospitalité* [Step of Hospitality/No Hospitality]" (Derrida and Dufourmantelle 75), which, following our discussion in "Shadows," we can also think of as "hospitality without hospitality."

2. Discussing *The Body Artist*, for example, Kessel suggests that literature "allows for at least a bracketing of the impossibility of absolute hospitality and at best allows for absolute hospitality to be glimpsed" (186).

3. And autoimmunity is necessary to ensure that what "is" is not only the self and that something of the other survives.

4. Thurston observes also that the "ghost story can [...] be seen as both a *host* story and a *guest* story" (3). Otherwise, however, he reads the ghost very differently, arguing that it is "a point of unbearable vital intensity" (4) and a "truth-event" (6).

5. In the context of mourning and melancholy, Del Villano describes "a melancholic '(g)hospitality,' where subject and ghost-object set up a relationship of hospitality, in which the former can be identified with a host and the latter with a guest, while the psyche is the 'home' where the meeting takes place. Obviously," she adds, "the two roles cannot remain so fixed" (90).

6. Derrida says, "There are many voices in me. I've not only one voice, and sometimes another voice speaks through me: my unconscious, a symptom; there are a number of inhabitants in me" ("Following Theory" 42).

7. Haunted Homes: Toni Morrison

The word "spook," that originally American term for the ghost which returns as a primarily American racial slur, reminds us of "the ways in which American culture represents racial and sexual minorities as dead—both figuratively and literally" (Peterson 4). As "an invidious term sometimes applied to blacks" (Roth, *Human Stain* 6), the word "spook" seems to be the twentieth-century product of a history of American slavery which, as Orlando Patterson argues, results in "the definition of the slave [...] as a socially dead person. Alienated from all 'rights' or claims of birth, [...] isolated in his social relations with those who lived, he was also culturally isolated from the social heritage of his ancestors" (5).[1] Denied a birthright, denied a name, denied an inheritance, denied roots, the enslaved are granted death so that their masters might take the greater share of life, might possess life fully and purely. As Peterson describes it, "The belief in my self-presence, which is also always a belief in my immortality, is [...] dialectically conditioned by the nonpresence of others" (4), and so, in an act of conjuration, the specter is exorcised so that the death of one is allotted to the other: "[T]he production of the socially dead describes the process by which the *hauntological* condition of the socially alive is disavowed and projected onto those who transgress the norms" (9–10, original emphasis), and "racial and sexual others stand in for the death that haunts every life" (4). And now, as Marisa Parham identifies when talking about another racially offensive term, "Niggers [...] are technically dead.

© The Editor(s) (if applicable) and The Author(s) 2016

D. Coughlan, *Ghost Writing in Contemporary American Fiction*,

DOI 10.1057/978-1-137-41024-5_13

They are assumed dead because it is assumed that the racist structures that engendered the term have already passed away" (2). It is not just slaves but slavery that is dead, racism that is dead and buried. And yet, says Parham, "'Nigger,' from the mouth of a white person. [...] Despite knowing that the nigger is not meant for me, the event of the nigger nevertheless snaps me into a ghostly and uncomfortable relation with the speaker" (2).[2] This is because "spook" does not only name a death but a return; it names a specter. It is the "spook," the specter of racism, that is heard in the word "nigger," and it is all the more terrifying for being thought dead (or believed dead, or hoped dead). But the surviving slaves were not dead, and racism is not dead now. So, if we are to speak of race at all, "the thing—that terrifying thing—that defines what America is" (Ramadanovic 136), then we need to learn to speak with ghosts, and even with those troubling spooks we would rather see consigned to the past, because to imagine them dead is to fail to attend to the living.[3]

Such a conclusion is familiar to any reader of the work of Toni Morrison, for whom any writing of American history, and therefore African-American history, is impossible without the ghost and the return of the figuratively and literally dead. Examples of the former include the Dead family in *Song of Solomon* (1977), while in *Paradise*, Connie wakes "to the wrenching disappointment of not having died the night before [...] in a space tight enough for a coffin" (Morrison, *Paradise* 221), and in *Beloved* (1987), all "the major characters struggle to regain life. Sethe's death image is her back [...] Paul D's dead part is his heart, [...] Denver has lived most of her life entombed within the house and yard of 124 Bluestone Road" (Page 145). Examples of the latter include the eponymous Beloved and the ghost of Macon Dead I, or Jake, in *Song of Solomon*. And what of Pilate in that novel, who births herself from the womb of her dead mother? Does what is born of a lifeless body return figuratively or literally from the dead? Anderson, for one, describes Pilate as one of Morrison's "[s]pectral figures, or characters who are open to spiritual realms" (11), but Anderson's work in general reflects the difficulties in coming to terms with Morrison's ghosts. She argues that "[s]tanding in contrast to the power of the spectral figures in Morrison's novels are the characters who are biologically alive, but who are ghostly because they are marginalized, silenced outcasts. I call these characters social ghosts" (11–12), she writes, of characters that others would surely call the social dead and that Morrison simply calls Dead. When Anderson speaks, therefore, of "Morrison's literary concern with 'unghosting' African American history" (13), she must have in mind the return of the (socially) dead to (social) life. Yet, as previous chapters have argued, not only is the ghost irreducible to death, but there is no life that is not a spectral living on, meaning the "unghosted" thing could never survive (and Anderson later acknowledges that "ghosts are necessary for cultural and personal survival—'learning to live'" [81]). It could even be said that, if the social dead are not ghosts, it is because they are not ghosts that they are dead. Or almost, because the spook attests to the ghostly return of the social dead (who are not, really, dead) to haunt the social living (who are not, really, alive); in the spook, "the invisible talks back" (Ramadanovic 136). The master may claim life for himself and decree that he can curse and cast out the impure ghost, but in the epithetic "spook" he uncannily names all the homely specters he believes he has evicted from his house. Peterson, therefore, is perhaps being inaccurate when he suggests, "To be socially dead, then, is in some sense to be *doubly ghosted*: for an African-American, this may mean that one's lived experience is one of being both a specter (in the generalizable sense) *and* a spook (to invoke the familiar racist trope of utter disembodiment)" (10). To be socially dead is in some sense to be unghosted; the dead as such do not haunt, but the spook is already haunting, working its way back not to life as immortal living but to "another place—neither life nor death—but there, just yonder, shaping thoughts" (Morrison, *Paradise* 307). This chapter, therefore, is about Morrison's concern with a haunted history, one that admits of more than the living and the dead. But because Morrison's ghosts are already widely studied, to an extent that exceeds the capacity of this one chapter, the main aim here is to address an important relation in Morrison's work between ghosts and hospitality.[4] The importance of being hospitable to the ghost, and yet the difficulty in accommodating the ghost, which is close to saying the difficulty in accommodating race, is illustrated via an initial return to the work of Marilynne Robinson, which, despite its best intentions, cannot, in the end, offer hospitality to the spook.

WELCOME THE STRANGER

In Robinson's *Gilead*, Reverend John Ames observes that you should "welcom[e] the stranger because you might be welcoming 'an angel unawares'" (234; see also 23).[5] The stranger is the *arrivant*, the unforeseen future whose appearance is so surprising and so unsettling. As discussed in the previous chapter, Lila is the central example of the stranger who arrives "from whatever unspeakable distance and from whatever unimaginable otherness" (24), but the other character involved here is Jack and his "inaccessible strangeness" (*Home* 260). Jack, thinks Glory, is "[l]ike a ghost" (32), a "[n]othing, with a body" that will "pass through the world" (301). As a ghost, however, Jack is the familiar stranger, returning to where he was before, to where he always already was: he "wasn't always gone, [...] was usually closer to home than [they] thought [he] was" (337). As such, he confuses the order of host and guest, so that Glory feels as if his return "were an inviolable claim on the place and her crossing the threshold an infraction" (38), as if he were the host now and she the guest who needs permission to enter "a long-empty room" (38). She thinks, "He makes me feel like a stranger in my own house. But this isn't my house. He has the same right to be here I have" (46), meaning of course that, for Robinson, the house is the father's, nominally Boughton's but truly God's. But whether the house is the spirit's or the ghost's, it means there is no present master, only guests.

For the others, it seems, Jack is a ghost who cannot escape his (pre-destined) death, the death he was born into, so that he is confronted with "this conjuration of himself [...], like Lazarus with the memory of cerements about him no matter how often he might shave or comb his hair" (Robinson, *Home* 250). The end of the novel, however, shows more clearly why Jack spooks the others by revealing him to be a spook, the return of all that was thought dead and buried with his namesake's violently abolitionist grandfather. Toward the end of *Gilead*, therefore, as previously noted, a blank page suddenly appears. And then Ames writes, "Jack Boughton has a wife and child. He showed me a picture of them. He only let me see it for half a minute, and then he took it back. I was slightly at a loss, which he must have expected, and still I could tell it was an effort for him not to take offense. You see, the wife is a colored woman. That did surprise me" (247).[6] The nameless stranger who enters with the spooky Jack, therefore, is the black person, the unforeseen guest whose return is so disconcerting, so destabilizing, that the narrative is momentarily derailed, blanked out, before Ames's voice reasserts itself.[7]

The explicit figuring of the black characters as ghosts comes at the end of *Home* when Jack's son Robert, his wife Della, and her sister come to the house in Gilead looking for him. Now, it is Della instead of Lila speaking to Glory "across an immeasurable distance" (Robinson, *Home* 333), while Glory wishes that Jack could know "that their spirits had passed through that strange old house" (337).[8] It is this apparition of Jack's black wife at the end of both *Gilead* and *Home* that confirms that these intensely personal novels ask also to be read politically. As in *Housekeeping*, the home expands by analogy, so that it is also Gilead, and Iowa, and the nation, with the tensions and conflicts of the growing civil rights movement condensed into the frictions and misunderstandings of the Boughton household; as Hungerford describes, "[O]ne could say that the work of both novels is to translate racial reconciliation into another mode of familial reconciliation" (119) though, given the general lack of reconciliation between Jack and his father, the novels show that race is hard to accommodate.[9] Indeed, the reconciliation of Jack and Ames serves, at the same time, to underline Ames's failure to honor his grandfather's political legacy. The words from *King Lear* with which Ames closes *Gilead*, if we can take them to mean that Ames shares also Lear's realization that he has taken "[t]oo little care of this!" (Shakespeare, *King Lear* 3.4.33), mean that the "novel's final events, in which Ames admits that a mixed-race family in 1957 [sic] cannot hope for security in Gilead, have forced him to acknowledge his own failure to defend racial and social justice" (Churchwell).

The problem with Robinson's well-intentioned racial politics is that she, too, has taken too little care of this. *Home* refers explicitly to events from 1955 to 1956, including those in "Tuscaloosa. A colored woman wants to go to the University of Alabama" (Robinson, *Home* 162), and in Montgomery, where the Bus Boycott was taking place. Though at one point, it is noted that the "protests in Montgomery are nonviolent" (213), earlier Robinson describes how "[o]n the screen white police with riot sticks were pushing and dragging black demonstrators. There were dogs. Police were pushing the black crowd back with dogs, turning fire hoses on them" (101–102). As Briallen Hopper notes, however, here "Robinson mixes up Montgomery and Birmingham" because, in "1963, when Birmingham cops attacked young people with dogs and water cannons, the images were considered so shocking and unprecedented that they appeared on the front page of newspapers around the country [...]. But neither the police attacks nor the media events happened in 1956," meaning that in "a scene in which remembering 'Montgomery' is equated with racial awareness, and forgetting it is equated with racial obliviousness, Robinson 'forgets' Montgomery." Not only does Robinson portray what didn't happen, she fails to portray what did happen, such as the bombing of black churches and the homes of activists, including Martin Luther King's, and, perhaps more significantly, the fact that the boycott proved a successful example of black activism. As Hopper argues, "[H]er displacement of the Montgomery bus boycott with images of brutality and suffering seems almost predestined by her theology. She is replacing a story of black people successfully coming together to transform their society with images of black people enduring pain inflicted by the powers that be."

It is for theological reasons that Della and Robert pass through "Gilead as if it were a foreign and a hostile country" (Robinson, *Home* 338). The reference is to Genesis (15.13), when God tells Abram, later Abraham, that his people will be enslaved and oppressed for 400 years before God judges that nation and compensates those who had been so long dispossessed. And it is for this reason that Della and Robert never actually enter Jack's home, "would not walk in the door" (337), but Glory, in a state of religious near-ecstasy, "knew it would have answered a longing of Jack's if he could even imagine that their spirits had passed through that strange old house" (337).[10] "Imagine they had walked in the door, Jack," Glory might say then, and it would be like imagining Ruth's house burning, something that only God sees happening and that only God has a name for.[11] The future is in God's hands, in other words, and one person "could never change anything" (337). For all that *Gilead* and *Home* are beautiful works, racial reconciliation in these novels can only be achieved by the grace of God, and a nation in which blacks and whites could live in the same house would be a heavenly paradise.

Morrison's Homes

Morrison's frequently quoted observation that "[t]he Bible wasn't part of my reading, it was part of my life" (qtd. in Ruas 97) is enough to illustrate the dissymmetry between her religious experience and Robinson's: the Bible was part of Morrison's life, but Robinson's life is part of the Bible. God has named Robinson's existence, and she takes joy in reading in the world the miracle of the divine text. The world cites the Word, as John Ames cites John Ames cites John Ames. But any attempt to repeat this with Morrison results in a somewhat different conclusion. In Morrison's *Song of Solomon,* for example, Macon Dead cites Macon Dead cites Macon Dead, but his name is not anything like pure soul embodied but is "scrawled in perfect thoughtlessness by a drunken Yankee in the Union Army" (18). The Bible is neither the first nor the last word in this world.[12] Therefore, if Robinson's *Home* puts its faith in a heaven which has room for all, in her essay "Home" (1998) Morrison expresses impatience with the belief that a world without negative race discrimination is so impossible that it can only be conceived of as a New Jerusalem: "[A] world, one free of racial hierar-chy, is usually imagined or described as dreamscape—Edenesque, utopian, [...] ideal, millennial, a condition possible only if accompanied by the Messiah" (3). In contrast, she desires something more humanly achiev-able, looking "to develop nonmessianic language to refigure the raced community" (11) and saying, "I prefer to think of a-world-in-which-race-does-*not*-matter as something other than [...] the father's house of many rooms. I am thinking of it as home" (3).[13] Morrison's influential thinking on home in this essay, which itself references *Song of Solomon*, *Tar Baby* (1981), *Beloved*, and *Jazz* (1992), feeds directly into her later novels, so that, as Yvette Christiansë observes, it "comments upon and cites *Paradise* while it is still being written, which novel later appears as the citation of 'Home,' itself cited by [Morrison's] novel *Home*" (5). This chapter, there-fore, moves from *Paradise*, and the idea of a community founded on the basis of an apparent covenant with God, to the idea of home, or, more specifically, from the idea of a spiritual paradise to a haunted home.

Quoting *Jazz* (221), Morrison writes in "Home" of a place "[w]ith a doorway never needing to be closed" (9), says that she wants to imagine "the concrete thrill of borderlessness" (9), and then, quoting *Paradise* (8–9), writes of a place where a woman "if she felt like it she could walk out the yard and on down the road [...] beyond, because nothing around or beyond considered her prey" ("Home" 9–10). She concludes that the "description is meant to evoke not only the safety and freedom outside the race house, but to suggest contemporary searches and yearnings for social space that is psychically and physically safe" (10). This home can be situated within the context of a self-contradictory hospitality. The thrill of borderlessness suggests Derrida's concept of an unconditional hospitality that says yes to whatever or whoever turns up, including to the woman who walks out beyond and is nowhere considered an enemy or target. But this unlimited hospitality of visitation is always already limited by a hos-pitality of invitation suggested by the (perhaps concrete) doorway which, while never needing to be closed, can be closed, or need not be open. Morrison knows this. When she asks for freedom outside and inside and for safety outside and inside, she knows she is addressing "a law of hospi-tality which violently imposes a contradiction on the very concept of hos-pitality in fixing a limit to it" (Derrida, "Hostipitality" 4). But she would welcome the necessary violence that any invitation inflicts on freedom over the greater violence of a "safe" world with no foreigners, no others, no future, because "the idea of absolute peace is the idea of absolute vio-lence" (Hägglund 84).

The terror of absolute peace is evident in *Paradise*. The quoted description above is being offered by one of nine men who, even as he thinks proudly of this untroubled woman, is "stalking females" he considers prey (Morrison, *Paradise* 9).[14] The security that he offers one woman, the right to a life and a home and a community, is what he denies the other, but more than this, he believes that to secure absolutely a home for one requires denying it to the other, that the conservation of the one is effected by the destruction of the other. There are then two places in play here: the town of Ruby is the home in this man's vision, where "people were free and protected" (8), but the Convent, where he hunts the "outside woman" (279), 17 miles from the town, is the place with "a door that has never been locked" (285), meaning that these two places become, in Morrison's "Home," the one hoped-for home. What is it in *Paradise* that divides this borderless home into a place that a man cherishes and a place that he must violently destroy? It is the ghost and the exorcism of the ghost.

Ruby's history begins with an original act of conjuration. In the USA of the Reconstruction Era and after, the future town's own Jacob and Esau are the twins "known as Coffee and Tea" (Morrison, *Paradise* 302). The two are close, but things change when the black brothers are told to dance by white men with a pistol, and Tea complies while Coffee takes a bullet in the foot. Coffee now sees in Tea "something that shamed him. [...] Not because he was ashamed of his twin, but because the shame was in himself" (303), and so, to drive out the shame that resides within him, he removes himself from his brother. Tea becomes the ghost that "[f]ew knew and fewer remembered" (302). Coffee, "a misspelling of Kofi, probably" (192), known to his descendants as Big Papa and known to the inhabitants of Ruby as one of the Old Fathers (like the Patriarchs of the Old Testament), renames himself Zechariah Morgan, perhaps after "Zacharias, father of John the Baptist? or the Zechariah who had visions?" (192).[15] After praying to his "Father" (96), he is visited by a more holy spirit than his lost brother, a small man in a black suit who appears to have been summoned by Zechariah to walk ahead of him and lead the way to a promised land. The journey takes time, "God's time" (98), and once there, "the man began to fade" (98). This is how Zechariah and 157 other freed slaves complete their exodus from Mississippi and Louisiana and, in 1889–1890, found the town of Haven in Oklahoma Territory, with God's apparent blessing even if not "at God's command" (Dalsgård 233). And when that town fails, it is Zechariah's twin grandsons, Deacon (Deek) and Steward Morgan, who lead the others further west, in what is by then the state of Oklahoma (following the amalgamation of Oklahoma Territory with the last existing Indian Territory and "the old Creek Nation which once upon a time a witty government called 'unassigned land'" [Morrison, *Paradise* 6]), to found Ruby in 1950. The Calvinistic belief in individual predestination found in Robinson's work, therefore, extends to a wider preoccupation in Morrison's novel with a community's believed or stated destiny.[16] She establishes the town's story within existing narratives of God-willed migration and settlement, both within the broader Abrahamic tradition and the related American one that extends from the Puritan vision of "a city upon a hill" (Winthrop 158) through to the idea of American exceptionalism and a manifest destiny.[17] The town of Ruby also displays a defining characteristic of some incarnations of American exceptionalism: its isolationism. The town's isolation, 90 miles from anywhere, seems both to nourish what is exceptional about it and avoid its corruption. But it is an instilled separationism.[18] As the town's story of its inception explains:

> [N]either the founders of Haven nor their descendants could tolerate anybody but themselves. On the journey from Mississippi and two Louisiana parishes to Oklahoma, the one hundred and fifty-eight freedmen were unwelcome on each grain of soil from Yazoo to Fort Smith. Turned away by rich Choctaw and poor whites […], they were nevertheless unprepared for the aggressive discouragement they received from Negro towns already being built. (Morrison, *Paradise* 13)

And, in response to this inhospitality, in response to a felt division or "a new separation: light-skinned against black" (194), the town becomes equally exclusive, repeating "the very violent 'disallowing' that generated the community's diasporic quest for home-as-haven in the first place" (Dobbs 110). They welcome no one who is not a member of the nine intact families who originally founded the community and who have skin of such a blue-black color that the teacher Patricia Best labels them eight-rock after a coal-mine's deepest levels. This is a pure black town, so self-contained that the "two words [outsider and enemy] mean the same thing" (Morrison, *Paradise* 212) and so closed to others that death itself cannot enter and there is only still life. "Was death blocked from entering Ruby?" (199); no one had died in the town for over 20 years.

The novel, however, also presents an alternative to the home as a promised land, or as the final destination of a chosen people, in a discussion between Pat Best and the Reverend Richard Misner. Misner wants the certainties of a home on earth and not the promises of a home in heaven, or even the expectation of a heaven on earth, or God's shining city on a hill. He asks Best:

> But can't you even imagine what it must feel like to have a true home? I don't mean heaven. I mean a real earthly home. Not some fortress you bought and built up and have to keep everybody locked in or out. A real home. Not some place you went to and invaded and slaughtered people to get. Not some place you claimed, snatched because you got the guns. Not some place you stole from the people living there, but your own home, where if you go back past your great-great-grandparents, past theirs, and theirs, past the whole of Western history, past the beginning of organized knowledge, past pyramids and poison bows, on back to when rain was new, before plants forgot they could sing and birds thought they were fish, back when God said Good! Good!—there, right there where you know your own people were born and lived and died. Imagine that, Pat. That place. (Morrison, *Paradise* 213)

Misner's answer to the empty dream of home as an impossible ideal or always-future utopia, a place that may never exist, is to believe that it did once exist, that it remains a reality to be tapped. This place is not an isolated fortress, nor does it have to be purchased from Indians, but it has God's blessing. For Misner, it is Africa, not a new Eden but the original Eden, the very same. This earthly home might seem at first to be closer to that which Morrison hopes for in "Home," but Africa and Haven, the origin and the end, are not the footfalls between which a step is traced, but instead each is the same return to the father's house of many rooms. Like Robinson's repetitions, they are the return of and to the spiritual home.

The alternative to a return to Africa, as Misner warns Best, is that, "[i]f you cut yourself off from the roots, you'll wither" (Morrison, *Paradise* 209), but she responds, "Roots that ignore the branches turn into termite dust" (209). Best is well placed to discuss the roots of Ruby because she has dedicated years to "a collection of family trees; the genealogies of each of the fifteen families. Upside-down trees, the trunks sticking in the air, the branches sloping down" (187). Misner would trace these lines back and further back to the presumed unity of the root, but Best is more than aware that such a tracing would exclude her because her branch has been rather grafted on to the Ruby tree and does not grow straight from the original ground. Her mother, Delia, was "a wife of sunlight skin, a wife of racial tampering" (197), from outside the eight-rock families. And Best believes that it was because of her mother's lighter skin that the men of the town (because the women did try) couldn't rouse themselves to help her and instead let her and her baby die in childbirth. Best's family tree, therefore, has a branch ignored by the roots, a phantom limb from which hangs the name of her dead baby sister, Faustine.[19] The ghosts must be remembered because, as Deborah Madsen argues, "To forget is to censor [...]. Morrison's work challenges the assumptions and exclusions of American exceptionalism by reinstating the history that exceptionalism would forget" (152); or, more radically, Katrine Dalsgård argues, "Morrison deconstructs the original ideal, suggesting that it is inevitably entwined with a violent marginalization of its non-exceptionalist other" (237).

Morrison's *Song of Solomon* addresses at greater length the nature of tracing roots, with its plot structured around the climbing of one such upside-down family tree and the discovery of the other voices that can be heard in any name or naming. The novel trails the youngest Macon Dead, known as Milkman, as he follows in his aunt Pilate's tracks on a journey which leads him first to learn his grandfather's "real name," Jake (Morrison, *Song of Solomon* 54), and then to discover his "original home" (270). Home is Shalimar (259), pronounced "*Shalleemone*" (261), misremembered as "Charlemagne or something like that" (244), repeated as "*Sugarman*" (6), and named for Milkman's great-grandfather, also known as Solomon.[20] It is the song of the Shalimar children, "singing '*Solomon* don't leave me' instead of '*Sugarman*'" (302), that enables Milkman to piece together the story of his family and to read it even in the landscape around him, in places called "Solomon's Leap and Ryna's Gulch" (302), the latter named for his great-grandmother.[21] The revelation that Solomon's leap was back to Africa, that "[s]ome of those old Africans they brought over here as slaves could fly. A lot of them flew back to Africa" (322), could be read as support for Misner's position that "Africa is our home, Pat, whether you like it or not. [...] There was a whole lot of life before slavery" (*Paradise* 210). But this would be to ignore the place of the phantom in this family tree also and the visitations of the specter of Jake, the first Macon Dead.[22] He appears to Pilate just after the birth of her daughter and, "[c]lear as day, her father said, 'Sing. Sing,' and later he leaned in at the window and said, 'You can't just fly on off and leave a body'" (*Song of Solomon* 147). What Pilate hears as an instruction, to sing, is really a secret bequest, her mother's name, which she "never knew" (294), passed on to her as she herself becomes a mother. This is also what Milkman learns, that his grandmother's "name was Sing. [...] She always bragged how she was never a slave. Her people neither" (243) because "Sing's name was Singing Bird" (322) and her mother, Heddy, was a Native American. The varieties of Solomon's name are matched now by the change from Singing Bird to Sing Byrd, the "[n] ames that bore witness" (330), prompting Milkman to consider "what lay beneath the names" of the New World and what it had been known as before its beginning: "The Algonquins had named the territory he lived in Great Water, *michigami*. How many dead lives and fading memories were buried in and beneath the names of the places in this country" (329)? Alongside the African root, therefore, the specter reveals a root in (what is called) America also. And, significantly, while the African root leads back to the oldest father in the family tree, the American root is aligned with the women in the family, springing from an unknown father and Heddy.[23]

Side-by-side with a lineage defined by the paternal flight to Africa, therefore, Morrison sets another maternal line of descent, defined now by the flight of "the Byrd family" (Morrison, *Song of Solomon* 284) and embodied in the figure of Pilate. Pilate, about whom it is asked, "Pilot Dead. She do any flying?" (283), and of whom it is said, "Without ever leaving the ground, she could fly" (336), is truly a Bird. It is even as if she were born from an egg since "[o]ne fact was certain: Pilate did not have a navel" (294).[24] What Milkman inherits from Pilate, he inherits through the egg: the day before he is born, Pilate tells his mother, "A little bird'll be here with the morning" (9); the baby comes "with a caul" (10), as if born with the "shell" of the womb (and meaning that "he'll see ghosts" [10]); when he and Pilate first meet, she offers him a soft-boiled egg (39); and when Milkman declares to Guitar, "I'm a soft-fried egg" (115), the response is, "Then somebody got to bust your shell" (116). When he leaps at the end of the novel, therefore, he is honoring Pilate's legacy and following as much in his great-grandmother's path as his great-grandfather's, leaping between the two. This is not unlike Jake also, who "was the only one Solomon tried to take with him" to Africa (323), but who is dropped and falls to Heddy, falling from one branch of the family to the other, between the old father and the new mother. Milkman's, Pilate's, and Jake's history does not in this way become, as Pat Best might fear, "some kind of past with no slavery in it" (*Paradise* 210) because the step between the absent father and the adopted mother takes in without naming it (like a specter) the origins of American slavery. Slavery does not have a single origin, a single root; it steps from one continent to another and does not find a foothold in either, like those who "perished on the slave ships midway between a place in African history and a place in the history of American slavery" and "never made it into any text" (Wyatt 479). The history of this slavery takes in the Middle Passage, Africa and America, lost parents, and all those unhoused not in an abstract but in a very real way: the systems of slavery, including kidnap, purchase, and rape, work to dissolve families and to deny parenthood and kinship. The systems of slavery deliberately obscure (biological, genealogical, familial, tribal, national) ties, so the story of slavery must step into these absences. As Pat Best insists, "Slavery *is* our past" (Morrison, *Paradise* 210), and that past is haunting.

MORRISON'S HAUNTS

For Morrison, as for Best, "a true home" (*Paradise* 213) has a past and a future, which is to say that it is not defined or limited by a God-given beginning and end. It is borderless for being between borders and not just between these God-set borders, which can only ever be part of the same, single, indivisible line, but between all the limits and differences that the branches of a spreading family tree might reach toward. That is how the Convent comes to be a home in *Paradise*. "Convent," of course, is a misnomer, because it was never a convent as such. It was formerly an embezzler's mansion and then the Christ the King School for Native Girls, but by 1976 it has evolved into a welcome and welcoming place of refuge for a group of four women, Mavis, Gigi, Seneca, and Pallas, who are enjoying the hospitality of Connie even though she might not be in a position to offer it. It's hard to know who the master of this house is, or who has authority over it:

> The title was in the hands of the benefactress' foundation (which was down to its principal now), so the house and land were not exactly church owned; the argument, therefore, was whether it was subject to current and back taxes. But the real question for the assessor was why in a Protestant state a bevy of strange Catholic women with no male mission to control them was entitled to special treatment. (232–233)

The Convent "is" between church and state, between Protestant and Catholic, between Native and American, between the appropriate, the inappropriate, and misappropriated, between the virginal and the promiscuous, between the gift and the theft, between women and men, between Ruby and a world. And it is when no one has sovereignty over the place, when the last figure of official authority, the Reverend Mother Mary Magna, would be dead but for Connie's light-giving life support, that the specter appears because living on land you can never truly own means living with the consequent ghosts.[25]

It is in 1968 (the year of Martin Luther King's assassination) that the Convent welcomes Mavis, although it would be more accurate to say that Mavis's arrival opens its doors rather than the Convent opens its doors to receive her.[26] The scene of her arrival establishes some of the important differences between the Convent and Ruby. Within minutes of their meeting, Connie, by identifying herself as a worker in the house rather than its owner and by unexpectedly declaring to Mavis, "Maybe I go with you" (Morrison, *Paradise* 39), and so suggesting a future of roles reversed, has thrown open also the categories of master, host, and guest. This continues when Connie goes upstairs, so that Mavis is alone in the kitchen to greet Soane Morgan when she visits from Ruby. The "Excuse me" (38) with which the newly arrived Mavis had hailed Connie is echoed in the "Oh, excuse me" with which Soane acknowledges Mavis, now the unfamiliar host. Unlike Connie, however, Soane, because she is from Ruby, is quick to set the proper boundaries: she is to be called "Mrs. Morgan" and not "hon" (43), and when she remarks that she "scared this girl to death. Never saw a stranger inside here before" (43), she draws clear and parallel distinctions between stranger and family, outside and inside, death and life. But, as Connie has already observed to Mavis, "Scary things not always outside. Most scary things is inside" (39); however much we want to believe that the inside is only ever that which does not terrify us (the inside thus being identified exactly as that which does not terrify us), it is always already scarily haunted by what we believe is out there. Between Soane and Mavis, therefore, between the insider outside of Ruby and the outsider inside the Convent, the novel's first ghost appears: "Connie's entrance was like an apparition" (43).

From that point on, the ghosts will appear on reclaimed ground and in the presence of women.[27] They do not appear to the men because the men will not admit to not being masters in their own houses; they have sought to "reproduce the master's voice and its assumptions of the all-knowing law of the white father" (Morrison, "Home" 4). The man will not countenance the ghost whose haunting provokes the laws of hospitality, the laws of guest and host, because the man would only ever be the master. Even when a woman extends a welcome, as Still observes, this "hostess implies hospitality offered by the master of the house, the true host, *by means* of his woman, the hostess. Her authority is thus only a delegated one, and she is an intermediary" (21). Hospitality stands at the threshold of sexual difference and of racial difference, as when a black maid answers the door of her white master's house, as when businesses have separate entrances for black and for white customers, as when there are hotels that do not admit black people, as when there is racial segregation of any form. This threshold dividing black and white does not exist in the Convent, which is borderless for having an infinite number of borders. It is a "new space [...] formed by the inwardness of the outside, the interiority of the 'othered,' the personal that is always embedded in the public. In this new space one can [...] iterate difference that is prized but unprivileged" (Morrison, "Home" 12). As written by Morrison, the five women's personalities, behaviors, speech, experiences, histories, sufferings, and longings are recognizable but individual, and they cannot be assigned to any particular ethnic group. Instead, they can be understood within Morrison's work on "[h]ow to be both free and situated; how to convert a racist house into a race-specific yet nonracist home" (5). Referring to the novel's famous first line—"They shoot the white girl first" (*Paradise* 3)—Morrison comments that she was "trying first to enunciate and then eclipse the racial gaze altogether" ("Home" 9), trying to write "a place where race both matters and is rendered impotent" (9). A reader might spend some time trying to identify the white girl before wondering why that should, in the end, be important. But Morrison's corresponding insight is to identify the point at which race appears, the way in which color as a racial marker only exists in the Convent when a man enters, "shoots open a door that has never been locked" (*Paradise* 285), and then shoots "the white girl" (3). The men commit violence here not by breaching the threshold but by establishing it, thereby defining sexual and racial difference.[28] An open door is marked so that it might be opened, a limit is established to that it might be transgressed, and this limitation is also the legitimation of that transgression as it sets the valued self against a threatening or unworthy other. So, there is sexual difference, racial difference, and then animal difference: the women run "like panicked does" (18) and the men hunt their "game" (18).

The actions of the men, and their every violent effort to defend an inside from a polluting outside, or to protect their community from degeneration, are ultimately an attempt to quarantine life from death: "Unadulterated and unadulteried [...]. That was their deal. For Immortality" (Morrison, *Paradise* 217). Indeed, the life of the community does seem guaranteed when all signs of their crime disappear, and there are "[n]o bodies. Nothing" (292). But death returns to Ruby, all the same, when Save-Marie, Sweetie and Jeff Fleetwood's youngest child, is the first to die in the town in 23 years. This return of death to the community, which means (recalling the earlier discussion of Robinson) the return of a future to the community, the possibility of a future and a future possibility, coincides with the reappearance of ghosts, without which there cannot be life and death. The ghosts in question are the five murdered, disappeared Convent women. After Save-Marie's funeral, Billie Delia wonders, "When will they return?" (308), and then they do return as a series of scenes shows us their unexpected afterlife: Gigi appears to her father, also enjoying a future after having his death sentence commuted; Pallas and her baby are seen by her mother; Mavis eats with her daughter; Seneca is found by her mother; and Connie is with Piedade "in Paradise" (318).

The question then is if these scenes occur inside or outside the book proper. The nine men who enter the Convent, and who stand for the nine families who established the town, are represented by the nine chapters of the book. However, the hyphenated title of the final chapter, "Save-Marie," reflects the fact that the chapter differs structurally from all the others in being composed of two parts. The second part, given over to the ghosts, might even be a new chapter except that it has no title of its own and "Save-Marie" continues to appear in the header. It stands as an addendum to the book, just as the Convent is situated outside of the town and just as the women of the Convent are outside of the cherished purity of the nine families. The ghosts are housed, therefore, in an annex to *Paradise* which, like the Derridean supplement, somehow also annexes the whole by taking possession of the name. As the last words of the novel put it, they are "here in Paradise" (Morrison, *Paradise* 318), which is to say "here in *Paradise*," here inside this novel from which they are excluded, haunting it.

These are not the first ghosts to haunt Morrison's texts. Another concluding word, "Beloved," names, of course, both Morrison's best-known ghost and the novel in which she appears (Morrison, *Beloved* 316). *Beloved*, like *Paradise*, is a spectral thing, because its 28 chapters mark 28 days of posthumous existence, of a life between two deaths, marking the days after Sethe's "death" as a slave and before the death by her own hands of her daughter. Kathleen Brogan reads the novel "as a literary 'secondary burial,' in which the victims of the slave trade, whom Morrison calls the 'unceremoniously buried,' are exhumed to be reburied properly in the novel's narrative tomb," but she finds that the "novel's troubled conclusion portrays trauma as an open grave, an ultimately irresolvable haunting" (27). Anderson transfers this haunting to the novel itself, arguing that "Morrison creates a specter and a spectral novel, two Beloveds that haunt both characters and readers" (81); Hungerford grants it a "sort of supernatural status" (103); and Petar Ramadanovic, too, proceeds "[a]s if the novel about haunting, this novel bearing in its title the name of a ghost, were itself a ghost. A ghost-writing, written by another hand. Written by the hand of another, Beloved" (98), he determines that "*Beloved* duplicates, repeats on the level of its structure, both the haunting effect of the ghost's appearance and the *revenant*'s trajectory" (105). Morrison's ghost writing is equally apparent in the novels *Jazz* and *Love* (2003), "whose narrators are like spectres who know everything and answer to every name" (Christiansë 42). As JaeEun Yoo shows, L, the first-person narrator in *Love*, "intimates that her full name is Love, the same as the title of the novel" (155), but the never-fully-present name "serves as a visual trace of haunting in/of the text" (155–156). Moreover, when it is revealed near the end of the novel that L is already dead when she begins her narration, then "the reader realizes that s/he has been haunted by L's ghost all the time s/he was reading" (155), and since "none of *Love*'s characters are affected by the existence of L's phantom, haunting in this case works exclusively on the reader" (155). Yoo argues that "L, the ghost narrator of *Love*, transforms the novel into a ghost [...] that intrudes into the reader's safe reading space" (154), but she notes also that L invites the reader into the novel's "spectral space" (165).[29] And Morrison herself declares, "I am very happy to hear that my books haunt. That is what I work very hard for, and for me it is an achievement that they haunt readers" (qtd. in Anderson 65).

In the end, the writing becomes a haunted home in which the reader— you—dwells. The final "Beloved" of Morrison's *Beloved* (316), the "Paradise" of *Paradise* (318), and the "*home*" of *Home* (147) all have the effect of returning you to the title of the novel, as if you have returned to 124 Bluestone Road, to the threshold of the text, to the doorway never needing to be closed, and are about to enter again a place you haven't ever left. Who invites you in, you who are always already within? *Jazz*, too, brings you face to face with the text when it concludes with the injunction to "[l]ook where your hands are. Now" (229), and in *A Mercy*, Florens opens her narration with "Don't be afraid" (1), as if she were a ghost who might scare you to death. True, she's addressing her former lover, the blacksmith, but her words sweep you in also, especially when she writes that "[s]trange things happen all the time everywhere. You know. I know you know. One question is who is responsible? Another is can you read? If a pea hen refuses to brood I read it quickly [...]. Other signs need more time to understand" (1–2). Who is responsible for what happens? Who is responsible for what happens when you read? And what happens when you can or cannot read (responsibly)? In discussing *Beloved*, Peterson responds:

> How do we begin to consider Sethe's act in such a way that it remains neither unintelligible nor fully intelligible? If to read is to make intelligible, and thus in some way to own or possess what one reads [...] then reading will always reveal its own violence. We must begin, then, by avowing this violence as the condition of our reading. (77)

As argued in "Haunts," no reading is absolutely faithful, absolutely respectful, absolutely responsible, or answers to the other so absolutely that there is no longer an other, only the same. To make absolute peace with the text would be to exact absolute violence on it. In place of this, we commit the lesser violence which Peterson describes, which is doubly hurtful for being also a betrayal of the other, and yet this is the only way to speak with the other. The responsible reading must be irresponsible. You can read only as you cannot read. Can you not read? Morrison asks you "to respond" to the text "on the same plane as an illiterate or preliterate reader would" (qtd. in Hungerford 104) because, Hungerford argues, "learning to read coincides with taking possession of supernatural power" (96). But this learning to read is always a learning to read otherwise, in other ways, in the ways of the other: "Often there are too many signs [...]. I sort them and try to recall, yet I know I am missing much" (Morrison, *A Mercy* 2).[30]

Florens is a black woman writing in a dead white man's house, "a grand house of many rooms rising on a hill" (Morrison, *A Mercy* 33) with "snakes in the gate" (159); it is the master's, the father's, God's now-forsaken house, a house that never accommodated a living soul, another American Paradise. When others see her "shadow," they believe that the master must have "climbed out of his grave to visit his beautiful house" (141), that "having died in it he will haunt its rooms forever"

(41): "They did not see him—his definitive shape or face—but they did see his ghostly blaze" (142). The black woman's shadow appears as a white specter.[31] Meanwhile, Florens writes on the fabric of the building, "carving letters" on the floors and walls of the house until "[t]here is no more room in this room" (158). Then, she is "remembering. You won't read my telling. You read the world but not the letters of talk. [...] If you never read this, no one will" (158). So, she imagines setting fire to the house, not to see the spirit of the words break free and transcend this plane but because "these words need the air that is out in the world. Need to fly up then fall, fall like ash" (159), like the ash from ovens or burning towers. Can you read these unwritten words in the world? Can you mark them? It would be like repeating the unspoken, or tracing a picture in the air, or finding graves in the falling snow, or stepping into fitting footprints. It would be like the way "It was not a story to pass on" (*Beloved* 316) is followed by "This is not a story to pass on" (316), and the "It was" translates untranslatably into "This is."[32] Each word, all of this, says, with Florens, "I last" (*A Mercy* 159).

Morrison's *Home*[33]

Morrison's *Home* is a, perhaps, too-brief novel with not enough flesh on its bones. And yet, the awkward articulation of its skeletal form also gives it a peculiar and useful directness. It is the story of the resurrection of Frank Money, and as it tells of the return of life to his body, it tells also of his return home. When the novel opens, he is restrained in a hospital bed, with no memory of how he got there, and "playing dead" (Morrison, *Home* 7) to get out of there, as he once did on the battlefield during the Korean War. Discharged and back in the USA for about a year, he remains traumatized by the experiences of war and of witnessing his friends Mike and Stuff die. These memories muscle their way into his being, so that "a dream dappled with body parts" (16) sees him waking to "socks folded neatly on the rug like broken feet" (17). Such experiences and the resulting episodes have already cost him his relationship with his girlfriend Lily, with whom, Frank says, "I felt like I'd come home" (68); they have left him unhoused, literally (like Robinson's transients) and figuratively (where, unlike in Robinson, to be unhoused does not equate to spiritual growth), to the extent that when "he mused about what it might be like in those houses, he could imagine nothing at all" (19–20). A letter calling him to help his sister Ycidra, or Cee, has given him renewed purpose. Cee's own rootlessness was guaranteed after she "was born on the road" (44), and now she, too, lies close to death, the victim of the eugenicist experiments of her white doctor employer: the summons from a fellow employee reads, "Come fast. She be dead if you tarry" (8), while the Reverend Locke's comment that "doctors need to work on the dead poor so they can help the live rich" (12) places her with the dead also. So, Frank is drawn by his sister back into "the real world" (17), still "haunted" (76) and "spooked" (77) by the war, and occasionally accompanied on his journey home to Lotus, Georgia by the "dream ghost" (34) of a "little man in [a] pale blue zoot suit" (33; see also 27).

The closer Frank gets to home, the more he can remember the war without being torn apart by those feelings and by the loss of his friends. But, more than anything, what haunts Frank is his wartime memory of a young Korean girl who, each day, would crawl through the bamboo to scavenge something from the trash, a reminder of Cee and him *"trying to steal peaches off the ground under Miss Robinson's tree"* (Morrison, *Home* 94). Frank cannot forget seeing a soldier approach her, and then "[s]*he smiles, reaches for the soldier's crotch, touches it. It surprises him.[…] [H]e blows her away*" (95). Says Frank, *"I think the guard felt more than disgust. I think he felt tempted and that is what he had to kill"* (96). But, when he rescues Cee and they are home again in Lotus, where Cee tries to reconcile herself to the fact of her ruined womb and to the ghost of a future baby, lost and "waiting to be born" now to "some other mother" (131), then Frank can admit to the truth of his memory: *"Maybe that little girl wasn't waiting around to be born to her. Maybe it was already dead, waiting for me to step up and say how. I shot the Korean girl in her face. I am the one she touched"* (133). But of course what Frank reacts so violently against here, it would appear, is not just the temptation that the girl offers but the relation between the girl and his sister, between *"the two missing teeth"* (95) of the Korean girl and Cee's matching "two baby teeth" (120). What he kills in her face is the recognition that he might once have been tempted in the same way by Cee, and this ghost of a girl that once was and of a child that will never be is the uncanny offspring of their incestuous bond.

Except, the Korean girl and Cee are most obviously linked in Frank's mind by the act of crawling through bamboo or grass, and the secret at the heart of his memory of creeping with Cee through long grass is not an incestuous desire but another repression, of the sight of a man being buried in a shallow grave. They had trespassed in a field in order to see the horses, but they found themselves also witnessing the black man's burial. Frank remembers "[g]*uarding her, finding a way through tall grass and out of that place, not being afraid of anything*" (Morrison, *Home* 104), but he remarks, "*I really forgot about the burial. I only remembered the horses. They were so beautiful. So brutal. And they stood like men*" (5). Morrison establishes that the horses stood like men even as men were being treated as animals, because the buried man is a father who was forced to fight to the death against his own son in "men-treated-like-dog fights" (138). Throughout the novel, the victims of brutality and war are seen by those who perpetrate that violence as other (or, in their eyes, less) than human, whether it is the army that treats returning soldiers "like dogs" (18), Cee being experimented upon like a lab rat (and then rescued in a "markedly nonviolent" way [114]), or the Korean girl who might be a "tiger" (94) or a "dog" (94) and picked through the garbage as "raccoons" do (95).[34] This violence haunts Frank, more generally in the form of waking dreams and more specifically in the specter of the zoot-suited man, the ghost of the father whose burial Frank witnessed and forgot. Creating a home, therefore, means reconciling himself to the ghosts of his past and tracing the chain of violence back through his war experiences to that earlier dehumanizing event. Once he admits to killing the Korean girl, Frank can also address the forgotten man; he and Cee return to the field, dig up the man's bones, and rebury him, observed by "a small man in a funny suit swinging a watch chain. And grinning" (144). "Here Stands A Man" (145), says the marker on the grave, to remind us that horses should rise up like men and men not fight like animals.

Frank and Cee bury the man in a quilt of "unimpressive pattern and haphazard palette" (Morrison, *Home* 142), placing "the bone-filled quilt that was first a shroud, now a coffin" (144) beneath a "sweet bay tree—split down the middle, beheaded, undead—spreading its arms, one to the right, one to the left" (144). If Pilate's name "looked like a tree hanging in some princely but protective way over a row of smaller trees" (*Song of Solomon* 18), does Ycidra's name somehow stand for this sweet bay tree? The tree's arms spread "in the glow of a fat cherry-red sun" (*Home* 145) certainly mirror Cee's "legs spread open to the blazing sun" (124) to heal her, the patchwork bundle in the grave like her patched-up, barren womb, and the bones of the father like the ghost of the child.[35] But this is not meant to be a grim ending. The tree is "[*h*]*urt right down the middle* [*b*]*ut alive and well*" (147), and indeed, the bay tree "is a symbol of resurrection, for seemingly dead trees often revive from the roots" (Watts 26). Morrison's *Home* has Frank and Cee revive from their buried roots and return to the mortal world. Nor is their story without its legacy. The final words of the novel—"*Let's go home*" (147)—deliberately name the novel also and mark it as the product of this sibling relationship.[36] The novel is both the issue of the damaged womb and its fertile likeness, switching voices and stitching together the stories of Ycidra and Frank, of Lenore and Salem Money, of Lily Jones's "yearning for her own house" (75), and of Sarah Williams and more.[37] The novel is the haunted womb, tomb, room, home for all who are no longer and are not yet, the "*already dead*" (133) and those "waiting to be born" (131). It births ghosts and lets them live again. And where ghosts live, so do we.

NOTES

1. In Morrison's *The Bluest Eye* (1970), the difference between a "peripheral existence" and "outdoors" was "like the difference between the concept of death and being, in fact, dead" (11).

2. For Parham, "To describe an object or event as haunting is to latch onto something important about the meaning it gains in representation and circulation" (2).

3. If we live in a world that needs to be told (and it does need to be told) that #BlackLivesMatter (following the movement begun by Alicia Garza, Patrisse Cullors, and Opal Tometi), then the terrifying specter of racism, always already there, has returned. Do you need examples? As I write this, at this very moment, here, now, in New York, hundreds march in Union Square in protest at the death of Freddie Gray, a 25-year-old black man, in police custody in Baltimore. That city is now under curfew after three days of sometimes violent unrest following Gray's funeral. Protests are taking place across the country, including in Ferguson, Missouri, where, just eight months ago, the fatal shooting by police of the unarmed 18-year-old black man, Michael Brown, following a robbery provoked scenes similar to what we see now in Baltimore. These scenes seem so frightfully familiar: during the eruption of civil disorder in the USA that followed the 1968 assassination of Martin Luther King, the rioting in Baltimore was so severe that the city still bears its marks today, even as black bodies and minds are marked again and again by white racism.

4. On Morrison's ghosts, in addition to Anderson and Peterson, see especially Brogan, Del Villano, Erickson, Gordon, Lawrence, and Ramadanovic.

5. The indissociability of a hospitality shown to the living and to the dead is signaled in one of the opening scenes of Robinson's *Gilead* where Ames and his father tend the graves of his grandfather and the "other folks" in a neglected graveyard in rural Kansas in 1892, and in turn, they experience the kindness of a local woman who "cried when we said goodbye" (14).

6. How easy it is to conjure the ghost, as the previous chapter does by speaking of Della and never acknowledging that she is black.

7. The novels repeatedly link blackness and namelessness: when Ames is con-
    sidering how Boughton might take the news of Jack's black son, he says,
    "He certainly took to that other child" (Robinson, *Gilead* 263), connect-
    ing the black boy to the nameless white child; in *Lila*, the Robert Boughton
    who is Ames's son receives two baptisms after the water spills during the
    first (248, 250), suggesting that one (but which one?) is meant for the
    Robert Boughton who is Jack's son. In both cases, the implication is that
    God will ensure that the black child is not denied a name.

8. Glory's observation that, "[i]f Jack had been here, he'd have felt that ter-
    rible shock of joy [...] that floods in like blood pushing into a limb that has
    been starved of it, like a wild rescue, painful and wonderful and humbling"
    (Robinson, *Home* 336–337), recalls Amy's comment to Sethe in Morrison's
    Beloved that "[a]nything dead coming back to life hurts" (46).

9. In her interview with Painter, Robinson comments that "Iowa was one of
    three states where interracial marriage was legal, so it might have been a
    home to [Jack's] family" (Painter and Robinson 486), but she continues,
    "An irony of *Home* is that for Jack's wife and son Gilead might well be a
    foreign and perhaps a hostile country. I fervently wish that America will
    some time be a good, welcoming home to her whole family" (490).
    Robinson is here quoting from *Home*, in which Glory wonders "how
    would [Della] forgive this, that she felt she had to come into Gilead as if it
    were a foreign and hostile country?" (338).

10. Glory continues, "Just the thought of it might bring him back, and the
    place would seem changed, to him and to her" (Robinson, *Home* 337),
    and Hopper is rightly critical of this idea that "a dream of interracial con-
    nection (however partial and temporary) is enough to give meaning to a
    white person's entire life," especially when "Glory does nothing to make
    even this modest fantasy of a family reunion come true" because "mere
    longing is enough: It feels more satisfying than any real attempt at inter-
    racial community or racial justice could ever be."

11. If, as Robinson says, Lila's "destitution has made her purely soul, unac-
    commodated" (qtd. in "Interview"), Della and Robert are purely black
    souls who cannot be accommodated in Gilead but must pass through, like
    ghosts, before arriving in God's promised land. These properly black souls,
    whose future is determined by their blackness, can be contrasted with the
    "spooks" (6) of Philip Roth's *The Human Stain*. The "self-incriminating"
    (6) use of the word "spook" leads to the retirement of Coleman Silk
    because the absent students to whom he applies it turn out to be black.
    But Silk himself is black and has been passing as white since he was 27. It
    would seem natural, therefore, to argue that Silk's use of the word
    "spooks" names his blackness, raising the specter of his secret racial past
    and consequently, and ironically, banishing him from the white life that,
    Robinson seems to suggest, could only be God-given in 1953 (and yet,

Coleman's brother Walter, in contrast, goes "through civil rights to get to his human rights" [327]). However, countering this, at no point does Roth equate Silk's use of the word "spooks" with his blackness, or reduce his secret to his blackness; Silk "doesn't just want to be white" (335), and it is hardly "[a]s though his accomplishments were rooted in nothing but shame" (335). Instead, "all the excess goes into the secret" (335), so that the word "spooks" does not mean only black souls. Where Robinson twice at the end of novels presents the (same) secret of blackness as a revelation, Roth introduces the fact that Silk is a black man relatively early on and without fanfare, with a reference to the Silks as "a model Negro family" (86). It is not his color but his secret that so confounds Zuckerman at the end, the secret that meant Silk "never again lived outside the protection of the walled city that is convention. Or, rather, lived, at the same moment, entirely within and, surreptitiously, entirely beyond" (335). Therefore, what Robinson presents in terms of "the fairy tale of purity" (341), Roth presents in terms of mere, devastating propriety. For Robinson, the excluded, the properly black, are promised a future by God; for Roth, the excluded, the improperly white, are denied a future by a very human idea of what is proper, of what is conventional. The message is that, in a world that is not given by God but shaped by humans, things can change.

12. Robinson's God knows all the secret stories that attach to a name, but in Morrison's novels, God's story itself is embellished as characters read it in wholly surprising ways and generate from it new or unseen names. Turning to the Bible for his daughter's name, therefore, Pilate's father, "since he could not read a word, chose a group of letters that seemed to him strong and handsome; [...] he had copied the group of letters out on a piece of brown paper" (Morrison, *Song of Solomon* 18). He responds to the appearance of the word, its materiality, and when he then returns the piece of paper to the Good Book saying, "It come from the Bible. It stays in the Bible" (19), he also adds to the Bible. This family tradition, as it becomes, of "the getting of names out of" the Bible (207), such as Magdalene called Lena and First Corinthians, both acknowledges and also supplements the traditional authority of the Bible as it reads the canonical text in noncanonical, illiterate ways. Hungerford observes that much "criticism argues that Morrison is revising or criticizing the aspects of the Bible she invokes [...]. What she borrows, more than anything else, is the Bible's status as a sacred book" (99), so that it "becomes one with her personal, writerly authority" (105).

13. Morrison and Derrida were among the group of writers who, in 1993, founded the International Parliament of Writers, which sought to create a network of Cities of Refuge for writers suffering persecution in their own states.

14. Each man has his own reason to kill: "to own it [...] no control [...] to blame [...] the shame [...] loose women [...] another grudge [...] betrayal [...] pride" (Morrison, *Paradise* 277–279).

15. See also Burr: "As Jacob changes his name to Israel to become the father of many nations, Coffee changes his name to Zechariah to become the Big Papa of his own people" (161).

16. The same enlargement from the self to the society applied also for the Puritans of the Massachusetts Bay colony, who, as Madsen notes, "believed that God intervened in human history to work the salvation not only of individuals but also entire communities or nations" (3). On *Paradise* and exceptional destiny, see Dalsgård, who is "aware that arguing that Morrison discerns an exceptionalist strain in African American discourse is risky business" (235) but does so convincingly, noting that to "say that *Paradise* narrates the African American community's aspirations in exceptionalist terms, however, is not the same as to say that Morrison accepts such terms" (236); and Fraile-Marcos, who, in contrast, argues that "Morrison does not eschew the aspiration, characteristic of the Puritan rhetoric and passed onto American civil religion, of creating an ideal community identifiable with an earthly paradise" (30).

17. When Madsen says, in a summation which references all three ideas, "America and Americans are special, exceptional, because they are charged with saving the world from itself and, at the same time, America and Americans must sustain a high level of spiritual, political and moral commitment to this exceptional destiny" (2), she underlines the extent to which these ideas have helped foster a single, seemingly incontrovertible narrative of America as both singular and exemplary. The myth of this exceptional destiny, however, despite being the myth of a God-given future, has not been inherited by the USA from its colonial forebears simply and purely but, whether providentially or fortuitously, has repeatedly been adopted and adapted in a way that is a measure of its historical appeal and usefulness but cannot fail to remark also on its own origins and therefore its own evolution. Madsen shows how the Puritans explicitly "identified themselves as latter-day Israelites occupying the New Canaan by divine decree" (17), and even though the American Revolution reframes exceptionalism "away from its religious origins" (36) and "represents the American errand as the creation of a secular state that is purified of the corruption of European politics and a social structure based on inherited title" (37), the sense of the USA as God's country survives. In fact, as Stephanson recounts, "When the imposing trio of John Adams, Benjamin Franklin, and Thomas Jefferson gathered in the summer of 1776 to select a national seal, each of the last two—deists at best—suggested images from the story of Exodus, while the Calvinistic Adams was, oddly enough, the one to propose a theme from classical antiquity" (4–5).

18. Stephanson, who uses the phrase "manifest destiny" in the wider sense of a "providentially assigned role of the United States to lead the world to new and better things" (xii) rather than in reference only to American

expansionism, establishes that "[t]his vision has been a constant throughout American history, but historically it has led to two quite different ways of being toward the outside world. The first was to unfold into an exemplary state *separate* from the corrupt and fallen world, letting others emulate it as best they can. The second [...] was to push the world along by means of regenerative *intervention*. Separation, however, has been the more dominant of the two" (xii).

19. Nor does America's exceptional destiny have a simple, undivided root. Madsen notes, "There is a key difference between the Puritan colonies at Boston and at Plymouth in terms of their mission in the New World" because, whereas Winthrop and the nonseparatists "represented themselves as necessarily repeating the sacred history of the Israelites" (16), Bradford, on the other hand, "did not present the settlement as a necessary stage in salvation-history, nor did he extrapolate from scripture a future destiny for the colony" (17).

20. Milkman's quest is set in motion by the presumed contents of the green sack that is Pilate's "inheritance" (Morrison, *Song of Solomon* 163). Milkman's father believes it holds gold, and Pilate believes she has the bones of a slain white man, but Milkman, in the end, can tell her, "You've been carrying your father's bones—all this time" (333). Like a name, therefore, the green sack is loaded with competing narratives of power, historical violence, and family, and yet again, the true inheritance is the secret inheritance.

21. Like Auster's dead men when they are returned to their ghostly lives, once Milkman finds that the "children were singing a story about his own people," or singing his own story, then he is "as eager and happy as he had ever been in his life" (Morrison, *Song of Solomon* 304).

22. A recognizably Derridean specter, when Macon and Pilate see their father's ghost, they don't see their father but rather "a man who looked like their father" (Morrison, *Song of Solomon* 169), so they "didn't know it was him at first" (40). Pilate remarks that "he was lookin at us and not lookin at us at the same time" (43).

23. Again, Madsen reminds us that "[t]he early years of the nineteenth century saw the rising power of exceptionalist mythology translated into the concept of Manifest Destiny—the belief that the United States was destined to bring a perfected form of democratic capitalism to the entire North America continent—and a policy of forcible removal of those tribes that would not retreat before the advance of democratic civilisation" (47–48) and, moreover, that "[o]nce the tribal people have been destroyed or subjugated those forces of destruction do not simply go away; [...] the injustices, the destructiveness, the racial hostility, the lack of humanity evinced by those colonists who claimed to be God's elect would become the historical legacy inherited by the future generations" (68).

24. Thanks to the students of my American literature class for helping me to realize this.

25. Relatedly, in *A Mercy* (2008), set in America in the years 1682–1690, Morrison writes of "three unmastered women [...]. None of them could inherit; none was attached to a church or recorded in its books. Female and illegal, they would be interlopers, squatters, if they stayed on after Mistress died, subject to purchase, hire, assault, abduction, exile" (56).

26. On *Paradise* and the post-civil rights era, see Schur, who argues that "Morrison's novel translates paradise from a universalized concept that transcends race, class, nation, and gender toward a smaller, more local, and more 'manageable' version" (276).

27. In the Convent, the ghosts of Mavis's twins, Merle and Pearl, grow old; in a foreclosed house, Dovey greets an unfamiliar man and lets him "pass through" (Morrison, *Paradise* 91) but knows "once she asked him his name, he would never come again" (92); and Soane dreams of her dead sons, so dispossessed of their bodies in the Vietnam War that on their return their father asks, "Are all the parts black? Meaning, if not, get rid of the white pieces" (112).

28. Morrison says, "It's interesting and important to me that once the women are coherent and strong and clean in their interior lives, they feel saved. They feel impenetrable. So that when they are warned of the attack on the Convent, they don't believe it" (qtd. in Dalsgård 245); in other words, when "the Convent women [a]re no longer haunted" (Morrison, *Paradise* 266), they too believe they have full life and can keep death out.

29. Burr reads *Love* in the context of Derrida's work on hospitality, arguing that "hospitality appears in the novel as a readiness to welcome the other and a readiness not to be ready for the encounter" (169) but that the novel "becomes the documentation of what causes this idealized love or hospitality to fail" (167).

30. In Morrison's *Paradise*, the younger generation in Ruby howl "at the notion of remembering invisible words you couldn't even read by tracing letters you couldn't pronounce" (83). On Morrison and (il)literacy, see also Brogan (62); Christiansë, who refers to "a language of interruption, of stuttering, of lacunae, and of sound without meaning" (22); Erickson, who argues that "the spectral presence of Beloved, positing a figure that demands the reader's exploration and supplementation, foregrounds [Morrison's] wish to register the interpretive demands of the history of slavery" (113); Gordon (145–150); and Page, who points out that *Song of Solomon* "requires the reader, like Milkman, to develop new strategies and sensitivities of interpretation" (101). It is worth noting that, in Roth's *The Human Stain*, Faunia's "illiteracy had been an act [...]. A source of power? [...] Not rejecting learning as a stifling form of propriety but trumping learning by a knowledge that is stronger and prior" (297).

31. DeLillo's *End Zone* (1972) is and is not about Taft Robinson, "the first black student to be enrolled at Logos College," who, you are told, "rightly or wrongly, no more than haunts this book. I think it's fitting in a way. The mansion has long been haunted (double metaphor coming up) by the invisible man" (3), by the racial spook and the spiritual father. In Morrison's *Paradise*, the violation of the paradisiacal "mansion-turned-Convent" (10) reinforces the impossibility of exorcising the specter of racism, of patriarchy, of nationalism, of heteronormativity, of the "father who never stays quite dead but reasserts himself repeatedly in multitudinous reincarnations" (Friedman 242).

32. Remember, "the ghost is just passing through" (Derrida, *Specters of Marx* 136); "Time seems to pass" (DeLillo, *Body Artist* 7); "Nothing lasts, and yet nothing passes, either. And nothing passes just because nothing lasts" (Roth, *Human Stain* 52); "I pass through the world" (Robinson, *Home* 301); "It was not a story to pass on" (Morrison, *Beloved* 315); "Remember" (Auster, *Invention of Solitude* 172).

33. With Morrison's *Home*, Robinson's twinning novel has its own twin. It takes place earlier in the 1950s but could almost have been written to set Jack's family on a different path to home. Quite coincidentally, where Jack appeals to the church of Ames, Morrison's protagonist's first step on the way is the AMEZ Church (African Methodist Episcopal Zion Church). His, therefore, will be an alternative destination.

34. Even Lenore, Frank and Cee's grandmother, loses the services of Jackie, the one person who can abide her, when she beats Jackie's dog, named Bobby like the dog of which Emmanuel Levinas writes.

35. "Room and tomb, tomb and womb, womb and room" (Auster, *Invention of Solitude* 159–160). The rhyming of womb and tomb appears also in Morrison's *Beloved*, with Sethe's "knees wide open as any grave" (11) to buy Beloved a name on her headstone. The bone-filled quilt recalls Pilate's green sack in *Song of Solomon* holding her father's bones. And if Pilate is born of the lifeless body of her mother, what is born of the ghost of Beloved? Says Gordon, "The ghost is not other or alterity as such, ever. It is (like Beloved) pregnant with unfulfilled possibility" (183).

36. In the same way, Morrison notes that "the last word in the book" *Beloved* sees "the resurrection of the title, the character, and the epigraph" ("Home" 5).

37. Among those Frank encounters is Billy, whose son Thomas's arm remains paralyzed after he was shot by a police officer because he "had a cap pistol. Eight years old, running up and down the sidewalk pointing it" (Morrison, *Home* 31). In November 2014, a twelve-year-old black boy, Tamir Rice, was fatally shot by a police officer in Cleveland, Ohio, while playing with a pellet gun.

WORKS CITED

Aldrich, Marcia. 1989. The Poetics of Transience: Marilynne Robinson's *Housekeeping. Essays in Literature* 16: 127–140.

Alfano, Chiara. 2012. Strange Frequencies—Reading *Hamlet* with Derrida and Nancy. *Derrida Today* 5(2): 214–231.

Alford, Steven E. 1995. Mirrors of Madness: Paul Auster's *The New York Trilogy*. *Critique: Studies in Contemporary Fiction* 37(1): 17–33.

Anderson, Melanie. 2013. *Spectrality in the Novels of Toni Morrison*. Knoxville: University of Tennessee Press.

Appelbaum, David. 2009. *Jacques Derrida's Ghost: A Conjuration*. Albany: State University of New York Press.

Auster, Paul. 1990. Book of the Dead. In *Ground Work: Selected Poems and Essays 1970–1979*, 183–210. London: Faber and Faber.

———. 1992. *The Music of Chance*. London: Faber and Faber.

———. 1993. *Leviathan*. London: Faber and Faber.

———. 1994. *Mr Vertigo*. London: Faber and Faber.

———. 1997a. *City of Glass*. In *The New York Trilogy*, 1–132. London: Faber and Faber.

———. 1997b. *Ghosts*. In *The New York Trilogy*, 133–196. London: Faber and Faber.

———. 1997c. *The Locked Room*. In *The New York Trilogy*, 197–314. London: Faber and Faber.

———. 1998a. *The Invention of Solitude*. London: Faber and Faber.

———. 1998b. *The Red Notebook*. In *The Art of Hunger: Essays, Prefaces, Interviews and* The Red Notebook, 341–379. London: Faber and Faber.

———. 1998c. Twentieth-Century French Poetry. In *The Art of Hunger: Essays, Prefaces, Interviews and* The Red Notebook, 199–237. London: Faber and Faber.

© The Editor(s) (if applicable) and The Author(s) 2016
D. Coughlan, *Ghost Writing in Contemporary American Fiction*,
DOI 10.1057/978-1-137-41024-5

————. 1999. *In the Country of Last Things*. London: Faber and Faber.

————. 2003a. Invisible Joubert. In *Collected Prose*, 720–728. London: Faber and Faber.

————. 2003b. *The Book of Illusions: A Novel*. London: Faber and Faber.

————. 2004. *Moon Palace*. London: Faber and Faber.

————. 2005. *The Brooklyn Follies*. London: Faber and Faber.

————. 2006. *Travels in the Scriptorium*. London: Faber and Faber.

————. 2008a. *Oracle Night*. London: Faber and Faber.

————. 2008b. *Timbuktu*. London: Faber and Faber.

Auster, Paul, and Michel Contat. 1996. The Manuscript in the Book: A Conversation. Trans. Alyson Waters. *Yale French Studies* 89: 160–187.

Auster, Paul, and Joseph Mallia. 1998. Interview with Joseph Mallia. In *The Art of Hunger: Essays, Prefaces, Interviews and* The Red Notebook, 274–286. London: Faber and Faber.

Barone, Dennis. 1995. Introduction: Paul Auster and the Postmodern American Novel. In *Beyond the Red Notebook: Essays on Paul Auster*, ed. Dennis Barone, 1–26. Philadelphia: University of Pennsylvania Press. Penn Studies in Contemporary American Fiction.

Barrett, Laura. 2009. Framing the Past: Photography and Memory in *Housekeeping* and *The Invention of Solitude*. *South Atlantic Review* 74(1): 87–109.

Bennington, Geoffrey. 1993. Derridabase. In *Jacques Derrida*, by Geoffrey Bennington and Jacques Derrida, trans. Geoffrey Bennington, 3–316. Chicago: University of Chicago Press. Religion and Postmodernism.

Bergland, Renée L. 2000. *The National Uncanny: Indian Ghosts and American Subjects*. Hanover: University Press of New England. Reencounters with Colonialism: New Perspectives on the Americas.

Bernstein, Stephen. 1995. Auster's Sublime Closure: *The Locked Room*. In *Beyond the Red Notebook: Essays on Paul Auster*, ed. Dennis Barone, 88–106. Philadelphia: University of Pennsylvania Press. Penn Studies in Contemporary American Fiction.

Blanchot, Maurice. 1992. *The Step Not Beyond*. Trans. Lycette Nelson. Albany: State University of New York Press. Intersections: Philosophy and Critical Theory.

————. 1999a. *Death Sentence*. Trans. Lydia Davis. In *The Station Hill Blanchot Reader: Fiction and Literary Essays*, ed. George Quasha, 129–187. Barrytown: Station Hill/Barrytown.

————. 1999b. Literature and the Right to Death. Trans. Lydia Davis. In *The Station Hill Blanchot Reader: Fiction and Literary Essays*, ed. George Quasha, 359–399. Barrytown: Station Hill/Barrytown.

————. 1999c. The Gaze of Orpheus. Trans. Lydia Davis. In *The Station Hill Blanchot Reader: Fiction and Literary Essays*, ed. George Quasha, 437–442. Barrytown: Station Hill/Barrytown.

———. 1999d. *The One Who Was Standing Apart From Me.* Trans. Lydia Davis. In *The Station Hill Blanchot Reader: Fiction and Literary Essays,* ed. George Quasha, 261–339. Barrytown: Station Hill/Barrytown.

———. 2000. The Instant of My Death. In *The Instant of My Death. Demeure,* by Maurice Blanchot and Jacques Derrida, trans. Elizabeth Rottenberg, 1–11. Stanford: Stanford University Press. Meridian: Crossing Aesthetics.

Blanco, María del Pilar. 2012. *Ghost-Watching American Modernity: Haunting, Landscape, and the Hemispheric Imagination.* New York: Fordham University Press.

Blanco, María del Pilar, and Esther Peeren, eds. 2010. *Popular Ghosts: The Haunted Spaces of Everyday Culture.* New York: Continuum.

———. 2013. Introduction: Conceptualizing Spectralities. In *The Spectralities Reader: Ghosts and Haunting in Contemporary Cultural Theory,* eds. María del Pilar Blanco and Esther Peeren, 1–27. New York: Bloomsbury Academic.

Bonca, Cornel. 2002. Being, Time, and Death in DeLillo's *The Body Artist. Pacific Coast Philology* 37: 58–68.

Boulter, Jonathan. 2011. *Melancholy and the Archive: Trauma, Memory, and History in the Contemporary Novel.* London: Continuum. Continuum Literary Studies Series.

Boxall, Peter. 2006. *Don DeLillo: The Possibility of Fiction.* London: Routledge. Routledge Transatlantic Perspectives on American Literature 2.

Brault, Pascale-Anne. 1998. Translating the Impossible Debt: Paul Auster's *City of Glass. Critique: Studies in Contemporary Fiction* 39(3): 228–238.

Brauner, David. 2007. *Philip Roth.* Manchester: Manchester University Press. Contemporary American and Canadian Writers.

Brogan, Kathleen. 1998. *Cultural Haunting: Ghosts and Ethnicity in Recent American Literature.* Charlottesville: University Press of Virginia.

Brown, Mark. 2007. *Paul Auster.* Manchester: Manchester University Press. Contemporary American and Canadian Writers.

Budick, Emily Miller. 1996. The Haunted House of Fiction: Ghost Writing the Holocaust. *Common Knowledge* 5: 120–135.

Burke, William M. 1991. Border Crossings in Marilynne Robinson's *Housekeeping. MFS Modern Fiction Studies* 37(4): 716–724.

Burr, Benjamin. 2006. Mythopoetic Syncretism in *Paradise* and the Deconstruction of Hospitality in *Love.* In *Toni Morrison and the Bible: Contested Intertextualities,* ed. Shirley A. Stave, 159–174. New York: Peter Lang. African American Literature and Culture 12.

Buse, Peter, and Andrew Stott. 2002. Introduction: A Future for Haunting. In *Ghosts: Deconstruction, Psychoanalysis, History,* eds. Peter Buse and Andrew Stott, 1–20. Basingstoke: Palgrave Macmillan.

Castricano, Jodey. 2002. *Cryptomimesis: The Gothic and Jacques Derrida's Ghost Writing.* Montréal: McGill-Queen's University Press.

Channing, William Ellery. 1985. *William Ellery Channing: Selected Writings*. Ed. David Robinson. New York: Paulist Press. Sources of American Spirituality.

Christiansë, Yvette. 2013. *Toni Morrison: An Ethical Poetics*. New York: Fordham University Press.

Churchwell, Sarah. 2014. Marilynne Robinson's *Lila*—A Great Achievement in US Fiction. *The Guardian*, November 7.

Clark, Timothy. 1992. *Derrida, Heidegger, Blanchot: Sources of Derrida's Notion and Practice of Literature*. Cambridge: Cambridge University Press.

Cohen, Josh. 2000. Desertions: Paul Auster, Edmond Jabès, and the Writing of Auschwitz. *The Journal of the Midwest Modern Language Association* 33(3): 94–107.

———. 2007. Roth's Doubles. In *The Cambridge Companion to Philip Roth*, ed. Timothy Parrish, 82–93. Cambridge: Cambridge University Press. Cambridge Companions to Literature.

Coughlan, David. 2008. Paul Auster's Ghost Writers. In *Space, Haunting, Discourse*, eds. Maria Holmgren Troy and Elisabeth Wennö, 143–152. Newcastle: Cambridge Scholars.

Coughlan, David, Christoforos Diakoulakis, David Huddart, and Elizabeth Wijaya. 2016. Introduction: Survival of the Death Sentence. *Parallax* 22(1): 1–4.

Cowart, David. 2002. *Don DeLillo: The Physics of Language*. Athens: University of Georgia Press.

Dalsgård, Katrine. 2001. The One All-Black Town Worth the Pain: (African) American Exceptionalism, Historical Narration, and the Critique of Nationhood in Toni Morrison's *Paradise*. *African American Review* 35(2): 233–248.

Davis, Colin. 2007. *Haunted Subjects: Deconstruction, Psychoanalysis and the Return of the Dead*. Basingstoke: Palgrave Macmillan.

De Boer, Karin. 2002. Enter the Ghost/Exit the Ghost/Re-Enter the Ghost: Derrida's Reading of *Hamlet* in *Specters of Marx*. *Journal of the British Society for Phenomenology* 33(1): 22–38.

DeLillo, Don. 2000. *Mao II*. London: Vintage.

———. 2002. *White Noise*. London: Picador.

———. 2004a. *Cosmopolis*. London: Picador.

———. 2004b. *End Zone*. London: Picador.

———. 2007. *The Body Artist: A Novel*. London: Picador.

Del Villano, Bianca. 2007. *Ghostly Alterities: Spectrality and Contemporary Literatures in English*. Stuttgart: Ibidem. Studies in English Literatures 7.

Derrida, Jacques. 1972. *La Dissémination*. Paris: Editions de Seuil.

———. 1982. Différance. In *Margins of Philosophy*, trans. Alan Bass, 1–27. Brighton: Harvester.

———. 1986. *Glas*. Trans. John P. Leavey and Richard Rand. Lincoln: University of Nebraska Press.

————. 1989. *Memoires: For Paul de Man*. Trans. Cecile Lindsay et al. Rev. ed. New York: Columbia University Press. The Wellek Library Lectures.

————. 1991. *Of Spirit: Heidegger and the Question*. Trans. Geoffrey Bennington and Rachel Bowlby. Chicago: University of Chicago Press.

————. 1993a. *Aporias: Dying—awaiting* (*one another at*) *the "limits of truth"* (*Mourir—s'attendre aux "limites de la vérité"*). Trans. Thomas Dutoit. Stanford: Stanford University Press. Meridian: Crossing Aesthetics.

————. 1993b. Circumfession. In *Jacques Derrida*, by Geoffrey Bennington and Jacques Derrida, trans. Geoffrey Bennington, 3–315. Chicago: University of Chicago Press. Religion and Postmodernism.

————. 1994. *Specters of Marx: The State of the Debt, the Work of Mourning, and the New International*. Trans. Peggy Kamuf. New York: Routledge.

————. 1997a. Freud and the Scene of Writing. In *Writing and Difference*, trans. Alan Bass, 196–231. London: Routledge.

————. 1997b. Structure, Sign, and Play in the Discourse of the Human Sciences. In *Writing and Difference*, trans. Alan Bass, 278–293. London: Routledge.

————. 1998. *Of Grammatology*. Trans. Gayatri Chakravorty Spivak. Corrected ed. Baltimore: Johns Hopkins University Press.

————. 2000. Hostipitality. Trans. Barry Stocker and Forbes Morlock. *Angelaki* 5(3):3–18.

————. 2002. "Le Parjure," *Perhaps: Storytelling and Lying. In *Without Alibi*, ed. and trans. Peggy Kamuf, 161–201. Stanford: Stanford University Press. Meridian: Crossing Aesthetics.

————. 2003a. Following Theory. In *Life. After. Theory*, eds. Michael Payne and John Schad, 1–51. London: Continuum.

————. 2003b. *The Work of Mourning*. Eds. Pascale-Anne Brault and Michael Naas. Chicago: University of Chicago Press.

————. 2004a. The Double Session. In *Dissemination*, trans. Barbara Johnson, 187–316. London: Continuum.

————. 2004b. Outwork, Prefacing. In *Dissemination*, trans. Barbara Johnson, 1–65. London: Continuum.

————. 2004c. Plato's Pharmacy. In *Dissemination*, trans. Barbara Johnson, 67–186. London: Continuum.

————. 2007a. *Learning to Live Finally: An Interview with Jean Birnbaum*. Trans. Pascale-Anne Brault and Michael Naas. Hoboken: Melville House.

————. 2007b. My Chances/*Mes Chances: A Rendezvous with Some Epicurean Stereophonies. Trans. Irene Harvey and Avital Ronell. In *Psyche: Inventions of the Other*, eds. Peggy Kamuf and Elizabeth Rottenberg, vol. 1, 344–376. Stanford: Stanford University Press. Meridian: Crossing Aesthetics.

————. 2008. *The Animal That Therefore I Am*. Trans. David Wills. Ed. Marie-Louise Mallet. New York: Fordham University Press. Perspectives in Continental Philosophy.

———. 2011a. Border Lines. Trans. James Hulbert. In *Parages*, ed. John P. Leavey, 103–191. Stanford: Stanford University Press. Cultural Memory in the Present.

———. 2011b. Living On. Trans. James Hulbert. In *Parages*, ed. John P. Leavey, 103–191. Stanford: Stanford University Press. Cultural Memory in the Present.

———. 2011c. *Pace* Not(*s*). Trans. John P. Leavey. In *Parages*, ed. John P. Leavey, 11–101. Stanford: Stanford University Press. Cultural Memory in the Present.

———. 2014. *The Death Penalty*. Trans. Peggy Kamuf. Eds. Geoffrey Bennington, M. Crépon, and Thomas Dutoit. Vol. 1. Chicago: University of Chicago Press. The Seminars of Jacques Derrida.

Derrida, Jacques, and Anne Dufourmantelle. 2000. *Of Hospitality*. Trans. Rachel Bowlby. Stanford: Stanford University Press. Cultural Memory in the Present.

Derrida, Jacques, and Elisabeth Roudinesco. 2004. *For What Tomorrow: A Dialogue*. Trans. Jeff Fort. Stanford: Stanford University Press. Cultural Memory in the Present.

Derrida, Jacques, and Bernard Stiegler. 2002. *Echographies of Television: Filmed Interviews*. Trans. Jennifer Bajorek. Cambridge: Polity.

Dimovitz, Scott A. 2006. Public Personae and the Private I: De-Compositional Ontology in Paul Auster's *The New York Trilogy*. *MFS Modern Fiction Studies* 52(3): 613–633.

Di Prete, Laura. 2005. Don DeLillo's *The Body Artist*: Performing the Body, Narrating Trauma. *Contemporary Literature* 46(3): 483–510.

Dobbs, Cynthia. 2011. Diasporic Designs of House, Home, and Haven in Toni Morrison's *Paradise*. *MELUS: Multi-Ethnic Literature of the United States* 36(2): 109–126.

Domestico, Anthony. 2014. "Imagine a Carthage Sown with Salt": Creeds, Memory, and Vision in Marilynne Robinson's *Housekeeping*. *Literature and Theology* 28(1): 92–109.

Downey, Dara. 2014. *American Women's Ghost Stories in the Gilded Age*. Basingstoke: Palgrave Macmillan. Palgrave Gothic.

Eastman, Andrew. 2000. Paul Auster as Poet and Translator. In *Pioneering North America: Mediators of European Culture and Literature*, ed. Klaus Martens, 112–121. Würzburg: Königshausen & Neumann.

Erickson, Daniel. 2009. *Ghosts, Metaphor, and History in Toni Morrison's* Beloved *and Gabriel García Márquez's* One Hundred Years of Solitude. New York: Palgrave Macmillan.

Esteve, Mary. 2014. Robinson's Crusoe: *Housekeeping* and Economic Form. *Contemporary Literature* 55(2): 219–248.

Foster, Thomas. 1988. History, Critical Theory, and Women's Social Practices: "Women's Time" and *Housekeeping*. *Signs* 14(1): 73–99.

Fraile-Marcos, Ana María. 2003. Hybridizing the "City upon a Hill" in Toni Morrison's *Paradise*. *MELUS: Multi-Ethnic Literature of the United States* 28(4): 3–33.

Fredman, Stephen. 2004. "How to Get Out of the Room That Is the Book?" Paul Auster and the Consequences of Confinement. In *Paul Auster*, ed. Harold Bloom, 7–41. Philadelphia: Chelsea House. Bloom's Modern Critical Views.

Friedman, Ellen G. 1993. Where Are the Missing Contents? (Post)Modernism, Gender, and the Canon. *PMLA* 108(2): 240–252.

Garber, Marjorie B. 2010. *Shakespeare's Ghost Writers: Literature as Uncanny Causality*. New York: Routledge. Routledge Classics.

Gardner, Thomas. 2001. Enlarging Loneliness: Marilynne Robinson's *Housekeeping* as a Reading of Emily Dickinson. *The Emily Dickinson Journal* 10(1): 9–33.

Geyh, Paula E. 1993. Burning Down the House? Domestic Space and Feminine Subjectivity in Marilynne Robinson's *Housekeeping*. *Contemporary Literature* 34(1): 103.

Gooblar, David. 2011. *The Major Phases of Philip Roth*. London: Continuum.

Gordon, Avery. 2008. *Ghostly Matters: Haunting and the Sociological Imagination*. New ed. Minneapolis: University of Minnesota Press.

Hägglund, Martin. 2008. *Radical Atheism: Derrida and the Time of Life*. Stanford: Stanford University Press. Meridian: Crossing Aesthetics.

Hall, Joanne. 2006. The Wanderer Contained: Issues of "Inside" and "Outside" in Relation to Harold Gray's *Little Orphan Annie* and Marilynne Robinson's *Housekeeping*. *Critical Survey* 18(3): 37–50.

Hartshorne, Sarah D. 1990. Lake Fingerbone and Walden Pond: A Commentary on Marilynne Robinson's *Housekeeping*. *Modern Language Studies* 20(3): 50–57.

Hedrick, Tace. 1999. "The Perimeters of Our Wandering Are Nowhere": Breaching the Domestic in *Housekeeping*. *Critique: Studies in Contemporary Fiction* 40(2): 137–151.

Hedrick, Tace, and Marilynne Robinson. 1992. On Influence and Appropriation. *The Iowa Review* 22(1): 1–7.

Herzogenrath, Bernd. 1999. *An Art of Desire: Reading Paul Auster*. Amsterdam: Rodopi. Postmodern Studies 21.

Holy Bible: New International Version. 1992. London: Hodder & Stoughton.

Hopper, Briallen. 2014. Marilynne Robinson in Montgomery. *Religion and Politics: Fit For Polite Company*. December 22. http://religionandpolitics. org/2014/12/22/marilynne-robinson-in-montgomery/

Howe, Irving. 1972. Philip Roth Reconsidered. *Commentary* 54(6): 69–77.

Hungerford, Amy. 2010. *Postmodern Belief: American Literature and Religion since 1960*. Princeton: Princeton University Press.

Ibsen, Henrik. 2013. *Ghosts*. Trans. William Archer. *Project Gutenberg*. The Project Gutenberg Literary Archive Foundation.

Interview with Marilynne Robinson. October, 2014. *Goodreads*. http://www.goodreads.com/interviews/show/983.Marilynne_Robinson

Johnson, Barbara. 2004. Translator's Introduction. In *Dissemination*, by Jacques Derrida, trans. Barbara Johnson, vii–xxxv. London: Continuum.

Kelly, Adam. 2013. *American Fiction in Transition: Observer-Hero Narrative, the 1990s, and Postmodernism*. New York: Bloomsbury.

Keskinen, Mikko. 2006. Posthumous Voice and Residual Presence in Don DeLillo's *The Body Artist*. In *Novels of the Contemporary Extreme*, eds. Alain-Philippe Durand and Naomi Mandel, 31–40. London: Continuum. Continuum Literary Studies.

Kessel, Tyler. 2008. A Question of Hospitality in Don DeLillo's *The Body Artist*. *Critique: Studies in Contemporary Fiction* 49(2): 185–204.

Kirch, Claire. 2008. At Home with Marilynne Robinson. *Publishers Weekly*, July 14: 22.

Kirkby, Joan. 1986. Is There Life After Art? The Metaphysics of Marilynne Robinson's *Housekeeping*. *Tulsa Studies in Women's Literature* 5(1): 91–109.

Kohn, Robert E. 2014. Secrecy and Radiance in Marilynne Robinson's *Gilead* and *Home*. *The Explicator* 72(1): 6–11.

Kröger, Lisa, and Melanie Anderson. 2013. Introduction. In *The Ghostly and the Ghosted in Literature and Film: Spectral Identities*, eds. Lisa Kröger and Melanie Anderson, ix–xvi. Newark: University of Delaware Press.

Latz, Andrew Brower. 2011. Creation in the Fiction of Marilynne Robinson. *Literature and Theology* 25(3): 283–296.

Lawrence, David. 1997. Fleshly Ghosts and Ghostly Flesh: The Word and the Body in *Beloved*. In *Toni Morrison's Fiction: Contemporary Criticism*, ed. David L. Middleton, 231–246. New York: Garland. Critical Studies in Black Life and Culture 30.

Lee, Hermione. 1992. Introduction. In *To the Lighthouse*, by Virginia Woolf, ed. Stella McNichol, ix–xliii. London: Penguin Books. Penguin Twentieth-Century Classics.

Leise, Christopher. 2009. "That Little Incandescence": Reading the Fragmentary and John Calvin in Marilynne Robinson's *Gilead*. *Studies in the Novel* 41(3): 348–367.

Little, William G. 1997. Nothing To Go On: Paul Auster's *City of Glass*. *Contemporary Literature* 38(1): 133–163.

Loevlie, Elisabeth. 2013. Faith in the Ghosts of Literature. Poetic Hauntology in Derrida, Blanchot and Morrison's *Beloved*. *Religions* 4(3): 336–350.

Longmuir, Anne. 2007. Performing the Body in Don DeLillo's *The Body Artist*. *MFS Modern Fiction Studies* 53(3): 528–543.

Loomis, Taylor. 2009. Nathan Zuckerman: The Tantalized and Tantalizing Hero of History. *Philip Roth Studies* 5(2): 179–188.

Luckhurst, Roger. 1996. "Impossible Mourning" in Toni Morrison's *Beloved* and Michèle Roberts's *Daughters of the House*. *Critique: Studies in Contemporary Fiction* 37(4): 243–260.

———. 2002. The Contemporary London Gothic and the Limits of the "Spectral Turn". *Textual Practice* 16(3): 527–546.

Lucy, Niall. 2004. *A Derrida Dictionary*. Malden: Blackwell.

Luszczynska, Ana M. 2013. *The Ethics of Community: Nancy, Derrida, Morrison, and Menendez*. New York: Bloomsbury.

Madsen, Deborah L. 1998. *American Exceptionalism*. Edinburgh: Edinburgh University Press. BAAS Paperbacks.

Malmgren, Carl D. 1995. Detecting/Writing the Real: Paul Auster's *City of Glass*. In *Narrative Turns and Minor Genres in Postmodernism*, eds. Theo D'haen and Hans Bertens, 177–201. Amsterdam: Rodopi. Postmodern Studies 11.

Mattessich, Stefan. 2008. Drifting Decision and the Decision to Drift: The Question of Spirit in Marilynne Robinson's *Housekeeping*. *Differences: A Journal of Feminist Cultural Studies* 19(3): 59–89.

McKean, Matthew. 2010. Paul Auster and the French Connection: *City of Glass* and French Philosophy. *LIT: Literature Interpretation Theory* 21(2): 101–118.

McLennan, Rachael. 2012. Anne Frank Rescues the Writer in Paul Auster's *The Invention of Solitude*. *Journal of American Studies* 46(3): 695–709.

McMullen, Ken, dir. 2006. *Ghost Dance*. Perf. Pascale Ogier and Jacques Derrida. Mediabox.

Meese, Elizabeth A. 1986. *Crossing the Double-Cross: The Practice of Feminist Criticism*. Chapel Hill: University of North Carolina Press.

Moraru, Christian. 2001. *Rewriting: Postmodern Narrative and Cultural Critique in the Age of Cloning*. Albany: State University of New York. Postmodern Culture.

Morrison, Toni. 1994. *The Bluest Eye*. London: Picador.

———. 1998a. Home. In *The House That Race Built: Original Essays by Toni Morrison, Angela Y. Davis, Cornel West, and Others on Black Americans and Politics in America Today*, ed. Wahneema H. Lubiano, 3–12. New York: Vintage Books.

———. 1998b. *Song of Solomon*. London: Vintage.

———. 1999. *Paradise*. London: Vintage.

———. 2001. *Jazz*. London: Vintage.

———. 2004. *Love*. London: Vintage.

———. 2006. *Beloved*. New York: Knopf. Everyman's Library 268.

———. 2009. *A Mercy*. London: Vintage.

———. 2013. *Home*. London: Vintage.

Naas, Michael. 2008. House Organs: The Strange Case of the Body Artist and Mr. Tuttle. *Oxford Literary Review* 30(1): 87–108.

Nealon, Jeffrey T. 1996. Work of the Detective, Work of the Writer: Paul Auster's *City of Glass*. *MFS Modern Fiction Studies* 42(1): 91–110.

Nel, Philip. 2002. Don DeLillo's Return to Form: The Modernist Poetics of *The Body Artist*. *Contemporary Literature* 43(4): 736–759.

Nicol, Bran. 2009. *The Cambridge Introduction to Postmodern Fiction*. Cambridge: Cambridge University Press. Cambridge Introductions to Literature.

O'Donnell, Patrick. 1983. The Disappearing Text: Philip Roth's *The Ghost Writer*. *Contemporary Literature* 24(3): 365–378.

OED Online. 2015. *Oxford English Dictionary*. Oxford University Press.

Osteen, Mark. 2005. Echo Chamber: Undertaking *The Body Artist*. *Studies in the Novel* 37(1): 64–81.

Page, Philip. 1995. *Dangerous Freedom: Fusion and Fragmentation in Toni Morrison's Novels*. Jackson: University Press of Mississippi.

Painter, Rebecca M., and Marilynne Robinson. 2009. Further Thoughts on A Prodigal Son Who Cannot Come Home, on Loneliness and Grace: An Interview with Marilynne Robinson. *Christianity and Literature* 58(3): 484–492.

Parham, Marisa. 2010. *Haunting and Displacement in African American Literature and Culture*. New York: Routledge.

Patterson, Orlando. 1982. *Slavery and Social Death: A Comparative Study*. Cambridge: Harvard University Press.

Peeren, Esther. 2014. *The Spectral Metaphor: Living Ghosts and the Agency of Invisibility*. New York: Palgrave Macmillan.

Peterson, Christopher. 2007. *Kindred Specters: Death, Mourning, and American Affinity*. Minneapolis: University of Minnesota Press.

Pierpont, Claudia Roth. 2013. *Roth Unbound: A Writer and His Books*. New York: Farrar, Straus and Giroux.

Plato. 1973. *Phaedrus and Letters VII and VIII*. Trans. Walter Hamilton. Harmondsworth: Penguin. Penguin Classics.

Poe, Edgar Allan. 2008. The Man of the Crowd. In *Selected Tales*, ed. David Van Leer, 84–91. Oxford: Oxford University Press. Oxford World's Classics.

Radway, Janice. 2008. Foreword. In *Ghostly Matters: Haunting and the Sociological Imagination*, by Avery Gordon, new ed., vii–xiii. Minneapolis: University of Minnesota Press.

Ramadanovic, Petar. 2001. *Forgetting Futures: On Memory, Trauma, and Identity*. Lanham: Lexington.

Ravits, Martha. 1989. Extending the American Range: Marilynne Robinson's *Housekeeping*. *American Literature* 61(4): 644–666.

Robinson, Marilynne. 1987. Let's Not Talk Down to Ourselves. *New York Times Book Review*, April 5: 11.

———. 1993. My Western Roots. In *Old West—New West: Centennial Essays*, ed. Barbara Howard Meldrum, 165–172. Moscow: University of Idaho Press.

———. 2005a. *Gilead*. London: Virago.

———. 2005b. *Housekeeping*. London: Faber and Faber.

———. 2007. Onward, Christian Liberals. In *The Best American Essays*, ed. David Foster Wallace, 210–220. Boston: Houghton Mifflin.

———. 2009. *Home*. London: Virago.

———. 2014. *Lila*. London: Virago.

Roth, Philip. 1993. A Bit of Jewish Mischief. *New York Times Book Review*, March 7: 1+.

———. 1994. *Operation Shylock: A Confession*. New York: Vintage.

———. 1995a. *The Ghost Writer*. New York: Vintage.

———. 1995b. *Zuckerman Unbound*. New York: Vintage.

———. 1996. *The Anatomy Lesson*. New York: Vintage.

———. 2001. *The Human Stain*. London: Vintage.

———. 2005. *The Counterlife*. London: Vintage.

———. 2007. *Exit Ghost*. London: Cape.

Rowen, Norma. 1991. The Detective in Search of the Lost Tongue of Adam: Paul Auster's *City of Glass*. *Critique: Studies in Contemporary Fiction* 32(4): 224–234.

Royle, Nicholas. 1995. *After Derrida*. Manchester: Manchester University Press.

———. 2003a. *Jacques Derrida*. London: Routledge. Routledge Critical Thinkers.

———. 2003b. *The Uncanny*. Manchester: Manchester University Press.

———. 2008. Clipping. *Forum: University of Edinburgh Postgraduate Journal of Culture & the Arts* 0.7: n. pag.

———. 2010. *Quilt*. Brighton: Myriad Editions.

Ruas, Charles. 1994. Toni Morrison. In *Conversations with Toni Morrison*, ed. Danille Kathleen Taylor-Guthrie, 93–118. Jackson: University Press of Mississippi. Literary Conversations Series.

Rubenstein, Roberta. 1987. *Boundaries of the Self: Gender, Culture, Fiction*. Urbana: University of Illinois.

Russell, Alison. 1990. Deconstructing *The New York Trilogy*: Paul Auster's Anti-Detective Fiction. *Critique: Studies in Contemporary Fiction* 32(2): 71–84.

Saghafi, Kas. 2010. *Apparitions—Of Derrida's Other*. New York: Fordham University Press. Perspectives in Continental Philosophy.

Schaub, Thomas. 1995. Lingering Hopes, Faltering Dreams: Marilynne Robinson and the Politics of Contemporary American Fiction. In *Traditions, Voices, and Dreams: The American Novel since the 1960s*, eds. Melvin J. Friedman and Ben Siegel, 298–321. Newark: University of Delaware Press.

Schaub, Thomas, and Marilynne Robinson. 1994. An Interview with Marilynne Robinson. *Contemporary Literature* 35(2): 231–251.

Schur, Richard L. 2004. Locating *Paradise* in the Post-Civil Rights Era: Toni Morrison and Critical Race Theory. *Contemporary Literature* 45(2): 276–299.

Sconce, Jeffrey. 2000. *Haunted Media: Electronic Presence from Telegraphy to Television*. Durham: Duke University Press. Console-Ing Passions: Television and Cultural Power.

Segal, Alex. 1998. Secrecy and the Gift: Paul Auster's *The Locked Room*. *Critique: Studies in Contemporary Fiction* 39(3): 239–257.

Shakespeare, William. 1987. *The Tragedy of King Lear*. Ed. Russell A. Fraser. New York: New American Library. The Signet Classic Shakespeare.

———. 2006. *Hamlet*. Ed. Ann Thompson and Neil Taylor. London: Arden Shakespeare. The Arden Shakespeare.

Shiloh, Ilana. 2002. A Place Both Imaginary and Realistic: Paul Auster's *The Music of Chance*. *Contemporary Literature* 43(3): 488–517.

Shostak, Debra B. 2004. *Philip Roth: Countertexts, Counterlives*. Columbia: University of South Carolina Press.

Shy, Todd. 2007. Religion and Marilynne Robinson. *Salmagundi* 155/156: 251–264.

Smith, Rachel. 2006. Grief Time: The Crisis of Narrative in Don DeLillo's *The Body Artist*. *Polygraph: An International Journal of Culture and Politics* 18: 99–110.

Sorapure, Madeleine. 1995. The Detective and the Author: *City of Glass*. In *Beyond the Red Notebook: Essays on Paul Auster*, ed. Dennis Barone, 71–87. Philadelphia: University of Pennsylvania Press. Penn Studies in Contemporary American Fiction.

Spivak, Gayatri Chakravorty. 1995. Ghostwriting. *Diacritics* 25(2): 65–84.

Springer, Carsten. 2001. *A Paul Auster Sourcebook*. Frankfurt am Main: Peter Lang.

Sprinker, Michael, ed. 1999. *Ghostly Demarcations: A Symposium on Jacques Derrida's* Specters of Marx. London: Verso.

Stephanson, Anders. 1995. *Manifest Destiny: American Expansionism and the Empire of Right*. New York: Hill and Wang. A Critical Issue.

Still, Judith. 2013. *Derrida and Hospitality: Theory and Practice*. Edinburgh: Edinburgh University Press.

Sword, Helen. 2002. *Ghostwriting Modernism*. Ithaca: Cornell University Press.

Tabbi, Joseph. 2002. *Cognitive Fictions*. Minneapolis: University of Minnesota Press. Electronic Mediations 8.

Tanner, Laura E. 2006. *Lost Bodies: Inhabiting the Borders of Life and Death*. Ithaca: Cornell University Press.   .

Thomas, Calvin. 2013. *Ten Lessons in Theory: An Introduction to Theoretical Writing*. New York: Bloomsbury.

Thurston, Luke. 2012. *Literary Ghosts from the Victorians to Modernism: The Haunting Interval*. New York: Routledge. Routledge Studies in Twentieth-Century Literature 27.

Tigchelaar, Jana M. 2013. Those "Whose Deaths Were Not Remarked": Ghostly Other Women in Henry James's *The Turn of the Screw*, Charlotte Perkins Gilman's *The Yellow Wallpaper*, and Marilynne Robinson's *Housekeeping*. In *The Ghostly and the Ghosted in Literature and Film: Spectral Identities*, eds. Lisa Kröger and Melanie Anderson, 29–43. Newark: University of Delaware Press.

Uchiyama, Kanae. 2008. The Death of the Other: A Levinasian Reading of Paul Auster's *Moon Palace*. *MFS Modern Fiction Studies* 54(1): 115–139.

Varvogli, Aliki. 2001. *The World That Is the Book: Paul Auster's Fiction*. Liverpool: Liverpool University Press.

Walker, Karen. 2012. Autonomous, But Not Alone: The Reappropriation of Female Community in *The Women of Brewster Place* and *Housekeeping*. *Contemporary Women's Writing* 6(1): 56–73.

Watts, D.C. 2007. *Dictionary of Plant Lore*. London: Academic Press.

Weinberger, Eliot. 2004. Mallarmé's Cat. *Harper's Magazine*, June 22.

Weinstock, Jeffrey Andrew. 2004. Introduction: The Spectral Turn. In *Spectral America: Phantoms and the National Imagination*, ed. Jeffrey Andrew Weinstock, 3–17. Madison: University of Wisconsin Press.

Wilson, Alexis Kate. 2005. The Ghosts of Zuckerman's Past: The *Zuckerman Bound* Series. In *Philip Roth: New Perspectives on an American Author*, ed. Derek Parker Royal, 103–117. Westport: Praeger.

Winthrop, John. 2007. A Model of Christian Charity. In *The Norton Anthology of American Literature*, ed. Nina Baym, vol. A, 7th ed., 147–158. New York: Norton.

Wirth, Eric. 1995. A Look Back from the Horizon. In *Beyond the Red Notebook: Essays on Paul Auster*, ed. Dennis Barone, 171–182. Philadelphia: University of Pennsylvania Press. Penn Studies in Contemporary American Fiction.

Wood, Sarah. 2012. Some Thing, Some One, Some Ghost (about the Fires of Writing). *Derrida Today* 5(2): 165–179.

Wyatt, Jean. 1993. Giving Body to the Word: The Maternal Symbolic in Toni Morrison's *Beloved*. *PMLA* 108(3): 474–488.

Yoo, JaeEun. 2008. The Site of Murder: Textual Space and Ghost Narrator in Toni Morrison's *Love*. In *Space, Haunting, Discourse*, eds. Maria Holmgren Troy and Elisabeth Wennö, 153–167. Newcastle: Cambridge Scholars.

Zilcosky, John. 1998. The Revenge of the Author: Paul Auster's Challenge to Theory. *Critique: Studies in Contemporary Fiction* 39(3): 195–206.

INDEX

© The Editor(s) (if applicable) and The Author(s) 2016
D. Coughlan, *Ghost Writing in Contemporary American Fiction*,
DOI 10.1057/978-1-137-41024-5

217